His Light in the Dark

Natasha Madden

Magic Mist Publishing

Trigger Warnings

Blood, Gore, Violence, Explicit Sex, Language, Intrusive thoughts, Possession, Kidnapping, Torture, Death

When you're lost in the darkness, search for the one light that will lead you out.

Vincere aut mori
Conquer or Die

Chapter One

Salena

Music blares from the stage as I make my way through the crowded bar toward the tables at the back. I can't help but grumble under my breath as I do. I don't enjoy kicking people out, but my bar is no halfway house. I walk purposefully toward the booth and the guy slumped over in the cushioned seat. His chin rests on his chest, thick ebony hair draped over his features. I knock my knuckles on the table but get no response.

I turn to the guys seated across from him in the booth. "Hey . . . Is he with you?"

The two men stop laughing and glance over at me. Their eyes slide over my body, landing on my cleavage and lingering there.

I huff out a frustrated breath and roll my eyes. "Eyes up here, boys, or I'll cut them out and feed them to you," I snap, clicking my fingers in their faces.

Both men's eyes jerk to mine, and I watch them swallow roughly.

One of them mumbles a quiet, "Sorry."

The other answers my question. "No, he was here when we arrived."

Huh. Okay, then.

I turn to the unconscious man and sigh in frustration. He isn't a regular. There's an air of unfamiliarity about him, as if either new to town or passing through. I reach over to shake his shoulder, but something stops me. Frowning, I tilt my head, curiosity getting the better of me. Instead of waking him, I brush the hair from his forehead aside so I can get a look at his face.

I draw in a sharp breath, my fingers lingering on his temple. He is handsome. Not model handsome, more the rough type of handsome. The kind of man that would draw eyes in a crowd. He has a firm square jaw, clean shaven, dark eyebrows that even in sleep are drawn together in a frown. Without thinking, I swipe my thumb over his brow, as if to soothe whatever might be causing him trouble. My hand travels down his face and cups his jaw. Slowly, I lift his face. My heart thumps hard against my ribcage at the sight of three scars that run down his cheek, starting at his hairline near his temple. Whatever happened to him happened a long time ago. The cuts have healed, but were deep enough they left thick scars.

As I look at him, my pulse quickens, as if I'm doing something forbidden. I take in his expensive black suit; his tie is loosened around his neck, and the top button undone on his white shirt. He looks important, put together. Apart from being passed out in my bar, that is. Something gold glints inside his suit jacket, drawing my attention. Being the nosy person I am, I slowly pull the edge of his jacket aside and draw in a breath at the police badge clipped at his waist. Or should I say detective badge. Shit.

A throat clears behind me, and the floor drops out from beneath me. I let my hand fall, stepping back quickly. I turn to see my brother smirking at me, his head slightly tilted, deep blue eyes regarding me with amusement.

"Hey, sis. Whatcha doin'?"

I cross my arms over my chest, beginning to feel a tad foolish. "Nothing."

"Didn't look like nothing."

"I was going to kick this guy out," I reply, gesturing to the man in the booth.

"And now?"

I shoot him a glare. "Now I'm not. Take him upstairs to my apartment, Kai."

My apartment is tiny, with only one bedroom, a bathroom, and a small living area. It definitely isn't the Ritz, but I love it.

Kai crosses his arms and narrows his blue eyes. "Say what?"

"You heard me. When he wakes, I will deal with him." I push past him and head back toward the bar. I have work to do.

Kai's hand wraps around my arm, stalling me. "You think that's a good idea?"

"Kai," I warn.

"What? I'm your brother. It's my job to look out for you," he says, a look of exasperation crossing his face.

"No, it's not. Really."

"But–"

I love my brother, but I wish he would just follow orders, for one; and for two, I wish he'd do his job without giving me a hard time. I stare up at him, letting my eyes flash in warning. "No buts, Kai."

Kai releases my arm and holds up both hands in mock surrender. "Yes, Alpha." There is a twinkle in his eyes as he continues, "Whatever you say, sis. Should I put him on the sofa or in your bed?"

My mouth parts, and Kai lets out a laugh as he moves past me. "Sofa it is."

With a sly wink, he moves to pick up the guy from the booth. I give his shoulder a playful smack before I turn to leave.

"That's a good little Beta," I mock.

Kai's shoulders relax and a chuckle escapes him as he hoists the man over his shoulder. A wave of relief washes over me as I watch my brother and best friend carefully carry the detective up the stairs to my apartment.

I question what could have caused him to drink so much. Why was he here alone?

The sun is just starting to rise as I walk into my upstairs apartment. Stretching my neck from side to side, I drop my keys on the kitchen table. With a tug, I pull my jacket off and hang it over the nearest chair. Sighing heavily, I grab hold of the back of the chair with one hand, and reach down to unzip my leather knee-high boots, pulling them off. My feet are absolutely killing me.

I groan at the pure relief as I sink my toes into the plush rug under my feet. Two of my bar staff were no-shows last night, so I had to stay and work longer than I would've liked, but it was one of the busiest nights of the week. The band always brings in a crowd on Friday nights. I took a risk at hiring two college students, but humans repeatedly have excuses for not showing up. I don't think they'll end up lasting the month.

Walking into my small kitchen, I open the fridge, reaching for the orange juice. I'm just about to grab a glass when I hear a shout from the parking lot out back. My gaze swings to the sofa on the far side of the room. No passed out detective there anymore. *Damn it.*

I sprint out the door, the cold air slapping me in the face as I descend to the ground level. My bare feet barely make a noise as I run down the stairs. My feet hit the pavement and I round the bend before skidding to a stop at the sight in front of me. Three of my wolves are surrounding the detective, who is slowly backing up toward a gray Ford Explorer. *That must be his car.*

He hasn't noticed me yet, so I have a moment to take in his features now that he's awake.

He looks like shit. His ebony hair's a disheveled mess, with pieces that seem to stick up in all directions. Bloodshot eyes lift, taking in each of my wolves. They're a striking pale blue and hold a haunted look. He's not afraid, just resigned to his fate. I hate that look.

Rose snaps at his feet in warning, and he steps back again. Grady moves too close, and I'm not prepared for the fury that sweeps through me at seeing their aggression directed at the detective. The urge to protect is instantaneous, and I can't control the shift. Before I know it, I'm barreling into Grady, sending him rolling across the asphalt.

I plant my paws in front of the detective and give a low snarl, snapping at them to back off. My stance is protective and threatening as I stand in front of the man with the haunted look in his blue gaze. I back up until I hit his legs and sit at his feet.

'You will all leave now,' I growl.

'We found him sneaking out of your apartment, Alpha,' Grady says in confusion.

'And what? You decide to attack him?'

I stare over at Rose, a young gray wolf, then turn my gaze on Grady and Lucy, the mated pair each having a coat of a darker gray with white markings. I can sense their confusion stirring through the pack bond like a rippling wave. They thought they were protecting me. So, they don't understand why I'd be protecting this man.

I can't say that I blame them. I'm at a total loss as to how to explain the overwhelming urge to defend this man. I don't know him at all. I don't fully understand what's happening with me. My thoughts and emotions in this moment are conflicting.

A flash of guilt stirs in my belly as Rose slowly slinks back, her head lowered and tail between her legs. Grady and Lucy are slow to follow their daughter, but after a moment's hesitation they turn to run into the woods.

I sense the detective shift on his feet behind me, but I don't move yet. I watch the woods until I'm sure the coast is clear. Once I'm sure they're gone, I stand and wrap my body around the detective's legs. My head comes to his chest in my wolf form. I know exactly what I'm doing. I just can't seem to stop myself from marking him with my scent.

I haven't had this sort of primal reaction to anyone. Ever.

Chapter Two

Logan

I stand stock still, mesmerized by the sight of the snow-white wolf as it circles me. To say I'm taken aback by the sheer size of these wolves would be an understatement. Their bodies are immense compared to the size of ordinary wolves.

When the others cornered me, I thought I was going to be their breakfast. Wolves generally don't come into town, but the bar does back onto the woods.

I slowly reach out, unable to control the temptation to stroke the fur, and trace my fingers along the wolf's back as it circles me. The wolf pauses at my touch, and my heart thumps wildly in my chest. This is not helping the massive hangover I'm currently sporting. It sends nausea rolling through me, making me take quick shallow breaths until the feeling passes.

The wolf looks up at me and I'm captivated by its eyes. They're a strange mixture of green, blue, and yellow. The yellow seems to glow, but I'm sure I must be mistaken. That's not possible. My heart pounds against my ribcage, and I take a shaky step back, which seems to break through whatever spell's had us trapped.

The wolf shakes its head like it's confused and starts backing away. My body jerks, stepping forward in response. I want to stop it, to call out, but that's stupid. What I need to do is get home and sleep this hangover off. My day to grieve has passed. Now I need to pull my shit together.

I watch as the wolf turns and bounds off toward the side of the building, disappearing from sight. I release a long breath and stand there for a few seconds, gathering myself before I turn to unlock my car. Sitting in the driver's seat, I tip my head back, closing my eyes. A headache is forming in my temples, and I need to get home before it hits hard. I had way too much to drink last night. *How did I even end up in the apartment upstairs?* I guess I should just be happy I'm fully clothed still. This time of the year is always hard for me, especially yesterday.

Thoughts of my brother flash through my mind. We were inseparable until the day everything changed. His screams still echo in my head twenty-five years later. But I will never forget what happened. It will haunt me every single day. The wounds still ache as if they were fresh. The taint on my soul will be with me forever. Like the moon, there will always be a part of my heart covered in darkness.

I sigh, putting the key in the ignition and pulling out of the parking lot, taking note of the name of the bar as I drive away. The Crescent Moon. Maybe I'll come back and thank whoever it was who helped me upstairs last night to sleep off my drunken stupor.

My mind whirls with thoughts of the wolves. Replaying the moment over and over. I can't seem to free myself from these thoughts, or those mesmerizing eyes. They will be permanently etched in my memory. They're unusual, even for a wolf.

When I get home, I check my phone and realize the battery's dead. *Shit.* The captain will be pissed if he can't get a hold of me. I plug it in and take my jacket and shirt off. My phone beeps with a string of incoming messages and I reach for it. My heart thumps hard at all the missed calls from Sander. I know what they'll all say. I flip open one of his texts.

Sander: Hey Logan, I can't get a hold of you. I'm hoping everything is okay. If you need me, call. I'm here.

Guilt pricks at my chest. I know he means well, but yesterday was a day I spent alone. Sander knows this, but every year for the past twenty years he has always called me, just to make sure I knew he was there for me. Sander was my one and only friend growing up. I met him when I was seven in foster care, and even though I bounced from house to house, Sander always found me. Sander knew everything about me. He befriended me when no one else would, everyone else too scared to be around the freak kid with scars. He never once questioned my story, never once made me feel like I was crazy.

I scrub my hands over my face and get in the shower. My mind goes blank as I stretch my neck under the warm spray. I brace my palms on the wall in front of me and hang my head, letting the water wash away all the feelings last night dragged up. I thought being transferred out here would be good, but being this close to the woods was probably a bad idea. I should have stayed in Portland. In the city.

Turning the shower off, I reach for a towel. I run it over my head before wrapping it around my waist, then reach up, wiping the fog from the mirror and stare at my face. My blue eyes seem dull and lifeless, just like always. Dark portions of my hair fall over my forehead. It desperately needs a cut as well, but I just don't care. My fingers flex and

I reach up, running them over the scars on my face. Screams echo in my head, haunting me. I brace my hands on the sink, dropping my head as I try to control the anguish that strikes like a dark storm. It lashes at my insides as I try to block out the screams of my brother.

This will never get easier.

I close my eyes, taking several deep breaths as images of my brother's terror-stricken face flash through my mind. A deep sorrow whispers from every corner of my mind, howling from the darkness, from the void that will never fully heal.

"Fuck!" I yell, pushing from the sink and storming through the door, my fist connecting with the door as I pass. I'm aware of the pain as I flex my fingers, but it's nothing compared to the searing ache I live with daily.

Dressed, I head for the kitchen and pop two Advil. There's no point trying to sleep now. It would only be filled with nightmares, anyway. I walk outside and climb into my car. I drive without thought for hours, not noticing the sun set until I pull up to the bar I left only this morning. The parking lot's full. It is a Saturday night, so I should have expected that. I sit there for a while, just watching people walking in and out.

New town, new house, new car, new life. This is what I wanted. What Sander pushed me to do. Told me a fresh start might help me live my life. I wasn't so sure, especially if the last twenty-four hours were any indication.

I push through the doors and instantly feel several sets of eyes on me. I look around, but don't notice anyone watching me. I roll my shoulders, trying to dispel the feeling, and make my way toward the bar. The bartender has her back to me, but I know the moment she senses me behind her. Her delicate shoulders stiffen.

Slowly she turns and it feels as if someone has pulled the ground out from under me. The air is completely knocked out of me. Bright turquoise eyes clash with mine and widen.

Fuck, she is gorgeous.

Absolutely stunning.

Her long silver hair is pulled back in a high ponytail, drawing attention to her sharp features. My eyes drop to her bright red lips as her mouth parts. Pale, snow white skin shimmers under the bar lights. I want to reach out and touch her, just to see how soft it is. Her eyes roam my face, and I have the urge to turn away. I can feel my scars burning under her perusal.

Suddenly, an arm is draped over my shoulders and my body locks up.

"Good to see you awake tonight," says a deep, jovial voice.

I instinctively step away and turn to the newcomer.

He has a bright smile, a knowing one, and his blue eyes shine happily back at me. He's around my height and build. His blonde hair is cropped close to his head.

"Do I know you?" I ask gruffly.

The guy laughs, "Nah, man. I just helped you upstairs last night."

I stilled at that bit of information. "Thank you for that."

"All good. We've all been there. Anyway, you can thank my sister here."

I look back at the stunning creature who's glaring daggers at her brother.

"Okay . . . " I draw out. "Thanks. And I wanted to apologize for getting so drunk I passed out."

Her gaze moves back to me, and it's like the air is sucked from the room. Smiling softly at me, a look of understanding passes over her face. I ignore the tug in my chest, and the attraction that follows.

"My name is Kai. And this here is Salena," the guy says in a friendly tone, breaking the bubble we seem to have put ourselves in.

I look between the two and feel like I'm missing something. But I can't seem to drag my gaze off her. She's wearing the sexiest red bustier and leather pants. But it's her face that hits me. Her striking features have me captivated.

"Logan," I reply roughly.

"What brings you here tonight, Logan? Round two?"

"Kai!" Salena snaps, irritation flashing in her eyes.

Kai leans on the bar, his blue eyes twinkling with mischief. "What?"

Salena rolls her eyes and mutters something under her breath I don't catch. She sends me a quick glance before turning and moving further down the bar. My eyes follow her as she goes, for some reason unable to pull my gaze away just yet. I'm drawn to her, and I don't understand why.

Kai is still watching me, but now it is with curiosity. I stare back. I've never been a big talker. I find if I remain quiet, it makes people uncomfortable, and they'll usually leave me alone. It's how I like it.

"So, what's your poison?" Kai reaches over the bar and pours himself a beer. I raise an eyebrow at him, and he winks. "Perks. Salena owns the bar."

I give a curt nod. "I only came here to thank whoever helped me last night and apologize."

"Stay for a drink," Kai says.

Hesitating, I look around, noticing a few stares directed our way, and frown. "Sure."

"What are you having?"

"Whatever you're having."

Chapter Three

Salena

Do not look, do not look.

I glance over my shoulder at Logan and Kai and gulp around the knot forming in my throat.

What's he doing back here?

My emotions are all over the place. I'm finding it hard to concentrate on the task at hand with him so close. Every inch of that man is magnificent.

I am enamored.

I am also screwed.

All I can think about is his intoxicating scent, and the way my heart beats faster, my breath catching at his proximity. It's as if I'm pulled to him by an invisible thread. I don't know where these feelings are coming from.

Logan's frowning at my brother, and I can't blame him. Kai can be absolutely infuriating, but he always means well. I know he thinks he's watching out for me, but I don't need looking after. I also know he can smell my scent on Logan, and I know he has the wrong idea. He thinks we slept together last night.

I watch as Logan runs a hand through his thick ebony hair. His pale blue eyes hold so much pain it tugs at my chest. His eyes are the kind of blue that's unusual—not the warm sunny day sky blue, but more like a winter sky when a snowstorm is coming.

A throat clears, and my gaze snaps back to the customer patiently waiting for his drinks.

"Sorry. Here you go." I place the drinks on the bar, and he hands over some cash, his eyes glued to my cleavage the entire time.

Logan's never looked at my cleavage. His eyes have stayed on my face. I don't know why I like that so much, but I do. I smile to myself, and go about serving other customers. Though I do my best to ignore Logan, my gaze just keeps drifting back to him. A few times our eyes meet, and I feel like I'm free falling, my stomach twisting with anticipation. Kai catches our exchange, and he's been trying to meet my eye for the last hour.

A commotion by the door draws my attention as Reaper walks in, followed by his entourage.

Just great.

I silently hope they won't come in and disrupt the peaceful atmosphere tonight. I may be the alpha of the local pack in Boulder, but Reaper is the alpha of the Denver pack. His pack is larger than mine, and their savage energy makes it feel wild and untamed.

I let him come here once a month to keep the peace. He and I have a deal of sorts. My brothers Kai and Felix hate the shifter, but sometimes you have to make a deal with the devil to keep the peace.

I watch as Reaper walks right to the bar as if he owns the place. Fire burns in my stomach at his arrogance.

"Looking mighty fine tonight, Salena," he purrs, resting his forearms on the bar and leaning closer. His eyes slowly drag over my body, and I fight the urge to cross my arms.

"What are you doing here, Reaper? You know the rules, we have them for a reason. It stops friction building."

"Once a month isn't enough. I needed to see you. Plus, a little friction could be nice."

I ignore the last comment. "Too bad. This is my territory. You need to back the fuck off," I say, my voice filling with my alpha magic.

"Come on. Don't be like that. You know you want some of this," Reaper says, while gesturing to his crotch.

"Don't be gross, Reaper," I snap, throwing a slice of lemon at him.

Anger ignites in his eyes, and he slams his hands on the bar. I raise an eyebrow in challenge.

His voice lowers. "You'd be lucky to get me, you know."

"I'm not looking for a mate, Reaper. I told you that. Or a quick fuck."

Reaper flexes his arms, his hand planted firmly on the bar. His arms are covered in tattoos from his knuckles to god knows where. His dark blonde hair is styled messy, and his brown eyes are always edged with a craziness I don't want to explore.

His jaw clenches. "Not many women would turn me down. This little game of yours, playing hard to get, is getting old, Salena."

I lean my hands on the bar, mimicking his posture. "It's not a game. I'm. Not. Interested."

Reaper stares at me long and hard. I don't blink. I hold his stare, demanding he take me seriously and back the fuck down. I will not fall at his feet. I am an alpha, and I didn't get that title by being a pushover.

Reaper pushes off the bar and raps his tattooed knuckles on the wood. "A round of beers."

I nod and turn, letting out a slow, quiet breath. I start pouring Reaper's beers, mulling over how quickly I could get him out of here. I feel a warm caress skate over the bare skin on my back and turn my head. Logan's staring at me from where he stands at the bar with Kai, who has a woman hanging off his arm now. Our eyes lock and it feels like all the oxygen has been sucked from the room. I quickly look away and finish up the drinks, sending Reaper and his buddies on their way. They nod in thanks and move over to the pool tables.

I feel eyes on me again and look around, my gaze catching on Logan. My heart gives a little flutter as we stare at each other. His gaze narrows, those artic blue eyes taking me in from across the bar like he can see straight through me. I give him a small, nervous smile and turn to the next customer. After that, things seem to get hectic. I lose sight of Logan and Kai, but I try to not let myself panic. Why I feel that rush of panic anyway is beyond me. Logan can take care of himself. And everyone knows the rules here. Strictly no fighting or shifting in the bar.

I feel it the moment the air shifts. Tension and hostility slam into me, and I spin to see Reaper cornering Logan. He leans in and sniffs the air in front of Logan. Shit!

I leap over the bar. *'Kai!'* I yell down our pack bond.

'Kinda busy, Salena.'

I really don't want to know what or who my brother is doing right now. *'I don't care. Tell whoever you're with you'll meet her later,'* I snap.

'Okay, okay.'

I'm across the bar in less than five seconds, the look on my face warning people to get out of the way. Logan looks over Reaper's shoulder, his eyes locking on mine. Scanning my face, fast and brutally efficient, searching for an explanation.

I don't hesitate when I reach them, grabbing Reaper's shoulder, and tearing him away from Logan.

A snarl rips from his throat as he spins on me. "Him?"

In the space of a second, his eyes lose their humanity, as he gets in my face. A shiver ripples down my spine, but I stand straighter.

"Back off," I growl, only loud enough for him to hear.

My gaze flickers to Logan's, confusion and anger swirling in the deep depths of his pale blue eyes. I see his mouth settle in a straight line, and he goes to step forward, but Kai is suddenly there, holding him back. Relief sweeps through me, and I step up to Reaper, getting in his face.

"Get the fuck out of my bar," I seethe.

A low growl rumbles up Reaper's throat, and his buddies move in closer. I sense my pack go on alert. Kai is fuming. Without looking, I know he's signaled Tyler and Grady, the older ones in our pack. I need to get Reaper out of my bar before I break my own damn rules. I snap my hand forward, gripping his balls in my hand and squeezing. Reaper makes an unintelligible sound and falters. I lean closer to whisper in his ear, letting my claws lengthen, piercing his jeans.

"Stay the fuck away from me, from him, from my pack. You are not welcome here anymore."

I let go, and he takes a moment before straightening. When his gaze meets mine, something seems to click in those depths. I want so badly to ask him what he's thinking right now.

Reaper shakes his head, his fist clenching at his sides. "You know this won't end well." His tone cools, and he frowns.

I tilt my head to the side. "I said get out."

When Reaper doesn't move, Kai steps forward. "You heard her. You're not welcome here anymore."

Reaper's eyes flash as he glares at Kai and then back at me. It promises payback for humiliating him publicly. Turning, he walks from the bar, his friends following. I take a deep, fortifying breath when he disappears out the door. I blink and glance around, realizing we have an audience. Fuck.

Avoiding Logan's gaze, I look at Kai. "Make sure he leaves quietly."

Kai hesitates and opens his mouth to say something, but I hold up my hand. "Please. And take Grady and Tyler with you."

Kai nods and walks toward the door. I watch as Tyler and Grady fall in step behind him. The implications of what I just did are still exploding like fireworks in my chest as Logan steps closer. He is so close I can feel his body heat. Logan's eyes are troubled as he frowns down at me. Sometimes, as an alpha, I wish I were taller, so I wouldn't have to look up at everyone. I'm not short at five foot seven, but compared to the men, I am. Logan isn't a shifter, but he still stands a bit taller than me, and I'm in heels.

"You didn't have to do that." His voice is rough. It rolls over my skin, making me shiver in response. That tug in my chest pulls me toward him again, his scent rolling over me like a soft breeze. It takes every bit of self-control I have not to go to him. We stare at each other for what seems like an eternity but is probably only seconds before I find my voice again.

"I know. I've been looking for an excuse to kick him out for a while. So, thank you."

Logan's frown deepens. "Is he going to be trouble?"

"Definitely." My eyes widen at my response. I didn't mean to say that out loud.

"If you need me to–"

I hold up my hands. "No, I have it under control."

"You sure?" He steps closer. He smells incredible. Masculine and clean. Like whiskey and oak. The smell is *intoxicating. Why am I even noticing?*

A dizzy feeling sweeps over me, and I rub my forehead with the back of my hand. Logan reaches over and touches my face. We both still at the touch. Surprise coats his features as if he moved without thought. He takes a quick step back, dropping his hand and shoving it in his pants pockets, as if to stop it from happening again. He seems like he wants to say more but has changed his mind.

"I better get going," Logan says slowly, his arctic blue eyes taking in those around us, observing them, me.

Nerves make me shuffle on my feet, and I nod, glancing at the bar. "I better get back to work. Sorry about tonight."

"Nothing to apologize for."

I want to laugh, because little does he know, this was all my fault. If I didn't mark him, we wouldn't be in this mess. I watch as Logan walks toward the front doors and out into the cool night.

Chapter Four

Salena

"**I**'m worried about you." Kai's voice floats down the phone the next morning.

"I'm fine," I reply, putting my phone between my ear and my shoulder as I finish up making my coffee.

"I'm not sure I believe you."

My lips pull into a tight smile, even though he can't see it. "Well, believe me."

Grabbing my coffee, I make my way over to my sofa to get comfortable. I cross my legs, and Ghost jumps up next to me, purring as she creeps onto my lap. Ghost strangely made her home here, after she realized I could see and touch her. The rather adorable Maine Coon cat has the thickest, softest black and white coat, with a unique white marking on her chest, standing out among her fur. Ghost's chest vibrates as she purrs, pushing her head into my hand.

"Reaper will not let it go. Logan will be a target now."

I can't help but grumble in annoyance, knowing all of this already. I've been searching for a way to take the heat off Logan without him having any knowledge of it.

"What were you thinking? Marking him?"

I blow out a breath. "That's the thing. I wasn't. When I saw Rose snap at him, and Grady moving in, I lost all sense of thought and defended him."

"What do you mean, 'lost all sense of thought?'"

"My first response was anger and the need to protect. Even though I know they wouldn't have attacked him. I just, I don't know, Kai. It's weird, it's almost like he's . . . " I trail off.

"What?"

I hesitate. *Do I tell him?* I tell Kai everything, we have no secrets between us. I don't think I've ever kept anything from him. I don't think I'd be able to, he can read me like a damn book.

I run my thumbnail along my bottom lip as I mumble the next words. "My mate."

Last night, I tried to go for a run and clear my head. Next thing I knew, I was standing outside a small ranch style home on the outer edge of town. When I realized where I was, the awareness hit me like a lightning bolt. It played over in my mind all night. I barely got any sleep.

The other end of the phone is silent, and I pull it away from my face to see if we're still connected. We are. "Kai?"

"Your mate? Are you sure?"

I blow out a breath. "I don't know, Kai. I've never had a mate before," I deadpan.

"Right, sorry."

"No, I'm sorry. It's just weird."

"He's human."

"I know," I whisper.

Kai blows out a deep breath. "If he is your mate, he'll be an even bigger target."

I grumble, tipping my head back to rest on the sofa, and staring up at my ceiling. This is a huge bloody mess. I need to get myself together, but every time I think about Logan, my pulse speeds up, and my mind races. I just can't get those haunted eyes from my mind. He seems to carry a dark shadow on his shoulders. I could feel the weight of his despair in the air of the parking lot, his face etched with defeat. It was like he accepted he was going to die, and he was okay with that. It makes my heart hurt to know he felt that way.

"We will need to have Reaper watched, at least for a few weeks. Who knows how he'll take this. He has been vying to be your mate since you became alpha."

"I know," I sigh.

Reaper is unpredictable and dangerous. I want someone watching Logan as well. If something happens, I want my pack there to help him.

"Who do you want on it?" Kai asks, his voice firm, the voice of a protective brother.

My mind automatically goes to Felix. My younger brother will make sure Logan stays safe. "I'll get Felix to watch Logan."

"Logan? He's a detective. I'm sure he'll notice someone following him. I was talking about Reaper."

"Well, what do you suggest, then?"

Kai blows out a heavy breath, and I can just imagine him pacing with his hand on his head. "What if we just tell him about Reaper?"

I scowl, even though he can't see me. "Absolutely not."

"Okay, fine. We can have someone watch his place at night. I don't think Reaper would be stupid enough to attack a detective in the middle of the day."

"True, I'll get Felix to sort out shifts. As for Reaper, he'll notice another shifter in his territory, so we need to send a contact in," I murmur, and take a sip of my drink.

"You can't mean–"

"Yes," I cut him off. "I will call Ashwiyaa."

I hear his muffled groan, and can't help but smile.

"You sure?" he asks.

"I'm not the one she has a problem with, Kai," I reply, running my finger over Ghost's head and down her back, her tail wrapping around my wrist.

Kai curses and I hear him shuffling around. "Fine, call Ash," he says, using her preferred name.

"Thanks for your permission," I respond sarcastically.

"Ha ha ha . . . Look, it's not my fault–"

"That you can't keep it in your pants?" I laugh, cutting him off.

Kai growls, "We were casual, and when I found out what she was . . . " he trails off.

Ashwiyaa is what most would call a dark witch. She shares the same traits as a skin-walker, having the ability to shape shift into any animal she chooses but with the unique difference to walk the veil between the living and the dead. I heard from some sources she is a world walker. They're extremely rare, and Ash, she is exceptionally powerful. It's a little unnerving, to be honest. Kai completely freaked when he found out the woman he'd been hooking up with when she was in town was a powerful dark witch with special abilities. And he doesn't even know about the fact she is an assassin for the Kotov mafia family, who runs the west coast. That last detail isn't common knowledge, but I did some digging when she first showed up in town. I don't blame Kai for how he acted, but he definitely could have dealt with the situation better.

"It's alright, Kai. You know I understand. I'm sure everything will be fine."

"Sure, fine," he mutters.

I feel bad, but I need someone who can go by unnoticed, someone who can be a ghost, and keep tabs on Reaper. If he's plotting some sort of payback, I need to know. Especially if it has anything to do with Logan. And Ash . . . She's the best.

We chat a bit more and hang up. I know I need to get some rest, but first I need to contact Ash. Sighing, I type out a quick text.

Salena: Ash.

Salena: Need a favor.

The text bubbles appear instantly, and I don't have to wait long.

Ash: 8 p.m. Old Mill.

Well, at least she replied.

I have eight hours before I have to open the bar, so I shower and try to take a nap. Too wired to sleep, I grab my phone and keys, and head to the café down on Main Street. Rose is working today. It'll be nice to see her and apologize face to face for how I acted the other day. I owe my pack an explanation.

"Here, drink this. It'll help you wake up," Rose says, passing me a coffee cup.

I smile over the rim, and take a deep inhale of the sweet sugar caramel scented coffee. I love coffee. I love the way it smells. The way it tastes. I can surround myself with the earthy sweetness all day.

"Thanks," I reply, taking another sip.

I take my cup over to a seat by the window and peer out, watching everyone going about their afternoon. Boulder isn't huge, but it isn't small either. I can't imagine living anywhere else. I love the mountains. It doesn't matter which way you drive out of town, either way you'll be in the mountains within a few minutes.

Rose plonks down in the chair opposite me, her warm brown eyes taking me in. Rose is a natural beauty with soft brown skin and caramel colored hair that she keeps shoulder length. She always says it looks better short, because it suits the beanies she loves wearing during winter. I have to agree; she is super cute in her beanies. Some people collect books, others crystals or even shoes. But Rose, she collects beanies.

Rose leans on the table, her voice dropping to a whisper. "So, what's the plan for Reaper?"

I take another sip of my coffee and put it on the table, my hands cupping the warm cup. "I don't know yet."

"You know we have your back, right?"

"I know. Thanks," I say, taking another sip of my coffee, my nerves rattling around in my chest. My leg is bouncing under the table. My vision trembles, and I blink, trying to dispel the odd feeling.

Rose squints at me. "Are you okay?"

I groan and tap my fingers on the table. "Yeah, just on edge. I'm meeting with Ashwiyaa tonight."

Rose's eyes widen. "Shit."

"Yep."

"You're not taking Kai, are you?"

I can't stop the laugh slipping from my mouth. "Hell no."

Rose grins and sighs in relief, taking a sip of her drink.

Felix strolls in at that moment and makes his way over. I watch as Rose's cheeks flush, and lift my cup to hide my smirk. My younger brother has this effect on most women. He's tall and lean, his muscles more defined than bulky. Being as Rose is only seventeen and thus new to boys, she's extremely obvious in her reactions, but my brother has never embarrassed her about it. Always the gentleman, Felix.

"Hey," Felix says, pulling another chair over and sitting on it backward. He looks bright-eyed and bushy tailed. I hate it.

"Hey," Rose and I say in greeting.

I put my cup down, before shifting in my seat to face Felix. Resting my chin on my hand, I smile at my brother. He looks just like Dad, with his silver hair and blue turquoise eyes. Felix and I both take after our dad, whereas Kai takes after our mother, with the darker blonde hair, and eyes a darker shade of blue. Though, I've been told my eyes shift between blue and green depending on my mood.

The table shakes from my leg bouncing under the table. What is wrong with me? I'm not usually this edgy.

Felix raises an eyebrow at me. "You good, Salena?"

"Sure, just peachy." My smile is tight, and I squint my eyes to stop my trembling vision.

Rose giggles. "You are wired."

Felix watches me closely. "What's wrong with you? You seem extra . . . twitchy today."

"I am!" I exclaim loudly. "Why can I suddenly see sounds in colors?"

Rose laughs. "I did add an extra shot to your coffee. Plus some caramel syrup for some sweetness."

My gaze snaps to her, and my eyes widen.

Oh, shit!

I am highly sensitive to caffeine. I'll be bouncing around for hours now.

"What? Don't look at me like that. You said you needed the boost."

"Shit," I swear. "No wonder it tastes so good."

Rose and Felix chuckle at my expense, and share a knowing look.

"Kai told me what happened last night," Felix says, growing serious. Even though he's twenty-two he acts like he's older, Felix seems to have skipped over the teenage stage, and matured overnight. Our parent's death probably has something to do with that.

I look into my brother's eyes, "I feel like I've set something in motion that I don't fully understand. What if I got it wrong?"

"Got what wrong?" Rose asks, curiosity making her lean in closer.

"That man Salena marked is her mate."

My hand shoots out and smacks Felix across the back of the head. "Hey!" I snap.

"What?" Felix replies with laughter in his eyes.

Rose's hand covers mine on the table, drawing my attention back to her. "Salena, you basically threw Dad across the carpark when you thought we were going to hurt that man. If he's not your mate, I'd be completely shocked."

I wince. "I'm sorry about that, by the way."

Rose chuckles, waving me off. "It's fine. I was confused at first, but when you marked him, it all clicked."

Felix's blue eyes lock on mine, and some of his silver hair falls on his forehead as he leans forward. "I can't believe you found your mate." His voice is filled with awe. Felix is a romantic at heart. He'll make one girl very happy when he finds her.

"I know . . . I'm scared. He doesn't know about us. What if he leaves?"

Felix smiles softly and knocks my chin gently with his knuckles. "Chin up. You got this, big sis. I have complete faith in you."

I relax back in my chair, and Rose sends me a wink. "How can he not fall in love with you?"

I feel my face heat at the praise, and bump her knee with mine, mouthing *thanks*.

"He's human," I whisper.

"So?" Felix says.

"Since when do we mate with humans?" I mumble.

Felix shrugs. "What does it matter? He's yours, you're his. You're meant to be together."

I like how simple he makes everything sound, but Logan might not feel the same way. This is a lot for a human to take in. They don't know about our ways; it'll be a hard thing for him to accept.

"You sure meeting with Ash is the right call?" Felix moves on as if all has been settled.

"She's the only one who can keep an eye on Reaper without being detected."

"Want me to come with you?"

I shake my head. Things would go much smoother if I were on my own. I tip my cup up, finishing the last of my coffee, and stand.

"I will be fine."

Rose stands and picks up our cups. "I better get back to work. Be careful tonight."

I nod to her, and she smiles softly at me, then Felix, before turning and walking toward the kitchen.

Chapter Five

Salena

I'm early, but I am not taking the risk of Ash leaving if I'm late. She hates tardiness. I pull up at the old mill, my headlights washing over the area. Sure enough, I spot Ash sitting on the hood of an old rusted out car, her long black hair gently moving around her in the breeze. She looks every bit as intimidating as I remember.

Her dark brown eyes zero in on me as I get out of the car and make my way over to her. Ash has one leg bent up to her chest, and is cleaning her nails with a dagger, her dark skin seeming to glow in the moonlight. Ashwiyaa is an anomaly. She originated from a native American tribe called the Krythodens. They are considered warriors, strong and militaristic, everything she radiates, in troves. I'm not sure just how old she is, but the magic I sense from her, it feels old.

"Hi Ash," I say as I walk toward her, trying to suppress my nervousness.

Her dark gaze is searching as she watches me approach. "You've found your mate," she says, surprising me.

I halt my steps, my heart thumping wildly in my chest. "How could you possibly know that?"

"I can smell it." She shrugs as if it's nothing.

"Oh . . . "

Wow, what a great comeback Salena, I chide myself.

Ash tilts her head, eyes narrowing in concentration. "Oh, I see."

My stomach drops, and I'm almost afraid to ask. "What?"

"He's human," she says, with a chuckle.

"How could you . . . " I trail off. "Never mind."

I shake my head in bewilderment as I close the distance between us. This is the thing about Ash, she seems to know everything about you, like she can simply read you like an open book. It's freaky, and more than a little unsettling.

"So, Kai didn't want to face me?" she asks, sheathing her dagger behind her back.

I bark out a laugh. "He's going for smart, not brave tonight."

Ash's eyes twinkle and she laughs. "Fair enough. Good choice."

I make my way over to the car, the metal frame creaking as I take a seat next to her. "I need a favor."

"So you said."

"I need someone to keep tabs on Reaper for a few weeks."

Ash lets loose a low growl. "Really. Reaper? What did you do to piss him off?"

I sigh, crossing my legs, and look over at her. Understanding dawns and she laughs, "Oh, he found out about your mate. He isn't happy to lose."

"Something like that." I tilt my head back, looking up into the dark night sky and the many stars twinkling above. "I actually don't think he knows yet."

"Then why do you need me to watch him?'

"I may have embarrassed Reaper publicly. I need to make sure he isn't going to retaliate."

"I see."

"I just need a heads up, that's all."

Ash considers my words for a long moment. "Okay. I'll keep an eye on Reaper and his pack and report anything you might need to know, on one condition."

I knew this was coming, and this is why I've been so nervous. Payment.

"What is it?"

"One meeting with your brother." A wicked gleam enters her eyes, and I sigh.

Kai is going to kill me for this.

"Deal."

I reach my hand out to shake, but Ash is quicker than me. Her dagger slices across my palm and hers before I can comprehend what's happening, sealing our hands together.

A flare of magic erupts from our clasped hands, making my skin tingle.

When she lets go, I jump from the car, spinning on her. "What the hell was that?"

Ash shrugs, putting her dagger away again. "Just sealing our deal. Tell Kai I'm looking forward to our date." She winks, and I watch as her body swirls in magic, her form shifting and changing into a beautiful gray timber wolf. Ash gives me one last look before she turns and bounds off into the dark. I blow out a long breath, shaking my hand. Well, that went better than I was expecting. Ash can be unpredictable and unstable, but she's a good ally to have.

Kai isn't going to be happy that I threw him in the deep end with Ash, but he knows how to swim, and I'm sure Ash won't drown him. Kai, whether he chooses to believe it or not, brings out a softer side in Ash, and I know he hurt her with his reaction when he found out she's dark witch.

I'm ten minutes from the bar when my phone starts ringing. I press answer on my steering wheel without checking who it is, but I already know.

"Hey," I answer.

Kai's voice fills the car. "So, how did it go?"

"Better than I was expecting. She's going to keep an eye on Reaper and his pack, and let me know if he makes a move."

"And?"

I cringe, tightening my hands on the steering wheel. "She wants to see you."

Kai groans. "You didn't agree, did you?"

I chew on my bottom lip.

"Salena?"

"Look, Kai, you owe her, and now I owe her."

"Shit!" Kai curses.

"Look . . . Stop being a baby. She isn't going to hurt you."

Kai mumbles something I don't quite catch. I'm about to answer when a loud bang startles me and my car rips across the road.

"Shit. Look, I have to go, Kai. I've blown a tire."

"Really?! I just replaced them last week. They should be fine."

"Maybe I ran something over." I pull off onto the side of the road and turn my hazard lights on.

"Want me to come out?"

I roll my eyes. "I can change a tire, Kai."

"I know but . . . "

I sigh. "Look, I'm not completely helpless, Kai. I'm the damn alpha remember. I can look after myself."

Kai sighs. "You're still my baby sister."

My tone softens. "I know."

I turned twenty-nine a couple of months ago. With an age difference of fifteen months, Kai's the oldest in the family, and Felix is the baby at only twenty-two.

"I'm always going to look out for you."

"I know that too. Love you, Kai."

"Love you too."

Pressing the disconnect button on my steering wheel, I hang up the phone and climb out of the car. Sure enough, my front passenger side tire is completely shredded. I look down the road, but I don't see anything that could have done this, though it is dark. I pop the trunk and pull out my spare. Now to try my best not to get my new silver, off-the-shoulder corset dirty. I just get the new tire put into place when my skin prickles. Suppressing a shiver, I slowly stand, the tire iron gripped in my hand. I put my back to the car and scan the area for danger, trying to pinpoint what's causing my sense of unease. I stand stock still, listening, watching. The feeling is still there, but whatever's watching me isn't going to make a move. Not right now.

I turn and quickly tighten the bolts on my tire, then toss everything in the trunk. I'll put it away properly tomorrow. I'm not getting a good feeling right now.

Chapter Six

Salena

The pack knows better than to bother me on Mondays unless it's an emergency, so I'm surprised when I hear an abrupt knock at the door. Monday is my day to unplug, enjoy myself, have a bath, read a book, go for a long run. Aside from sleep, there is precious little time I have completely to myself. Sometimes it just becomes too much. So, Mondays, I step away, reset.

Without checking who's there, I swing open the door. "This better be good," I say with a slight whine.

My eyes widen as I take in the tall, imposing man on my front step. Logan looks sharp in his navy suit, crisp white shirt, and light blue tie. His pale arctic eyes pop against his dark hair, creating a striking combination. My eyes roam his face, taking in every detail in the morning light. Every fiber of my being reaches for him, aching to be folded in his strong arms.

Several long seconds stretch out as we take each other in. Logan turns his face away, hiding his scars from view, and I hate that. I don't want him hiding from me.

Clearing his throat, Logan rubs the back of his neck. "Sorry to bother you so early."

He keeps his gaze averted, and for some reason that bothers me. I want his eyes on me.

"You can bother me anytime, detective." I smile, leaning against the door frame, and cross my arms.

His eyes snap back to mine, a look of surprise flitting across his face. His expression turns serious again a moment later. "I came to make sure you were okay."

Puzzled, I regard him. Looking closer, I realize he's tense, on edge. Something's wrong.

"Why?" I ask.

"There was an animal attack close to here last night. The victim fits your description."

I straighten up from the doorframe, my arms dropping to my sides. "What?"

Logan shifts on his feet, just a slight movement. The tension rolling off him draws my attention. His icy blue eyes are fierce, so many emotions warring within—relief, anger, desire, sorrow, and need.

He wants me, but he doesn't want to want me.

When he doesn't answer, I ask, "Where?"

"Not far. It happened on the walking trail about five miles from here. A girl was mauled."

"Is she okay?"

Logan turns his face away again, burying his hands in the pockets of his pants. "No."

"Is she alive?" I whisper, a feeling of dread washing over me.

"No."

My stomach drops, and my mind frantically tries to think what could have happened. Was it the thing I sensed last night, watching me? Did it go after easier prey?

I watch as Logan squats down and picks up Ghost, and my mouth drops open. I figure the best course of action right now is to ignore the fact he just picked up my cat. Whom, I might add, is not a real cat, but a spirit of sorts. Ghost just showed up one day and refused to leave. It wasn't until Felix came over that I realized Ghost was, well, a ghost. No one else has been able to see her or touch her.

Logan's hand runs over Ghost's back, making the cat purr in pleasure. "I just needed to make sure it wasn't you before I attended the–" Abruptly, he stops speaking and swallows.

I reach out my hand and rest it on his arm. He flinches, and my heart pinches in response. I drop my hand and look down at my feet.

"Sorry," I whisper.

"It's fine. I better go." His response is quick as he puts Ghost down.

"Okay."

I watch as he turns and jogs down the stairs and over to his car. When a breeze sweeps through the door, I realize I'm in my lazy clothes, which just so happen to be some loose track pants and my favorite white t-shirt, which is so old it's completely see through. Embarrassment heats my face, and I shut the door quickly, but not before I catch a whiff of his scent lingering in the air.

Crisp whiskey and aged oak . . .

Chapter Seven

Logan

I hate murder scenes. I can't imagine there are many people who enjoy them, but it is by far the worst part of my job. Even though this has been classed as an animal attack, I have a gut feeling it's more than that. A nagging sensation telling me to look closer. Over the years, I've learned to trust that feeling.

Although, you'd think after being rounded up by wolves a couple of days ago would have me jumping on this bandwagon. But something just doesn't sit right.

The fact that the woman fits Salena's description has me on alert. At the very thought of it being her who'd been killed, it tore at my insides.

I don't even remember the drive to her place or pulling up. And when she opened the door, the sense of relief that washed through me was instant. Then I noticed her top was see through. The cat was the perfect distraction to keep my mind on topic. Not on her perfect handful-sized tits.

I get out of my car and make sure my badge is clipped to my waist before making my way over to where the coroner is bagging the body. I raise the crime scene tape and flash my badge at the officers, each nodding in return.

"Hey, Doc," I say as I come up behind him.

Doc's warm brown eyes peer up at me, the corners crinkling with age as he smiles. "Logan. Good to see you."

"You, too, old man."

"Wish it was over a beer instead of a body though," Doc mumbles gruffly.

I've only been here a month, but in that time, I've met Doc a few times around the station. Mostly when we both sought some peace and quiet on the roof.

I grunt in response and point to the victim. "How long until we know the cause of death?"

"I can say with great certainty that this was due to an animal attack. Most likely a coyote or wolf."

Doc finishes zipping up the bag and stands. I look around the area and see signs of a struggle, she didn't go down without a fight. Someone has to have heard something.

"Do we know who she is?" I ask.

Doc shakes his head, "There was no identification on her, and she doesn't look like a local. Not that I know all 108,250 people in Boulder, but she does have old injuries, and looks to be slightly malnourished."

I lower my brows and stop him as he goes to walk past. "What kind of old injuries?"

Doc pauses to consider the question. "I'd have to take a proper look at the body, but from what I could see, it looked like she'd been whipped.

She had several lacerations on her back and thighs. Also, what looks like an old break to her collar bone that didn't heal right."

"Okay, well, maybe we aren't looking at an animal attack," I say, shaking my head in frustration.

Doc frowns and thinks about it. "You could be right, but everything here suggests otherwise. It was an animal that killed her, but whatever happened before that . . . " He trails off, a concerned look creasing his face.

My jaw tightens, and I pat him on the back. "I know. I'm going to find out who she is."

I shift my focus to the jogger who discovered the body, her face etched with shock. She stands as still as a statue, huddled by the police cruisers, her arms wrapped tightly around herself.

I'd better get a statement from her, so she can go home and put this shitty day behind her.

"Let me know when you're ready to move the body," I say absently to Doc.

Doc glances up at me and nods. "Will do."

I head over to the jogger with a deep sigh, my feet sinking slightly in the wet ground.

After taking a statement from the jogger, I then proceed to knock on a few doors of the surrounding homes. No one saw or heard anything. Although the houses are widely spaced, and there is a considerable distance between the wooded trail and the yards, it's strange that no one mentioned any disturbance.

A million thoughts run through my head as I make my way back to the station.

It's late afternoon when I finally turn onto my street and see a group of teenage boys on the street ahead playing basketball. Someone must've dragged a freestanding hoop to the end of the driveway. Not the safest place, but this is a pretty quiet street. My house is the last on the street in the cul-de-sac. Behind my house is a small creek, then the woods. The neighbors on either side of me are young families.

I slow down the car so I can pass the kids safely and pull in my drive. Turning the car off, I stretch my neck side to side before getting out. A quick glance around shows nothing out of place, and I start for the front door when one of the teenagers calls out.

"Yo. You a cop?"

I pause at the bottom of my steps and turn, all of them now standing there watching me.

"Who's asking?" I call back.

"Totally a cop," one of the boys says, eyeing me up and down.

"You got a problem with us playing in the street?" the tallest one pipes up.

I run a hand through my hair and walk toward the street. They're two houses away and I'm heading inside, so I don't know why they'd be asking me that.

"Why would I?" I call out.

"So, you weren't going to call your cop buddies to come and shut us down?" a dark-skinned teenager says, stepping away from the group.

I grin at the way he holds his head high. I remember feeling the need to prove myself as a teenager, especially against the adults who tried to tell me what to do.

"Nah, I was heading in to wash off the day."

My eyes drift to one of the boys standing at the back of the group. A slight tug pulls at my chest, and I'm overwhelmed with a sense of urgency. When the boy's green gaze meets mine, a wave of loneliness and sorrow hits me, so strong it almost knocks me back a step. I've seen that same expression in the mirror many times.

They all eyed me skeptically, and I don't blame them. Some cops like to puff out their chests, but not all of us. I sigh and walk closer, signaling them to throw me the ball. The teenagers all exchange looks and shrug before the tallest one throws the ball my way.

I catch it and smile. "What's your name?"

"Jacob, and this is Mack, Leif, Peter, and Ro," he says, pointing at each of the boys.

"I'm Logan. I promise you won't have a problem from me."

They all wear a mixture of looks. Doubt, confusion, uncertainty and amusement.

"Well, Jacob. Care for a game? Three on three?"

All the boys holler except for Ro—the one with the haunted, sad eyes. He just seems to stand there, nervously shifting from foot to foot. His light brown eyes hold a deep sadness that keeps him distant from the others. I can tell without asking that something's off.

"Okay, Logan, you can team with Peter and Ro," Jacob says.

I shrug and toss the ball back to him. "Sounds good to me."

"Need to warm up, old man?" Leif quips, waggling his eyebrows at me as he bounces back and forth on his toes. At the look of mischief on his face, I tip my head back and laugh. It feels good.

"Thanks for your concern, pipsqueak, but I'm good."

The boys all laugh, "Okay old man show us what you got," Jacob teases.

Jacob bounces the ball, his eyes jumping between Mack and Leif. He throws to Mack, who dribbles forward. He attempts a fake pass, and I intercept, knocking the ball free. Ro snatches the ball up and dribbles the ball toward the hoop, the sound thumping off the road and echoing around us. He pivots and jumps, launching the ball as it hits the rim before going in.

A small grin tugs at Ro's lips, and I flash him a smile. "Nice shot."

Ro nods, a nervous look crossing his face before he jogs off to the side. Peter has the ball, but Leif makes a quick grab, throwing it at Jacob. I move quickly, intercepting the throw, and bounce the ball once before I spin around, and jump, letting the ball go. It arcs perfectly in the air and straight into the center of the hoop.

We end up playing for around half an hour, when the streetlights start to come on. My shirt is sticking to my skin under my jacket, but I don't want to take it off with my holster on, so I snatch the ball and dodge to the side, spinning around and taking the shot. It goes in.

"You're the rain maker," Leif says, looking at me in awe.

"Nah, just had a lot of practice," I reply, holding my fist out.

Each of the boys gives me a fist bump and a pat on the back, except for Ro. He's already gathering his shit and making his way home. With a frown, I turn and head for my house, thoroughly worn out. I can't get Ro's sad eyes from my mind all night. The next time I see him, I'll make sure I ask him if he's okay.

Chapter Eight

Logan

Walking into my house, I remove my jacket and throw it over the back of the couch. I unclip my badge and holster, placing my gun on the kitchen table before walking to the fridge and grabbing a beer. It has been a long day. No one seems to understand my need to follow up on the girl's death. Animal attack is all anyone's saying, all they'll accept. They're happy just to put out her details on the missing person's profile and clean their hands of her.

At least I finished the day without hitting someone. *That* was another reason for my move, I was on thin ice in Portland. The officers in my precinct there were useless, and I have trouble holding my tongue and my temper.

And if that damn lieutenant doesn't quit ogling me, I'm going to snap at her. That won't be pleasant for anyone. All she ever does is make heart eyes at me all day. Makes my skin crawl. I don't understand why women are drawn to me. The scar scares most people off, but sometimes I get those women who see instead a man to comfort and fix. A wounded animal. I am no wounded animal, and I will not get involved with anyone from work. I can't count the number of reasons why that would be a disaster.

Sitting down on the nearby couch, I tip the beer up to my lips. The cool liquid is just what I need. I kick off my shoes and unbutton my sleeves before rolling them up. I hated wearing suits when I first became a detective, but they grew on me, and now I actually enjoy wearing them.

I should probably get a workout in, but all I want to do is jump in the shower and sleep for the next eight hours. Taking another sip, I pull out my phone and open up my emails. Seeing one sitting there from Sander, I click on it, opening it up and quickly reading it.

A photo of him and his family is attached at the bottom. I miss them already. I've only been here a month, but it's enough to know that not seeing my best and only friend whenever I want is going to suck.

Kyra looks happy, her warm brown eyes smiling up at Sander. The boys are five and eight, and almost identical. They're a perfect mix of their parents. I feel a sharp pang in my chest, a sense of longing at something I will never have.

I must have dozed off, because I'm woken by the vibrating of my phone. I look down to see its Sander calling.

"Hey," I answer hoarsely.

"Did I wake you?" Sander's warm voice replies.

I huff out a breath. "Yeah, but I needed to be woken. Haven't even eaten today."

"Is everything alright?" Concern bleeds down the phone line, his voice wary.

I rub a hand over my head and stretch it side to side. "Yeah, just work."

"How's the new job going?"

"Okay."

"Playing nice?"

I let out a rough chuckle. My friend knows me well. "Of course."

"Sure. Well, I just wanted to check in and see you're alive since you haven't responded to my messages or emails."

"Shit, sorry."

"All good. Now I know your alive. Go eat."

"Will do."

I hang up and make my way into the kitchen, opening the fridge. It's bare; only some milk and eggs in there. Sighing, I shut the door. I could order in, but I need some fresh air, and there is a small café I've been wanting to check out. So, I grab my keys, slip my shoes back on, and head out the door.

It only takes around five minutes before I'm pulling into a spot on Main Street. The nights are getting cooler now, and I really have to get around to unpacking the rest of my shit. All my winter gear is still boxed up in the garage. I'm just not sure if I'll be staying yet. The thought of unpacking makes the move seem official. I open the door to the café and make my way to the back corner, giving the young waitress a nod as I walk by. I can see surprise register on her face, and am curious as to why.

I don't bother reading the menu, I know what I want. The young waitress makes her way over, and I can feel her nervousness. I tilt my head up as she approaches, and she sucks in a sharp breath before trying to compose herself. I guess she's never seen scars like mine before.

"Hi, my name is Rose, and I'll be serving you tonight. What can I get you?"

"Steak, medium, and salad," I reply. I don't mean for my words to come out clipped, but I can't stop it. It doesn't make an ounce of difference to the young girl as she writes down my order.

"Drinks?" she asks softly.

"Water."

Rose offers me a warm smile before she leaves, and I frown after her. People come in and out, but I pay them no mind as I go through emails while I wait for my food. A sudden sense of awareness washes over me, followed by the sweetest smell. I close my eyes briefly, drawn in by the scent, my shoulders drop as I relax. I didn't realize I was so tense.

"Detective."

My eyes snap open at the sound of the most alluring voice. "Salena."

I stare up at her beautiful face, her striking blue eyes focused solely on me.

"Can I join you?" she asks softly, almost as if she's afraid of my answer.

"Sure," I say, clearing my throat.

For some reason, I don't want to keep her at arm's length like I do everyone else. But I need to. For her own sake as much as my own. Salena slides in the booth across from me and leans her arms on the table. She's dressed differently tonight, having traded her leather pants and bustier for a plain black tank, jeans, and leather jacket. I swear, this woman could wear a potato sack and still draw gazes. There's something magnetic about her.

"How are you?" she asks.

"Fine."

Salena's lips tip up at the sides. "You always talk this much?" she teases.

My pulse picks up, and warmth spreads through my chest. It's a feeling I'm not used to. "Yep."

She laughs, and damn that sound. My stomach clenches and my eyes drop to her mouth. Fuck, I want to kiss her. I must be staring at her mouth, because she stops laughing, and her eyes spark. Blinking several times, she clears her throat and lowers her voice. "Have you gotten any leads on who the girl was?"

I lean back in my seat, my fingers tapping the table. "No. She hasn't shown up in any missing person databases yet."

"Oh . . . Someone's surely missing her, right?"

"Maybe," I say, looking off to the side.

I freeze as Salena's soft, warm hand covers mine on the table, my gaze moving back to her. Concern lines her eyes. "Are you sure you're okay, detective?"

I want so badly to turn my hand over and link my fingers with hers. Instead, I slowly withdraw my hand and reach for my water.

"I'm fine. Thank you for your concern."

Salena's brows dip and she chews on her bottom lip. A sick feeling twists my stomach, and I think it's guilt at making her uneasy.

The young waitress returns then, glancing between Salena and I. A small secretive smile pulls at her lips as she places my meal down.

"Thank you, Rose," I say.

I don't think she was expecting me to use her name, because surprise shines in her eyes, and she takes a moment to respond.

"You're welcome."

Salena stands. "I'll leave you to it, Detective. Have a good night."

Salena links arms with the waitress and they walk off to the counter. Rose disappears for a moment then reappears with a bag, and the two walk out the door. Salena quickly glances at me over her shoulder before she disappears from sight. My chest tightens, making it hard to breathe when I can no longer see her. I don't know why that makes me nervous, but it does. I don't have time for pretty girls or feelings. But seeing her leave has protective instincts pushing to the surface, and I do my best to rein it in. Now is not the time to let my feelings get the better of me.

Chapter Nine

Logan

I add another file to the stack on my desk and settle into my chair with a heavy sigh. I catch a glimpse of Kallie, the lieutenant, out of the corner of my eye as she makes her way toward me. I can't help how tense my body gets as I grit my teeth in annoyance and count to ten. I get to eight when my phone rings. *Thank fuck.*

I swipe it up and see the unknown number.

"Hello. Detective Sinclair speaking."

"Detective," a voice greets me on the other end, one I recognize.

"Kai?"

"Aww, how sweet. You remember me."

"How could I forget?" I reply sarcastically. "Wait, how'd you get this number?"

Kai chuckles then clears his throat. "Listen, we have a situation at the Crescent Moon."

That has me immediately standing and reaching for my keys. "What's going on?"

Kai blows out a breath and mumbles something, he must be talking to someone else. I start for the front door of the precinct while I wait.

"Look, someone left a dead cat at the front door."

"Ghost?" I ask, my chest squeezing at the thought.

"No, It's a stray, but it's what was done to it that's concerning."

I halt in the doorway. "What?"

"I'll let you see."

"On my way," I reply, seeing that Kallie's followed me. I hold up my hand to stop her approach and shake my head. Her face drops, and she tucks her short, wavy brown hair behind her ear. Her light brown eyes cast downward, understanding the message.

Kai clears his throat. "One more thing."

"What?"

"You've met Ghost?"

I frown as I open my car door. "Yeah. Why?"

I slam my door closed and start the car, listening to the silence on the other end of the phone. I pull it from my ear to make sure the connection's still there.

"Kai?"

"Yeah, sorry. See you when you get here."

The line goes dead. I internally shrug and pocket my phone, then pull on to the street. Ten minutes later, I pull into the parking lot and see Kai talking with another man and Salena. Her eyes move to my car, and she blanches. I can't hear what's being said, but I think Kai's getting a tongue lashing right about now.

The other man looks to be in his early twenties, and could easily pass as Salena's twin. Sucking in a deep breath, I pause before climbing out of the car, and stroll over to where they're standing by the front of the building.

"Kai, Salena," I say nodding in greeting.

Kai steps forward and holds his hand out to me. I reach out and shake it. His usual easy going demeanor is gone as he says, "Thanks for coming, man."

It takes all my willpower not to look at Salena. "No problem."

Salena huffs, and I allow myself to finally turn to her. Despite the fact that I have prepared myself to see her, I'm still floored by her beauty. Even with a frown firmly in place and her arms crossed defensively in front of her, she is stunning. Today, she's in black skinny jeans that mold to her slim body like a second skin, and an off-the-shoulder red top. It's classy and casual.

Salena looks off to the side before returning her gaze to me, her silver hair shimmering in the sunlight as she moves, casting a radiant glow that looks like starlight.

"Sorry to waste your time, detective, but this was nothing but a prank. We can handle it," she says through gritted teeth.

"Why don't I just take a look anyway?"

Kai steps forward. "Sounds good to me."

The other man standing next to Salena steps forward, hand outstretched, a serious look in his eyes. "I'm Felix. Salena's younger brother."

I shake his hand, his grip firm. He squeezes, a warning, and I nod with a smirk tugging at my lips.

I don't need warnings. I have no plan to get involved with his sister. "Logan."

"I can see you're a man of many words." Felix grins, stepping back.

My eyes move to Salena. "Yes."

Kai snickers and motions for me to follow him. The four of us make our way over to the front door of the building where a ginger tabby cat lies. It's been placed in a manner that suggests the person who left it wanted to gain maximum attention. The cat was not simply killed, it was skinned, its stomach cut open. A single word is written in its blood across the door: *Leave.*

Rage courses through me so hot and hard, I struggle to contain the tremble in my hands. I curl my hand into a fist, acid burning my stomach. I spent years learning to control this shit. To curb the violence that would send me spiraling. As I crouch down, getting closer to the cat, I sense Salena approaching me.

"Can we clean it up now?" she grumbles.

"Do you know who left this?" I ask.

When no one answers, I stand, making Salena take a step back. I turn and stare down at her, the look on her face making my chest tighten. Possession coils through me. I want to shield her from this.

"No," she finally replies after several seconds.

"Enemies?" I ask, doing my best to stay calm and focused as I wait for her reply on who the fuck I'm hunting down.

Kai scoffs and Felix elbows him in the ribs, a scowl on his face. You can tell they're siblings even though they have slightly different colorings. Felix looks more like Salena. They have about the same hair and eye color. But Salena's hair is a brighter silver, her features more sharp.

I raise an eyebrow and glance down at Salena.

"Nope," she replies, popping the p.

"Right . . . And that tattooed guy from a few nights ago?" I ask.

Salena frowns. "Reaper?" She raises her hand, waving me off. "No, not him. I would've smelled him."

Her expressive turquoise eyes widen and her brothers both startle.

"Okay, then. Well, I can make a note of it and take some photos, but there isn't much else to be done. If anything happens, it's best to have a paper trail."

Salena nods, her bottom lip clenched between her teeth. My eyes are glued to it. I want to suck her lip from between her teeth and bite down on it myself. My fingers twitch to reach up and touch her. It's like everything else melts away and it's just us.

I register movement in my periphery, and blow out a breath, steadying my heartbeat. Without another word, I walk over to the car and grab the camera. Best to get some proper pictures. I study the poor cat. Whoever did this was not right in the head; this poor creature has suffered greatly. Once I'm done, I pack up my stuff and make my way over to where they're standing.

"I'm done. If you think of anything, let me know."

Kai steps forward, shaking my hand again. "Thanks man, I appreciate it."

"Was nice to meet you, Logan," Felix says with a boyish smile.

Salena tucks her hands in her pockets and looks at the ground. I hear her brothers intake of breath and frown. Salena's eyes dart up to them and then to me. "Thanks, Detective."

"Anytime," I reply gruffly.

Chapter Ten

Salena

I turn on my brother the second Logan's car is out of sight. "Why would you call him?" I snap. I do my best to control my anger, but the minute I noticed Logan pull into the bar my stomach dropped.

Kai runs a hand over his head, looking sheepish. "I thought–"

Flustered, I step back. "No, you didn't think at all. We handle our own shit, Kai. Not the cops."

"I didn't call the cops. I called Logan," he volleys back, clearly annoyed with my response. He thought he was being helpful. Well, this isn't helping.

"We handle our own shit, Kai," I growl.

"What harm is it letting the detective know?" The concern in Felix's blue eyes sends shame through me.

"You know why." I sigh heavily. I shrug one shoulder, hoping it looks more casual than it feels. "Nothing good comes from involving them."

Kai steps forward, his face softening. "I get that, but–"

I hold up my palm, stopping him, and shake my head before turning and storming for the back.

"Told you she'd be pissed," Felix says.

"Just clean it up," I call over my shoulder. Guilt slithers through me at my harshness, and I stop, looking over my shoulder. "Please."

Kai nods. "No problem."

I make my way inside. "I can't believe some asshole would kill an innocent cat," I mumble under my breath.

When I heard the car approaching, Logan was the last person I was expecting to see. When he stepped from the car, I couldn't breathe, he was so handsome. His navy-blue suit oozed power and masculinity. I couldn't drag my eyes from him. His broad shoulders, pale blue eyes, and the scars, draw me in like a moth to a flame. The whole look makes him seem like a real-life superhero. As my eyes darted down to the police badge clipped to his trim waist, the gun strapped there, I couldn't help but wonder if he was.

I want to get to know him, and I know it's a bad idea. He's not only a human, but a cop. I'm not sure if this pull to him is a mating bond, but . . .

I could kill Kai for calling him. I know he wants me to be happy, and he will try and push to see if Logan really is my mate, but the haunted look in his eyes scared me. I don't think he's ready to hear what I have to say.

Ghost winds between my legs glancing up at me. *'Meow . . .'*

I reach down and pick up the cat. It's weird that Logan is the only other person to see Ghost and be able to touch him. I wonder if it's that Ghost is only visible to those she trusts, or if Logan has some sort of second sight. Being able to see beyond the veil is rare, and I'm a hundred percent sure he'd know if he had that gift. There's so much about him I'm curious to know. He seems extremely distant and cut off from others. The few times I've seen him, he has barely pulled together a full sentence.

Chapter Eleven

Salena

Once a month, the pack all gets together out at Kai's house, which is further out of town on a large property. I've always enjoyed the drive out here. The view is breathtaking and is made even better by the crisp mountain air blowing through the windows. It's where the mountains meet the woods. I've been thinking of buying something like this for myself. I can't help but smile at the idea of a peaceful retreat surrounded by nature, and the possibility of owning horses. Living upstairs from my bar is convenient, but the noise and traffic from the street below are constant. I crave a place where I can be alone and won't be disturbed by noise or chatter. I blame spending so much time at the bar for that. The last couple of years I've been dragging my feet when it comes to buying a property. Mostly because I've been waiting for my mate. But now that I've found him, and know nothing can come of it, maybe I should start looking into it.

I push the thought of Logan from my mind and walk up the steps of my brother's beautiful farmhouse. As soon as I pull open the door and step inside, I can hear everyone's voices out on the deck and make my way through the house. A picture of my parents on the wall catches my attention, and a pang hits my chest. It's been five years since they died, and we still aren't sure what happened. One day they just didn't wake up. At least they went together. They were so in love. Most mates are, but I'm talking *real* love. The kind of love I hope to have one day. Releasing a long, drawn-out sigh, I turn away from the picture and continue on toward the deck. My heart is full, and my mood instantly picks up at seeing my pack gathered.

"Salena, you're here." Lola grins, skipping over to me and linking her arm in mine. Lola's the youngest of our pack at sixteen. Her short pixie cut is the color pink today, and her hazel eyes shine with happiness. She is exactly what one would expect of a teenage girl, bright and overly bubbly, and I adore her. Her parents passed away in a freak accident when she was ten and she now lives with Grady and his wife, Lucy. The oldest pack members and good friends of my parents.

"I'm here," I reply, bumping shoulders with her. "What's the hot goss?"

Lola leans into me and whispers, "Kai hooked up with Naomi."

I tip my head back and groan. "Seriously?"

Naomi has been after my brother since high school. She's always hanging around trying to get in with him. Now it's going to be even worse. Plus, she's human, so that makes it even more difficult. When I step up to the grill to give Felix a hug, I spot someone standing off to the side. My body locks up and nerves fill my stomach as Logan's distinctive blue eyes take me in. I stand there speechless until Logan closes the distance between us. Blinking once, I crane my neck to peer up at him. My stomach erupts in a flurry of tremors.

God, those eyes are so alluring.

My toes curl in my boots as excitement and trepidation send my pulse racing. Logan stops just out of arm's reach, looking all sorts of sexy. This is the first time I've seen him out of his suit. The jeans and plain t-shirt look good on him, really good.

"Your brother invited me." His voice, so low and rough and charged, has my mouth going dry.

I blink, trying to find my voice as I stare up at him. "Cool."

Cool? *Cool?* God, what am I? Like, fifteen?!

Logan stares down at me, his face stern, as if he were searching for something. I bite my lip to stop the smile that wants to appear, and his gaze falls to my mouth. A muscle ticks in his jaw, and he looks toward the yard. Seems he isn't as unaffected by my presence as he'd like me to think.

I sense my brothers' stares and roll my eyes in mock annoyance. '*A heads up would have been nice, you turds,*' I say down my link with Kai and Felix.

Both my brothers laugh from their spot off to the side. Rose and Lucy make their way over to us, and I make introductions. Though, Logan already met Rose, and I'm surprised he actually remembers. Lucy's like a mother figure to the group, her warmth and kindness make her easily approachable. When my parents died, she was there to help us. She and Grady's support was invaluable, and without them, the outcome would have been much different. Lucy's long auburn hair sparkles in the sunlight, and her complexion has a few creases from wisdom earned with age.

I don't realize Kai has disappeared until he comes out the back sliding door, a shit eating grin on his face.

"What have you done now?" I sigh, exasperated.

"I got you a present."

I groan, and I hear Lola laugh, followed by Lucy and Rose.

"What?" Kai asks, looking around the deck at everyone.

"Dude, you are a shit gift giver," Declan yells from the back lawn.

"Yeah, do you know what a present is?" Felix adds.

Kai looks confused as he looks around. Taking pity on him, I walk over.

"What is it?"

"I don't want to give it to you now," he pouts, and I can't help the burst of laughter that falls from my mouth.

Kai's arm wraps around my neck and he pulls me into his chest, his knuckles rubbing on top of my head.

"Get off me, you giant baboon." I laugh, trying to free myself from his iron grip.

Kai lets go, and I punch him in the arm before trying to straighten my hair. "You're such a shit," I grumble, but the smile on my face gives me away.

"What are big brothers for?" He smirks at me, then pulls an envelope from his back pocket. I eye it warily.

"What is it?" I ask cautiously.

"Your present," he replies, pushing the envelope at me.

I reach out and pluck it from his hands, opening it immediately. Inside is a signed contract for the Vesperas to play at the bar Friday and Saturday night in two weeks. My eyes widen and a squeal escapes my throat. "How?!"

Kai shrugs. "I know someone."

"But . . . "

I have been trying for months to secure a spot in their schedule. I jump at my brother, wrapping my arms around his neck.

"Oh my god. Thank you!" My enthusiasm is uncontainable, and I dance around the deck, feeling my heart pounding with excitement.

"See, everyone!? Not a shit gift!" Kai says loud enough for everyone to hear.

Lola bounds over and enthusiastically gives him a high five. My gaze catches on Logan's and he seems to be lost in thought as he watches us.

His eyes flicker to mine, as if sensing my gaze, and I'm caught up in the swirl of emotions there. Then he blinks, and his face is a blank mask, as if I imagined it.

"Grub's up!" Felix shouts.

"So much food," Logan muses.

"It'll all get eaten," I reply with a chuckle.

"Really?"

"Yep!" Kai slaps him on the back.

Shifters eat a lot. Food waste is never an issue with us.

We all take a seat at the benches around the large outdoor table that takes up most of the back deck. It's easier this way to fit everyone in. Though, today Mercy isn't here. She's got work at the hospital.

Lola's sharp intake of breath has us all looking at her. Reaching for her mouth, she touches her tongue and laughs. "You don't realize how hard you chew your food until you bite your tongue," she says, blood coating her fingertips.

"Goodness Lola, are you alright?" Lucy looks ready to jump up.

Lola waves her off. "Of course. The tongue is the fastest healing part of the body."

We all stare at her silently for a long moment before Kai clears his throat and turns to Grady. "What were you saying, old man?"

Grady blinks a few times, looking lost. "I forgot what I was going to say."

"Where does a thought go when it's forgotten?" Lola pipes up, popping another piece of meat in her mouth as she looks around at all of us.

"That's an excellent question," Felix admits.

Lola looks at me and I shrug. "Beats me."

Kai laughs, pointing a fork in Lola's direction. "You and your weird ass thoughts."

"What?" She looks affronted.

Rose giggles. "You always have us thinking outside the box."

Dinner passes with easy conversation, and I find it hard to tear my gaze from Logan. Every time our gazes meet, butterflies erupt in my stomach. Logan seems relaxed. I don't think I've heard him speak more than ten words at a time. But here he is, chatting with my brothers and indulging Lola in her stories. My pack is overjoyed to have him here, to get to know their alpha's mate. I'm lost in my own thoughts when I hear Kai say my name.

"Salena's heading that way. She can take you home."

My gaze snaps to Logan, nerves filling me, making my pulse speed up.

"Where's your car?" I ask.

Logan scratches the back of his head. "Kai picked me up."

"Yeah, so he wouldn't bail!" Kai yelled over the group.

I rub my lips together with a smile, making Logan's eyes drop and linger for a moment. He swallows roughly, and for a moment, I think he might kiss me. I can sense that he wants to, but he seems to shake it off and step away. I try not to show my disappointment.

"Yeah, I can take you back," I say.

"Are you sure? I don't want to be a burden," Logan replies.

I wave off his concerns. "It's fine."

I tap my fingers on the steering wheel, trying to hum along with the music. The sun's setting, casting the sky in reds and oranges. I look over in the fading light at Logan and smile. As I turn my head back to the road, my body freezes, muscles locking up tight as my stomach drops. I whip my eyes back toward Logan and gasp. Not a second later, I have the brakes locked up and am out of the car, my heart pounding.

"Oh my god. Oh my god. Oh my god," I chant, my entire body shaking while jumping on the spot. I tip my head down and run my hands through my hair. Goosebumps break out over my arms, sending a course of shivers racing over my skin. It feels like tiny ants are crawling all over me. I run my hands over my clothes, wiping down my arms. When I look back up, Logan is looking at me over the top of the car, one eyebrow raised in question.

"Any reason you're dancing all over the middle of the road?"

"There is a *spider* on the back of your headrest!" I shriek, patting my body down again.

Logan's head ducks back into the car and he comes back out holding the massive spider. I leap back another few feet, even though there are already several yards between us, plus the car.

Logan looks up at me and smirks. "This tiny thing?"

I gasp, absolutely horrified. "That thing is *huge!*"

"Only because it's carrying babies."

"Oh my god!!" I screech as another round of full body tremors rack my body.

"It's more scared of you–"

I hold up my hand, stopping him, and shake my head. "Nope. I've heard it all before. Just get rid of it."

Logan shakes his head, smirking, and turns, walking to a tree. Unable to watch, I turn on the spot and pull out my phone from my back pocket, quickly sending a text to Kai.

Salena: My car's on the main road into town. Can you collect it for me and burn it, crush it, I don't care. Just get rid of it.

Kai: What?

Salena: I don't care what you do with it but I'm never driving it again.

Kai: Where are you?

I turn my screen off and pocket my phone just as Logan approaches. "There. All taken care of. Now we can go."

"I– I'm n– not getting back in that car," I stammer.

Logan's eyes brighten with amusement. "You can't be serious."

"Deadly."

I turn and start walking down the road toward town. I hear a sigh and Logan falls in step with me.

"Are you seriously just going to leave your car here because of a spider?" he asks, tone incredulous.

"I needed a new one anyway," I bite.

Logan laughs. "Really?"

"I hate spiders."

"I couldn't tell."

I grunt and keep walking, wanting to get home and shower, to make sure none of those babies got on me. Another shudder runs down my spine.

"It wasn't even that big."

I growl, and feel my eyes flash, so I look down at my feet quickly. "It was huge, and it was covered in hundreds of babies. The car is dead to me."

Before Logan can respond, a set of headlights come up behind us and Kai slows down next to us. "Really, Salena?"

I glare at him, and he tips his head back, laughing at me. His hand hangs out the window and he taps his car door, then looks over to Logan. "Seems the big bad wolf is afraid of spiders," he jokes, and I want to strangle him.

Kai stops the truck and motions to get in. "Come on, I'll drop you off."

"Thanks," I say, moving toward the truck.

I jump in the backseat, leaving the front for Logan. Kai eyes me in the rearview mirror. The mirth in his eyes makes me want to hit him. I cross my arms and stare out the window.

"She has always been terrified of spiders," Kai decides to voice.

Before I have a chance to yell to Kai, Logan's voice cuts through the cab. "We all have things we're afraid of."

"Touché," Kai replies, looking at me in the mirror.

Kai drops me at the bar first, and I watch as he and Logan drive away. The quietness of the night settles around me, and I sigh. I have never experienced this before, and the sensation of inadequacy is overwhelming. When Logan starts to open up, it's as if he can feel himself wavering, and quickly retreats. A shadow moves behind his eyes, and I sense his walls go back up. I desperately want him to open up and accept me, but I'm not sure I can make it happen.

Chapter Twelve

Logan

I feel an ominous presence behind me, the soft sound of a woman singing drifting on the wind. A cold sweat breaks out all over my body. I snap open my eyes. I don't see it, but I can sense it.

The shadow is there, lurking just beyond reach, watching, waiting.

A sharp pain steals my breath as something stabs into my back, causing me to arch in pain as if I could somehow escape.

I cannot breathe or scream. The only sound coming from me is a wheezing sound as my heart rate triples.

There's a disturbance in the air behind me, and a cold breath caresses my cheek, before a hauntingly soft voice whispers in my ear, "Your time's almost up. I can't wait to taste all that misery and loneliness that's eating you up on the inside."

My eyes snap open for real this time, and I jolt up in bed, panting as I swallow my fear. I glance around the room, searching those darker corners for the source of my unease. The phantom pain still lingers in my back. I reach my hand around and touch the area, finding it slick with sweat. I take my hand away only to see it's darker. Frowning, I reach for the lamp and switch it on. Blood coats my hand, and I spin, looking down at the bed sheets, seeing them smeared with blood. What the hell . . .

It was a dream. It wasn't real.

I walk into my adjoining bathroom and look over my shoulder in the mirror. Five large puncture wounds are seeping blood, like someone stabbed their long sharp nails into my back. My eyes travel over the other scars on my back, and I turn, looking over the rest of my torso, the angel wings I have tattooed across my chest, the only thing I try to focus on. The name etched in the wings across my heart.

I step into the shower to wash away the blood, then do my best to patch myself up, pulling on an old Portland PD t-shirt and some loose track pants. I make quick work of stripping the sheets and remaking the bed. I can't help the fear that tightens my chest as I ball up the bloodied sheets, and make my way downstairs, giving up on sleep.

The nightmare hovers over me as I enter the kitchen and toss the sheets in the corner to take out to the trash in the morning. I draw up short when I hear a muffled noise coming from the back porch, followed by a clicking sound. Without turning on the lights, I move quickly to the drawer and grab a handgun I keep hidden there. My pulse is steady as my brain flips modes. I check the magazine and flick off the safety, moving slowly to the back door. Without much thought behind it, I swing open the door and raise my gun as I step onto the porch.

A heavy thud comes from my left, and I swing my gun, my gaze clashing with the white wolf I saw in the Crescent Moon parking lot a few days ago.

I blow out a breath as I lower my gun. I don't say anything as we stare at each other. The wolf slowly steps from the shadows and approaches me. I stand stock still, unsure if I should step back inside or wait to see what it's going to do.

I decide to wait as the wolf steps up to me, its head tilted. It circles me, pausing at my back, its nose sniffing my shirt. The wolf whines before moving back in front of me. It pushes me with its head until my knees meet the deck chair and I sit. I stare straight into its unique eyes, blue ringed with yellow. It's an odd combination, and yet I feel as if I know this animal as something familiar is reflecting back at me in those eyes. I reach my hand out and gently stroke over its ears, its white coat extremely soft and thick. It shuffles even closer, leaning into the touch, and I smile. The nightmare seems to evaporate with that touch, all my worries and fears quieten down, and my head goes silent. It's wonderful.

"You are gorgeous," I murmur, reaching my other hand up and stroking down its neck.

The wolf's eyes seem to glow, and it nuzzles me. My lips tug up, and I sigh, a feeling of contentment washing over me.

"I don't know why you're here, but I'm glad you are. I need the distraction." I relax into the chair, a slight hiss falling from my lips as my back hits the chair. The wolf's ears perk up at my pain, but I smooth a hand over its head.

"I'm okay," I grunt.

The wolf doesn't take its eyes off me as I try to relax in the deck chair. "You know, I've had these nightmares since I was a kid. They feel so real. And I always wake up with marks . . . " I trail off, feeling foolish for talking to an animal.

The wolf nudges my hand gently, and I let out a stuttered breath. "It's not something you forget, you know. That moment you think you're going to die. There's no white light, no peace, no calm. It's pain, and fear. You remember every second of it, and it doesn't fade over time."

The wolf's head rests on my leg, and it whines. As my hand runs over its massive head, I can't get over how soft and thick the fur is. Accepting the comfort, I settle in and wait for the sun to rise.

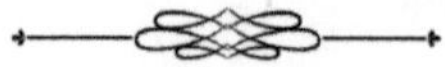

I'm sitting at my desk draining my third cup of coffee, but my mind is on Salena. I had a great afternoon at Kai's house yesterday. I was way more relaxed than I thought I'd be.

But then nightmares plagued me all night, flashes of my brother's death and animal attacks on a constant loop. I have this awful sense of dread curdling my stomach, and I can't shake the feeling. It's like I somehow know something bad's going to happen, and I'm on edge.

"Sinclair!"

My head snaps up at the gruff voice. "Captain?"

"There's another body. I want you out there."

Shocked, I feel fiery anger surge through my veins, and I'm already gathering my shit before he finishes speaking. "Sure thing."

My mind is running over a hundred different scenarios as I make my way out to the hiking trail north of town. It's a popular area, not a great place to leave a body.

I pull up at the crime scene and flash my badge, ducking under the tape. I overhear a couple of cops as I pass.

"Another animal attack?"

"I don't know."

"We don't get many animal attacks here."

Annoyance grows in my chest. I don't believe the first was an animal attack, and my intuition is very rarely wrong. I see Abby up ahead, her red hair glinting in the sunlight as she stares down at the body in front of her.

"Hey, Abby," I say, making my way past her to the body.

Abby's head snaps up, as if she wasn't expecting me.

"Hey, detective."

I squat down next to the victim, and pressure builds in my chest as I stare down into her terror-stricken face, her mouth open in a silent scream. This poor girl suffered, and not just in her final moments. The bruises and swelling across her body suggest long term abuse.

Abby, the crime scene specialist, snaps some photos, getting close-ups of the victim's hands and feet, which have been rubbed raw from rope marks. The first victim didn't have rope marks. This woman looks as if she was held longer, starved and tortured.

"This is the second body. Both victims have the same characteristics. This doesn't seem like an animal attack to me," Abby says, lowering her camera.

"I don't think so either."

Abby's warm brown eyes meet mine and she pauses, dropping her voice to a whisper. "The two girls both show signs of abuse."

I grunt in response and look around the body. "ID?"

Abby's bright red hair dances around her face as she shakes her head. "None."

I let my eyes drift over the body again as I stand, every mark on the victim's body lit up by the harsh LED lights. "She looks half starved," I note.

Abby hums and snaps another photo. "I know. I think she was kidnapped and basically fed to the wolves when she outlived her purpose."

My blood runs cold as Abby voices my thoughts. This girl was put through hell. The suffering and depravity inflicted on her was unimaginable. She was probably praying for death to come for her.

I'll have to wait for the official cause of death, but I know some fucked up person tied this poor girl up and tormented her then tossed her away like garbage. It's my job to find this fucker and bring him to justice, help make sense of this crime. But it won't help the family left behind. They rarely get the answers they're looking for.

Just like me.

"Sexually assaulted?" I can't help how harsh my voice is when I ask.

Abby froze and looks up at me from her camera, "I– I don't know. Doc will have to–"

"Detective Sinclair?" a loud voice interrupts.

I turn to the newcomer. "Yes?"

It's the captain, and he looks worried as he makes his way over. "I need your full focus on this, and to keep it quiet. I can't have the city of Boulder thinking we have a serial killer on the loose. For now, it's an animal attack." Stress lines his face, making him look ten years older.

"Understood," I reply. I don't like it, but if it gets out into the public that we might have a serial killer on our hands, we'll have panic and vigilantes running around, causing god knows what kind of havoc.

"Good." The captain's eyes drift to the body behind me, and I can see the tension there, behind his eyes and the way he's holding his body.

He runs a hand over his mouth. "Poor girl," he mutters, then turns, walking back to the parking lot.

It takes me a couple of hours to go over the crime scene and talk to the poor jogger who found the body. The younger woman takes this path three times a week, and says it's a quiet path that doesn't usually have many people around. I don't think she will be running this path again, if the haunted look in her eyes is anything to go by. I reach into my pocket for my wallet, find the card I'm looking for, and hand it to her. The woman looks down at it, surprise lighting her eyes.

"A shrink?"

"The best counselor in the city," I reply, and turn on my heel, heading for my car. I do my best to shake off the lingering weakness I feel.

Everyone is spooked. I can sense it in the way they hold their bodies, hear it in their voices, and see it in their eyes. It started out as an animal attack, now it's two Jane Does torn apart like ragdolls, who looked so similar they could have passed for sisters.

I drive back into town, my mind numb, not really paying attention to where I'm going. I stop the car and look out the window to see that I'm at The Crescent Moon. I don't know how long I've been sitting there when there's a tap on the passenger window. My gaze connects with a set of brilliant blue eyes in the dark. Salena.

The door opens, and she slides into the seat and shuts the door. It traps her smell in the car, her beautiful scent surrounding me, smoothing down my frayed edges and calming my nerves. What is it about her that is just so alluring and comforting?

"Are you okay, detective?" Her voice is soft, almost a whisper.

I break eye contact and stare out the front window. "It's been a long day."

"I heard about the animal attack," she says, laying her hand on my arm. "Did you want to come in and I will pour you a drink?"

"No."

Even without looking at her, I can feel her hurt at my sharp tone.

"Okay. Is there anything I can do?" she asks.

"It wasn't an animal attack."

Her hand spasms on my arm, and I hear her intake of breath. I look over at her, and I can see the shock in her eyes and the tightening of her mouth. She's worried, and not just about the attacks, but about me.

How do I feel like I've known her my whole life, after only meeting her a week ago? I take a deep breath and force the thoughts out of my head, violently and mercilessly shoving them back.

"She looks just like you," I breathe the words into the car.

Salena's eyes widen. "Both of them?"

"Yes. With the threat you got, I think it's the same person, or it could be two people. Both targeting you."

"Me . . . " she says, her voice trailing off.

"There's no proof, but it's just my gut is telling me it's connected. With the message left for you at the bar, it seems like a stalker. But the girls, the way it's escalating, I think it's two different people. They seem to be targeting girls who look like you. Making them look like animal attacks or even using an animal. Either they are in on it together or they are working alone. I don't know yet, but you need to keep an eye out and call me immediately if something happens or if you feel unsafe."

I pull out my card and hand it to her. The slight brush of our fingertips sends a jolt through my hand and up my arm. Salena's blue eyes drop to where our fingers are touching, and she seems transfixed. My heart thuds hard in my chest, and I slowly pull my hand away. Blinking, she looks back at me, a blush staining her snow white cheeks, her full red lips parting on a soft inhale, and I want nothing more than to lean over and take her mouth. This . . . might be a problem.

Chapter Thirteen

Killer

It's possible he might have gotten a bit excited with his plans and killed the girl more quickly than he was supposed to. He just couldn't help himself. Sometimes, he forgets just how fragile humans are.

Looking over at his other prizes, the collection of women he's gathered from all over the state, his gaze is drawn to the one who hasn't stopped crying since she woke this morning. The sound is doing his head in. Humans are so weak. They have too many emotions.

He hates emotion.

Salena wouldn't cry, she would snarl and bite.

Crying is a weakness.

This one doesn't have *her* strength, which is a pity.

She won't fight.

He sighs heavily and walks toward where the three women are bound and gagged along the wall. They all look strikingly similar in appearance. All platinum blonde hair and blue eyes. No one would have Salena's hair color, of course. Her hair color is unique. Her eyes switch between blue and green at any given moment. He has spent months watching her. Learning all about her.

He ignores the cries and whimpers from the others as he selects his next prize. Reaching for her chains, he undoes the lock and drags her by her hair over to the table.

Chapter Fourteen

Salena

I press my lips together firmly, inhaling slowly. "It's not that bad."

"Not that bad," Kai snaps. He takes a full step back, placing his hands on his hips as he glares at me. "It sounds pretty fucking bad to me, Salena."

"It doesn't mean anything."

"The fuck it doesn't. Someone's out there targeting girls that fit your description. Leaving you goddamn threats. You can't tell me it means nothing."

I want to scream my frustration to the sky. I didn't know what to tell him. Whoever is behind the threats knows what I am. They're smart in keeping their tracks covered and scent hidden. Kai is fuming as he paces the living room. Felix stands off to the side, arms crossed and frown firmly in place.

"Look, we need to find out how they're able to mask their scent. It's odd we can't find even the smallest amount of scent to trace."

Felix nods. "I'll take Declan and go to see Old Myrtle. See if she can tell us anything."

I cringe at the thought of seeing Old Myrtle, and am thankful Felix is offering. Myrtle is a seer who was shunned from her coven twenty years ago. The details surrounding her departure from the coven are murky at best, and I don't like to speculate. Myrtle isn't so bad as far as old ladies go, but she is eccentric to say the least, us shifters don't enjoy being around her.

"Okay. Thanks, Felix." I look between my brothers. "Everything will be fine. I have work, but make sure the pack is made aware and to be careful."

Kai nods, his fists clenching. "Has Ash gotten back to you?"

I shake my head. "Not yet."

He blows out a long breath and nods. "Okay. I'll drive you to the bar."

The night is busy, which helps to keep my mind off the events of the day. I've just delivered another round of drinks and head back to the bar, stepping around a group of men. One grabs my arms, managing to catch me off guard, and swiftly spins me around. My palms land on his broad chest and I grunt, pushing him away. I peer around to see there are five of them, all dressed in leather cuts, closing in around me. They really don't know what or who they're dealing with. The guy who grabbed me steps into my space, his hand grabbing my waist.

"Get your hands off me," I say in a low, calm voice.

"Come on, sweetheart. A pretty girl like you, dressing like that, wants attention. You're practically begging for it," the sleaze bag sneers. He looks at his friends and his shoulders jerk as he laughs.

Anger and fury explode in my veins at his audacity. It's men like this who make women feel unsafe. I tug my arm free, and I look for an escape route, but I am surrounded. I'm not worried, but I also don't want to make a scene.

Jerkface in front of me takes a sip from his beer. "You got a nice rack. Bit skinny, but enough for a good romp." His tongue darts out, licking his lower lip, as his eyes travel my body, stopping on my crotch.

"I bet you're real tight, too."

I wrinkle my nose in disgust, my stomach churning at his crude words.

"Sorry, boys, but you all fall way under the bar I've set for myself."

Jerkface steps forward, his chest brushing mine, but I refuse to back down. I glare up at him, his green eyes filled with a crazed wickedness. He's used to getting what he wants. Whether it's consensual or not. I can smell it on him.

"Come on, sweetheart, don't be like that," he jeers, earning himself some chuckles from his friends.

"Back the fuck off and get the fuck out of my bar," I grit, my teeth, aching with how tightly my jaw is clenched.

Suddenly, the man is ripped away from me and swung around. My eyes widen as Logan's face is in his, as he pins the man to the closest wall, his forearm across the man's neck.

"She said back off!" he snarls, the sound ripping through the air like thunder.

The man makes a choking sound that snaps me from my shock, and I dart forward. "Logan."

Logan's gaze stays glued to the man he holds against the wall. He presses his forearm a little harder against the man's throat, making his next words seem even more threatening as he leans in close.

"You ever fucking touch her again and I will end you. Understand?"

The man makes a gurgling noise, and my hand reaches up, landing on Logan's arm.

"Is– is that . . . a threat?" he chokes out.

Logan pushes a little harder, making the man's eyes bulge,

"No, it's a fucking promise. Touch her again, and it will be the last thing you fucking do," he snarls in the man's face.

My heart is thundering in my chest. "Logan?"

Logan releases the man, letting him fall down the wall, his eyes watering. "Fuck you, man. And fuck her," he says, holding his neck.

Logan takes another step forward, fists clenched. "One more word. I dare you," he snarls.

I can see the muscles under his shirt bunch, he wants to lay this guy out, but is holding himself back.

The man stumbles to his feet, and he glares at us as he and his friends walk toward the door. I watch them go, making sure they don't cause trouble on the way out. I startle when Logan's fingers brush along my hand.

"Are you okay?" he asks, looking down at me. And the way his eyes drill into mine steals my breath. He is so damn handsome.

"Always," I whisper.

Logan grunts and steps closer, his eyes bright and full of desire, making my heart thump loudly.

"I hate them watching you," he says, lowering his voice.

At first, I'm confused, but I follow his gaze and see several men looking our way. My hand reaches out slowly, and I link my pinky with his. "Good thing I'm not watching them."

Logan's finger tightens around mine as we stare at each other, everything else fading out. A body bumps into mine, breaking the spell, and Logan steps away, clearing his throat. He turns his face away as if to hide his scars from me.

His gaze briefly flicks back to me. "I'll let you get back to work."

When he turns to leave, everyone parts for him like the Red Sea. Women watch as he walks past, and I feel my claws extend. I shake my head at my own ridiculousness and watch him step through the door, a pang of longing hitting me square in the chest. The night before flashes through my mind, along with what he said. Whatever happened to him left him with scars deeper than the ones on his face. I make my way back behind the bar, and Declan slides up and leans over so only I can hear.

"He's scary for a human. And strong. He basically threw that guy against the wall," Declan whispers harshly in my ear. When I turn to look at Declan, his distinctive grayish blue eyes sparkle with delight, and his blonde hair with blue tips tumbles over his forehead.

"I noticed," I say, biting my bottom lip.

It's hot.

Chapter Fifteen

Logan

I tuck my hands into my pants pockets as I make my way down the street. It's getting cooler now, the air crisp as autumn slowly fades away. I don't know how the others roped me into joining them for a drink at the small bar down the road after our Friday shift. I silently follow Milo into the bar; this is the last place I want to be, but Sander's been pushing me to open up and try to make friends. I've barely spoken to anyone down at the precinct, except for Milo. He's young, and a new Dad. I like him because he respects my boundaries and doesn't push for more. Milo moves to the bar, pushing his shaggy brown hair from his face as he orders a round of drinks. From the corner of my eye, I see

Kallie approach, her shoulders pulled back and head high. She comes to a stop next to me, and I groan internally. I have a feeling I'm going to have to be direct and firm with her or she's just not going to leave me alone.

"So, how are you liking our small city, Logan?"

I drop my gaze to hers, and her eyes widen a little at the full weight of my stare. "It's different," I answer, unable to keep the bored tone from my voice. I look around the bar. It's a fairly busy night, even though it's still early. All the tables are full, and a few people are out on the small dance floor. I feel the weight of my age as I glance around the room. Thirty-one is far from old, but half the people here don't look old enough to be drinking, or even to grow facial hair.

A flash of silver hair catches my eye, and my pulse picks up. My eyes scan the crowded bar, hoping it's *her*.

Kallie moves in closer to me, and I stiffen as her hand lands on my bicep. My gaze snaps to hers. Her smile is forced, betraying her nerves.

"So, what do you do in your down time?" she asks, trying to make small talk.

I fucking *hate* small talk.

I move my arm, making her hand fall. Her brows crease and she shifts nervously on her feet. I fold my arms and slowly raise my gaze to survey the crowded bar. Another flash of silver hair catches my attention, and I turn in time to see Salena making her way over to a group of girls who are standing around a high table. They all cheer and raise their drinks before taking a sip.

"Logan?" Kallie says my name, reminding me I haven't answered her.

I look down at her. "Hiking. I like hiking," I say, making something up on the spot. I've never been hiking one day in my life. I can't think of anything worse than the idea of walking through the forest.

"Oh, me, too. Maybe I could show you some trails next time we have a matching day off."

"I hike alone," I reply.

Just then, Milo appears in front of us with a beer held out for me, his steel gray eyes lingering on mine in amusement. I take it, nodding my thanks, and Milo strikes up a conversation with Kallie. Two other officers join the group, Sam and Mark. Sam's a newbie to the force, and he looks it. Mark is in his sixties and almost set to retire. He's been in Boulder his whole life.

My gaze remains trained on Salena. She must feel my eyes on her, because she looks over her shoulder, her crystal-clear turquoise eyes locking on mine. A smile slowly spreads across her face before she turns back to her friends.

The conversation continues around me, but I barely say a word unless the questions are directed at me. I've never been one to socialize, though when I was at Kai's with Salena and her friends and brothers, I somehow felt at ease in a way I'm not used to. Like the tightening of my throat loosened, allowing my words to flow freely. I haven't felt like that in such a long time.

Milo draws my attention. "What's it like in Portland? My wife has been wanting to go there for a while."

"It's nice. Wet." I take another sip of my beer. Milo gives me a smile and shakes his head at my short answer. I glance back at Salena and freeze. A man stands a few feet from her, openly staring at her ass. My hands clench around my beer, and I fight the growl that works its way up my throat.

The man edges closer to her, his eyes never moving from her body. Yes she has a great body, and I don't blame him for looking, but I fucking hate it. His short blonde hair is styled messy, and he's dressed in blue jeans and black buttoned shirt. His jewelry screams rich boy, which means he's probably used to getting things he wants. The thought of him having Salena has my jaw clenching to the point of pain. The man stops just behind her as she laughs at something her friend said. She is absolutely gorgeous with her head tipped back, the brightness of her skin and eyes making her look like a goddess. A goddess I want on her knees in front of me.

The guy reaches out, grabbing her wrist and spinning her around to face him. I freeze, a possessive wildness creeping into my veins. I don't like anyone but me touching her. The other night was bad enough when I stopped into Crescent Moon for a drink after work and saw that a guy and his friend had her cornered. My heart was pounding in my ears, and I had to struggle to keep myself in check. I walked out of the bar that night without ever having a beer. This time, I'm not sure I'll be able to hold back if he doesn't back the fuck off her. My stomach churns with the need to storm over there and rip his arm from the socket and beat him with it.

What the fuck is wrong with me? She isn't mine. I need to get it together. I've never been this worked up by anyone before. There's just something so captivating about her, something that has my dead heart beating for the first time in twenty-five years.

The guy steps closer to her, getting in her face, and my eyes narrow on where his hand is wrapped around her arm. Salena's hand lands on his chest as she pushes him back, but he doesn't budge.

Jealousy and possessiveness overtake me. Before I know what's happening, I'm pushing my beer at Milo, ignoring his questioning gaze, and storming across the bar. Salena must sense my approach because she manages to spin herself and the guy, so her back is to my chest, putting herself in between us. My arm wraps around her middle, and I drag her backward into me. The guy drops her arm like it's on fire and takes a quick step back at the thundering look on my face. I don't say a word as my other hand lands on Salena's hip and I lean down to kiss her bare shoulder. Her head tips to the side, giving me more room. I obey her unspoken words and kiss her neck, my hands squeezing her as my eyes remain on the dickhead in front of us, daring him to make a move. Salena turns in my arms, and I drop my gaze to hers. A coy smile lights up her face, the look almost knocking the wind out of me.

Her hands loop around my neck, and she leans in, whispering in my ear, "Hello to you, too, detective."

A low growl rumbles from my throat at her teasing tone, and I grip her waist, anchoring her to me. When I look back up, the guy is nowhere to be seen, and her friends are all openly watching us, broad smiles on their faces. My gaze narrows slightly on one of the girls, it's Rose, and she didn't look much older than eighteen.

Salena turns her head and follows my gaze. She grins and looks back at me, pausing when she sees the look on my face.

"Is she supposed to be in here?" I ask.

Salena pats my chest. "She isn't drinking, and we are all watching out for her. No one would dare mess with Rose."

The cop in me wants to debate this, but the moment Salena's soft warm hands cup my face, tipping it down to her, I'm gone. Completely lost in those eyes. I've been ignoring the way she makes me feel, the way my body responds to her. My fingers flex on her hips as I drag in a deep breath. Her sweet flowery scent is calming and mouthwatering, stirring my blood. Her lips curve up at the side as if she can read my mind. Slowly, Salena closes the space between us, her hands still holding my face, and places those soft, plump lips on mine. All thought flees my mind. I groan, deepening the kiss, my mouth moving over hers.

Fuck, she tastes like whiskey and something sweeter.

I pull back, my heart thumping hard against my ribcage as I stare down into her intense eyes.

"I want you so fucking bad I can't breathe. I should stay away from you. I tried. But something keeps pulling me back."

Her blue eyes glimmer with an emotion I can't name, and I watch in curious silence as her hand reaches up to trace my jaw, her fingers spreading over my cheek, my scars.

"Then stay," she says loud enough for me to hear over the music.

Her words fuel my desire, and I pull her closer, my lips brushing her ear. "Are you sure?"

I hear her intake of breath and feel her fingers tighten on my arms as she holds onto me. I pull back slightly, and she gives me a gentle nod of her head. Relief floods me. She wants this, too. Grabbing my hand, she pulls me over to her friends, all faces I remember from the barbeque.

I peer around the bar, my eyes catching on Kallie. Hurt that I don't understand is splashed across her face.

Chapter Sixteen

Salena

I noticed the second Logan walked into the club; I felt a warmth inside me that brought a smile to my face. I wanted to get to know him better, and I wasn't sure he would notice me. And when I saw that woman talking to him, trying to get his attention . . . The way she looked at him set my teeth on edge. It took all my strength not to storm over there and claim him.

But now, as we all make our way out onto the street, Logan stops next to me when I don't follow the others back to the car.

"Are you coming, Salena?" Rose calls, walking backward down the sidewalk.

"I'll walk," I call back, butterflies taking flight as Logan's warm palm lands on my lower back.

Rose's eyes twinkle as she winks at me. I shake my head, waving goodbye to them all. We watch as they pile in the car and pull away from the bar.

I turn to Logan. "Walk me home, detective?"

Logan's eyes burn with lust as he stares at me. "Lead the way."

I start walking in the opposite direction the girls went, stepping over a puddle. "So how long have you been in Boulder?" I ask.

Logan's body grows tense. I have a feeling he doesn't like small talk, or the get to know you questions. But I'm stubborn. I'll break him down eventually. My mother always said I never knew when to give up.

I look over at him expectantly. "Well?"

Logan shoves his hands in his pockets and looks at the ground, "About two months."

"Do you like it here?"

His gaze moves to mine. "Yes."

My body warms at his tone, his response causing my stomach to dip. I bite my lip, and his eyes drop to my mouth. Logan's hand reaches out, clasping my wrist gently, and he pulls me into his chest. His eyes are burning with desire as he glances at my lips. My whole body heats, causing my breath to hitch as he slowly lowers his head, his lips barely brushing mine when a drop of rain hits my cheek, then another and another. I look up at the sky and curse as the sky opens up and the rain soaks us in seconds.

We run up the stairs to my apartment, and I push open the door. Water slides off us, making a puddle on the floor as we step in. I can't help but laugh. We are soaked.

"I'll get us a towel," I say, already walking toward the bathroom. I bend over to grab two towels, and when I stand, Logan is right behind me. How did I not hear him? We stare at each other in the mirror, his eyes heating me to the core. He takes a step closer so his chest is pushed against my back. Dipping his head, his lips brush the shell of my ear, making me shiver.

"You have bewitched me."

His palm brushes my wet hair over my shoulder, and he places a soft kiss there, his pale blue eyes never leaving mine. I bite my lip to stop myself from saying something to ruin the moment. Logan brushes his lips along my neck back up to my ear.

"I want you spread out beneath me, screaming my name." His tongue darts out, swirling on my pulse and making my core clench. "I don't care if you come on my tongue or cock, as long as it's my name you're screaming." His voice is scratchy and rough, and I shiver. My hands grip the basin in front of me, needing something to hold me steady. "I want you writhing against me, as I worship this sexy as fuck body of yours." His teeth nip at my shoulder.

My heart lurches and my stomach clenches at the images those dirty words conjure. The look in his eyes is pure hunger, and it has butterflies rioting in my stomach.

"Don't tease," I say huskily.

"I'm not. I want to do so many dirty, wicked things to you. I honestly don't know where to start." His fingers play with the thin straps on my dress.

I turn to face him, and his hands drop away from me. I loop my arms around his neck, drawing him closer to me, and whisper against his lips,

"Start anywhere, detective. Anywhere you want to kiss, you can also bite. I want you to leave your mark on me . . . make it sting."

Logan's eyes flare and his lips crash with mine in a possessive kiss, fingers digging into my ass and hips as he pushes against me. His tongue glides against the seam of my lips, and I open my mouth to slide my tongue along his.

Shit . . . I feel like I'm on fire. My body trembles with need as his grip tightens on me. Logan growls into my mouth, causing another delicious shiver to race over me. He kisses me like he wants to consume me in the most wicked way.

He pulls back, both of us desperately trying to catch our breath.

"We should get–"

Logan growls, cutting me off, and his hands wrap around my waist as he lifts me up and places me on the basin, his large palm landing on my chest. Applying the slightest pressure, he pushes me back until my shoulders meet the cool glass. Then slowly he glides his palm down my chest, between my breasts to my legs, pushing up my dress. I'm panting with need, but content to watch him, waiting to see what he does. Gripping my hips, he pulls me until I'm seated on the very edge of the basin, then drags my underwear down my legs. The moment is so slow and torturous, I'm doing my best not to beg him to hurry. I love how possessive he's being. It calls to something hidden deep inside of me.

Leaning forward, he bites down on my bottom lip, hard. I hear the sound of his zipper echoing off the bathroom wall. He straightens, and I watch in fascination as he rips open a condom and rolls it on, not once taking his piercing gaze off mine. I'm breathless by the time he's positioning himself, and pushing in.

My head tips back, hitting the mirror with a thud. A loud moan falls from my lips as they part with a gasp. He's big, and the stretch is amazing. The pain mixed with pleasure is sending sparks firing through me.

"Fuck, you're tight," he growls, working his way in.

My hands land on his biceps, and I feel the tremble of restraint there. I lean forward to graze my teeth over his neck, and grip his shirt, tearing it open. The sound of buttons falling mingles with our breathing.

"Don't hold back, detective," I purr, running my hands over his abdomen and up his chest, pinching his nipple.

I don't have a chance to admire the angel wings tattooed on his chest as his hand wraps around my throat, tipping my head back. My core clenches at the heated look in his arctic gaze, making a small hiss fall from his lips.

"You're going to be the death of me," he growls, slamming into me, hard.

I bite my bottom lip, tipping my hips up. "But it will be a good death, right?"

His fingers flex around my neck. "The fucking best."

Logan picks up the pace, his hips slamming into me hard and fast as he grinds his pelvis into mine. My eyes roll back as I take everything he's giving me. Logan's grip on my neck tightens as his thumb presses on my pulse. My breathing is stuttered, and a rush of desire fills me at his possessiveness.

"Harder," I breathe.

Logan growls, slamming into me once more before pulling out. He lifts me from the basin and spins me, grabbing my hips and guiding himself back in. Oh my god, he feels so good. Our eyes meet in the mirror and hold. Logan's palms glide up my body, dragging my dress over my head, then banding his arm across my chest, he pulls me flush against his body. His tan skin against my pale white is a beautiful contrast. One hand cups my breast and his other hand glides down and hooks my leg, lifting it so he can drive in deeper. His eyes go to where we are joined, and my head falls back to his shoulder as he pumps into me over and over, drawing me higher. My muscles quiver and clench around him, and I feel my canines descend, wanting to mark him.

Shit.

I try to cover them with my lips, but Logan's thumb brushes over my clit, causing me to cry out as the orgasm rips through me like a lightning bolt. He groans into my neck, driving in harder as my muscles clench around him.

"Fuck, Salena," he growls, gripping me even tighter. I'm sure I'll have bruises.

His whole body goes taut and he shudders as his arm wraps securely around my waist, pulling me so tightly against him there's absolutely no space between us. His eyes lift to the mirror, the blue so vibrant it almost takes my breath away.

"You're so fucking beautiful," he breathes.

My stomach dips at his words, and I smile as I reach behind me to run my fingers through his hair. Logan's eyes fall closed at the touch. Placing a soft kiss on my shoulder, he pulls out and strips us of our clothes, then tosses the condom in the bin.

Lifting me up, his hands go under my ass and my legs around his waist, as he turns for the shower, carrying me in there. Turning it on, he steps under the water, letting the warm water cascade over us. I unwrap my legs, and slide down his naked body, his hands gently gliding over me as I do. Grabbing the soap, we wash each other slowly and meticulously. My hands linger and trace over the three deep scars on his abdomen. What on earth happened to him?

Logan's palms smooth over my breasts, the lather of soap making us slippery. I lean into him, pressing my soapy chest to his, kissing the underside of his jaw. Slowly, I trail a path of bites, nips, and kisses down his body, his fists sinking into my hair as I get on my knees. I peer up at him through wet lashes as I grab hold of his thick cock and run my tongue over the tip. Logan's fists tighten in my hair, and I moan, loving the stinging sensation. I do it again, then run my tongue over the full length of him and take him in my mouth. I use my hand as I go, taking him as deep as I can. My other hand is braced on his thigh, the muscles tense and trembling under my touch. I take him to the back of my throat and swallow, my throat tightening around him, dragging a deep guttural groan from him. My nipples peak at the sound, but I don't pick up my pace. I tease him with aching slowness, until I can feel him barely holding back his control.

Pulling away, I drop my hands to his legs and peer up at him. The fire in his gaze makes my core throb. I open my mouth, and wait, his eyes flaring with a feral need as he understands what I'm doing. His hands pull my hair back from my face into a ponytail which he wraps firmly around one fist while the other hand opens my jaw wider. Then his cock fills my mouth, the tip of him hitting the back of my throat, before drawing out to the tip, a few more slow strokes and his hips pick up the pace.

"Fuck, Salena. You're even more beautiful on your knees taking my cock into that pretty mouth."

A delicious tremor runs over me at his words, a dark feral anticipation fills me at the tone. It makes my core pulse in response, and I squirm, rubbing my thighs together. Logan tugs and pulls at my hair as he moves his hips, making him go deeper. I grow dizzy with need as his thrusts get faster. Suddenly, he releases my hair, grabbing my face with both hands and holding me steady while he moves his hips, hitting the back of my throat each time. He fucks my mouth with ruthless force, and I fucking love it.

Logan's pace falters, his body tensing as he trembles. "Fuck . . . " he roars, tipping his head back. Water cascades down his body, the tendons in his neck standing out. He pushes in all the way to the back of my throat and stays there, his release spilling down my throat, forcing me to swallow around his throbbing cock. The taste of him is sweet and comforting.

Logan's face tips down to mine, water dripping from the ends of the dark strands. The way his eyes are burning into mine makes my stomach flutter as he pulls from my mouth. He strokes my cheek and across my lips with the pad of his thumb. My tongue darts out, swirling around his thumb, and he curses, pulling me to my feet and drawing me into his chest, his mouth covering mine. Surprise has me frozen for a second before I return the kiss. Most men would demand I rinse my mouth out first before kissing me.

Logan pulls back, looking into my eyes. "Tasting me on your tongue is fucking hot," he says, nipping at my bottom lip.

How a human can be this animalistic I have no idea, but I love it. Shutting off the hot water, I step out of the shower and reach into the cupboard for the towels, tossing one to Logan before snagging one for myself. I watch as he dries off, his broad shoulders flexing with the movement. Every muscle is well defined, which can only come from hours of vigorous training. His abs and obliques are masterpieces, and his legs bulge with strong muscles. I notice more scars on his back, questions burning the tip of my tongue.

Chapter Seventeen

Salena

I lie here listening to the steady sound of Logan's breathing. We're laying on our sides facing each other, his muscular arm draped over my waist, keeping me close. I softly trace the name Riley on his chest. I wonder who Riley was and what happened to him or her.

I also notice more faint scars marring Logan's side. The three on his stomach are remarkably deep, as if the wound didn't heal properly. I have so many questions about what happened to him, but I know I can't ask them. He'll open up to me when he's ready. I close my eyes, knowing I need to get some sleep.

I must drift off, because I wake warm and comfortable, my whole body relaxed. Slowly, I blink my eyes open. My head is resting in the crook of Logan's arm, soaking in his warmth. I press my nose to his neck, breathing him in, savoring his scent. I lift my head to stunning blue eyes staring into mine. His hand is drawing slow small circles on my lower back.

"Good morning." His voice is deep and rough from sleep.

"Morning."

Reaching up, I run my palm up his chest, loving the hardness of his muscles. My thumb runs over his nipple, and he sucks in a shaky breath. I smile at his response and continue my exploration. My fingers idly trace over the wings tattooed on his chest. The angel wings stretch across both pecs from the middle of his sternum to his shoulders. Over his heart, the name Riley is woven in with the feathers. I look up into his pale blue eyes as they stare down at me.

"Who's Riley?" I whisper.

Logan's hand reaches up and threads into my hair behind my ear, his thumb stroking my cheek. I'm not sure he's going to answer when he drops his forehead to mine and closes his eyes. When he opens them, the look there is pure devastation.

His voice is barely above a whisper when he speaks,. "My brother."

The absolute heartbreak in his voice and the sorrow in his eyes tells me Riley has passed. I touch his cheek, keeping my eyes locked with his. "I'm sorry," I whisper back.

He lets out an uneven breath, his head lifting, and in a moment his mouth is on mine. My hands slip into the hair at the back of his head, and I pull him closer. Logan's massive hands wrap around me, pulling me tight against his body. I moan into his mouth, biting down on his bottom lip.

Logan breaks the kiss, and skims his nose over my jaw. "When I kiss you, it's like you set my soul on fire. It almost–"

"Consumes you?" I pant.

"Yes . . . "

Logan rolls us so he's on top of me, staring down into my eyes. There are no clothes between us, and as I feel Logan grow harder, I instantly become wet. My legs wrap around his hips, and I rock upward. Logan's eyes fall closed, his head dropping to mine as we rock against each other.

"Logan."

At the sound of his name, his blue eyes flash open. "I'm clean, are you . . ."

"I'm clean and protected," I say, answering his unasked question. I can't fall pregnant until I'm fully mated.

Logan's mouth covers mine, his tongue plunging into my mouth, making me dizzy. With another rock of his hips, he enters me, bare. I break the kiss, arching my back off the bed at the sensations of him being inside me without any barrier. He is hot and silky as he slides in and out. Every sensation is a little more intense and a little warmer than before. I've never felt anything like it. The feeling is indescribable. Perfect. Logan's lips clamp over my breast, sucking hard, a wave of pleasure rushing over me.

"Oh my god," I cry out, my hips lifting off the bed.

"Fuck," Logan grinds out.

My nails dig into his arms, trying to find purchase as he moves deeper with each thrust. His lips drop to my neck, biting down on the sensitive skin before laying a soft kiss over it, making me quiver and clench around him.

"Salena," he growls, slamming into me harder. "I could fuck you all day and never tire."

His words fill me with contentment, making nerves take flight. Logan pulls out and flips me over with no effort, sliding a pillow under my hips. Then his teeth bite down on my ass cheek and I shriek in surprise. He chuckles, nipping and kissing up my spine. When he reaches my neck, I'm basically panting with need. I want him inside of me now.

"Logan, please," I beg, my chest heaving.

Logan's fingers trail up my back and fist my hair, angling my head to the side. His mouth crashes down on mine, his tongue sweeping inside my mouth. I lift my hips slightly as he pushes back in. We both groan as Logan releases my hair and cages me with his powerful arms, pounding into me with renewed fervor that has dark spots dancing in front of my eyes. I grip the bedsheets in both hands, taking everything he's giving me. His hand slides around my stomach and down to find my clit, one swipe of his thumb, and I am gone.

"Logan!" I scream, burying my face in the mattress as I ride the waves cresting my body. I grind my hips into his hand as he draws out my pleasure. I feel him getting closer, his movements erratic. Both his hands move to my waist, pulling me into his thrusts, and my stomach tenses, my limbs trembling. I turn my head back. My eyes meet Logan's and hold, the muscles in his neck strain, his mouth drops open, and a flood of warmth spreads within me. The moment makes me shatter into a thousand pieces, moaning into the bed, milking his cock as pleasure lights me up from the inside out.

Logan collapses onto my back, his heavy breathing ruffling my hair. "Fuck, Salena."

I hum in response, unable to answer him just yet.

Chapter Eighteen

Logan

I'm pacing the small area of the break room, reading the file on the missing girl. Victim one is still a Jane Doe, but victim two is from Lincoln, Nebraska. Hannah disappeared after leaving work around four months ago.

Movement from the side has me stepping out of the way of an officer as I mumble an apology. My eyes glue to the page in front of me. A throat clears from the doorway, and I glance up at Milo.

"Yes?"

He frowns, looking around the break room. "Who were you talking to just now?"

I tense up and quickly look away from him, my eyes scanning the now deserted break room. "The officer," I mutter. But I'm alone.

I could have sworn someone was standing there waiting to get past me. My jaw is clenched so tightly it feels like my teeth will shatter as I spin away and leave the break room. I'm not going down this fucking rabbit hole again. I'm stressed, and when I'm stressed, I start seeing things. Things that aren't there. Mostly shadows, or a disturbance in the energy around me.

I slam the file down on my desk and take several deep breaths, placing my hands on my hips.

"Everything alright, Sinclair?" Milo asks, having followed me.

I turn to meet his warm friendly gaze, a ball sitting at the bottom of my stomach, and I can't shake the feeling of discomfort that's hanging over me today. I run a hand over my hair, realizing it desperately needs to be cut.

"I'm fine. It's just this case is . . . it's hard to swallow. These girls, they all look like Salena. I can't help feeling like it's connected somehow." Then there is the threat she got.

Milo takes a seat at my desk and picks up the file. "So, you and Salena are close?"

My gaze snaps to him and I growl, "That's none of your concern."

Milo shrugs and keeps flicking through the file. "Just asking. No need to get pissy."

I stare down at him, wondering why he is here at my desk. My general unfriendliness keeps people away, but not Milo. It's like he doesn't even notice the wall I put up around myself.

"So, you think it's someone targeting Salena?"

"Possibly." With a huff, I take a seat and pick up my pen, tapping it on the desk. "The first body showed up just over a week ago. Then the next day a cat is killed and left on Salena's doorstep. That isn't a *someone* escalating, that is two different MO's. They have completely different patterns."

"Salena doesn't seem like the type to easily scare," Milo muses.

"She doesn't, does she?" I say thinking back on the way she reacted to the cat.

"If you need help just let me know."

"I'm fine."

"Still . . . "

"I said I was fine," I grumble, opening up my file.

"You should be nicer, you know," Milo says, tapping his knuckles on my desk as he stands.

"You know I'm not nearly as mean as I'd like to be. You should really appreciate that more," I reply, leaning back in my chair.

Milos eyes crinkle and he laughs. "Fuck, man," he says, shaking his head and walking off, his shoulders shaking with laughter. I feel my own lips twitch in response.

"Sinclair, in my office," the captain booms from the door of his office.

"Yes, captain," I call.

My phone dings with a message, and I frown, picking it up and swiping my thumb over the screen. Kai.

Kai: You busy?

Logan: Give me 5 mins.

Kai: Oh, okay. On the shitter then?

Logan: What? No. Meeting.

Kai: Sure it is. Don't forget to wipe.

I can't help the tug of my lips. Kai is relentless.

I pocket my phone and head to the captain's office. Hannah's parents will be here in the morning, and he wants me to meet them and ask questions.

Chapter Nineteen

Salena

"Salena, there's a delivery out back. Want me to take it?" Declan yells through the empty bar. We don't open for another hour, and this delivery is late.

I throw my cloth down on the bar, "That's okay. I got it."

Declan salutes me as he ducks back into the storeroom. Declan's one of our quieter pack members, he showed up here without any family last year, needing shelter.

I push out the back door into the loading zone and smile at Hank as I make my way over to his truck. Hank's in his sixties and has a great sense of humor. I enjoy our chats. He always talked about his wife Mary-Jane and his two granddaughters. His hair is more gray than blonde now and smile lines crinkle around his eyes. He keeps his beard neat and tidy, which is surprising. Most men his age don't bother.

"Hey, Hank."

"Salena, you get prettier every time I see you."

I wave a hand at him and laugh. "Oh, stop it, you charmer."

Another man steps out of the truck, his boots crunching on the gravel as he lands. His head is shaven, and I can smell the distinct scent of cigarettes on him. I scrunch up my nose and raise an eyebrow at Hank. He twists around and sees the younger man approaching,

"Ah, Salena, this is the new guy, Ray. I'll be handing this route over to him."

"What? Why?" I ask. I love my weekly chats with Hank.

"Mary-Jane took a bad fall over the weekend and broke her hip."

I gasp, covering my mouth. "Is she okay?"

"She's in the hospital for the moment, but I'll need to stay home and take care of her for a while."

"Oh, Hank. I'm so sorry. If you need anything, please call."

Hank winks. "I'm sure we will be just fine."

That's one thing I've always loved about Hank. He's so easy going, takes everything as it comes and with a smile.

Ray steps up next to Hank, his blue eyes raking over my body, in a predatory way.

I cross my arms, frowning at him. "There will be none of that," I snap.

Ray's eyes jump to mine, and he smirks. "I was just looking."

Hank's hand comes up and smacks him on the back of the head. "Watch it, boy. Salena will put you on your ass if you're not careful."

"Damn straight," I say.

Ray looks between us. "Whatever," he mutters, turning around and walking to the truck.

Hank shakes his head as Ray opens the back of the truck. "No manners, these young ones." He says the words under his breath.

I chuckle, agreeing with him. I help the two of them get the orders inside and Hank waves goodbye as he climbs in the truck. Looking at Ray, who's lingering, I decide to play nice. "Thanks, Ray," I say and turn to head inside.

I only make it two steps before Ray's hand grabs my ass. I spin, ready to tell him where to go, when he's pulled away and a fist connects with his face.

"Logan!" I exclaim.

Ray falls to the ground, holding his face. "Fuck, man!"

"Get the fuck in your truck, and don't ever touch a woman without her permission again," Logan seethes.

Ray looks between the two of us and scrambles to his feet, bolting for the truck. I take a deep breath and roll my shoulders. Logan turns me toward him. His hands are gentle, but his eyes are fierce as he peers down at me.

"Salena. Do men always touch you like that?"

I step away from him, hating the distance, but I need it in order to think straight.

"No, Logan. This is my place of business, you can't just show up here and make demands. Bossing people around."

Logan grits his teeth and nods. "I'm sorry, but . . . "

"No. No buts!" I snap. "I can take care of myself."

Logan swears and shoves a hand through his hair.

I've said all I'm going to say on the subject. It's up to him to accept it or not. I turn, ready to head back inside. The bar will be opening in a few minutes.

"Baby, don't walk away right now," Logan says.

I freeze, because he called me baby.

My pulse kicks up, and I forget why I was mad in the first place. How can that one word stop all thought processes?

Logan spins me around, his hand reaching up and cupping the back of my neck as his lips descend on mine. I open my mouth for him, and his tongue sweeps inside, everything flaring with need. I gasp at the feel of him, and step closer, my arms wrapping around his neck as the blood in my veins turns to liquid fire. Logan's hands grip under my thighs and lift, and I automatically wrap my legs around his waist. Deepening the kiss, he takes a couple of steps forward until my back is pressed gently but firmly against the wall and his hand wraps around my hair. His other hand moves up my ribs, running a thumb over a taut nipple as his body molds against mine.

My hands stroke the muscles of his back, and I can feel him tremble under my fingers. My head spins. The feeling of being this close to him is intoxicating.

"Can you be quiet?" he whispers against my ear.

"What?" I breathe, my mind clouded with desire.

"I need to be inside of you."

I jerk in his hold, surprised. "Now?"

"Yes," he growls against my neck, the vibrations of his voice sending my pulse skyrocketing.

"There's people inside."

"So?"

I laugh into his neck. "You're a cop. Do you want to get caught for indecent exposure?"

He grunts, nuzzling my neck and nipping at the sensitive skin behind my ear. My fingers thread into his hair, and I tug on the ends. I squirm as his hands skim down my sides and cup my ass, lifting me a little higher. I wrap my legs around his waist a bit tighter. The rough brick wall behind me digs into the soft skin on my back.

"I don't know if I can wait to get you home."

"I'm literally around the corner," I laugh huskily.

Logan's head drops to my shoulder, and he groans, "You're right."

His hands spasm on my thighs. "Having you in my arms, your legs wrapped around me, is becoming one of my favorite things."

I squeeze my legs, adding more pressure between us. His hand skims higher, the pad of his thumb brushing over my center. I bite my lip to hold back my whimper. How does this man make me lose all sense of self-control when he so much as touches me?

Logan pulls away and gently places me on my feet, taking several steps back. He straightens up his suit as he watches me, the corner of his mouth going up. Holding out his hand, he murmurs, "You look so fucking beautiful in that dress. It's going to be the first thing on the floor as soon as we get upstairs."

I decided to wear a corset dress with a gothic flair and the soft touch of lace trim tonight. Seems like Logan loves the look. I take his hand, feeling heat rise to my cheeks, and I grin back, "Your words are dangerous weapons, detective."

"Is that so?"

"Yes, but I have to work tonight. Think you can wait for me?"

"Fuck, yes."

Logan chooses a seat at the end of the bar. Something tells me he wants to be left alone. The one seat next to him is currently being occupied by Kai, leaving no other chairs available. They're both sitting there talking while watching the football game on the television. A group of girls approaches the two of them, and I watch as Logan doesn't take his eyes from the game. Kai is more than happy to entertain them though. I can't help shaking my head, a smile playing across my lips. I love my brother, and he loves women.

I pour a beer and smile as I hand it over to Gary. He's a regular. And by regular, I mean he is here every night from seven until closing. Gary's in his late fifties, and lost his wife to cancer last year. He has no other family that I know of.

"Thanks, Lena," he grunts, taking his beer and going to his table in the back.

I go to the next customer but stop short when I see one of the girls take a deep breath and move to Logan's side. He doesn't look over at her or acknowledge her in any way, and I feel a slither of relief move through me. I sense Declan move to my side.

"She is brave."

I snort, but don't take my eyes off Logan. "What makes you say that?"

"Logan has only had eyes for you since he got here. That chick has to be blind not to notice. She is about to crash and burn."

I quirk an eyebrow at Declan's enthusiasm to this girl's impending rejection.

"Well, someone here will surely cheer her up," I reply.

I tense up as I watch her lift her hand and place it on Logan's arm. Anger ignites in my stomach, but I don't have to worry because Logan tips his beer back and stands, saying something to Kai and completely ignoring her. She opens her mouth to say something, but before she can, Logan lifts his gaze to mine. He smirks when he sees I'm watching, and makes his way over. I step around the bar to meet him, and he pulls me into his arms, placing a soft kiss on my lips.

"Mind if I meet you upstairs?" he asks.

That's when I notice the exhaustion hanging off him.

"Of course not," I reply.

Logan grins and backs away, raking a hand through his hair, his shirt lifting with the movement, and I catch a glimpse of his abdominal muscles sculpted to perfection. When I lift my gaze, I find myself staring into heated eyes. Groaning, I quickly spin away.

Damn that man. I need him. I want him so badly.

Relief when we finally close is palpable. I am so over this night, which is new for me, I usually love being down here and around people, but tonight has been different. Having Logan waiting upstairs is a new special kind of torture. Kai disappeared just after Logan, probably entertaining one of the girls from earlier, or several, knowing my brother's womanizing ways.

I just finish wiping down the tables when the door swings open, and I spin on the newcomer with a growl, but it dies in my throat.

"Ash?"

"Salena."

"What are you doing here?"

"I heard about the two girls found dead."

"Yeah . . . "

"It's not Reaper," she says, taking a seat at the bar as I move around to grab two glasses and a bottle of bourbon.

"I know. Doesn't seem like his style."

"I've been watching him and his pack like you asked. None so much as sniff your way. Whoever is stalking you and killing these girls is a new threat, one I can't pick up on. It's concerning. Do you have any leads?"

"Nope. Whoever it is, can cover their tracks and their scent. Logan seems to think that it's two different people."

Ash takes a sip from her glass. "You're letting the cops get involved?"

My stomach drops at her words, and I straighten. "I didn't have much of a choice."

"But after your parents . . . " Ash's voice trails off and a sharp pain stabs at my chest, making it hard to breathe.

I pause, closing my eyes and taking a deep, unsteady breath. "I know. I've been avoiding thinking about that."

Ash knocks back her shot. "I have to go away for a while, but I will be back."

It was a gentle reminder about my half of the bargain. "Okay," I reply.

Ash pivots on her stool, her dark gaze holding me hostage. "Be careful."

Her eyes shift to the door, mercifully releasing their relentless hold on me. I sag in relief and tip the last of my drink back. The burn of my throat is nothing compared to the turmoil of emotions Ash just brought up.

I follow Ash to the front door and let her out, locking it behind her. I take several deep, calming breaths before I make my way through the bar to the back. I unlock the door that leads upstairs to my apartment. There's another door at the top of the stairs, but Logan has left it unlocked. I walk into my apartment, trying to be quiet in case Logan's asleep. I sneak into the bathroom and shower quickly, then dry off, wrapping the towel around myself while walking into the dark room. When I reach the bed, I realize Logan isn't in it. Confusion sweeps through me, because I know he's close. Before I can turn, I let out a shriek as I'm tackled to the bed from behind, all of Logan's weight presses down on me. His lips brush my ear.

"You are fucking irresistible."

Then he bites down on the side of my neck, making me moan in a mixture of pain and pleasure. One of his hands slides around, cupping my breast as his hips rock into my ass.

"And you denied me the pleasure of removing that sinful, sexy as fuck dress."

Chapter Twenty

Logan

With a gentle push, I lift myself off her, rolling her onto her back and slowly opening the towel. I stare down at her naked body, my breath catching.

Salena squirms under my heated gaze. "Forgive me?" she whispers.

I fall down, bracing my hands on either side of her shoulders and drop my head. My mouth moves over her skin, placing an open mouthed kiss on the hollow of her neck, making my way down her body. When I reach her pussy, I look up at her as my mouth covers her.

Her gasp fills the air, and her hips lift. I grip her hips tightly in my hands as I explore her, tasting, sucking, and nibbling. My tongue spears inside of her, her hands flying to my hair as I angle her hips higher.

"Logan!"

I feel her body tremble with the beginnings of her orgasm, and move up her body, gripping her wrists and pinning them above her head before thrusting in.

Fuck . . .

I move in, out. Deep and hard.

Fuck, she feels so good, her first orgasm warming us both up.

I drop my head, needing her mouth on mine, our kisses desperate as if we're trying to climb inside each other.

I move faster, my grip on her wrists firm as I pound into her.

"Logan," she breathes against my lips.

"I forgive you."

Letting go of her wrists, I sit back, bringing her with me. I turn my back against the headboard and Salena lowers herself onto my cock. My head drops back on a groan, and her mouth finds mine.

My hands grip her ass, squeezing and helping her rock against me.

"Yes, yes, yes," she chants with lust burning in her eyes.

Her breathy moans are driving me fucking crazy. "You better hurry up and come, baby."

My cock swells inside of her, her tits bouncing in my face as I grit my teeth, trying to hold off. "Fuck, Salena," I growl.

I curse under my breath as I feel my release slam into me. Not a second later, she follows me over the edge, her walls squeezing me. Her mouth crashes down on mine, and I swallow her cries.

God, that was . . . fuck.

We both sit here panting, Salena limp in my arms. I feel a connection with her—one I never knew was possible. She turns her face, kissing up the column of my neck and biting down on my earlobe.

A full body shiver goes through me. Chuckling, she crawls off me, and we slide under the covers. I pull her over to me, tucking her into my side, and we settle in. It doesn't take long for sleep to take me.

Chapter Twenty One

Logan

T he night is unusually cold. Clouds hang heavy over the sky, blocking the moon and stars. From the cabin we're staying at, the view of the lake looks like a void of inky blackness, mist swirling over the surface.

"Riley, this is a bad idea. We should go back," I whisper-shout, as I follow my brother down the dark path in the woods. Tripping over a tree root, I stumble forward and catch myself on a tree, the rough bark digging into my palms.

"Careful," Riley says as he flashes the torch my way.

"Can we go back?" I whine, looking around at the dark and creepy woods. I don't want to go to the lake. I have a very bad feeling about this.

Our family's vacationing for a week in a cabin on Priest Lake in Idaho. It's just the four of us. Mom and Dad are in bed, and Riley begged me to go down to the lake with him. At eight and five, we know better, but he's my older brother, and we do everything together. We are inseparable, and he always takes good care of me, so I trust him.

Riley shakes his head at me and continues forward. I start to follow when movement out of the corner of my eye causes me to still. I slow my breathing down, and my ears strain, listening for any sound of movement. A soft whisper of a hum drifts toward me, not particularly loud.

"Do you hear that?" I whisper, too scared to talk any louder.

A sudden coldness creeps into my body, and I don't think it has anything to do with the temperature out here. My body is shaking uncontrollably, and I have an unfamiliar feeling in my stomach. Riley stops and turns back to me. Our breaths puff out in front of us as we stand there silently.

Riley's eyes find mine in the dark as we both stand frozen to the spot, listening. We can faintly hear the humming of a voice, but as it draws closer, it becomes clearer. I reach for Riley's hand, gripping it in mine, too afraid to move. My breathing was getting faster and faster, and I want to run back to the cabin and get into bed with my parents. We never should have come out here.

Riley's voice is shaky when he speaks. "We should go back."

I frantically nod my head, gripping Riley's hand tighter. He tugs me on my arm as he starts forward, my feet slipping in the dirt.

"Come, Logan," he urges.

Together, we run back the way we came, the uncomfortable feeling getting worse, our feet constantly tripping on rocks and tree roots. I watch as a mist rolls over the forest floor, growing thicker. I don't like it. I'm scared. I want Dad.

A burning sensation shoots across my stomach, and I slow my pace. I place my hand over my stomach, only to feel something wet and sticky. I stop running and look down. Even in the dark, I can make out the dark liquid coating my hands.

"Is that blood?" Riley asks, panicked.

I look up at my brother and frown. "I– I don't know."

The burning sensation spreads and I start crying, warm tears coating my cheeks. Riley's arms wrap around me as he tries soothing me.

"We're almost back at the cabin, come on. Mom will know what to do."

Suddenly, Riley is jerked away from me, and I watch terrified as he flies backward through the air. I look around, frantically trying to see what threw him, but I can't see anything. Only the mist as it swirls around us.

A soft, eerie voice floats around me as I watch Riley stand up, his blue eyes wide on mine.

"Run, Logan!" he yells.

My body goes cold with dread, and I don't hesitate this time. I turn to run, but something I can't see strikes my face, sending me sprawling in the dirt. Crying, I reach up and touch my face. Dark liquid coats my fingers, and I start shaking. Riley is by my side in an instant, helping me up.

"I'm sorry!" he cries.

Why is he saying sorry? He didn't hit me.

The burning feeling from my stomach races through me, and hot fire burns my body, making me stumble. I fall to the ground again. Riley tries to pull me up, but I can't move. I'm hurting too much. I don't think I've ever felt pain this bad before, even when I broke my arm jumping out of the tree at school.

Rushing footsteps approach us, and Riley jumps to his feet. I see a dark shadow wrap around his leg and pull, causing Riley to fall heavily next to me, his head smashing the hard ground. His hand reaches for mine, gripping it. Tears roll down my cheeks in quick succession.

"I'm sorry," Riley whispers, our eyes locked.

Suddenly Riley is yanked away from me. I scream his name, reaching for him, but he's dragged away from me into the mist. Riley's hands claw at the dirt, desperately trying to get away. Before he disappears, his eyes lock on mine in pure terror. Then he's gone.

I cover my ears, crying as the sound of bones cracking fills the air, my brother's scream joining them. There is a loud crunch, and then silence. My body aches, but I manage to lift my head and look around the dark forest.

"Riley!!" I cry into the dark night.

My heart is hammering so hard in my chest I feel sick. My tears mingle with the blood on my face. Having no energy left, I lay my head back down in the dirt and close my eyes.

"Riley," I sob over and over.

A gentle hand strokes my face. No one has ever been gentle with me. I shift, feeling soft silk sheets under me, and realize I've been dreaming. I pry my eyes open, not ready for the set of turquoise eyes that will be looking down at me.

Salena bends, kissing my cheeks softly, wiping away the tears that have been falling. My stomach twists at her seeing me like this. This is why I don't have sleepovers. These damn nightmares. Embarrassment floods me, and I go to roll off the bed, but she's quicker than I expect, and straddles me. Against my wishes, my cock hardens.

"Don't leave," she whispers.

My voice is rough when I manage to speak. "I think it's best."

The emotions from my nightmare are still swirling around in my chest. I don't have them as often as I used to, but when I do, it's the same every time.

"You don't have to talk. Just, don't leave. Please," she begs.

Drawing in a deep breath and releasing it slowly, I give a small nod in response.

Sliding off me, she curls into my side, her fingers tracing Riley's name on my chest. I bring my hand up and cover hers over my heart.

"No one believed me," I whisper hoarsely into the dark.

"What happened?" she asks, and quickly adds, "You don't have to tell me."

I squeeze her hand gently before answering, "They all thought I was in shock. Maybe I was, but . . . "

"You don't have to tell me," she murmurs again, stroking my face.

She never looks at my scars with disgust or pity. I like that, with her, I don't feel like I need all that heavy armor wrapped around me. I can just be. It is so freeing. I'm tired of keeping everyone at a distance, and I don't want to do that with her. She's the first person apart from Sander that I've wanted to open up to.

"When I was five, my brother and I went exploring the woods one night. He was my older brother, and we did everything together. I knew something wasn't right that night, I tried to get him to go back, but he wouldn't listen." My voice lowers as I continue, "Something was stalking us in the dark, and my brother was killed. After the attack, my parents withdrew from me, they couldn't even look at me. I was a reminder of my brother. The scars on my body are a reminder of what happened. A week after I was released from the hospital, my dad dropped me off at a bus station and put me on a bus heading for Portland. That's the last time I saw him. My parents just abandoned me. I lost everyone I loved, all in one week."

Salena's body trembles. I think she may be crying, and I don't think I can handle that. But she is suddenly sitting up and launching herself off the bed. I sit up, startled by her sudden movement. Her wild eyes lock on mine in the dark, burning like the hottest flame. I notice her fists are clenched and her shoulders are bunched.

"Are you fucking kidding me right now!" she shouts.

My brows drop and I tilt my head as I watch her. I reach over and turn on the bedside lamp, needing to see her better. I wasn't expecting this reaction from her.

"Sorry?" I ask, confused.

Her jaw clenches and her hands ball into fists. "They fucking left you?! You were just a kid. You witnessed your brother getting killed. What selfish fucking–" she cuts herself off and starts pacing, muttering under her breath. I am completely bewildered by her reaction. She's so angry, it looks like she's ready to go to war for me. I was expecting pity. But this . . . this is . . . this is unbelievably sexy.

I push from the bed and stalk over to her. She spins to face me, fuming. She opens her mouth to speak, but I grab her face in my hands, and swoop down, taking her mouth with mine. When our lips meet, she melts almost instantly into my arms. Her hands wrap around my neck, fingers threading through my hair. Her lips on mine spark a flame inside of me, and I pull her flush against me. I devour her mouth, taking every last breath until we're both pulling away, panting.

Her bluish eyes are blazing with desire, mirroring my own. Her voice is soft when she speaks. "You deserved better. So much better."

I reach down and wrap my hands behind her thighs and lift her into my arms. Salena's long legs wrap firmly around my waist, and I walk us back to bed.

She is still wrapped around me when I put my knee on the bed then my hands, crawling to the middle of the bed. My lips drop to her, and she opens her mouth immediately. I fucking love how responsive she is to my touch. She seems to crave me as much as I do her.

I reach between us and tear the side of her underwear. Her small gasp makes my cock twitch. I tear them off her and push down my boxers.

"So your underwear stays in one piece, I see." She smirks.

I don't answer, just roll my hips, sliding into her. She is warm, wet, and tight. She fits me perfectly. My hands grab her wrists and pin them above her head, holding them firmly in place. I pull all the way out and thrust back in hard, drawing a gasp from her. I do it again, relishing in the feel of her tight pussy. My hand tightens around her wrist as I pick up my pace, her soft moans driving me even more insane.

My other hand slides under her back, and I wrap my hand around her silky hair and pull downward, making her back arch off the bed, exposing her neck, her breasts pressed firm against my chest. I have this unexplainable need to mark her, to bite her. Without warning, I bite down hard on her neck, a deep growl rumbling from my chest. Her hands reach up, delving into my hair to hold my mouth to her neck.

My hips drive into her, my pace unrelenting.

"Logan!"

I feel her body start to quiver and pulse around me.

"Fuck," I groan, pulling back to cover her mouth with mine as we move, riding out our orgasm together.

Chapter Twenty Two

Salena

Fire burns through me at what Logan went through at such a young age. I want to find his parents and shred them to pieces for this. For leaving their little boy like that. Fuck.

It's no wonder he's so closed off and keeps his emotions so tightly locked away. I would, too, if it were me. To be abandoned that way would hurt far deeper than any of the wounds on his body.

Sleep doesn't come easy, even though I'm thoroughly worn out. Logan has stamina, that's for sure. I'm still not sure of what happened the night of Riley's death, but I have a feeling his scars are a part of it. Whatever happened, Whatever he saw, it haunts him every day.

I lie here watching him for the longest time. I'm not sure when I fall asleep, but it isn't a pleasant one. My mind spinning around Logan's heartache, I wish I could take it all away.

"Wake up, baby," Logan whispers across my lips.

At his softly spoken words, my eyes blink open, adjusting to the sunlight creeping through the window. Logan is leaning over me, warm hands sliding down my sides, his fingers lifting my tank top. He glides it up, his fingers caressing my skin as he goes. My back arches to allow him to slip it over my head. He takes advantage of my position, his hand smoothing over my stomach and sliding up to cup my breast, his thumb running over my nipple. Then he leans down and sucks a nipple into his mouth, drawing a groan from me. I savor the touch, my hands running over his abdomen and chest.

His mouth descends on mine and our tongues stroke each other. Hunger deep and primal rushes through me. I need him, I need more. I clamp my legs around his waist, urging him closer.

His head pulls away just enough to gaze into my eyes. "Fuck, I love touching you. You're like the sweetest addiction. I would go absolutely mad if I couldn't touch you."

I run my hand over his jaw and smile. "I love touching you, too."

Desire fills his eyes, making them change color, then his mouth crashes down on mine again, the kiss lighting a fire deep within me. He releases a deep raw sound that vibrates through my soul, taking hold of me and setting me on fire. Our kisses become harder, more possessive, and I cling to him. Our underwear is discarded without breaking our kiss. Then he's inside of me, hard and thick. My hips move in rhythm with his as he pushes all the way in and slides out. He braces his arms on either side of my shoulders as he continues to thrust into me, our eyes never leaving each other's. It seems different this time, our emotions mingling and intensifying. I can't look away.

His hands move, pinning my hips to the bed as he thrusts harder into me. My legs wind tighter around him, holding him closer. I feel my canines tingle, and my orgasm hits me without warning, Logan following, his hips slowing, savoring the feeling. My eyes slide over the scars on his face, and I lean up, placing a soft kiss on his heart. His scent surrounds me, filling me. He rolls off me and onto his back, pulling me with him. I close my eyes and rest my head on his chest. Our heartbeats race and I listen closely as they settle into the same beat together. A slither of guilt works its way into my chest. I need to tell him about me. About the pack. About our bond.

What if he rejects me? What if he thinks I'm crazy? Or worse, hates me? I couldn't bear it if he looked at me with contempt or distrust.

Chapter Twenty Three

Logan

I can feel all the muscles in her body tense, her anxiety filling the air around us, and I tighten my embrace. I'm scared that any minute I will wake, and this will all have been a dream. I don't want to let her go. She chases away the darkness that has been my constant companion since that terrible day when I was five. Salena gives me a sense of hope. The kind of hope that lets me feel like I can finally breathe.

For so long, I have been terrified to let anyone in. But with her, it's different. The thought of losing her like I did my family makes me want to tear the world apart. I feel the weight of the day ahead, knowing I have to leave for work soon. First, I need to go back home and change.

I take her chin in my hand and lift her face to mine. "I need to go."

She pouts, but her turquoise eyes are sparkling with happiness. "Okay."

"See you tonight?" I ask, tucking some wayward hair behind her ear.

With a hint of hesitation, she bites her lip and nods in agreement. I run my thumb over her lip, feeling the softness as I pull it away from her teeth before taking another kiss. Her gaze stirs something within me that I have been trying to ignore—a yearning for something I thought was impossible.

With a groan, I pull away and climb out of the bed before I decide to stay there all day. I quickly dress and grab my phone, seeing I have a missed call from Sander. I really need to call him back before he shows up here to see if I'm alive.

Salena follows me to the door and wraps her arms around my neck, pulling me in for a kiss. The moment her lips meet mine, I want to drag her back to bed.

I step away and open the door, stepping aside for Ghost to stroll in. One step out the door, and I immediately know something's wrong. I hold my hand up, halting Salena in the doorway. I scan the area and don't immediately see anything wrong, but Salena gasps and rushes past me and down the stairs in nothing but a night shirt which only just covers her ass. I try grabbing her, but she's quicker.

I follow her down the stairs to the side door of the bar where the words *You will pay* are written in red.

The blood drains from Salena's face as she stares at the door, her face whips around to stare into the woods, a low growl rumbling up her throat. With a furrowed brow, I cast my attention toward the woods and find nothing.

"Salena, who is doing this? It's the second time–"

"Third," she says, cutting me off.

I grip her arm, spinning her to face me. "You serious?"

She runs a hand through her silver hair and sighs. "Yes, I had someone sabotage my car a couple of weeks ago."

Fury whips through me. "Why didn't you say something? Report it?"

Salena shrugs, her teeth biting down on her lip.

"Was it that guy you kicked out?" I demand.

"Reaper? No, he wouldn't do something like this."

"I'm calling it in."

Her eyes widen in surprise. "What? No."

She puts her hand on my arm, and I look up from my phone and pin her with a glare. "No, Salena. This needs to be reported. Someone is clearly targeting you. Go get some pants on and I'll call it in. We need to get a report done."

She looks like she's going to argue, but I place my hands on her shoulders and squeeze. "Please."

Her eyes soften a fraction, and she nods before leaning in and placing a kiss on my scarred cheek. Then she jogs around the corner to her stairs.

I hit speed dial, and Mack answers the phone. "Mack, I need some officers down at Crescent Moon Bar. There has been some vandalizing and threats made against the owner."

"Okay, sure I'll send some officers now."

"Thanks, Mack."

I hang up and look around the area. There isn't much on this side of the building, just an access road for deliveries and then the woods. I'll be talking to Salena about getting security cameras installed. I don't like how secluded this place is.

Salena comes around the building. She's put on some black leggings, but left her night shirt on. I can't help but stare at her stunning, effortless beauty and those unique eyes, which seem to have a hypnotic effect on me.

I want to pull her into my arms, but a police cruiser pulls in the parking lot. Salena comes to a stop beside me, and we watch as Milo and Kallie get out of the car. I suppress my groan at seeing the young lieutenant. Her eyes bounce between me and Salena, and I know she's adding up in her head the time and our casual dress.

I also notice the stiffening of Salena's shoulders as the two approach. Milo's face is friendly and concerned as he takes in the door behind us and holds out his hand for Salena.

"Miss Cartwright?"

Salena nods, staying by my side.

"I'm Milo, and this is Kallie."

Kallie doesn't so much as look at Salena, she's looking at me.

Milo frowns at Kallie and turns his concerned gaze back to Salena, but before he can ask her anything, Kallie cuts in, her tone ice cold and bitchy.

"So what, you called us because someone painted your door?"

My anger at the lieutenant rises, and I clench my jaw, looking at Milo.

"I called it in. Not Salena."

Kallie's breath comes out in a rushed huff as she averts her gaze. Milo opens his mouth to speak, but before he can get a word out, Salena interrupts.

"It's blood," she states, crossing her arms defensively.

My protective instincts flare, seeing her discomfort, and I wrap my arm around her shoulders, pulling her into my side. She comes willingly. I notice Kallie's eyes narrow further.

"How do you know that?" Kallie snaps, her tone suggesting Salena had something to do with this.

Milo shoots her a look that reads *what the fuck?* But I can tell he also wants to know the answer to that question.

"I can just tell. It looks the same as the cat blood that was smeared on my front door a couple of weeks ago."

Milo's brows drop as he glances at me, and I nod.

"I put in the report," I say, reminding him.

Milo nods. "Right, I'll take some notes and get a statement, and then we will get forensic out here."

"Thank you," Salena says, her perfect, delicate face contorts into a frown as she peers back at the door.

I abhor the sight of it there.

There's something about Salena that has my protective instincts flaring to life.

I hate that some asshole is targeting her.

Kallie steps toward Salena, her gaze calculated. "And where were you last night?"

"I was home all night, after the bar closed." Salena answers easily.

"Do you have anyone who can confirm that?"

Salena doesn't even get a chance to answer or even look my way before I step between them, my eyes hard as I look down at Kallie. "She was with me all night."

Kallie's face went bright red, and her mouth drops open. Milo steps forward to save the situation. "And your relationship with Miss Cartwright?"

"She is my girlfriend," I growl.

Kallie's eyes widen before she narrows them on Salena. I've seen that look on women before, and I don't like it directed at Salena.

I can't seem to stop the words spewing from my mouth. "And I know she didn't leave the apartment, because we barely slept last night. We were occupied." I let the insinuation settle between us, and Salena's hand grips the back of my shirt as she tugs me back a step, her arm sliding around my waist. I lift my arm, fitting her to my side. I peer down at her, and she smiles softly up at me. Her other hand pats my stomach in a *down boy* kind of way.

Milo clears his throat, trying to hide his smirk. "Right, well, I will take a statement, and Kallie, you can make some calls. Get the team down here."

Kallie spins on her heels and storms back to the cruiser.

"That was awkward," Salena mumbles.

Milo barks out a small laugh, then his eyes widen. "Sorry, it's just she has been gunning for Detective Sinclair since he arrived, and she isn't used to being told no."

"She needs to learn," I grumble.

Salena squeezes me and pulls away. "Come on, we can take a seat inside while we wait."

It took a couple of hours before forensic was done with the door. Statements were taken, and then I helped Salena clean up before heading home and showering.

I'm heading into the office when my phone rings.

"Detective Sinclair," I answer.

Complete silence greets me on the other end. I frown, pulling the phone from my ear, and see the line is active.

"Hello?" I say.

Still, nothing but silence greats me. I'm about to speak again when the line goes dead. I glance around the busy street, my eyes scanning everyone. I think it's time to call in a friend. I dial Sander's number and he picks up on the first ring.

"About time you called me!" comes my friend's cheery voice from the other end.

"Yeah, sorry I've been MIA. I've been settling in, and there's a case that's taking up a lot of my time."

"Anything you need help with?"

"Actually, yes."

I mention the call just now and hear Sander typing away on his end,

"What are you doing?"

"I'm tracing the number now."

"You don't have to waste your time with that, that's not why I called."

"I'm not wasting my time. You're family," he replies instantly.

I turn back and head into the station. "Thanks, man."

"It's a burner phone, but it looks like it pinged off a tower two miles from you."

"He's close, then."

"What's going on? Should I be worried?"

"This woman in town has a stalker. Leaving her notes in blood and sabotaging her car. There have also been a couple of murders. The victims closely resemble her."

"Shit."

"Yeah."

"Sounds like you could use the help. I'm booking the next flight out."

Before I can argue, the line goes dead. Sander has always had my back, he's the friend I can always count on. I never have to ask Sander for anything; he always just does it.

Chapter Twenty Four

Salena

A thump from below startles me awake, my gaze going to the alarm clock beside my bed, 2 a.m. I hold my breath, trying to calm my racing heart, and strain my ears, listening for any noise out of place. All while trying to pull my brain from the fog it seems to be in, it feels like I've been dragged from a deep sleep. Blinking my eyes, I move them over the room, my brain trying to focus on what I heard. Another thump sounds below, and I swing my legs off the bed, a cloud of unease rolling in the pit of my stomach.

Adrenaline courses through me as I slowly tiptoe to the door that leads downstairs and into the bar. Someone is down there. As I carefully flip the latch on the door and pull it open, a cold chill washes over me, and I feel my skin pucker, the tiny hairs on my neck standing on end.

After a moment's hesitation, I turn and quickly swipe up my baseball bat that's behind the door and tiptoe down the stairs. I know which steps to skip, ones that will give my presence away. My eyes are quick to adjust to the dark, my shifter genes kicking in. I don't smell anything out of place, and I prick my ears to listen. Nothing.

I make my way down the hall, past the bathrooms, and pause where it opens up into the bar. I hear bottles clinking and frown. I close my eyes, tilting my head, trying to pinpoint where exactly they are. I feel a slight movement in the air, and I can sense them behind the bar. I snap open my eyes, ready to step into the light, when Ghost winds through my legs and meows loudly. I shriek out of surprise and curse the damn cat as I rush from my hiding spot out into the now empty bar. I swing an accusing gaze back at the cat and move around the bar. Nothing looks out of place, I sniff the air, and there is a fresh scent. My brows lower as I inhale again. Declan?

It's an hour before opening, and Felix is here helping me get ready. Declan called in sick. I can't say I'm surprised. I have some questions, and I think he knows it.

My brothers now refuse to leave me alone until whoever's threatening me is found. I don't need a babysitter, but they sure do like to remind me that I'm important and worth protecting.

The front door to the bar swings open, and I sense an unfamiliar shifter. I spin, my eyes flashing and claws extending instantly. Felix is by my side in a second. The tall man raises his hands.

"I come in peace," he says calmly.

I eye the newcomer. He is tall with a military look about him, close-cropped brown hair, and his eyes are a soft brown and hold a kindness to them, an easiness. I relax instantly, recognizing him as no threat.

"We're closed," I say, retracting my claws.

"I know. I just wanted to stop in and see the alpha of this territory, and announce my presence in town for a week, maybe two."

I get busy with pouring myself a whiskey, I take a shot, and pour another, taking it as well. I relish in the warm liquid burning my throat and settling in my stomach. I hold the bottle up to the newcomer who shakes his head.

I clear my throat and raise my eyebrow. "Okay, and why are you here?"

"I'm visiting a friend who has asked for my assistance."

"Do I know this friend?" I ask.

The man shrugs. "Probably."

Felix gestures to the stool in front of us. The newcomer slowly makes his way forward and takes a seat.

"So, what's your name, and who is this friend, and what are you helping him with?" I ask, crossing my arms over my chest.

"That's more information than you need. I only need to announce my presence in your territory, and I come peacefully."

"Well, we've been having some trouble as of late. Can't be too careful." I shrug. "If you want to stay, you'll answer my questions."

The man studies me for a long moment, neither of us breaking eye contact. Finally, he relents.

"My name is Sander, I'm from Lukas Black's pack. I'm here visiting Logan Sinclair, and helping him with a case."

My mouth pops open and closed several times. All words have fled my mind. Lukas runs the largest and strongest pack in America. He is well respected, and his Luna's rumored to be a Legacy. A descendant of a goddess and a shifter.

Felix chuckles under his breath and pats me on the back before he takes his leave. "I will go tap the kegs and do a stock count. Call if you need me."

Sander watches him leave, confusion on his face. I walk around the bar and take a seat next to him. I hold out my hand to him. "I'm Salena. The alpha of the Crescent Moon pack here in Boulder."

He takes my hand, smiling. "Nice to meet you, Salena."

"So, how well do you know Logan?" I ask, unable to help myself.

"Very well. We grew up together, and then we work together occasionally."

Huh.

"Do you know Logan?" he asks curiously.

"Yes."

Sander must sense something in my voice. "How well do you know Logan?"

"We're dating."

Sanders eyes widen and he jerks back in his seat. "You're dating Logan? Logan Sinclair?"

"Yes." It's on the tip of my tongue to tell him about us being mates, but I hold off.

It's Sander's turn to be speechless. "Huh." He looks perplexed, as if the thought of Logan dating anyone is absurd.

I shift in my seat. "Logan called you here?" I ask, curiosity getting the better of me.

"Kind of. Do you know about his gift?" Sander asks.

"I suspected something, but I haven't spoken to him about it. He has the second sight, right?"

"Yes, he does. But he also doesn't know about it."

"Does he know about you being a shifter?" Hope rises in my chest at the thought of him already knowing about us. Maybe telling him won't be as bad as I've been imagining.

"No."

My shoulders drop. "How is that possible?"

"Logan is different. He has been through a lot, and he had many people tell him he was crazy. He bounced around a lot of homes as a child after his parents left him. I was the only constant in his life, and

I didn't know how he would take the fact that there were things that lurked in the dark. That what he thought he saw the night his brother died was real. He is damaged, Salena."

Logan may be damaged, but that doesn't mean he doesn't deserve love. He just needs to be loved a little differently. I am his mate, I will shield him and protect him.

I lift my gaze to Sander's, the warmth in his brown eyes making me feel safe. He just has this way about him, this calming presence. I feel deep down he is someone I can trust. He is Logan's friend, and from one of the most respected packs in the world.

"He's . . . my mate."

Sander's eyes widen in alarm. "Shit."

"That bad, eh?" I laugh.

Sander shakes his head. "No. No, not at all. It's just, I can tell you, he isn't going to be the easiest person to love, and honestly, you are probably going to go through hell with him. He is one of those people who thinks that they're just too hard to love. As soon as he begins to feel more than he can handle, his defense will go up, to protect himself."

"I can handle that. I'm not easily scared away, Sander. I care deeply for him, and not just because we're mates. I felt something for him before the mate bond showed itself."

"Logan's never had a girlfriend before, never dated."

My mouth drops open, and I make a choking sound. "What? Really?"

"He has been through plenty of women, but never–"

My low growl cuts Sander's words short, and he holds up his hands. Jealousy burns through me at the thought of Logan with other women.

"Sorry. Look, Logan's been through so much, and on the outside, he might seem invincible, but on the inside, there is a war raging because he is terrified to love, to let someone in his life who he cares for so deeply."

I blink at Sander and rub my forehead.

"If he is really your mate, you're going to need to be patient. He will push you away."

I glance to the side, considering his words. "Patience isn't one of my stronger attributes. But I won't let him go easily."

"Well, all I can say is if you really love him, fight for him. Give him time to accept this. To accept you. He'll come around."

"How does he not know about us? You guys have been best friends since childhood, he's a detective, he should have known something was up."

Sander shrugs. "I was careful."

I run a hand through my hair and turn, pouring two shots of whiskey and hand one to Sander before tipping my head back and letting the liquid burn a path down my throat. I can't shake the feeling that all his affections for me will scatter like dust once he finds out everything.

Chapter Twenty Five

Logan

"Hey, why's Ro here?" I ask, stopping at Milo's desk.

Milo's surprised gaze jerks up to mine. "You know Ro?" he asks, dropping his pen on the desk and leaning back in his chair.

I shrug. "I played some ball with him and his friends a week or so ago."

Disbelief fills Milo's eyes, and he glances between the two of us. "Really? You play basketball?"

"Yes. Now, why is he here and looking like someone pissed in his breakfast?"

Milo sighs, rubbing the back of his neck. "He got caught shoplifting. His dad died two years ago in the line of duty. Since then, he's been distant, angry, always getting into trouble."

Shock rolls through me, and I tense. "How did his dad die?"

Milo shakes his head. "It was a domestic call gone wrong. Charlie got in between two wolves on Kai Cartwright's property, and one of them mauled him. From what I heard, a white wolf came to his rescue, but Charlie succumbed to his injuries before the ambulance arrived. Mack was his partner at the time and blamed himself for a long time. Sometimes I still think he does," Milo says, nodding toward the older officer. My gaze then moves to Ro, who's seated at Kallie's desk. My pulse kicks up. Was the white wolf my wolf? What happened at Kai's house?

"Those two girls are the first animal attacks we've had since Charlie. It's an extremely rare occurrence."

Without another word, I make my way over to Ro.

"Hey, Ro. What's going on?"

Ro jerks at my sudden appearance and glances around, a flush covering his cheeks. He doesn't speak, just stares at the ground.

"Want to get out of here? I can take you home?"

He looks up. A flash of anger goes through his eyes, and they narrow on me. "You're not my dad. And I don't need your help."

I exhale and put my hands in my pockets. "I'm not trying to be your dad, Ro. I just understand what you're going through."

Ro stares at me long and hard, his gaze lingering on my scars. Finally, his shoulders drop, and he pushes his mop of brown hair from his face. "Fine," he mumbles, looking defeated. My chest squeezes painfully at that look.

"But Detective–" Kallie starts arguing.

I step closer to her, lowering my voice, "I'm not cutting you out, Kallie. The boy isn't leaving town, but I am taking him home."

Kallie opens her mouth to argue, when the captain speaks from behind her. "He's right, lieutenant. Let Ro go home."

Kallie flushes and drops her gaze. "Fine," she responds, sinking into her chair and turning on her computer, Ro and I forgotten.

I lead the way out of the precinct and over to my car. Ro hesitates before climbing in. The drive is silent, and I don't push for conversation. I know from experience how much it pisses me off. Ro only speaks when telling me when to turn. He points out a house that looks in dire need of care. I pull over at the curb and he jumps out, his pace clipped as he makes his way to the house. I follow him up the path and he glares at me. "You can leave," he snaps.

The front door swings open and a woman around my age with long brown wavy hair and green eyes stands there, worry lining her face.

"Ro, where have you been? I've been worried sick looking for you. You wouldn't answer your–"

"I'm fine, mom. Geez, back off!" Ro yells, jogging up the stairs to the front door. She steps aside, letting him pass, and he disappears inside.

Her face is strained when she faces me, her olive eyes fixating on my scars. I roll my shoulders to dispel the tension building there, and she pales a little, her eyes finally flickering to mine. "Who are you?" she asks, her voice trembling.

"I'm Detective Sinclair."

Her mouth drops open. "Oh . . . " She looks behind her into the house and sighs. "What has he done now?"

"Shoplifting. I will talk to them to see if they can drop the charges."

The woman throws me a grateful look. "Thank you. Ever since Charlie died, he's been closed off. He won't talk to me. I can't seem to break through to him. He does this stuff, and I don't know what to do." Tears fill her eyes, and my heart throbs in response to her pain.

At least Ro has a mother who cares.

I reach up and put a hand on her shoulder, squeezing softly. "You're doing a good job. All you can do is be there for him. He'll come around. The pain won't go away, but he'll learn to live with it."

Her eyes drop, and she nods slowly. "Thank you."

"He's a good kid. He just needs more time. Right now, he's angry at the world for taking his dad away."

Green tear-filled eyes blink up at me and she offers me a wobbly smile, "I'm Hayley, by the way," she says, wrapping her arms around her middle.

"Logan. Now get inside where it's warm. If you need anything, here's my number." I hand her my card.

She looks down at the card, turning it over in her hands. "Thanks," she whispers, stepping backward into the house, and closes the door with a soft click.

The ground crunches under my shoes as I make my way back to my car. Thoughts of Ro's dad, Charlie, circle my head. What happened at Kai's house to warrant the police being called? Something is telling me to look closer. Maybe I need to ask Salena about it. I get in my car, letting my head fall back against the headrest. I look at the time and decide to head home. I'm done for the day.

I only live a couple of streets over, so I reach home in under five minutes. I notice a truck parked in my driveway, and curse under my breath. Who the fuck is at my house? My gaze moves over my yard and I see Sander seated on my front step. The tension drains out of my shoulders, and I'm filled with relief that he's here. I step out of my car, and he stands, making his way over. We grip each other's hands, pulling each other into a hug, our hands clasped between us.

"Good to see you, brother," Sander says lightly.

"You, too. Thanks for coming," I reply, leading the way into the house.

Sander chuckles. "Anytime."

"Want to order pizza?"

"Hell yes. I'm starved."

I shake my head with a laugh. "You're constantly hungry."

I call up, ordering us a pizza each, then we grab some beers and head for the deck out the back.

"So, what's bothering you about this case? It seems personal," Sander says, kicking back in the deck chair.

He has always been way too perceptive. "It's not personal," I lie.

Sander raises his eyebrow. "Really? Because I happened to run into a striking silver haired woman on my way here today. She says you're dating."

My breath stalls, and I squirm under his stare. "Yeah, I'm dating Salena."

"That's awesome. It's about time you got a girlfriend." When I don't return his smile, he pins me with a bizarre look. "What's the problem, exactly?"

"It's hard to explain," I reply, not wanting to get into it right now.

Sander reaches over to grab another slice of pizza and leans back in his chair. "Well, try. I'm here to help."

"A cop was mauled by a wolf on her brother's property two years ago, after being called out to a domestic situation. It is the only fatal animal attack here, and then the two girls. I feel they are somehow connected. Someone has something against Salena. They want to scare her off, or worse."

"Maybe you need to talk to Salena about it. Find out what happened out there two years ago," Sander suggests before tipping the last of his beer back.

"Yeah . . . " I pause, struggling to collect my thoughts. Sander knows me well and doesn't rush me.

"I like her," I whisper.

Sander tips his head back, gazing up at the stars. "I know."

"I don't know if I can do it."

"Do what?" he asks, looking over at me.

I meet his gaze in the dark and speak honestly. "Give her my heart."

Chapter Twenty Six

Salena

I walk into the police station the next day and look around. I spot Logan sitting at his desk in the back, his head bent as he flicks through a folder, dark strands of his hair falling on his forehead. I wonder if he would let me cut his hair. I step up to the counter and smile at the young blonde receptionist.

"Hi, I'm here to see Detective Sinclair."

The receptionist's honey-colored eyes look up at me, and she smiles warmly before she looks over her shoulder. Returning her gaze to me, she nudges her head to the door leading into the office.

"Of course. Head on through, honey."

"Thanks," I reply, beaming at her.

I walk through the gate that separates the reception area from the precinct. I keep my eyes trained on Logan, ignoring all the stares I'm getting.

"Detective," I say as I stop in front of his desk.

Logan's head whips up. "Salena?" I watch as his eyes fall to the box in my hands, and his brows furrow in confusion. "What do you have there?" he asks.

"Donuts."

Logan doesn't say a word, as he stares at me in question.

"What? Cops like donuts," I reply, feeling heat rise to my cheeks.

Milo walks past then. "Hey, Salena. Oh, donuts! Mind if I pinch one?"

I grin. "Of course." I hold them out to him.

"Thanks!" he calls over his shoulder as he makes his way to his desk.

"See," I point out, raising my eyebrow.

Logan eyes me suspiciously. "Why did you come here with donuts?"

Okay, so Logan is way more astute than I gave him credit for. I let out a deep breath and glance around. I shuffle on my feet and watch as his lips curl up into a smile, the hard expression in his eyes shifting to something gentler. I itch to run my hands through his dark hair, it's tousled enough to be sexy but not messy. He looks fierce and gentle all in the same breath.

"Well?" he asks.

Right, the real reason I'm here.

"Fine. I got another note."

Logan's body tenses, "And you stopped to get donuts before coming to me?"

"Well, yes. I thought it would help your mood."

"Salena," he growls, making goosebumps scatter across my arms.

"Yes, detective?"

"Not now!" he exclaims, standing from his chair. He reaches into his drawer and pulls out some blue surgical looking gloves.

I exhale and open my bag, pulling out a folded piece of paper.

"Anyone else touched it besides you?" he asks tersely.

"Nope, it was stuck to my door this morning."

Logan pulls on the gloves, and I hold out the letter to him. Opening it up, I watch as his face hardens, and his brows slam down. His steel blue gaze meets mine, the icy hardness in it making it hard for me to breathe.

"Salena, what the fuck?!" he shouts, struggling to control the anger in his voice.

Okay, the donuts did not help.

"I know," I answer quietly, biting my nail. I fall into the seat on the other side of his desk, my knee bouncing up and down rapidly as I stare at the note in his hands.

"Your stalker confessed to killing those two girls." He lets out an angry huff and slams the note down on his desk, making me jump. His full lips are pulled into a straight line, his fist clenched at his sides he tries to rein in his frustration. But I can sense fear coming from him —he's scared for me.

"I'm sorry," I whisper.

The note is . . . it's disturbing, sick, and completely frightening. While I know I would fare better than the girls he's already killed, I also know this stalker is a genuine threat.

"For what? This isn't your fault."

I bite down hard on my lip, and Logan's eyes soften. He steps around the desk and squats in front of me. His hand reaches up to cup my face and sees he still has the gloves on. With a snarl, he yanks them off and cups my face. "Baby, I'm not angry at you. I'm angry at this fucker."

"Okay," I whisper.

"Are you okay?"

I nod, even though my stomach is twisting in fear and trepidation. My heart hammers in my chest as I voice my thoughts. "Those girls died because of me."

Logan's eyes harden to ice chips. "No! Fuck no. Don't do that, Salena. This is all on him."

Logan leans forward, his mouth gently brushing mine before he pulls back and stands.

"Milo!" he calls.

Milo, who has been watching everything, stands and strolls over, concern etched on his face.

"What's going on?"

"Log this evidence. I need to make some calls."

Milo's eyes fall to the letter and widen. "Shit."

Salena,

Do you like my gifts? They are pretty, aren't they? Not as pretty as you, though.

I love the color red. I cannot wait to bathe us both in red. To watch the blood run over your snow white skin, soaking the ground beneath us.

Your screams of pain mixed with my screams of pleasure will sound like a symphony.

Soon, we will be together.

Chapter Twenty Seven

Salena

I pace the living room of Kai's house, waiting for my pack to arrive. Everyone's here except for Rose and Felix. A restless feeling buzzes through me. The note has put me on edge. I don't think it fully sank in until I left the police station.

I whip my head up as the back door slides open and Rose slips inside. "It's bound to snow any day now," she says, taking off her jacket, a smile on her face. She's always loved winter here. Her smile drops when she sees everyone's grim expressions. Quietly, she makes her way over to the sofa and takes a seat next to Lola, who has, for once, been quiet while watching me wear a hole in the floor.

Rose looks around warily. "What's going on?" she asks softly.

I don't answer, just continue to pace, shaking my hands out at my sides to hide the tremble in them. I want to break something, scream, howl, and fight. Every cell in my body is driving to hunt. Hunt this killer and deal with him once and for all. I am beginning to feel threatened, as if being backed into a corner, and that is far from ideal. As I pace, the tension in the air is palpable, my negative mood reflecting onto my pack.

"Where is he?" I yell.

Panic threatens to overcome me as I stare at each member of my pack. Felix hasn't been seen or heard from all day, and it has me nervous as fuck. Mercy stands by the door, arms crossed, watching me. Her long blonde hair is wind tousled, and her blue eyes sharper than ever as she observes me. Grady stands with Lucy at the back of the room, his light green eyes grim, his face a mask of rage. Kai stands at my back, his presence growing more agitated by the second. Declan and Tyler quietly walk in from the kitchen, their gazes averted as they go to stand with Mercy.

My phone dings, and I grab it from my back pocket, swiping my thumb over the screen to open the message.

Unknown: You could save them from this. Just leave.

I let out a throaty rumble, my phone cracking in my hands. When I hear the car pull up, my attention immediately snaps to the driveway, and I take off running toward the door. I feel a wave of release, like a balloon deflating, in my chest, as a sudden sense of relief floods me. I double over, my hands braced on my knees as I gasp for breath. Thank god he's okay. Felix is alive and okay.

Felix steps out of Sander's rental truck and they both make their way to the house. The second Felix enters the door, I punch him hard in the shoulder.

"What the hell, Felix? I've been worried sick!" I snap. "Don't you ever do that again!"

Felix's wide eyes dart to Kai.

"She found a note," he says.

"I'm sorry. My phone went dead, and I was helping Sander. I didn't think–"

"Keep in contact, Felix. If anything happened–" I choke on the words and spin on my heels, putting my back to them. Tears sting my eyes, and I cover my face, taking several long, deep breaths. Maybe my anger isn't just anger. A sob works its way up my throat, but I force the emotions down to the bottom of my stomach. I will not break down in front of my pack. Not now, not ever.

Felix's powerful arms wrap around me, turning me into his chest.

"I'm sorry, Salena," he murmurs, resting his chin on the top of my head.

My arms wrap around his middle, and I hold on to him tight. If anything ever happened to them because of me, I wouldn't survive. If anything happened to any of them because of something I did . . . I pull away and clear my throat.

"As you all know, there have been several messages left warning me to leave."

A chorus of growls erupts around the room, and it warms me that they don't like the idea of me leaving.

"Then there are the girls, the two who looked like me." I take a shaky breath before continuing. "I think we have two people behind this. The stalker is more interested in scaring me away and leaving warnings. Whereas the killer is actually targeting girls who look like me and killing them in ways to show me what he has planned for me." I shiver and wrap my arms around my middle.

"So we have a stalker and a serial killer after you?" Declan says, pushing from the wall.

I nod and throw him my phone. He catches it and reads the message.

"Why were you in my bar two nights ago?"

Declan's eyes lift from my phone and widen. He backs up slightly from the look on my face, and fidgets as all eyes turn to him.

"What do you mean? I'm always at the bar," he replies, but there's an underlying nervousness there.

Kai stalks toward Declan, a growl rumbling up his throat. "Don't lie right now."

Declan looks to the side and then back at me, ignoring Kai's hulking form in front of him.

"I've been sleeping in the basement."

Shock rolls through me at his words. How have I not known this? "Why?"

His cheeks flush with embarrassment. "I got kicked out of my apartment a few weeks ago."

I walk over to him, stepping between him and Kai. Declan drops his eyes, and I reach out for his hand. "What happened?"

"I kept missing rent," he mumbles.

"Don't I pay you enough?"

"You do," he rushes to reassure me, "It's just . . . I . . . have a problem."

"What kind of problem?"

I don't smell drugs, and he never drinks. Not that I've seen, anyway. "Gambling."

"What the fuck, Declan?" Kai growls, and I spin on my brother, sending him a warning glare.

"You are not sleeping in my basement. You can stay in Kai's guest house until you get on your feet."

I can feel Kai's irritation down the bond I share with him, but tough. He'll get over it. We take care of each other here, and Declan needs help.

"It's okay. I can find somewhere else. I'm sorry I didn't tell you."

"It's okay. Now I know why Ghost gave me away when I heard you in the bar."

Declan frowns, and I shrug. "I think my spirit animal likes you."

"It's weird you have a pet, let alone a ghost cat," Declan mutters, rolling his shoulders, like the thought of my cat liking him makes him uneasy.

"Is not. He's sweet," I reply.

"Why can't we get a scent on this guy?" Lola says, interrupting us.

I blow out a frustrated breath. "Whoever it is has help. There are only a few who can mask their scent from a shifter."

"Could they be helping each other?" Kai asks, moving to take a seat next to Lola. There really isn't any room, but he squeezes in.

"I don't think so. Both have different motives," Sander says, piping up.

Felix grips the back of his neck. "We know some witches and demons are powerful enough to mask scents."

Lola jumps to her feet, her eyes bright and angry. "Who would do this? It's fucked up. And that's saying something coming from me."

Rose reaches out and grabs her hand, tugging her back down. "We will figure out who it is. Don't worry, Lola."

"What about Old Myrtle?" Grady asks. "Maybe she has some idea."

"I can go back out and ask her, but she didn't seem to know last time I was there," Felix says.

Kai curses and Lucy steps forward, her hazel eyes lined with resolve. "I will go out and see Old Myrtle. She has to know something. Even a spell to help us."

"Thanks, Lucy," I whisper.

"Did Ash have much to report before she disappeared?" Kai asks.

"No. Only that Reaper was in the clear," I answer. My bottom lip starts to swell, and I realize I've been biting it hard.

"Mercy, can you find out if any girls fitting Salena description have come through the hospital?" Felix asks.

Mercy straightens from the wall. "I can certainly try. I don't know why I didn't think of that earlier."

Mercy is a doctor at the major hospital in Boulder. She runs a tight ship and is well respected. "If it jeopardizes your job, don't do it," I warn.

She nods, smiling mischievously. "I can be sneaky."

After everyone has their tasks sorted, Sander pulls me out onto the deck, shutting the door behind us. I have a feeling I know what he wants to talk about.

"What happened two years ago on this property?"

I startle. That wasn't what I thought he was going to say.

"How do you know about that?"

"Logan."

The ground tilts under me, and I stumble to the chair and fall down. "He knows?" I whisper.

"No, all he knows is a cop got killed by a wolf."

I put my elbows on the table and my head in my hands and take several deep breaths.

"What happened?" Sander asks quietly.

"Some idiot called the cops. That's what happened."

Sander sits down next to me, his shoulder bumping into mine. "Listen, I'm not here to judge. I'm here to help. Logan says he's been seeing a large white wolf. That it seems friendly. Is that you?"

I nod, unable to get words past the panic building in my throat.

"Who killed Charlie?"

My heart squeezes painfully at the name. "Fuck . . . " I breathe, trying to calm down my racing heart. I'm starting to feel sick.

I sit back and look over at Sander. His kind brown eyes hold compassion as he waits for me to speak. "My brother Samuel killed him. He went feral and attacked the officers when they arrived. I don't know who made the call that day. Who told them to come out here, but humans should never have been here. Especially not that day."

"Why? What happened that day?"

"I don't want to talk about it."

"She was defending herself," Felix answers, coming up the back steps.

Where has he been?

"Samuel wanted the pack and attacked Salena. She fought him and won, but he couldn't accept it. He lost it. And when those officers arrived, all hell broke loose."

"Felix . . . " I croak, wanting him to stop.

"He should know," Felix replies.

Sander blows out a breath. "What happened to Samuel?"

"I banished him. He can never set foot in Boulder again," I murmur.

Images of him attacking Charlie push to the front of my mind. I tried to save him, but Samuel had torn into his carotid artery, causing too much damage. I knew Charlie, he had come into the bar plenty of times. He had a wife and teenage son. I tried to see them after everything happened, but Hayley got so mad and told me and my family to stay away from her and her son. I don't blame her one bit.

"I'm sorry. Logan may ask you what happened, so I want you to be prepared."

My stomach is in knots just thinking about it. There is so much I need to tell Logan, the list just seems to be getting longer by the day. The secrets are killing me.

"How did he find out?" I ask, looking over at Sander.

"He knows the boy, Ro."

Pressing my lips together and bob my head, feeling tears sting my eyes. I press the heels of palms to them, trying to get myself under control. Today has been rough.

Chapter Twenty Eight

Salena

After the day we've had, everyone decides to stay at Kai's house for dinner. I'm in the kitchen with Rose and Lola cutting up the salad, my mind tuned out with the slicing of the knife until Lola lets out a little laugh. I raise an eyebrow as I glance over to her.

"You alright?" I ask.

Her brown eyes fly to mine, and she shrugs. "I was just thinking how easy it would be to chop off my finger right now. These knives are super sharp."

I blink once, twice. "What?"

Rose giggles. "She constantly says this stuff and you're still surprised?"

I look between the two girls and shake my head, smirking, and continue chopping the carrots.

"Just ease up on the intrusive thoughts, yeah?" I murmur.

"I'll try." Lola grins, her pink hair falling over her eye. She uses the back of her hand to push it back behind her ear.

"Is Logan coming tonight?" Rose asks, her eyebrows jumping up and down.

I chuckle, feeling my face heat. "I think so."

"He's good for you," Rose replies dreamily. "The way he stares at you . . . " she trails off on a sigh.

"Really?" I grin.

An arm wraps around my neck and Kai leans in, placing a kiss on my head. "We approve."

I roll my eyes. "Good to know."

I hear a car pull to a stop out front and a car door close. The fluttering in my chest appears, letting me know my mate is close by. I can't keep the smile from my face. He came.

"I'll go let lover boy in," Kai states, letting me go and walking away.

I point the knife at each of the girls with a wide smile on my face. "Not a word."

They both laugh at me and go on chopping. I feel it the moment he enters the kitchen. I put the knife down and turn on the spot. God, he's handsome. He stands in the doorway in his work suit, badge still clipped to his waist and his hair a mess. He must have spent the day running his hand through it. The girls put their knives down and gaze at me. "We will give you guys a moment," Rose says, winking at me.

Then it's just the two of us. My heart pounds in my chest as Logan stalks forward, his intense gaze never leaving mine.

Something tugs in my chest, a familiar sensation that constantly draws me to him. I read the intention in his gorgeous blue eyes before they lower to my mouth. My stomach tightens, then I forget how to breathe.

His hands circle my waist, and he lifts me onto the counter, stepping between my knees, close enough I can feel his body heat.

Logan's eyes remain locked on mine as the air in the room grows hot and thick, as the world around us blurs. His hand rises and his thumb runs along my jaw in a featherlike touch that makes me want to melt into him.

His voice is strained as he drops his forehead to mine. "Fuck, I wish we were alone."

I bring my palm up to rest on his chest. I can feel how fast his heart is beating under my palm. Logan pulls back and curls his fingers under my chin, lifting my mouth to his. All thoughts flee when his lips touch mine. My arms wrap around his neck, and I push my chest into his, needing him closer. His mouth is warm and firm against mine as he slowly explores my mouth.

My head swirls with all that is him; the touches, his warmth, his scent. I heard my mom once say that when you're smelling someone you love, logic goes out the window and the scent of their skin becomes more captivating than a fresh-baked pie floating on the air from an open window.

I'm not certain how long we'll stay here, but we aren't in a rush. We both need this. I run my fingers through his thick black hair.

"I know. I need a haircut."

I run my fingers through again and smile. "I like it."

Logan smirks, leaning down to whisper in my ears. "You just like having something to hold onto when I go down on you."

A shiver runs up my spine, and my cheeks warm. "I do. But if you want a haircut, I can do it."

I don't want anybody, male or female, running their fingers through his hair. The thought sends a rush of possessiveness through me. Thankfully, I manage to suppress my growl. Shit. I lower my eyes as I control myself, but Logan lifts my chin, his mouth covering mine. The kiss is tender and sweet, unrushed. I sigh into his mouth, and when he pulls away; he places a soft kiss on my forehead.

"You can cut my hair anytime, baby."

Chapter Twenty Nine

Logan

I've been on edge ever since Salena showed up at the station with that note yesterday morning. I knew by the tightness in her shoulders that something was wrong. She tried to play it down and almost succeeded. Salena is strong and independent, and I know this is getting to her. You'd have to be made of stone if the prospect of a serial killer targeting you was like a walk in the park. She refuses to have police stationed outside her bar, saying it's bad for business. Which I fully understand, but this is her safety we're talking about. If anything happens to her . . . The thought causes my blood to boil. I will kill anyone who touches her. The feeling is so primal, so possessive. I pause. I'm not used to feeling this way.

Dinner last night was just what I needed. I have to say, it surprised me to see Sander there. If he weren't my best friend and totally in love with his wife, I'd have been jealous.

Steam fills the bathroom as I undress. All day I've felt as if a dark, ominous cloud has been hanging over me. It's been weighing me down with doubts and self loathing. In the foggy mirror, I can just make out my blurred reflection. The scar on my face stands out, a reminder of why I can never have normal. That I am damaged and unlovable. The night I got these scars changed everything. It turned me into an abomination, one my parents couldn't even stomach. Salena deserves better. Someone who doesn't have demons.

I step into the shower, and the hot water cascades down my body, soothing my aching muscles. Soothing my frayed edges. I let my mind go blank and stand there, letting the warmth soak into me.

Turning off the shower, I step out, feeling a little more grounded than before. I run the towel over my head and pull on my sweatpants. I'm planning on ordering dinner and going over the case files tonight. I feel like the answer is staring me right in the face. There must be something we've missed. No one is this good at keeping their tracks hidden.

What if it's someone close to Salena? But who?

The thought that someone close to her would betray her like this is doubtful. All her friends and her brothers adore her.

I make my way to the kitchen and pick up all the takeaway menus and start flicking through them. I'm not sure what I feel like tonight. Even the thought of eating is unappealing. I know I need to eat. It's something I find I have to force myself to do. The doctors are quick to throw depression my way, and it could be a possibility, just one I won't entertain. Yes, I am tormented by nightmares and feel hollow on the inside. It isn't depression. Though lately I have been feeling less empty and lonely, Salena's presence sparking life into me, bringing her inner light and pushing back the darkness that threatens to consume me.

The doorbell rings, and I frown; I'm not expecting anyone. Not this late. Slowly, I open the drawer next to me and snatch up my gun. I slink toward the front window and peer out and see Salena's back to me. My gaze scans the yard and driveway quickly before I put my gun away and make my way toward the front door, swinging it open, and I'm met with a gorgeous set of blue eyes.

"Salena?"

She's wearing something so simple tonight, but fuck if she doesn't look stunning. She's wearing a pair of black tights and an oversized off the shoulder gray sweatshirt, her hair down around her face. I watch as she bites her lip, her eyes lock on mine, and it feels like she's looking deep into my soul. We stand there for only a moment, but it feels like an eternity getting lost in those eyes.

My heart beats faster in my chest as her eyes roam my naked torso. Then Salena takes two steps inside and flings her arms around me. I can feel her heart racing and immediately draw her in closer.

"Is everything okay?"

She nods into my neck, and I look past her outside, but don't see or sense anything wrong. I take a step back with her clinging to me, and shut the door.

I back her up against the door, releasing her and placing my palms on either side of her head, caging her in. I stare down into her blue eyes. This close, I can see flecks of green and gold shining in their depths.

Salena's hand comes up and cups my cheek, her fingers lightly brushing over my scars. My soul feels as if it's reaching for hers. I bend down, my lips skimming the shell of her ear.

"I don't usually like people showing up at my door, but baby, you're welcome here any damn time." My words come out in a rough rumble, and I watch her shiver slightly. I pull back and look down at her.

"Careful, detective," she purrs, tracing her fingertip over my jaw.

My eyes sharpen on hers, and I nip at her finger, making her let out a small yelp.

I chuckle darkly. "Baby, careful is the last thing I want to be."

Chapter Thirty

Salena

God, he is gorgeous.

And shirtless.

Wearing nothing but a pair of gray sweatpants that, of course, are hanging dangerously low on his hips. What is it about a guy in sweats that makes women's minds go straight in the gutter?

His dark hair is wild, disheveled, and wet. He obviously just got out of the shower. I can still smell the soap clinging to him.

He reaches up, grasping my hair in his fingers, and I feel my breath hitch at the touch. Logan's lips twitch at my reaction.

"I was about to order dinner. Did you want to join me?" his voice turns deep and rumbling, sending shockwaves through me, and it takes a moment for his words to sink in.

"Yes," I reply, my voice husky. Desire has flooded my entire body at his nearness.

"You have two choices, Chinese or pizza?"

"Pizza."

"A girl after my own heart. Extra cheese?"

My eyes light up. "Of course! All the meats? I love meat."

Amusement shines in his eyes before his head dips to my neck, breathing me in and placing a soft kiss on my collarbone. Goosebumps break out over my skin, setting me on fire.

"I know you like meat, baby. Especially my meat," he chuckled.

Laughing, I lightly slap his chest. "I meant meat pizza."

He looks down at me, a smirk tugging at his sinful full lips.

"You're in a good mood," I note.

"You're here. How can I not be?"

I tilt my head back and let out a small chuckle. "Well played."

Logan steps back and immediately I want him close again, but he grabs my hand, pulling me into the living room. I haven't been inside his house yet. It's spacious and open planned.

I see the case files open on his coffee table and point to them. "You were planning on working tonight?"

Logan follows my gaze and rubs the back of his neck. I can't help but watch in pure fascination the way his abs bunch and his biceps flex as he does. He is a work of art. Scars included.

"Yeah, but it can wait." His gaze lifts to mine, and he catches my look. "Like what you see, baby?" he asks, dropping his arm.

"How can I not? You're perfect, detective."

Logan's face clouds over, and I see his fingers twitch. I know he's thinking about the scars that litter his body and face. I step up to him, gently tracing over the long scars on his stomach.

"These don't take away anything, Logan. You went through something horrible, and you came out on the other side. If anything, it shows you're a survivor."

His arctic blue eyes soften as he reaches up, brushing the hair off my face. "Do you always see the best in people?"

I shrug and step closer, tilting my head back further. "Not always, but you are good."

Doubt crosses Logan's face, but before he can object, I push up on my toes, pressing my lips into his. His arm immediately wraps around my waist, anchoring me to his chest. Our kiss is a slow, languid dance, as our lips explore each other's warmth and softness.

Logan draws back slowly, releasing me.

"Wait here. I will order pizza," he says, dropping a quick kiss on my head before turning and walking off to what I presume is the kitchen. I hear him on the phone. Then a moment later, he strolls back in with two beers, and a t-shirt on.

Damn it.

"Thanks." I grab a beer from him when he holds it out to me.

We take a seat on the sofa, him on one end, me on the other. I tuck my feet up under me and face him, resting my shoulder along the back of the sofa.

"Any new leads?"

Logan takes a deep sip of his beer. "No. The only prints on the note were yours."

"He'll slip up soon, right? They all do?"

"I hope so. I hate that someone's out there targeting you like this. It's unusual we haven't gotten any leads yet."

I hum my agreement, my stomach sinking. The cops haven't been able to get anything on this guy. The pack hasn't either. No scent or trail, nothing.

"I've been meaning to ask you something." Logan's voice is gentle, almost apologetic.

My pulse kicks up and a sick feeling takes up residence in my stomach. Before I look at him, I school my expression. I know what he's going to ask. I've prepared myself for it.

"Yes?"

"Two years ago, an officer was killed on Kai's property. What happened?"

I look down at the beer in my hands. "We had a bit of a family issue. Someone called the cops, and when they arrived, a pack of wolves came out from the woods." My fingers tear the label off the beer bottle as I speak. "Kai tried to get the officers back in the car, but it all happened so fast. One wolf attacked Charlie. I know those wolves, so I was shocked when it happened."

I take a stuttering breath and look up at Logan. Now is my chance to tell him about me.

"There was a white wolf outside your bar the morning I was leaving your bar. It seemed friendly, protective."

I bob my head up and down, pressing my lips together.

"She is."

"So it really was just an animal attack?"

"Yes," I whisper.

Logan has a frown on his face, his mind working over what I said. Movement behind him catches my attention. A shadow moves across the front window, and I draw in a breath, my heart slamming against my rib cage.

Logan follows my gaze, and his brows lower. "What is it?"

"Nothing, I just thought I saw something?" I get up, walk toward the window, and peer out. But I see nobody.

Logan pulls me away from the curtains. "You thought, or you did?" he asks.

"I don't know. Maybe the pizza's here."

Logan moves to the front door, opening it and stepping outside onto the porch. I follow behind, anxiety eclipsing my thoughts. Logan and I look around, but no one's there. He looks back at me just as headlights turn down the street. Now the pizza's here.

We wait for the teenager to get out of the car and grab our food before heading inside. We eat in relatively comfortable silence, talking about our favorite shows, music and food.

I stand, taking the plates to the kitchen with Logan, placing the rest of the pizza in the fridge.

I feel him come up behind me, his hands firmly gripping my hips as he leans down, kissing my shoulder. I turn in his arms, leaning back against the sink. A small smile tugs at my lips as I look up into his eyes.

"I should go."

Logan shakes his head, stepping even closer, his body brushing mine, lighting every nerve on fire.

"You're not leaving until I remind you how fucking perfect it feels to be mine," he whispers against the shell of my ear, making goosebumps cover my entire body. I shiver in delight. I know he feels it.

"Is that what I am? Yours?" I ask breathlessly.

Stepping back, Logan looks down at me, his eyes roaming my curves. "You were always mine."

My heart races as our mouths melt together. Logan picks me up and makes his way up the stairs. He drops me down on the bed and hovers over me, his eyes filling with a fierce tenderness.

"I swear if anything happens to you, I will kill anyone involved."

My eyes widen at his admission as a surge of emotions rush through me. I reach up, cupping his face. "Detective."

"I mean it, Salena," he stresses, cutting me off. His eyes flash in warning, making me think he's being completely serious.

His gaze drops to my lips and my tongue darts out, wetting my lower lips instinctively. Then we're in a frenzy as we rip each other's clothes off. Logan's mouth drops to mine, kissing me with a dominance that has me dizzy and panting with need. His tongue strokes mine as our lips move together. I let out a low moan, grinding my body against his, making his fingers dig deeper into my flesh. He pulls back, looking into my eyes as he nudges my entrance, spreading my legs wider. I stare up at him, my hands roaming over his chest as he pushes roughly into me. He grabs my hands, his fingers entwining with mine, and pins them above my head, as he slams into me over and over.

I can feel my release coming as my toes curl and my fingers clutch his. "Logan . . . fuck . . . I'm . . . I'm . . . "

"I know, baby. Fuckkk," he groans, his voice pure velvet, sending me spiraling into an orgasm. Logan follows me over the edge, panting. He collapses on top of me before rolling to the side and dragging me with him. I snuggle into Logan's chest, his breathing already deepening and evening out.

"Stay," he mumbles into my hair.

"Okay," I whisper. I can't bring myself to tell him. I will do it tomorrow night.

Chapter Thirty One

Logan

"Did you know our sixth senses are all different and are unique to every person?" Salena's voice floats to me across the table.

We're in my kitchen at my small table enjoying the Chinese food she brought over. When she showed up at my door for the second night in a row, I was surprised, but a sense of calm came over me. Having her here sets me at ease. Apparently, her brothers are running the bar this week, wanting her to stay out of the public eye. I have to agree with them, though Salena seems pissed by it.

"Sixth sense?" I question.

"Yes. It's that part of us that guides us unknowingly; intuition."

I pick up my beer and have a sip, the cool liquid wetting my now parched throat. For some reason, this conversation is making me uncomfortable.

"You mean a gut feeling?" I ask.

Salena beams at me, the sight taking my breath. Fuck, she's bewitching. Those eyes are so unusual, so mesmerizing, I swear they can see straight into my soul.

"Yes, it's like we tap into our primal instincts."

"Cops have gut feelings all the time."

"No, it's more than that. Some people can act as the in-betweener, their senses more open than others. Some even have the ability to see spirits, just as clearly as humans and all else living."

I frown, placing my beer on the table. "Okay. Why are you telling me this?"

Salena rolls her shoulders back and blows out a deep breath, staring up at the ceiling. "Logan, you've met Ghost, right?"

"Your cat?" I ask, confused.

Where is she going with this?

Her turquoise eyes drop to mine. "Yes."

"Is this a trick question?"

"No. But Ghost is, well, a ghost. He is a spirit animal that has attached himself to me. I'm the only one who has ever been able to see or interact with him. That first day when you picked him up, I was so shocked I didn't know what to think. I mean, you picked up a spirit, for starters, like it was some normal ass cat. I've been the only one who could do that."

I stare at Salena as she blurts all this out, my hands clenching in my lap. My brows slam down and my jaw clenches as I look away from her.

"Who put you up to this?" I grit out.

"No one. It's the truth. You're a medium, or something like that."

"I don't believe in that spiritual crap, Salena," I snap, my gaze swinging back to her.

Why is she saying this? Did she find out about my past? The way they tossed me from foster home to foster home, everyone claiming I was mentally unstable and a freak?

Salena's voice is firm. "It's not crap. Did your mother, father, or maybe grandparents have any psychic abilities?"

I huff out an irritated breath. "Not that I know of. I never had the chance to find out."

I see guilt slide across her face.

"I know, and I'm sorry about that, but don't you think–" she starts again.

"No, I don't," I interrupt her, and pick up my beer. I push my food away, suddenly not feeling very hungry anymore.

"You saw something the night your brother died, didn't you?" Her voice is small, almost apologetic when she speaks.

I freeze, beer halfway to my lips. My eyes land on hers. I feel a sliver of ice work its way into my chest. A cold distance moves between us. She must sense it, because her eyes widen, and she lets out a small gasp.

"Why do you say that?" I ask, my voice void of emotion.

"Because you can–"

"I'm not some psychic or medium who can see spirits and shit, Salena, and I don't want to fucking talk about it!" I yell, slamming my beer down on the table.

"Logan."

"No." I stand abruptly and grab my jacket off the back of my chair. "I've got to go."

"Logan, please just listen. I know you see things; you know it, too." Salena stands, her beautiful eyes pleading with me to hear her out.

I would, but her words bring up too many memories, too many emotions from my past. My nightmares have been becoming more frequent lately, a feeling of dread and doom lingering around me for hours after. Her words hit me hard.

"I'm sorry." Turning, I leave her standing in my kitchen as I walk out the door.

Chapter Thirty Two

Salena

Sander said he would pull away, but watching it happen is harder than I thought. A sharp pain pierces my chest as the door slams closed behind him and I hear his feet pound across the wooden porch and down the stairs. He was so desperate to end the conversation that he left instead of asking me to leave.

I groan, tipping my head back. If he can't accept his own differences and gifts, how did I expect him to accept mine?

I rub at my chest, my heart pulsing with anxiety. He didn't even give me a chance to explain. I inhale through my nose and growl when all I manage to do is drag his scent in. I'll give him a chance to cool down, then I'm going to make him listen.

I look around and think I better tidy up and take the trash out before I leave.

Crescent Moon comes into view, and I shift into my human form, surprised to see the lights are still on. It's past closing, and Grady should have this place closed by now. Felix is supposed to be here helping him as well.

I walk into the bar and see Reaper sitting on one of the stools, beer halfway to his lips. What in the hell is he doing here? I storm over, holding my hand up to Grady, stopping his approach.

He and Felix are sitting in a booth watching Reaper.

"Reaper, what the fuck?" I snap, coming to a stop behind him.

Reaper freezes and spins around on his stool. "Salena. Looking gorgeous, as always."

"Cut the crap."

Reaper smirks, lifting the beer to his lips.

"Why are you here?" I growl, narrowing my eyes at him.

"What? I've come alone to check on you. I hear you have a stalker."

"Who told you that?"

"A little birdy."

Fuck.

With a low groan, I take a seat next to him. "How much do you know?"

Reaper shrugs and places his beer on the bar. "Not a lot."

"Any of your pack been coming on my land attacking girls?"

Reaper snarls, spinning to face me. "Don't, Salena. It's not us. Call off your fucking spy and look at your own pack."

"What's that supposed to mean?" I scowl.

Reaper stares at me long and hard before he shakes his head. "Nothing. Just watch your back."

"Ash left a week ago, so I'm not sure who you're referring to."

Reaper's brows drop, and he studies me. "Is that what she told you?"

The ground tilts as I absorb his words. "She's still around?"

"Yes," he bites out, his tone harsh.

I bite my lip and reach over the bar for the whiskey and a glass.

"Want one?" I ask.

Reaper grunts, which I take as a yes.

"I'm not sorry I sent Ash to watch you. You're unpredictable, Reaper, and I wasn't sure how you were going to react."

"You would have deserved any retaliation I decided on. You embarrassed me in front of members of my pack and yours."

"I know that. I wasn't thinking clearly when you had my mate cornered–"

"Wait, he is your mate?" Reaper blurts out, cutting me off.

My eyes widen and I curse myself at my slip up. "Yes."

Reaper goes quiet for a long moment, then reaches for the whiskey and takes a swig from the bottle. I don't say a word. He can have it.

"I'm happy you found your mate, Salena, but there needs to be consequences. From now on, we are not on friendly terms. We will not enter each other's territories unless it's for important pack business."

"If you hear anything on the streets about who's responsible for the killings . . . "

Reaper holds up his palms, and purses his lips. "Not my place."

A growl rumbles up my throat. "Reaper, so help me–"

Reaper stands up, meeting me head on. "You'll what? You know, once, I'd let you talk down to me, but not anymore."

"Reaper, you can't force a mating bond. That's not how it works," I reason.

His hand runs over his head, and he grips the back of his neck. "Fuck! I know that. I just thought the imprint would take after . . . Look, I've always liked you, Salena. I've never hidden that."

"You like my body Reaper. Nothing more," I state, cutting him off.

This whole thing is awkward. I'm not used to Reaper sharing so much. Reaper lifts his piercing gaze to mine. "It was so much more, but like I said, I understand. I don't have to like it, but I understand. I wish you the best, Salena. I really do."

With that, he turns, walking out the door. Felix and Grady are still at the bar, waiting. Having heard everything. I pull out my phone and dial Ash's number. It goes straight to voicemail.

Growling, I hang up, my fingers flying over the screen.

Salena: Ash, I just spoke to Reaper. Call me.

Chapter Thirty Three

Salena

It's been quiet all week. No messages, no dead animals and no dead girls showing up. I know it's stupid, but I'm hoping maybe whoever it was has lost interest. It would be stupid to let our guard down, though. Someone wants me gone.

Ash hasn't replied to the several messages I've left her. I don't know what she's playing at, or if what Reaper said is true, but I need to find out. Logan apologized for the way he left things the other night, but said he didn't want to talk about that stuff. As much as I hate it, I've decided to wait until after they catch my stalker to tell him everything.

I'll show him what I am, and explain he's my mate. I just hope it goes better than trying to explain to him about his gifts.

"Hey, Alpha," Lola says, skipping into the house and slamming into me.

"Hey, Squirt."

"I ain't no Squirt."

"You're the baby of the pack, so you're Squirt," Felix says, coming up behind her and ruffling her hair.

"By six months!"

She and Rose are six months apart in age, but Rose is definitely the more mature one. Both girls don't have parents and were adopted into Lucy and Grady's house.

I tip my head back, laughing at her outrage. Lola lightly punches my arm as Felix wraps his arm around my shoulder and places a sweet kiss on my head. I hate that he's so much taller than me. I'm the big sister.

"Hey, do you think a candle shop would smell pretty if it caught on fire?" Lola's curious voice cut through the silence.

Startled, Felix and I whip our gazes back to Lola.

"What?" I choke.

"You are now banned from all candle shops, Lola. Do not go near them," Felix declares with all seriousness.

I pat his stomach and move from his arms to link elbows with Lola. "She wasn't serious. Right?" I say, looking down at her.

"Right," she responds with a nod, a cheeky grin spreading across her face.

"You know what though? I think it would," I say in a mock whisper.

Lola's face lights up. "I knew it!"

Felix groans. "Don't encourage her and her intrusive thoughts."

Lola leans in closer to Felix, "Do you think–"

"No," Felix says, grabbing her shoulders and steering her the other way. I laugh and wave to her as she is escorted from the room. Felix grumbling under his breath.

Grady walks into the room and hands me a beer. "Anyone know where Kai went?"

I feel down the pack bond for him and I'm hit with his sudden anger and rage. Spinning on my heels, I run for the backdoor, racing out onto the deck that overlooks the yard. Kai is dragging an unconscious man by the foot over dirt and leaves as he emerges from the woods.

Shit!

I race down the steps and across the backyard. "Kai, what the fuck?" I yell.

"He was in the woods taking photos," he says, tossing a camera at me. I catch it and turn it over in my hands. My eyes widen as a shiver works its way over me. He was watching us?

Kai drops a bag at my feet and photos spill out across the ground, all of me.

The blood drains from my face, and I meet Kai's eyes. His are borderline feral, the yellow flecks flickering through the blue.

"Do you think . . . " I trail off and Kai grunts, letting go of the man's foot.

I walk over and peer down at him, but I don't recognize him. Felix and the others all surround us. Lola lets out a small gasp, covering her mouth.

"Is he dead?" she asks softly.

"I wish," Kai grunts in response, and I flash him a warning look.

"Incoming," Rose says, and we all spin her way.

Instinctively, the pack takes a defensive position around me, facing outward. Logan's car is making its way down the long driveway. There's no way we are going to be able to hide this. Logan is way too perceptive.

"Shit," I hiss.

"We could tie him up and gag him until Logan leaves," Lola says.

Slowly, I turn back and stare at Lola in shock. I did not just hear her right, right?

"We will do no such thing," I scowl.

Lola shrugs. "Just an idea, I mean we–"

I hold up my hand, stopping her. "Look, just stay here. I'll bring Logan over. We won't be able to hide . . . this," I gesture to the unconscious man on the ground, surrounded by photographs of me.

Quickly I make my way back toward the house, my feet crunching over the leaves that have fallen and now covered the ground in a thick blanket. I watch as Logan pulls to a stop next to the other cars and gets out. His brows lower as he closes his car door, watching me approach.

"What's wrong?"

My heart is hammering so hard in my chest I can barely hear myself speak.

"What makes you think something's wrong?"

He growls and storms toward me. "I can see it in your eyes, Salena, so don't even try hiding it from me."

I hold up my hands in surrender at his glare. "I'm sorry."

Logan follows me over to the others, and I gesture down to the unconscious man at Kai's feet.

Logan squats down and picks up some photographs. His pale blue eyes narrow, and instead of the tension in his body releasing, it increases tenfold. A deep knot forms in my stomach as I wait.

Rose shifts around on her feet, rubbing her hands together. I can sense her nervousness down the pack bond. She doesn't like confrontations of any kind.

Logan stands abruptly, an odd sound falling from his lips. It's a mix of a growl and a rumble that seems to vibrate from his entire being.

Rose freezes for a moment at the sound, before grabbing Lola by the arm and dragging her back to the house.

"You guys go with them," I say, motioning to the others. Declan, Grady, Lucy, Tyler, and Mercy all shuffle nervously on their feet. I can sense their unease and worry. They don't want to leave me out here.

"Go," I repeat, motioning to the house.

Begrudgingly, they all turn and shuffle toward the house, following Rose and Lola.

When it's just the four of us, Logan slowly turns to face us.

"Why wasn't this called in?" Logan growls, stabbing a finger at the unconscious man.

"Kai found him like five minutes before you turned in the driveway," I state.

"He was fucking spying on you, taking photos." Logan's chest heaves, and I watch as his fists clench and unclench at his sides.

He is furious.

My heart thumps wildly against my ribcage as I watch him. His gaze lifts to mine, and the intensity in his eyes sends me into a spiral of emotions.

Logan grabs my wrist, pulling me into his arms. My forehead falls against his chest as his arms wrap around me. "If anything had happened . . ."

I huff out a light laugh, drawing back. "You're not going to kill him, are you?"

"No," Logan grunts, looking down at the man.

Kai's eyes go wide at Logan's tone, then look at me. "Why don't you go inside, Salena? We'll wait out here for the cops to show up."

"I think that's a great idea," Logan voices before I can tell Kai to stick it.

"Fine," I growl, sending him a dirty look.

Logan leans in, kissing my forehead. "I'll be inside as soon as he's in cuffs."

"Okay," I whisper.

Felix steps up and links his arm in mine. "I'll walk you in," he says with a small smile.

I take deep breaths as I go into the bathroom and quietly shut the door behind me. I turn the tap on and hold my wrists under the cold water. This is beginning to get to me. Who is that guy? I've never seen him in my life. With a sigh, I turn off the tap and dry my hands, making my way out into the hall. I pause at the sound of hushed voices coming from the living room.

Rose gasps. "You think he was here to hurt her?"

"She has a stalker, Rose," Declan deadpans.

"Plus, Kai doesn't freak out and knock people unconscious for no reason," Grady adds.

"Do you think whoever it is knows what we are?" Lucy asks nervously.

"Could be hunters," Rose adds.

"No, we would smell them," Felix reassures her.

Taking a deep breath, I round the corner and enter the room. Felix twists around, his gaze locking on mine. Worry bleeds down the pack bond. Everyone is on edge. I know I have to be strong and a leader, but at this moment I have no words. I see Logan and Kai making their way up the stairs to the back porch. The cops must have come and gone. Kai opens the sliding door and Logan steps inside, his eyes immediately finding mine. The fire burning in them catches my breath, and I feel my hands tremble. Logan stalks toward me and frames my face. I feel a flood of calm and warmth surge through me. Logan's eyes search mine, and I hate the sting of tears that burn my eyes, making my nose twitch. I turn my head and look out the window, trying to gather my emotions.

"Baby," he whispers, drawing me into his chest, his powerful arms wrapping tightly around me. A few tears fall, but I refuse to let my emotions get the better of me. His chest rumbles against my ear, and my fingers grip his shirt.

"I'm going to the station to watch the interrogation," he murmurs into my hair.

"You're not doing it?"

"I can't, I'm too close. I don't think I'd be able to hold back."

I lift my head to look up at him, words stalling on my tongue as he stares down at me. Logan's palm cups my cheek, a dark deep energy pulsing from him. His thumb swipes across my bottom lip before his mouth descends on mine, stealing my breath, causing my heart to pound frantically.

Logan is hulking, intimating, and rough but also soft, kind, and real.

Chapter Thirty Four

Logan

Possession winds me tight, making it hard for me to draw in a calming breath. Salena's worried turquoise eyes flash in my mind as I park my car outside the police station. I sit there a moment to gather myself, then get out of my car. The way she turned her head away and looked out the window like it could somehow cover up her distress, it was like she thought she could hide them from me, but I could feel her emotions. They pulsed from her in waves. When I saw the tears line her eyes, I almost snapped. It took all my willpower not to get in the car and chase that piece of shit down.

I reach the doors and push them open, stepping inside the station. Sander's eyes snap up from my desk and he stands waiting for me. I make my way over, running a hand through my hair.

"You heard?" I ask, my voice sounding rough.

"Yes."

I grunt and grab my case file, heading toward the interrogation room. Sander follows close behind.

"So, Kai found the guy taking pictures in the woods?"

"Yeah, all photos of Salena. He had a whole bag full of them." Just thinking about it had my body tensing with barely contained fury.

"Did he say anything?"

"He was unconscious when I got there," I reply, opening the door for Sander to go through first.

Sander's brown eyes flare, and he tries but fails to hide his smile as he steps into the viewing room. I enter after him and my gaze immediately goes to the fucker seated across from Milo on the other side of the glass.

"Sinclair. Kellan," the captain greets us.

"Captain," I respond.

Sander nods and walks up to the glass, his head tilted to the side as he studies the guy. One thing I've always admired about Sander is his ability to see right through people's bullshit. He has always seen through mine. It's one of the reasons he knows everything about me.

The three of us stand there quietly, waiting for Milo to start. Milo is currently staring at the guy, who looks extremely uncomfortable. Good, make him sweat.

Milo leans back in his chair. "What's your name?"

"Alexander Hastings."

"Where are you from Alexander?"

"Denver."

"What are you doing in Boulder?"

He hesitates before answering, glancing at the glass. "I'm a private investigator."

"You're a PI?" Milo asks skeptically.

Sander steps back, sitting down in one of the chairs and whipping his phone out.

"Yes. I was on a job," the man says.

Milo leans forward, resting his elbows on the table. "Who's the job for?"

The man shrugs. "I couldn't tell you. I never met the guy. We did everything over the phone."

"What about payment?"

"Cash left in my mailbox."

"So you had no idea who you were working for?"

"No," he replies like it's no big deal. I can feel my temper rising, I must make a sound, because the captain gives me a quick look.

"What was the job?" Milo asks.

"Just said he wanted me to follow that woman and find out where she was going and who she was with."

"You realize she has a stalker, right?"

The guy's eyes widen. "What?"

"Two girls are dead. Two girls who look just like the woman you've been photographing."

The guy's face pales, and his mouth drops open as the implications hit.

"Doesn't look good for you," Milo states calmly.

"No, I was hired to take those photos. I didn't know she had a stalker!" he exclaims, panic creeping into his voice.

"Seems like something a PI should know, right?" Milo says coolly.

"I swear I didn't know."

"How long have you been following Miss Cartwright?"

"Only two days."

Milo stands and makes his way to the door without another word. A second later, he's in the viewing room with us.

"What do you think?" he asks, folding his arms over his chest.

Sander is typing away furiously on his phone. "His story checks out. He is a PI from Denver. Only got into town Monday night."

"So he was, what? A decoy?" Milo asks.

The captain turns to us, a firm frown on his face. "Yes. Someone's trying to throw us off their scent."

"Or trying to scare Salena," Milo adds.

My fists clench at my side. A nagging feeling spreads through the pit of my stomach, and I pace the small room. My eyes continuously flicker to the man on the other side of the glass. My mind races as I think about everything we know. Which isn't a lot. This was the first lead we've had.

My phone rings, and I look down at the unknown number. I swipe my finger over the green button and bring the phone to my ear.

"Hello."

"Detective Sinclair?" a deep, gravelly voice says.

"That's me."

"My name is Reaper, and I have some information for you."

Chapter Thirty Five

Salena

"Logan's been avoiding me."

Kai stops wiping down the bar and turns to glare at me. "Why? What did you do?"

"What makes you think I did something wrong?" I grumble, throwing the hand towel at him. I peer down at my phone for the millionth time in the last few hours. Still no messages. I sigh. Logan and Sander have been busy with my case. There's a new lead, one everyone has been tight lipped about, and it seems to have Logan on edge.

"Well, why else would he be avoiding you?"

I shake my head, running my tongue over my teeth. Kai's expression is soft as he pulls me into his chest. I love my brother's hugs. They always make me feel loved and protected. I sense Felix enter the bar, followed by Declan. The music starts up from the stage as the band begins their set. I pull from Kai's arms and turn to face Felix and Declan. I'm immediately alert, with the concern on both their faces.

"What's your man doing at that club? The one Reaper owns, the Den?" Felix asks, taking a stool.

"What?" I stammer, confusion and worry slamming into me. I lean my palms on the bar in front of me, mostly to hold myself steady.

"The Den. I saw Logan heading in there about an hour ago," Felix says with a shrug.

I stare at him, a mixture of emotions running through me. Yes, we've ruled Reaper out of being my stalker, but it doesn't mean he isn't still an enemy. Why would Logan be going into his club in Denver? Why are Felix and Declan in Denver?

"What were you doing in Denver?" I snap.

Felix and Declan share a look.

I let loose a long growl, which draws the attention of the young couple a few seats down. "What?"

"I paid off my loans," Declan mumbles, his voice barely audible above the band.

"Oh, well that's good, but we are not supposed to go into Reaper's territory."

"We were quick," Felix assures me.

"Are you sure it was Logan?" Kai asks them.

"Definitely. Walked straight in, no lining up."

Thump.

"He didn't tell you?" Felix asks.

"No," I choke out.

Thump.

"Huh."

My heart rate begins to pick up, a sick feeling twisting in my stomach.

Thump. Thump. Thump.

Felix frowns at me. "When was the last time you spoke?"

"Yesterday." I scan the bar. It is fairly quiet tonight, these guys would be fine without me. "I'm leaving to check it out."

Felix and Kai both jerk their heads to me. "What?"

"I need to know what's going on with him."

Felix eyes me. "Maybe you shouldn't go."

I feel the darkness closing in. I have to know, or it's going to eat at me.

"Stay here and work the bar," I snap.

Gritting my teeth, I ignore the stares from my pack and storm out the doors, getting into my car. Logan has been brushing me off all week. He told me he was busy working on the case. But doubt is starting to creep in. He can't dodge my calls and texts forever, and he certainly can't avoid me if I go to him.

I skip the line to the club, walking straight to the front. The bouncer's eyes widen on me, and he moves to intercept me. My eyes flash and I growl in warning. Being the smart boy he is, he moves aside to let me in the door. The club is busier than I was expecting. I notice people staring as I move through the crowd. A group of women turn to look at me and start whispering. A few of them even point. My heart sinks and speeds up at the same time.

I shouldn't be here.

I veer to the closest bathroom and check my reflection in the mirror. I shouldn't be this nervous. Yes, I'm here looking for my mate. Yes, I'm in enemy territory, but I am an alpha. I sweep my hair up into a high ponytail and smooth my fingertips under my eyes. The pack here wouldn't dare touch me. I know they all recognize me.

Stepping out of the bathroom, I notice even more people watching me than before. I frown at them and turn to slip into the crowd, but come to an abrupt stop almost immediately. The air leaves me, and everything stops. My heart freezes before it gives a hard thud and drops like lead in my stomach. A new type of pain slices through me, one I've never felt before, as everything shatters at my feet.

I'm not prepared for what I see. I have a deep sense of unease, like something isn't right. But this . . . this hurts.

Logan is sitting at a table by the wall, a woman on his lap, straddling him. Her long blonde hair is swaying to the music, her breasts are pushed up against his chest, with her arms wrapped around his neck. I watch as she rubs her sparsely clothed body all over him. Her lips drop to his and his hands come up, but I can't watch anymore, it's like a dagger is slicing at my insides. I spin on my heels and move quickly through the crowd, my gaze glued to the ground.

Someone grabs my arm and spins me around. I come face to face with Reaper. The threat of violence swims in the depths of his dark eyes,

"What are you doing here?" he snarls, his breath smelling of whiskey and cigarettes.

I open my mouth, but the only noise that comes out is a whine. It feels like my insides are being ripped out.

Reaper pulls back a fraction and frowns at me. "Shit. Salena, are you okay?"

He glances over his shoulder, and when he looks back, sympathy and anger reflect in his eyes. Swearing under his breath, he grips my arm and turns me toward the exit.

Reaper pushes open the door, and cool air slaps me in the face. Grasping my hand, he drags me down the sidewalk and into the alley. I'm too numb to even put up a fight right now.

Letting go of me, Reaper spins, pinning me with a savage look. "What were you thinking coming here? It's dangerous. You are fair game now. My pack are pissed at you."

"I was told Logan was here. He hadn't . . . He didn't . . . Did you know?" I'm not making much sense, but Reaper sighs, running a hand over his head, his teeth raking over his lip ring.

"Yes," he bites out. "Of course I knew he was here."

Images flash in my mind of Logan's mouth on hers, her hands in his hair. The hair I love running my fingers through. I can't stop the onslaught of images. My stomach rolls, and pain pierces my heart. I growl, the sound ripping from my soul as I turn, slamming my fist into the brick wall. Pain flares in my hand. It feels good. It takes over the pain in my heart, so I do it again and again, the skin on my knuckles splitting, my bones cracking with the force.

Reaper curses, grabbing my hands. "Salena, stop."

I shake my head and try to push him away. But he is solid and strong. Frustration wells up, so much pressure builds. A sob escapes me. Reaper lets go of my hands, pulling me into his chest. At first, I resist his comfort, but sobs rack my body, and I cling to him as more tears fall.

Reaper's hand cups the back of my head. "You're strong, Salena. So strong and fierce. It's okay to cry, but don't you ever stop fighting, not for one minute. It's not what you think."

I nod, my tone barely above a whisper as I cling to his shirt. "Is he fucking her?"

"No."

"How would you know?"

"Why ask, then?" Reaper snaps. "Look, he is here working a case. Your case. I don't know what you saw, but it's not that."

I stare at Reaper, confusion clouding my mind. My hands are throbbing, and my chest is cracked wide open. I can't think straight. A small spark flares in my chest, the kind I get when Logan is close. Butterfly wings beat fiercely in my chest as I glance over my shoulder, seeing Logan round the corner of the building.

"What the fuck is going on?" Logan's voice rips through the night air.

Reaper steps in front of me, shielding me. It's odd. He's being nice for a change. Maybe he isn't a complete asshole after all.

"She saw you and that whore," Reaper spits.

"I know," Logon snarls. "Leave us."

"Careful, detective. You're on my territory here."

I sense the hostility rise in the air and I step out from behind Reaper.

"I don't want to talk, Logan."

"Salena."

"No."

"Reaper, can I have a word alone with her?" Logan growls.

Reaper looks down at me, waiting. I heave a deep sigh before nodding my head. He doesn't need to be in the middle of this. Reaper purposely bumps Logan's shoulder as he goes past. I stare at Logan. His icy blue eyes are hard, and I can't get a good read on him, his face is set like stone. The only thing I feel is hurt. He touched another woman, and I am not okay with that.

"Salena."

I close my eyes at the way he says my name.

"No."

"It was all work."

"You had your tongue in her mouth!" I scream, my voice turning hoarse.

Logan's hands fist in his hair. "Fuck."

My arms wrap around my waist and I watch him closely as he turns his back on me. I have never felt so vulnerable before. My heart is aching fiercely.

"She caught me off guard. I didn't want that," he says, pointing back at the club. "You weren't supposed to be here," he growls, turning to face me again.

"Who is she?"

"Reaper called and said she came in asking for me. Won't talk to anyone but me. I've been trying to get information out of her for three days. The normal methods weren't working. She said she had information on your case. Then she asked to meet me here. Said she would tell me everything over a few drinks."

"So you what? Thought you'd sleep with her for the information!?"

"No!" he snarls, frustration causing his temper to show.

"She was grinding on your lap!" I snap. "You could have called her down to the station."

"Salena." My name comes out as a warning. "She wasn't grinding on my lap, and Sander already tried that."

My shoulders drop, I am so tired. I want this all to be over, and I know he does as well, but I can't get what I saw out of my head. Reaper could have told me, but he doesn't owe me anything.

"Salena," he murmurs softly this time. His hand glides up my arm, but I take a step back, putting more space between us. I am hurting, and all I want to do is step into his arms, but I can't. Especially not when he smells like *her*.

Logan's gaze drops to my hands, seeing the blood on them.

His voice comes out edged with fury. "What happened?"

Logan tries to grab them, but I take another step back, flexing my fingers. Understanding dawns in his eyes and he ignores the space I've put between us, stepping in front of me.

"You hurt yourself? Because of me?" he says as he strokes his thumbs over my knuckles. I can't take my eyes off of his. The fury swirling in his eyes is mesmerizing. "Don't ever fucking do that, Salena!" His voice is deadly, and I have the urge to submit, but I push those feelings away.

"You had your mouth on another woman," I croaks.

"I'm sorry, Salena." He holds up my knuckles and sees the dried blood and light bruises. I'll heal soon enough. Lifting them to his mouth, he places a kiss there. The touch is so gentle, so tender, it brings a fresh wave of tears. One slips down my cheek and I swipe it away angrily.

Pain slashes across his face, and he steps forward, but I step back, holding out a hand to stop him. Another tear slides down my face.

"Salena," he chokes out.

I shake my head, backing away.

"Please?"

My heart throbs painfully. I try speaking over the lump in my throat. "Just. Stop."

"I won't," he declares.

I turn my back on him, walking a few paces away. "I need time," I call over my shoulder. I don't wait for his reply as I take off running down the alley. I hear his curse as I run, making more tears fall down my face.

Chapter Thirty Six

Logan

S hit!

I knew I should have listened to Sander and explained to Salena what was happening. I just needed to do this without worrying about her interfering. From what she vaguely mentioned to me, Reaper is a family rival, and someone who has wanted her for a very long time. So, I knew she wouldn't want me going. Now everything is a mess.

Fucking Jenna. I didn't expect her to sit on me like that. One minute we were talking, the next she was on my fucking lap. Something caught me off guard at that moment. I had a strange sensation in my chest that I couldn't quite place. It was like a million butterfly wings beating.

Next thing I knew, Jenna was straddling me, her mouth on mine. Instinctively, I shoved her away, my body shaking with rage at her unwanted advances. But before I could rip into her, my eyes were drawn to the long silver hair shimmering in the lights of the dim club, walking away. I brushed past Jenna without a second look, yet she still reached out to keep me from leaving.

I feel like I've been set up, played. Someone is trying to fuck with me, with Salena, and I won't let that slide. She is mine.

I need to fix things with Salena, explain what really happened.

Somehow, she's wormed her way into my heart, and I think she's here to stay.

I sense Sander's approach, which I've always been able to do. I never would have thought much of it before, but what Salena said the other night is making me notice things I normally wouldn't. Things I've always brushed off as nothing, or an overactive imagination.

He comes to a stop beside me and looks in the direction Salena ran.

"She'll be fine. She'll understand once she's had time to cool down," he says softly.

"You didn't see the look in her eyes," I huff, lacing my fingers behind my head.

Tonight has been nothing but a fucking disaster. Why would she show up here? I feel like this has all been a big fucking waste of time. Like someone wanting to mess with me. The lead with the private investigator turned up nothing. Whoever he spoke to on the phone was using a burner phone, and all we know is the calls were coming from the Denver area. Everything was paid in cash and left in his mailbox, as he stated. There's only one street camera in the area, and there is no way to trace any who come and go. We have no fingerprints, no ID, no clue whatsoever.

Sander's phone lights up and he peers down at it before cursing. "The woman left," he says apologetically.

"Fuck!" I storm toward where we parked the truck.

She was our only lead, and she was fucking stalling, and now we have no clue where she is.

Chapter Thirty Seven

Logan

The sound of a forceful knock reverberates through my house as I'm putting on a pot of coffee before work. Frowning, I make my way to the front door. I swing the door open, and feel the tension in the air as I stare at two very pissed off men.

With a heavy sigh, I step out of the way to let them pass.

"Kai. Felix."

Kai spins on me as I shut the door. "What the fuck, man?!" he snaps. His fists are clenched, and I can see the effort it's taking to keep his anger in check.

My gaze moves to Felix. He looks equal parts pissed and disappointed.

I take a deep breath, then rub my temples in an attempt to relieve the throbbing. "Look, it wasn't what she thought."

"You were kissing another woman, meeting her behind Salena's back. Looks pretty obvious to me!" Kai snaps.

"It was work. I didn't expect that woman to kiss me."

Kai scoffs and spins, putting his back to me. I look over to Felix and he seems more hurt than angry now.

"I'm sorry. The last thing I wanted to do was hurt Salena. I was caught off guard, and no, not by Salena. Something else. And the woman took advantage of my distraction."

"Why were you distracted?" Felix asks, finally speaking.

I furrow my brow, thinking back on the night before. "It was weird, and you'll probably think I'm crazy, but one minute I was trying to get information from her, the next my heart began almost fluttering. It was weird, and it only seems to happen . . . " I trail off, not wanting to sound ridiculous.

"Around Salena?" Felix guesses.

I notice the look Kai sends Felix, a silent understanding passing between them.

"Yeah. But I didn't think it could be her. I had started scanning the dance floor looking for her when the woman straddled me. I barely had time to react when she kissed me. I pushed her away immediately, but it was too late."

Kai slumps against the wall, scrubbing his hands over his face. "Look, man, Salena is hurt, angry, and just . . . " He blows out a breath. "You need to make this right."

"I know," I reply, my heart beating faster with a sense of foreboding.

The possibility of her not forgiving me hangs heavy in the air, and I can almost feel it pressing down on me. If the situation were reversed, I'm confident I'd be behind bars right now. I need to explain what happened, if she will just take a moment to hear me out. I tried calling her last night, and even stopped by her apartment, but she wasn't home. Even Ghost wouldn't come over to me. She just perched above the door, her eyes never leaving mine as I paced around the small porch at the top of the stairs.

"I'll go to see her after work," I say.

"Just stay away from her. Give her some time," Kai says in warning.

I bristle, feeling anger take root in my stomach, making my skin prickle.

"Why were you meeting this woman?" Felix asks, drawing my attention.

"Reaper called–"

"Fucking Reaper. If this is his fault, I'll kill him!" Kai snaps angrily.

"No. Reaper called me a few days ago, saying there was a woman asking around about me. I went there and he pointed her out. She obviously knew by asking around that Reaper would call me. How, I have no idea. I've never been to that place in my life. She told me she had important information regarding the murders. But kept stalling. I think she was setting me up. Maybe setting Reaper up, too. I don't know."

"You need to fix this. You fucked up." Kai pushes off the wall and heads for the door.

"I know."

Felix hesitates as he goes to pass me, his brother a few steps ahead. My heart pangs as I stare into his eyes that are identical to Salena's.

"Just be honest with her. It's not cool you kept any of this a secret."

I dip my head in acknowledgment.

"Bad night, Sinclair?" Mack asks as I push through the doors of the station later that morning. I didn't get any sleep last night. I grit my teeth, wondering if it's worth mentioning. I've never been one to share anything about my personal life, but it seems I'm way out of my depth here. I decide against it and go straight to my desk. My stomach is twisted in knots over how things went with Salena last night. The look of pure devastation that reflected back at me in her gorgeous eyes almost broke me. I hate that she saw what she did and that I had hurt her. I never wanted that. I want to protect her.

"Detective," a woman purrs, the sound causing a shiver of revulsion to run over me.

What the fuck is she doing here?

"Jenna, if that's even your name," I reply, leaning back in my chair.

She shrugs and takes a seat across from me. "It is."

"Are you finally going to tell me what you know? Or are you going to keep fucking me around? Because I'm really not in the mood." I can't keep the bite from my tone.

"What I know is, someone paid me to set you up, to drive a wedge between you and your girl," she says with a sardonic smile.

A gnawing feeling spreads through the pit of my stomach, anger heating my veins. "Who?" I reply calmly.

Jenna just smiles. "The two dead girls look a lot like Salena Cartwright, don't they?"

My heart misses a beat at her name, her name from this woman's mouth. "What do you know?"

"I don't know anything,"

"How do you know Salena?" My jaw hurts from how hard I'm clenching it.

"I don't."

I growl in annoyance. "What about the girls? How do you know they look like her?"

Jenna shrugs and looks off to the side. "I just assumed."

"That's bullshit!" I snap, slamming my hand down on my desk.

Jenna grins like she's won some bet, then slowly stands. I follow suit, leaning my hands on the desk. "You're not leaving until you tell me everything you know."

Jenna tips her head back and laughs as if I've said the funniest thing. I frown, completely confused by her behavior.

"Are you going to arrest me, detective?"

Before I can respond, I see someone approach. My gaze swings to the side, and I see Salena standing a few feet away, glaring daggers at Jenna. I place my palm out and step between the two.

"What is she doing here?" Salena growls, a sound I haven't heard from her before. It seems to rumble from deep in her chest.

"She has come to give a statement," I say, my eyes pleading with Salena to understand.

"Trouble in paradise?" Jenna mocks from behind me.

Salena's eyes flare and a red flush works its way over her skin. I can see her vibrating with anger.

"Did you need something?" I ask, and immediately curse myself. That sounds so rude and informal. I suck at this, but she always sets my pulse racing, and right now my emotions seem to be mingling with hers—if that's even a thing—and I can't concentrate.

"I can't think straight when all I'm picturing is ripping her throat out." Salena snarls.

Jenna's laughter rings out. "Oh, honey, this was all a setup. But he is an extremely good kisser."

Salena lunges forward, and I wrap my arm around her waist, spinning her so her back is to my front. I motion for Milo to come over and take Salena.

"You need to calm down, baby."

Salena rips from my arms and spins to face me. Her eyes search mine with such a raw intensity that I swallow roughly. A knot of guilt tightens my stomach. I did this. Without another word, she turns and leaves, taking the light with her. It feels like something has pulled the very breath from my lungs as I stand there in the middle of the station. Everything grows cold and dark. The way I felt before I had Salena in my life. Before she reached the darkest parts of my heart and brought light and warmth with her. Slowly, I turn to face Jenna and see her smirking, her arms crossed, and her hip cocked to the side.

Anger burns up my throat and I snarl, grabbing her by the arm and dragging her toward the interrogation room.

Refusing to heed Kai's advice and leave her be, I make my way to the Crescent Moon after work. But she isn't here. Declan's body goes rigid, and he pauses for a moment before answering when I ask about her whereabouts. Some vague answer, saying she's on a run. So I head upstairs, but nothing. She's avoiding me, and I don't blame her. After last night and this morning, I'll be lucky if she even lets me explain. I get in my car and head home. Jenna's been charged with hindering an investigation, so she's spending the night in a cell. She was seething mad about it, but she should have thought about it a bit harder before taking cash to ruin someone. I can feel my anger rising at having been manipulated.

With a glass of bourbon on the rocks in my hand, I step out onto my deck, feeling the cool wood beneath my feet. The cold outside is unbearable, but I still crave the icy breath of the fresh air. The air has a sharp edge to it, and I can feel my skin tingle. That fluttering sensation fills my chest again, and I look around. Could Salena be here? I walk through the house and out onto the front porch, but no one's there. Confused, I make my way back outside and take a seat on a deck chair. My eyes adjust to the dark, and I see a flash of white in the forest over the back fence. I can feel the white wolf's presence close by, and I find myself hoping it will come and greet me.

I feel my phone buzz in my pocket and take it out to read the incoming message. Sander's checking in with me and updating me on his progress. He's still in Denver, chasing leads from Jenna. I tip back my drink and decide to get an early night. I double-check the locks on the house and slowly head up the stairs.

I don't remember falling asleep, but I know this is a dream. I'm enveloped in darkness, but the chill of the night air is palpable, and I can see my breath in a faint white cloud. I turn in a slow circle, but see nothing.

The air is filled with a beautiful, feminine voice. Her voice drifts softly through the air, but I can't make out the lyrics. Suddenly, I'm airborne, a wicked laugh taking over the sweet singing. I'm thrown backward and land hard on the ground, the wind knocked from my lungs. I let out a long groan as I roll onto my hands and knees. I feel a hand wrap around my throat, lifting me from the ground. I struggle against its grasp, my vision still blocked from the darkness.

A whisper of air caresses my ear. "*You're all mine, remember?*"

The grip around my throat releases, and I feel my heart pounding in my chest as I keep falling, never touching the ground. I suddenly jolt awake on the floor next to my bed, sweat coating my entire body as I lie there panting.

Chapter Thirty Eight

Salena

I knock twice on the door in front of me and take a deep breath as I step back. Logan swings the front door open, a deep frown on his face making his scar more prominent. But damn, he's shirtless and wearing only a pair of loose gray sweatpants. His defined chest and abdomen are on full display, the scars in no way, shape or form taking away the beauty of his body, only adding to it.

"Salena?" he steps onto the porch and looks around. "Are you okay? It's snowing. Why are you out in this weather without a jacket?"

Shit, why am I here? Soft snow falls on my face, the wind whipping around my bare shoulders. When I left the bar and went straight to the woods, I was still dressed in my bustier and jeans. I needed a run and have just been playing in the snow, not really paying attention to where I was going until I got here.

I know why. I missed him. It has only been a couple of days since I tried to see him at the police station, but I needed to hear his voice.

When I don't answer, he takes a step outside and looks around. "Did you walk?"

"I shouldn't be here," I blurt, then turn and jog down the stairs. I make it two steps down the path before Logan has my arm grasped in his hand and spinning me.

"Wait." His voice is desperate, a plea.

"I'm sorry. I don't know why I'm here," I whisper.

My heart thumps loudly as I let Logan draw me into his chest. Every nerve in my body is firing in rapid succession at being this close to him. At the feel of his warm hand on my skin, I want nothing more than to dive into his powerful arms.

"How is it you calm me? Just one look into your eyes and I'm instantly home. One touch and I'm more alive than I've ever been. You make me feel things I've never felt in my life," he whispers against my skin as his lips move over my bare shoulder to nuzzle my neck.

I try to step away to put some space between us, but his glacier blue eyes lock on mine, freezing me to the spot. His hands thread in my hair as his lips descend on mine. I don't stop him. I've missed him so damn much. The kiss is soft, his lips moving over mine with purpose. He pulls back a fraction and stares into my eyes. I'm speechless for a moment, then I remember he's half naked in the snow.

"Shit, you must be cold," I blurt, looking down at his bare feet.

"Not with you here. I don't feel anything but you."

My pulse picks up and anxiety fills me with what I need to tell him. "Logan, we need to talk."

His eyes close, and his forehead drops to mine. "I know."

I grab hold of both his wrists and pull his hands from my face. He doesn't resist, just lets go and grabs my hand, and starts pulling me toward his house.

"Logan–"

I'm cut off by the sound of a gunshot and spin around just as Logan's body takes me to the ground. Another shot rings out in the night, and I can just make out the sound of someone running away through the brush. I try pushing Logan off me. I know I can catch the guy. He isn't being quiet, and he must be leaving an easy enough trail. But then, that could be the point. Maybe it's an ambush. But who would know I was coming here when I didn't even know? Maybe they were here for Logan. That thought has my inner beast snarling and snapping.

I hear Logan grunt in pain as he lifts off me, and I snap out of my haze. I sit up and reach for him. "You're hurt."

"It's just a graze," he says as he looks around the yard.

"Let me see."

"Salena, I'm fine."

I can't stop the snarl that rips from my throat as I jump to my feet. "Show me, Logan."

My eyes must flash, because he looks stunned for a moment before he slowly moves his hand from his shoulder. I move closer and inspect the wound. The bullet just grazed his shoulder.

"Come on. I'm fine. Let's call it in," Logan says lightly, then guides me to the house.

I look behind me toward the trees and whip my phone out to quickly type out a message to Kai.

The police cruiser arrives within five minutes, followed by an ambulance. Logan gets his arm bandaged, and a quick once over, then we head inside to give our statements. Milo comes downstairs and throws a black long sleeve thermal at Logan, who tugs it on. The temperature has dropped significantly since it started snowing.

I wait by the front window, my eyes scanning the street and woods nearby. Kai, Felix, and Declan are out scouting the area. How did I not realize we were being watched? My mate just got hurt while I was right there. I feel my chest rumble with a low growl, a mix of fury and fear toward the shooter. I dig my fingernails into my palms and close my eyes, trying to calm myself before I wolf out in front of the cops. I open my eyes, feeling a tad calmer, until my gaze catches on Kallie in the reflection of the window as she approaches Logan. Her hand lands on his arm, and I bite down hard on my lip, but a growl still rumbles from my chest. I clear my throat to hide it, and I sense Logan's irritation toward her, which helps ease my jealousy. I watch in the reflection as Logan pushes her hand away and gestures toward me. My ears prick, and I can't help but listen in on their conversation.

Logan's voice hardens. "You know I'm with Salena. Why do you keep at me?"

"Word around town is you broke up."

I watch as she steps closer again and lowers her voice.

"She runs a bar on the edge of town, and dresses in skanky clothes, Logan. She isn't someone you take home to your mother, and everyone knows it. You deserve someone better, someone who has class."

Hurt worms its way into my chest at her words. I love what I wear, but I didn't realize that's how others saw me.

"You are way out of line. You need to shut your fucking mouth now and walk away. Who I date is none of your concern, because I sure as hell wouldn't date someone like you. Salena is fucking amazing, and if I had a mother, I sure as fuck would take her home to meet her."

I turn around to face them, and even though they're on the other side of the room, a tear slips from my eye. I brush it away. "You would?" I whisper, not knowing he'd be able to hear me.

Logan's gaze swings to mine, his face softens, and he rounds the sofa to approach, Kallie totally forgotten.

"Baby, I would show you off to the world as long as it was my hand you were holding."

Another tear falls. "Your hand is the only hand I want to hold."

"I'm sorry for not telling you about the Den, and meeting with that woman. It was all a ploy to break us apart, but I never once thought of her that way. You're the only one, Salena. You left the other night before you could see me push her off me. She set up the whole thing . . ." He trails off, a pleading look in his eye for me to understand. And I do. Kai has explained what happened, but god, it still hurt to see him with another woman.

"I know you were only working, but it . . . it hurt so much to see you with someone else. To have someone else touch you." I shiver, hating the images of that night that still repeat in my head.

Logan drops his forehead to mine. "I know. If things were reversed, I probably would have killed the guy."

"You're a cop. You can't say things like that," I chide softly.

Logan's eyes are open, and the fire burning in them says he isn't joking.

I swallow hard and sense someone approaching from the side. A throat clears and Milo stands there, a small grin on his face, before getting serious.

"Sorry to interrupt, but just thought I'd let you know we lost the tracks when they got to the lake. Looks like they may have had a boat waiting there for them."

Logan shifts to the side to face Milo with me, his massive hand engulfing mine. "Okay, so he or she knows the area well, then."

"Looks like it."

"Do you think they'll try again?" I ask.

Logan squeezes my hand as Milo talks.

"We haven't gotten any new leads, and we haven't determined yet if this is related to your stalker, Salena," Milo says, hooking his thumbs in his belt loops.

"Sander is looking at street cameras to see if he can find something on there," Logan adds.

I nod and look out the window, my eyes instantly connecting with Kai's where he's hiding in the bushes. *Find anything?* I ask.

'*No. We followed the tracks to the river. But Salena, it's weird. This guy doesn't have a scent. I can't smell anything. The tracks are there, but no scent.*'

'*So, it is the stalker, then?*'

'*Yes.*'

The ball of anxiety in my body is growing by the minute. '*He was so close.*'

'*I know. Do you think he was after Logan? To get to you?*'

I stretch my neck from side to side and release a deep, internal sigh. I just want this to be over with. My pulse skyrockets knowing Logan is in danger, and the need to protect him with every fiber of my being is overwhelming. Logan suddenly gathers me in his arms, his hand resting gently on the back of my head.

'*Your eyes were glowing, Salena, get it together,*' Kai's voice floats down the mental link.

My hands grip Logan's shirt at his sides. '*Did they see?*' I ask.

'*No, I don't think so. You must have made a noise and Logan pulled you to him.*'

I take a deep breath and re-focus on the conversation.

"We'll assign a patrol to stay outside tonight," Milo says, directing this at Logan.

Logan is still holding me to his chest, and I step back, his hands falling to my lower back, concern on his face.

"Thanks, Milo," I murmur, ignoring Kallie, who is waiting by the front door.

"No problem, Miss Cartwright. This person is bound to make a mistake. When they do, we will be ready."

Logan shakes Milo's hand and leads him to the door and opens it for Kallie and Milo. He completely overlooks Kallie, and I glance over to watch them head to the car. Kallie turns to stare at me, anger and jealousy shine in her eyes. I pivot away from her and look at Logan.

"I should go," I state.

Logan's hands land on my shoulders. "Please stay."

I nibble on my bottom lip and quickly look out the open doorway. A primal instinct rises inside of me, demanding I go hunting, eager to track my prey. To find the person responsible for hurting Logan.

Logan's warm hands side down my arms and grab hold of my hands. "Please."

My stomach twists with indecision.

'Stay, sis, you need each other. We will keep looking. We have rounded up the pack.'

'I should be out there.'

'No, you need to sort things out with Logan.'

Logan squeezes my hands. "Hey, are you okay?"

I blink, breaking my connection with Kai, and stare up at Logan. I reach up, lightly touching his cheek, and his eyes fall shut as he leans into the touch. My thumb runs over his scars and Logan's breath comes out stuttered.

"I missed you," he whispers, opening his eyes. Warmth spreads all the way to my toes at his words and I stare up into his eyes, the blue seems to glow as he stares at me, making my pulse speed up.

"I missed you, too."

He wraps his arms around me. "Can you forgive me?"

My mouth opens, but then shuts again. I have already forgiven him. But I'm overcome by an inexplicable need to stake my claim on him. Mark him in a way that indicates he is off limits.

"I forgive you. But Logan, if another woman so much as touches you, I will claw their eyes out." I speak softly to keep the growl from rumbling up my throat.

Logan stares down at me in silence. My heart is pounding against my ribs as I wait for his reply.

"Why?"

I know he's asking why I forgave him, and I can see the relief in his expression. "Because I know you would never intentionally do anything to hurt me."

Logan closes his eyes briefly, and when they open, they hold so many emotions I can't track them all.

"I would never cheat on you. Never hurt you like that."

"I know."

Logan bends, sweeping me up in his arms. I startle. "Your arm!" I shriek.

"Can't even feel it."

He carries me into his bedroom and puts me on the bed. "Shirts are in the top drawer, get comfortable. I'm going to check the house." He turns and leaves without waiting for my reply.

I run my hands over the comforter and lift the pillow to my face. His bed smells like him. It's all woodsy and spice. Taking a deep breath, I inhale his scent, then stand up and walk over to the dresser. I slowly open it and pull out a t-shirt from the top and walk to the adjoining bathroom.

I remove my jeans and bustier, placing them folded on the basin and pull the t-shirt on until it falls to my mid thighs. I pull my hair tie out and run my fingers through the long silver strands. A calmness has fallen over me since he brought me in here, where the familiar scent of his cologne surrounds me.

I make my way back to the bed and pull the cover back, slipping in between the cool material. Logan walks in, and I watch as he flicks off the light and walks toward the bed. He tugs his shirt over his head with one hand and tosses it aside before slipping in the other side of the bed, pulling the cover over his waist. Silently, he moves closer, wrapping his injured arm around my waist and tugging me into him, my head resting on his chest. His arm slides around my back, his fingers threading through my hair. My hand slides under his arm and I hug him close. We hold each other tight, the only sound in the room the gentle rhythm of our breathing as we drift off to sleep.

Chapter Thirty Nine

Salena

I wake to a warm body pressed against my back and a hand sliding under my t-shirt, cupping my breast. A muscular thigh slides between my legs and rolls me onto my stomach. Logan's scent wraps around me as his lips go to my shoulder and he nips, before moving his lips to the back of my neck. I draw in a sharp breath as goosebumps break out across my skin.

Logan's mouth disappears, and his hands slide my t-shirt up as he moves down my back, leaving me breathless as his lips and tongue move across my skin. He pushes my t-shirt over my head, and my hair falls over my naked shoulders as I struggle to remove it completely. Logan presses his chest to my back, his lips moving to my ear. I can feel the curve of his smile as he bites down on my earlobe.

"You're so fucking irresistible, Salena."

I shiver at the desire coating his words, and reach behind me, my hand sliding around his neck, my fingers twisting in his hair. He grunts, grinding his hips into mine. One hand moves over my side and down the front of my underwear. The fabric is pushed aside as he slides a finger inside of me. Then another.

A shudder runs through me. "Logan."

He chuckles, the sound making my stomach clench in anticipation as he nuzzles my neck, laying open-mouthed kisses along it. His fingers push further inside of me. An intense throbbing sensation pounds through my veins as I rock into his hand.

I turn my head to the side, and his mouth is there, waiting. He sweeps his tongue into my mouth, devouring me as his fingers move faster.

Logan breaks the kiss, burying his face in my neck. I need him inside of me. I push back so I'm kneeling in front of him, his chest against my back as he continues, his fingers sliding back and forth, going deeper each time.

"Logan," I pant, wrapping one arm around his neck, my head falling back against his shoulder.

"Yes?" he rasps, his thumb rubbing over my nipple.

"Fuck me."

A guttural groan leaves him. "Hold on to the headboard."

Shit.

My fingers curl over the wooden headboard, my nails digging into the wood. A frenzied energy fills me as I wait in anticipation.

I need him, all of him. Now.

His fingers leave me, and I hear his boxers get pushed down, then in one swift movement, he thrusts deep inside of me.

"Fuck." He grunts as his body curls over mine.

A delicious shiver rushes through me as his breath caresses my skin. I close my eyes, welcoming the heat that fills my body. He moves slowly, leisurely, and I growl in frustration, trying to push back into him.

Logan's large, warm hands cover mine. "Don't take your hands off that headboard," he growls into my ear.

His hands skim down my arms, down my back, and grip my hips tightly before he slams into me. Pleasure cascades over me from the rough way he's filling me. It is too much and not enough all at once. Using my grip on the bed, I push into his thrusts.

"Shit," he gasps, his fingers digging even harder into my hips.

I hang onto the headboard, panting, every muscle winding tighter. Keeping a steady pace, he thrusts into me, over and over. I can sense my orgasm getting close.

"Logan. Oh, god," I groan. I am there and so is he. My orgasm rolls through me in waves, making every inch of me tremble in ecstasy. Logan grunts behind me, biting down on my shoulder. Our pace slows, then he collapses onto my back, gently kissing my shoulder and neck.

"Are you okay?"

I nod, unable to answer verbally.

"You can let go of the headboard now," he chuckles.

I pry my fingers from the bed and let Logan lift me, placing me between his legs as he rests against the bed. I love how he can simply pick me up and place me on his lap.

"Are we good, baby?" he murmurs, nuzzling my hair.

"Yeah, we're good, detective."

God, I missed him. I never want to be without him again. I turn sideways in his lap, and my hand moves up, hitting the bandage on his shoulder.

"Are you okay? Does it hurt? I mean, of course it hurts. Do you need anything?" I'm rambling, but I hate seeing him hurt.

"I'm fine, baby."

I melt into his arms, laying my head in the crook of his neck. I idly trace my fingers over his abdomen and the scars there.

"Will you tell me how you got these?" I whisper.

I feel him tense under me, his whole body locking up. I wait patiently for his reply, not wanting to push him. Logan exhales slowly, his warm fingers intertwining with mine.

"I was five when it happened. My brother thought it would be a good idea to visit the lake one night. Riley loved doing stuff like that. He was the adventurous one. I made a desperate attempt to talk him out of it, but he refused to budge. I had a sinking feeling in my stomach, as if something terrible was about to happen. I had felt it the minute we entered the woods. But I followed anyway, pushing it down to nerves. First the mist rolled in, then I could hear singing. I was the only one who could hear it at first. Riley just shrugged it off, thinking I was making it up. The singing got closer and when Riley realized I was telling the truth, we turned and headed back. With our sense of direction gone, we started to panic, and our hearts raced. With the thickening mist, we couldn't tell where we were. Riley pulled me quickly through the woods, his fingers gripping mine so tightly that I could feel my knuckles aching. As we ran, I felt something slice through my clothes, leaving these." Logan runs our linked hands over the scars on his stomach.

"Didn't see a thing, I only felt it. Riley tried to help me, but he was thrown across the woods several feet. I felt a sharp stinging sensation across my face from whatever it was. Its sweet tormenting voice whispered from all sides, coming from everywhere at once. The mist circled us, it was like it was alive. Which I know sounds crazy. Riley managed to make it back to me, he was apologizing over and over."

Logan closes his eyes, pain lining his face. My heart is breaking for him, but I stay silent.

"We frantically tried to run away, but the menacing dark shadow blocked our path, knocking me down. It– It snatched Riley away. All I could hear were his screams, they filled the air around me. I was terrified. I couldn't move, my whole body numb as I lay there on the cold forest floor waiting for death to find me."

My heart is hammering in my chest so hard I swear it will burst free. I feel sick to my stomach at the thought of a five-year-old Logan alone like that. I pull back, my fingers tracing the ridges of his scarred cheek as tears roll down my face.

"I'm so sorry, Logan."

Logan's eyes have grown distant, and I know he's hearing his brother's cries. I close my eyes and gently press my lips to his. My fingers stroke his face softly as I whisper against his lips, "Logan, come back to me."

His eyes blink slowly, as if coming out of a trance, and he stares at me. "You were right."

I feel a wave of confusion sweep over me. "About what?"

"I can sense when shit is going to happen. I see things I can't explain. I just thought I was seeing shit."

"Well, technically, you are seeing shit. But you're not going crazy. It's there. You're not imagining it."

"I'm sorry I got mad at you for bringing it up." His finger brushes the hair off my face and over my shoulder.

"It's okay. I kind of thought you'd think I was crazy," I joke, giving him an easy smile.

"So, Ghost isn't real?"

"Oh, he's real. He's just a spirit of sorts. Ghost found me and hasn't left my apartment since."

"Huh."

I can tell he's absorbing all this. It's a lot to take in for anyone, and I really want to tell him what I am, what we are to each other. But I hesitate. He is only just accepting his own gift. I don't want to overwhelm him. I know I'm making excuses, but I can't bring myself to utter the words.

Chapter Forty

Logan

I descend the stairs and find Salena in the kitchen, her face illuminated by the morning sun streaming in from the giant window above the sink. She's standing there drinking from a mug of coffee, the smell wafting over to me. I walk over to her, wrapping my arms around her, and pulling her into me. I feel her body relax against mine as she releases a content sigh. I don't know how she can be this calm after everything I've put her through, everything I've told her. She must feel me tense because she pulls away, placing her coffee mug on the bench before turning in my arms and resting her cheek on my chest. She nestles into me so comfortably, it's like she's made to fit there perfectly.

"Logan?" she murmurs, placing a kiss in the middle of my chest.

"Hmmm . . . " I answer, my anxiety washing away at hearing my name on her lips.

"Can you pick Lola up from school today? I don't want her walking alone. I hate to ask but . . . "

I pull away from her and gently cup her face in my palm, my thumb stroking the soft skin of her cheek.

"I'm never going to say no to you. You get that right."

Salena beams up at me. "Thank you."

I drop my lips to hers in a soft, explorative kiss. Her lips move in sync with mine like a well-rehearsed dance.

"I made you a coffee," she whispers against my lips.

"Thank you, baby."

I press a light kiss to her lips and turn to the sight of my steaming coffee cup on the island bench, and wrap my fingers around the cup, savoring the flavor as I take a sip, my eyes tracking Salena's movements as she comes and sits at the bench.

"Are we good?" I ask.

"We're good." She smiles at me, and I swear the light in the room gets brighter.

A few hours later, I'm standing outside the school, my back resting against my car, scrolling through emails when I hear the sound of Lola's laughter, and then she comes into view with a huge smile on her face. Her pink hair is in Dutch braids today and she has on these brown cargo pants, and a tight long sleeve blue shirt. I notice another girl following behind her, but at a distance.

"Hi, Logan!" Lola exclaims, coming to a stop right in front of me.

"Lola," I greet her with a small dip of my head.

"Can you give my friend Amara a ride home? We're planning on studying at her house for a while. Her mom can drive me home." She turns to the girl behind her.

Amara looks scared as she nervously scans the parking lot, her eyes darting back and forth.

"Sure. Everything okay?" I ask.

Lola and Amara share a look before Lola spins on me. "Of course."

I give them both a look that conveys I think they're full of shit and motion for the car.

"Wait, can I drive? I have a learner's permit!" Lola shouts.

I pause and consider it. Lola pouts, putting her hands under her chin as if she's praying.

Chuckling, I shake my head. "Sure. Why not?" I toss her the keys and move to the passenger side.

Lola lets out a massive squeal and jumps into the driver's seat. Her friend hesitantly climbs in the back. I catch her mumbling, "This is a bad idea."

I find out why five minutes into the drive.

"Do you think if that semi-truck suddenly put its brakes on and I didn't, we'd get decapitated when we hit it?"

My head snaps to Lola. "What?"

"Never mind," she says as she absentmindedly rubs her neck, likey an involuntary motion from the thought of being beheaded.

We drive in silence for a couple of minutes. Lola glances over at me quickly before looking back at the road. I watch her hands tighten on the steering wheel and brace myself for whatever's about to come out of her mouth next.

"Do you think if I hit that divider at this speed, it would split the car in half? Or just crush it?"

"What the fuck, Lola?" I growl, seriously regretting my decision to let her drive.

"What? It was just a question."

"Why are you even thinking shit like that?" I snap.

"I don't know!" she exclaims. "It just pops into my head."

"This is why they keep failing you in driving. You need to keep that shit in your head," Amara says from the backseat.

"I have things I need to ask. You know, like when you're standing on a cliff and you have the sudden urge to jump . . . "

"Nope," Amara replies calmly, as if she is completely used to this shit coming out of Lola's mouth.

Lola huffs and looks back at her friend before returning her eyes to the road. "Well, I do. I have questions . . . "

"Like that random question about your tongue?" Amara says. I can sense the girl's exasperation.

"It was a legitimate question," Lola argues.

"Really?" Amara says, and I can hear the incredulity in her voice.

"Yes."

"What was the question?" I ask, curiosity getting the better of me.

Lola's cheeks turn a deep shade of pink as she glances over at me.

"What do you do with your tongue when you're not using it?" she asks.

I frown in confusion, my brows drawing in. "What do you mean?"

"Like, where do you put your tongue? On the roof of your mouth? Pressed against your teeth? Down? I don't know. My tongue felt too big for my mouth, and it was annoying me. I didn't know what to do with it. So, I asked what people did with their tongues." Her words come out in a rush.

I stare at Lola for a long moment, feeling my mouth tug into a smile despite my best efforts. I shake my head in bewilderment. This girl's head must be noisy as fuck.

"Don't ever change, Lola." I smile.

Amara finally speaks from the backseat. "What's the quickest way to a man's heart?" she asks, sounding sad. Ah, so the issue is with a boy, then. I give Lola a quick look and she shrugs sympathetically. I twist in my seat and peer back at Amara. Her hazel eyes look tired, and her face is pale.

"In all seriousness, through the fourth and fifth ribs," I say with a wink.

Lola cackles, slapping her hand on the steering wheel. Amara's lips curl in a half-smile as her cheeks flush pink, and she gazes out the window, her brown hair cascading around her face.

As I drive away from Amara's house, I can feel the weight of my responsibilities at the station settling back onto my shoulders. I still have a lot of shit to do. We have made no headway in determining who shot me last night. Every lead we follow ends up being a dead end.

With what feels like the weight of the world on my shoulders, I climb out of my car and make my way into the station. My shoulder aches, but the pain is nothing new to me. It's something I'm familiar with. From a young age, I have found that pain is an effective way to keep myself centered and focused.

Sitting behind my desk, I feel the rough texture of the manila folders as I pick up the files on the missing girls that fit Salena's description. There are precisely seven girls missing from nearby states, aged between sixteen and twenty-eight. All having disappeared in the last six months. I meticulously dissect every detail, analyzing each file, then sit back in my chair, feeling the wheels creaking underneath me. As I scan the station, I notice Betty is the only person here. She works the night shift at the front desk.

I look out the window and notice night has fallen while I had my head buried in all the files and photos scattered across the desk. I've managed to miss lunch and dinner. Besides picking up Lola, I've spent hours reviewing these files. The frustration builds as I let out a deep sigh, realizing that today has been a complete waste. I wonder where Sander is? I find it odd that he hasn't come looking for me yet.

I stare down at everything on the table in front of me and growl, frustration getting the better of me. I need a break. I push away from my desk and head for one of the private rooms where Sander has set up shop to work his way through video feeds on the street cameras. We also have a list of residences with security cameras in the area.

Sander is still here going over information with me. He offered to call in help from Portland, but I didn't think we needed help. What we need is for these guys to fuck up and leave a clue.

"Anything?" I say, pushing open the door.

Sander doesn't look up from his laptop when he answers me. "Nothing yet."

I make my way to the window and notice the eerie stillness of the street as I look out into the darkness. What are we missing?

Sander sighs, pushing his chair away from the table and rubbing his eyes. "I can't find anything but a fucking shadow."

I spin on him. "What?"

"There's a shadow that's standing just off to the side of the street camera."

"Show me," I demand.

Sander swiftly taps the keys and brings up footage from the camera down the street from my house. I see Salena knocking on my door, me following her down the path, then Sander pauses it and points.

The camera offers a sharp-angled view of the street, but the front yards are mostly obscured. I move my gaze to the outskirts of the neighboring yard, and I see someone standing there, just beyond the trees. The lack of light makes it impossible to make out any details. It's too dark and too far away. Whoever they are, they stayed mostly hidden a few feet in the shadows of the trees. We wouldn't have known they were there at all.

Sander hits play, and I watch as he or she stands there with statue-like stillness, a predator watching its prey. Then slowly they lift their arm, a gun in hand, and fire, then step into the shadows and meld into the night.

"Fuck."

"Yeah."

I stand, running my hand over my head, staring at the computer. "Wait, go back. I want to see something."

Frowning, Sander rewinds before hitting play, and I watch again. "There." I point at the screen. "Zoom in as much as you can."

Sander zooms in on the person, and I focus. There's a second as they lift the gun that the hand is bathed in light. The hand firing the gun is covered in tattoos. Sander and I share a glance. It's a lead. Our only lead.

Milo taps twice on the door, poking his head inside. "Hey, Sinclair. Report's come in of suspicious activity down at the old mill."

My eyes dart up to Milo. He wouldn't mention something like this unless I needed to know. This is something the uniform officers would deal with. I stand and grab my jacket, Sander following suit.

Chapter Forty One

Salena

I finish lighting the last flaming Dr. Pepper shooter, smiling at the three young men who all wear looks of apprehension, when a searing pain radiates through my chest. I stumble, my hand going to my chest, as I rub at the strange sensation. What was that?

Another sharp pain takes me to my knees, my body becoming uncomfortably warm. I can hear shouts, but can't make out the words as my body is filled with sharp stabbing pains. Blinding white light flashes in front of my eyes. A scream is trapped inside my throat, my breath coming out in ragged gasps. Next thing I know, I'm being swung up into Kai's arms and raced out the back door. Felix and Mercy following closely behind.

"Salena, what's wrong?" Kai's desperate voice penetrates the pain. He gently sets me down on the ground, and I can feel the chill of the icy ground through my jeans. I hold up my palm for them to wait. I take several deep breaths and close my eyes, trying to concentrate on where the pain is coming from. In my mind, I follow the pain down my pack link.

"Lola," I breathe.

My eyes flash open and I feel rage and fear overtake the pain. Within seconds, I've shifted and I'm racing into the trees toward the edge of town. I don't know how I know where to go, but I do.

'Lola is hurt. She is at the old abandoned mill,' I send out to the others.

The others shift and chase after me. I'm the fastest, though, losing them in the woods. I'm barely paying attention to my surroundings as I dash through the trees. Everything becomes a blur as I race ahead in a blind panic, my pace not slowing until I reach the mill.

I can feel the cold snow beneath my paws as I slowly move forward. I'm breathing heavily, my heart pounding as I run on pure adrenaline. The metallic coppery smell of blood floats in the air. Fear punches me in the chest as I creep around some old, rusted machinery.

A sudden wave of magic sweeps through the air, and I stop in my tracks, my stomach twisting in worry. I take a cautious step forward, and my hackles rise knowing there is a threat nearby. Before I can take another step, something large crashes into me, my body rolling across the ground with the impact. My fur prickles with magic like I've touched an electric fence. The aches and pains I'm feeling are pushed to the back of my mind as I rise and look around, finding I'm the only one here.

What was that?

A shiver of fear trickles along my spine, making me tremble, but I ignore it. I need to find Lola. There's a sense of dread rising inside of me as I follow the smell of blood. I don't realize what that means until I move around the next corner. Lola is lying in the middle of a ritual circle. Her body has been mutilated. Blood coats the entire snow covered ground in the circle. My steps falter and I shift into my human form, running toward her. I drop to my knees, lifting her limp, lifeless body into my arms.

"Lola? Lola, wake up," I croak.

I lightly stroke her cheek, blood smearing all over my hands in the process. "Lola?"

Frantically, I look around for any sign of who did this. I notice a pattern of rocks around the ritual circle and frown, my eyes blur with tears. I hear the moment others arrive. Felix swears and paces behind me, still in his wolf form. Shifting, Kai and Mercy look from me to Lola, to the circle full of Lola's blood.

"What does it say?" I ask.

Mercy moves over to the carefully placed rocks and turns even whiter.

"What is it?" I whisper hoarsely.

When she answers, her voice is unsteady. "You're next."

"FUCK!" Kai yells, gripping his head with both hands. "FUCK."

I close my eyes, tears falling and mingling with Lola's blood. I search down my pack for her link, her connection to me, and find nothing. She is truly gone. A tiny fracture goes through my chest, and I try so hard to be strong, but the dam breaks. A sob rips free as I bury my face in her neck. I failed to protect the youngest in my pack. I stroke her blood-covered face, pushing the clumps of hair away that are sticking to her cheeks.

"Oh, Lola. I'm so sorry," I cry, hugging her closer to me.

My anguish rushes down the pack link, and answering howls fill the night. We all feel the heaviness of her absence in the air. Whoever did this will pay with their life. I will tear them apart myself. I scream my sorrow and frustration at the sky for this cruel twist of fate.

The next moment, we hear the sirens and feel our hearts thumping as we exchange a silent gaze.

'*Who called the cops?*' Felix asks through our mental link.

'I don't know,' I reply.

I look to the others. I'm about to tell them to go when the first cop car swings in, headlights shining over us.

"Freeze! Police. Put your hands in the air."

"Fuck," Kai and Mercy say together.

I look over my shoulder and see Felix backing up into the long grass.

'Go.'

'I will meet you at the police station.'

'Okay.'

'I love you, Salena.'

I close my eyes, tears still streaming down my cheeks. *'I love you, too, Felix.'*

Chapter Forty Two

Salena

Slowly, I strip off my clothes, letting them thud to the floor in a wet heap. They are soaked in blood, Lola's blood. My chest splinters and I swallow the sob that works its way up my throat.

Numbly, I reach out, drawing the curtain back and turning the water on. I step under the spray, leaving the cold off. I need to wash off her blood. My skin turns pink as I relish the burn of the water.

My shaky fingers grip the bar of soap, and I slowly drag it over my arms, my skin turning pink from the scalding water. Another sob works its way up my throat, and this time I can't hold it back. It tears free from my chest, making me double over in pain. My eyes find the red water swirling at my feet and I break. My legs give out, and I hit the tiled floor, curling my body into a ball. I draw my knees to my chest and feel the tears streaming down my face.

Faintly, I can hear a wailing sound and realize it's coming from me, my cries so violent my body convulses with the sheer force of them. Suddenly, the door to the bathroom bangs open, the noise bouncing around the bathroom. I don't bother looking to see who it is as the curtain is ripped open.

Logan's loud curse startles me, and I curl in tighter on myself.

"Salena?"

I don't look up, just continue to heave, my sobs ripping my body apart. The water temperature changes to something cooler, and I vaguely hear Logan's clothes hit the floor.

Next thing I know, I'm being pulled upright and into a warm, firm chest. Logan is sitting in the shower naked, his back to the wall, and cradling me on his lap.

He tucks my head under his chin, smoothing my hair back, whispering words of comfort to me. I can't hear them though. Not through the sounds of my cries and the water beating down on us. But his voice, smell, and arms bring me the comfort I need; the sound of his voice, the scent of his skin, and the embrace of his arms like a blanket of security.

My heart feels wrecked, everything raw and aching. Lola is gone. I failed her. I am the Alpha, it's my responsibility to keep my pack safe. But someone is stalking me, threatening me. My pack has paid the price.

We stay like this under the soft spray of water for a long while, him stroking my hair, whispering words I can't make out. I am desperately trying to regain my composure, my breathing still unsteady. Logan reaches over to the ledge and grabs something, but I don't open my eyes. He positions me between his legs, my back to him as his hands work my hair into a lather, gently washing it. I keep my eyes closed, soaking in the feeling of him taking care of me. The feel of his fingers running through the length of my hair.

When he's done, I turn around to face him, my legs wrapping around his waist. My head rests on his chest, as I breathe him in. His thumb and forefinger grip my chin, tilting my head up to his. When I look into his eyes, the palest shade of blue, the anguish and worry is unmistakable. God, they are beautiful eyes. I have never seen eyes like his before. They remind me of frozen glass, like when the temperature drops and your windows frost over.

"Stupid question, but are you okay?" he whispers.

I swallow hard and shake my head. Reaching up, his hand lands on the side of my face, swiping away water that's mingling with my tears. I fall forward to rest on his chest again, his arms wrapping tightly around me.

Logan reaches up and turns the shower off and somehow manages to stand with me cradled in his arms. He steps from the shower, grabbing two towels and walking us over to the bed. Sitting on the end of the bed, he gets one towel and gently rubs it over my hair, then dries me off. Standing again, he places me on the bed, pulling the covers over me and placing a soft lingering kiss on my forehead.

"Sleep, baby. I'll be here," he whispers.

I close my eyes and feel tears fall down my face, soaking into the pillow. I don't know how I have any more tears left to cry, but even though I'm not crying, the tears don't stop falling, one after another.

Not long after, I feel the bed dip behind me and Logan's warm body slides in behind me, his arms wrapping around me and pulling me tightly against his body. I bask in his warmth and contentment, and soon enough my eyelids droop with overwhelming exhaustion.

Chapter Forty Three

Logan

I will never get the sight of Salena covered in blood from my mind. When I pulled up at the crime scene and saw her sitting there, I lost all sense of thought. I raced over to her and checked her over for injuries myself, snarling at the paramedic who tried to tell me she was unharmed.

Salena clung to me as her friend was bagged and wheeled into the other ambulance. Kai and Mercy stood off to the side, talking in hushed whispers, both casting worried glances at Salena. I tenderly stroked her hair, breathing in the scent of coconut before laying a gentle kiss there and walking off to talk to the first on scene officers. They told me she was holding the body when they arrived, refusing to let go. An anonymous tip had come in of suspicious activity down at the old mill. The number, of course, was from a burner phone. Salena was first on scene, saying she was tipped off as well.

I won't rest until whoever did this has been taken care of. My chest aches with a dull, heavy pain that seems to reverberate through my entire body. Lola is gone. The bubbly seventeen-year-old is just gone.

I hold Salena in my arms all night, and as soon as the sun rises, I slide out of bed, tucking the blanket firmly around her. I grab my phone and step outside.

Sander picks up the first ring. "She okay?"

I blow out a deep breath and rub the back of my neck. "No."

"What can I do?"

"Come with me to Denver. I need to speak to Reaper."

"You sure that's a good idea?"

"It's my only idea."

I can sense the wheels turning in Sander's head. "You think he's the one?"

"I don't, but he is the only one I know who has tattoos like that. I think someone's trying to make it look like him, and I need to know who."

"Why don't I go, and you stay with Salena?"

I consider it. Sander can get the information I need. But I need to be sure. I need to look into his eyes when I tell him Lola is dead.

"No, I want to go. I need to speak to him myself."

"Okay, when do you want to leave?"

"Give me thirty minutes."

We hang up, and I dial Kai. He answers on the first ring. "Hey, Logan, how is she doing?"

"She's still sleeping, but I need you here. I have to go do something."

"Sure, I'll be there in ten."

I walk back inside and take a seat on the edge of the bed, reaching up to run my fingertips across Salena's soft cheeks. Her face is still red and puffy from crying, and her hair's a knotted mess from drying in bed. I'm not used to caring for someone like this. Her heartache is like my own, sharp and deep.

Lola was a sweet young girl with her whole life ahead of her. This time, the killer didn't target someone who resembled Salena. This time, it was someone she loved.

Sander and I saunter through The Den's back door, the dimly lit hallway illuminating our path. Sander seems extremely on edge, almost as if his hackles are raised. He's gone to make a call to his friend Lukas from Portland. Apparently, Lukas knows of Reaper and needs to be made aware of what's happening. I'm not sure why, but I never question my friend.

There's a young woman standing at the bar cleaning glasses when we enter. Her eyes instantly whip to us, and she frowns. "What are you doing in here?"

She has short pixie cut blue hair and piercings all over. Her dark black makeup is thickly applied to her eyes and lips, making her blue eyes stand out, even from where I'm standing.

"We are here to see Reaper." I flash my badge.

Before she can answer, Reaper appears at the top of the stairs leading to the upper level. "Up here."

I share a look with Sander before we make our way up the stairs.

Reaper guides us to a table at the back of the room. He cracks his knuckles, his eyes on me as we settle into our chairs. "What do you want now, detective?"

I don't waste time with pleasantries. I'm in a bad fucking mood.

"Where were you last night?" I growl, my fists clenching on the table.

Reaper's eyes drop to my hands, and he frowns. "Here."

"One of Salena's pack was killed last night," Sander says, leaning in.

My brows slam down at his choice of words. *Pack?* There's something in his voice, something I've never heard before. Almost animalistic.

Reaper's head rears back. "The fuck?"

"Lola. She was only *sixteen*. Any idea who would do something like that?" I ask.

Reaper's brown eyes go hard as he stands abruptly. He starts pacing in front of the table, muttering under his breath before turning on us. His hands slam down on the table.

"Someone fucking killed *Lola?!*" he snarls, half crazed. "I'll fucking rip them to shreds. I may not have gotten Salena, but I would never hurt . . . " he trails off, shaking his head.

My heart thumps hard at his admission. Reaper's whole body is tense. Agitation rolls off him in waves. I look to Sander, confused; his reaction is extreme, but Sander seems relieved.

"Look, do you know anything? Anyone who would want to hurt Salena or her friends? I know we've asked before, but . . . fuck. It was Lola." My voice betrays my emotions.

"I told you last time, no. If I did, I would have dealt with it."

My eyes narrow on him, and he raises his hands. "I'll send out my pack and help find this fucker. Enough is enough. Salena may not have chosen me, but I won't stand by anymore. This fucker needs to be taken care of."

There's that word again, *pack*.

Sander stands up and moves to shake Reaper's hand. Something passes between them, and I frown. What is that about? Sander is acting differently than I'm used to.

When we get back on the road, my hands clench around the steering wheel. "Well, that was a waste of time," I sigh.

"No, now we have help."

"What was up back there? You seemed different."

Sander looks over at me, his gaze lingering. "What do you mean?"

I shake my head, putting the car in drive. "I don't know. You just seem different."

On the drive back to Boulder, the only sounds are the steady hum of the engine and Sander tapping the keys on his laptop. All the while, I'm lost in my thoughts. How could someone kill sweet, bubbly Lola? She was so young and full of life. Whoever it is must have a huge grudge against Salena and wants her gone. Permanently.

Chapter Forty Four

Salena

I wake just before noon and can sense my brothers in the house, but no Logan. The crushing weight of last night comes crashing down on me, and I bury my head in the pillow and scream. The bedroom door bursts open with a loud bang, and Kai and Felix are there.

"Salena," Felix says softly.

Suddenly there is someone else in the room with us, and I jump from the bed and shift in a heartbeat, my emotions too raw and mind too fractured to control it. I let out a deep growl, my eyes trained on the doorway.

I'm shocked to see Old Myrtle standing there, a look of anguish on her aged, weathered face.

"It's okay, child. I'm not here to harm you. I heard about poor dear Lola."

I huff out a sharp breath before shifting back into my human form. "You scared me," I say, choking on the words. My throat is raw and achy from hours upon hours of crying.

The old witch never leaves her house in the mountains. This is an extremely rare occurrence.

"Sorry, we didn't think she would follow us up here," Felix apologizes, throwing her a dark look.

"How do you know Lola?" Kai asks, moving up next to me.

"Lola used to visit me once a week. I always looked forward to it."

Surprise filters through me. I had no knowledge she did that. Felix walks past Kai and me.

"Let's take this out of the bedroom, yeah?" he says.

We all move downstairs to the living area and take a seat. Except for Felix, who stands by the window, staring out at the snow covered ground. His shoulders are hunched, and stress holds every muscle in his body hostage. I can feel each and every one of my pack through our shared connection. Their pain, grief, and anger all adding to my own.

Lucy, Grady, and Rose are suffering the most. Grady spent all night hunting whatever attacked me and killed Lola. Kai's the one who went to get him, force him home to be with his family.

There's a soft knock on the door, and Felix leaves to answer it. He's only gone a minute when he guides Amara in. Her tear-stricken face is red and puffy. I have no idea how she knew this is where we would be or where Logan lives.

"Is it true?" she whispers, her eyes meeting mine.

"Yes."

Amara's legs give out, but before she can hit the floor, Felix scoops her up and places her on the sofa across from me.

Logan walks in, his eyes scanning the room and taking in the new-comers. I look at what he's holding and gasp. Ghost is nestled in his arms. He gives me a look that conveys he couldn't leave her there and I won't be leaving here. Old Myrtle regards him with a frown and a tilt of her head. I don't like that look one bit.

Logan scans Amara before his expression darkens in a frown. Stepping around the sofa, he carefully places Ghost on my lap and plants a gentle kiss on my head. Then, turning, he squats down in front of Amara.

"Are you okay?" he asks softly.

Amara squeezes her eyes closed tightly, shaking her head vigorously.

"Hey. Hey. It's okay," Logan says, grabbing her hands.

"It's not. It's all my fault," she cries, her red-rimmed eyes flashing open. There's so much pain and heartache reflecting there. I take a deep breath, suppressing my emotions and burying them deep inside.

"Why do you say that?" Logan asks.

"She got a call from a boy she liked last night before she left my house. I should have gone with her."

A boy?

"What was the boy's name?" I demand, my tone harsher than I intended.

Amara doesn't flinch though, her red blood-shot eyes rise to mine. "Ro. Ro Peterson."

I can hear the thudding of my heart echoing in my ears. If anyone has a reason to hate me, it's him. I am the reason his father was killed. But the humans don't know that, they think it was an animal attack on Kai's property.

"I shouldn't have let her go. I should have called you," Amara cried, dropping her face in her hands.

Logan stands and runs a hand through his hair. I put Ghost on the sofa and drop to my knees in front of her, pulling her into my arms.

"Hey. It's not your fault. You didn't know this was going to happen," I murmur.

"But I told her to go, and now she is dead," Amara screams, pulling from my arms. She stands swiftly and runs for the door and out into the cold.

Felix sighs and looks at me. "I'll make sure she gets home."

Logan's eyes meet mine as he turns to me. "It wasn't Ro."

"You can't be sure. He could blame me, us"—I motion to Kai—"for his father's death."

Logan's head drops. "I will go and see him. Ask a few questions. But I know he isn't a killer."

"Okay," I whisper.

Logan offers me his hand, and as I stand, he pulls me into a warm embrace. "Will you be okay?" he murmurs into my hair.

I nod, taking a deep inhale of his scent. I let my breath out slowly, my fingers gripping the back of his shirt tightly. Stepping back, Logan squeezes my shoulder gently.

"I'll be back as soon as I can."

He turns, giving Kai a firm pat on the shoulder before leaving the room. I hear the soft click of the front door closing and fall back into my seat on the sofa.

Old Myrtle remains silent and motionless as she watches, her dark gaze steady and unblinking. It gave me the creeps.

'You and me both,' Kai says down the link.

The old witch swings her gaze my way, as if she heard my thoughts, her dark coal-black eyes locking on mine. The air freezes in my lungs as images flash through my mind. Claws, teeth, blood, and shadows swirling together. I can hear my own screams echoing in my head. When she blinks, I double over, gasping for breath.

With a feral growl, I tilt my face up to her. "What the hell was that, witch?"

Old Myrtle is unfazed by my words. "You both have demons you need to overcome."

Kai steps forward. "What do you mean?"

Old Myrtle's gaze flickers to him and waves him off. "Not you, boy. Logan and Salena."

"What do you mean?"

"Those images you just saw . . . They are what await you."

Chapter Forty Five

Logan

I knock hard on the door in front of me and step back, waiting. I stare at the house, taking in the details of its worn exterior. It still seems run down like it did last time I was here. Maybe I can see if some guys from the station can come down and help tidy the place up. The thought surprises me. I'm used to closing myself off to anything and everything, but now, thanks to Salena, I'm more open and accepting.

I know deep down Ro had nothing to do with Lola's murder, but that doesn't mean he doesn't know something.

I step forward and knock again when there's no answer. After a moment, I hear a noise on the other side of the door.

"Hello, it's Detective Sinclair. I need to ask you some questions," I call through the door.

The door unlocks and opens only a couple of inches. I can see Hayley's shadowed face just barely through the crack.

"Mrs. Peterson, I need to talk to your son, Ro. Is he home?"

Hayley doesn't say a word, just shakes her head.

"Can you tell me where he is?"

"No, I don't know where he is," she croaks.

My stomach twists with trepidation as I take a step closer, and I hear Hayley's sharp intake of breath, her eyes widening a fraction.

"Are you okay?" I ask softly.

"Yes, everything's fine. I'm fine. I've got to go."

The door shuts, and the locks are engaged. I stare at the door for several beats before I make my way back to the car. Well, that was weird. Something is most definitely wrong.

I pull my phone out of my pocket, hitting recall.

Sander answers, "Everything okay?"

"I'm fine, but I need you to look into Hayley Peterson for me to see if anything stands out."

"The wife of the cop that was killed?"

"Yes."

"Okay. Anything I should know?"

I glance back at the house and movement at the upstairs window catches my eye. The curtain drops back into place when I glance up.

"No. I don't think so. Something feels off. Plus, I found out Lola was supposed to meet Ro the night she was killed."

I hear Sander's soft curse through the phone. "I'm on it."

I hang up the phone, shoving it in my pocket before getting in my car. I drive toward the local hang out spots the kids like to use. Jacob and the other boys saunter out of the diner on Main Street, the sound of laughter trailing behind them as they stop at the curb. I put the window down and call out,

"Hey, any of you boys seen or heard from Ro?"

"Hey, Logan, man. What's up? Nah, we haven't seen him. He left school and all. Walked right out," Jacob says.

"Okay, thanks anyway," I mumble, exasperated.

I look around the street, wondering where to start. I hear a gentle tapping on my window and quickly lower it again. Peter leans in on it, his disheveled blonde hair falling into his eyes.

"He usually heads to the lookout this time of year."

"The lookout?"

"Yep," Peter says, stepping back and nodding before jogging over to his friends.

Okay, I know where that is. But what's he doing all the way out there? The drive only takes me ten minutes, and when I arrive, I see Ro, his shaggy brown hair shining brightly against the sun as he sits on top of a boulder. I park the car and make my way over. The snow has been falling all night, so it lies fresh and thick across the ground, crunching under my feet. Ro turns and sees it's me and frowns.

"What are you doing here?" he grumbles.

"I need to ask some questions."

"What questions?" He pulls his jacket tighter around himself.

"Did you call Lola last night and ask to meet her?"

Ro glances away, a barely audible "Yeah" escaping his lips.

"Where were you going to meet?"

Ro drops his head, his shoulders hunched over. My heart twists at the look of defeat that comes over him. If I could take away his pain, I would. This kid has seen too much heartache. Then again, some would say the same about me.

"It was her, wasn't it?" His eyes meet mine, tears rimming them. "She was the one found murdered?"

I gently place my hand on his shoulder. "It was her. I'm sorry, Ro."

His eyes fall closed, and he trembles under my hand. I drop my hand and we sit in silence, staring out at the town beneath us. As the sun begins to set, the sky is awash with soft pinks and purples, casting a gentle glow over the landscape.

"We were going to meet at Jimmy's Diner at eight, but she never showed." His voice cracks and his eyes meet mine. "How could this happen?"

"I don't know, Ro, but we'll find who is responsible."

He gives a solemn nod, his eyes filled with emotion. "She was special. Made me laugh and forget about how miserable I was."

"I know that feeling," I murmur.

"Why would anyone want to hurt her?"

"I don't know."

After a moment of silence, I can tell he's gathering the courage to ask me something.

"How'd you get those scars?" Ro's eyes hold mine, still and waiting.

"Come on, I will drive you home. I don't want you out here alone."

"Why won't you tell me?"

"It's personal, Ro," I huff, annoyance coating my tone.

"I get that, but you know everything that has happened to me."

I blow out a breath. "When I was five, I was attacked by something in the woods one night."

Ro frowns. "What were you doing out in the woods alone?"

"Who said I was alone?"

Understanding dawns in his eyes. "Who did you lose?"

"My brother."

The silence between us seems to stretch on for an eternity until I finally break it with my soft apology. "I'm sorry about your dad."

I hear a soft intake of breath from Ro as his eyes move to mine. "I'm sorry about your brother."

"Let's get you home." I stand and make my way over to where I parked the car.

"Okay," Ro replies, trailing after me.

Once we're settled in the car, I twist to face Ro. "Do you mind if I ask you something?"

"Sure."

"What's going on with your mom?"

Ro frowns. "What do you mean?"

"Today when I stopped by, she wouldn't open the door and sounded anxious."

I don't want to say it looks like she was hiding something and sounded afraid. The look in Hayley's eyes was fear and dread. I know those looks, but she also looked like she was in fight-or-flight mode, and she was about to run.

"Mom always has a hard time around the date that Dad died. She usually will start drinking the day before and stay drunk until the day after."

Guilt churns in my stomach because I immediately got suspicious of her because of her behavior when, in reality, she was coping with the loss of her husband, the same way I cope with the loss and trauma of losing Riley. Getting lost at the bottom of a bottle.

We drive in silence after that, and ten minutes later, we are pulling up at the curb of Ro's house.

"Are you going to be, okay?" I ask.

"I'll be fine."

"You sure? I don't like leaving you like this," I reply, looking past him and at the dark looming house. I know he's more than capable, but the idea of him being by himself fills me with a sense of unease.

"I'll be okay. Plus, mom needs me."

Ro jumps from the car, and I wait until he's safely inside before pulling away.

Chapter Forty Six

Salena

I anxiously walk the length of the living room, my sock covered feet silent against the hardwood floor. Where is he? He has been gone most of the day. I know I've had Kai and Felix here with me all day, and the pack coming and going. But I need Logan. I need my mate. It's getting harder and harder to keep everything from him. This case needs to be over, this killer to be caught, so I can tell him about the mate bond.

The sound of my phone dinging with a message fills the room, and I quickly snatch it from the coffee table. I sigh in relief and look over at Ghost who is sitting on the windowsill watching me pace.

"He's on his way."

Ghost meows loudly and jumps down, strolling toward me and winding around my legs. I'm so grateful Logan went and got him.

Kai and Felix only left twenty minutes ago, after I convinced them I would be fine. I need to be alone with my thoughts. I need room to breathe. Dealing with the pack and all their emotions on top of my own all day has taken its toll. Along with the need to stay strong for the pack, meaning I have been holding all my tears in, all my emotions.

I see Logan's headlights shine through the living room window and feel my tension drain from my body. A moment later, the front door opens, and Logan walks in. The second his eyes meet mine, tears burn my eyes and my nose twitches. I rush to him, jumping into his strong arms. He is my home, my safe space. The tears fall as I bury my face deep into his neck, and my legs wrap tightly around his waist. Logan's palm cradles the back of my head, his other arm wrapped firmly around my waist as he holds me close to him. Slowly, he climbs the stairs and walks to the bedroom.

Logan sits on the end of the bed with me still tightly wound around him. His palm brushes my hair back, his fingers sliding through my hair. The motion is calming and relaxing. I slowly inhale, letting the warmth of his scent wash over me. My stomach clenches as his smell invades all my senses.

I pull back and stare into his clear blue eyes. With both hands, I cup his face and close my eyes as I lean in. My lips brush against his in a gentle kiss. Logan's hands grip my waist. He tries to keep the kiss light, but I want more. I trace the seam of his lips with my tongue.

"Salena."

"Logan, I need you, please," I whisper against his mouth.

We draw back an inch so he can see the emotions in my eyes. His forehead drops to mine and his hands flex on my waist. I lean forward and feel the warmth of his skin as I bite down on his neck. His fingers tighten almost painfully as he grinds me down on his lap. I tip my head back and groan as he does it again, his cock rubbing that sweet spot perfectly.

"We need these clothes gone," I pant, trying to push his jacket off his shoulders.

Logan stands abruptly and spins, throwing me down on the bed with a soft thud. A squeal of surprise escapes me, and I stare up at him as he undresses. I lay on my back, resting on my elbows. My teeth sink into my bottom lip as his full muscular body is put on display. My core throbs in need, and I rub my legs together. Logan smirks at the movement and leans over me, undoing the button on my jeans and slowly dragging them down my legs. I pull my top over my head, feeling the fabric brush against the bare skin of my breasts. Logan kneels on the bed, his powerful thighs pressing against my own. His hand wraps around his cock and he begins to stroke himself. I groan as I watch his hand move over his cock casually, his abdomen tensing with the movement. I lick my lips and grip his hips, my nails digging in, trying to urge him closer.

"I want to taste you," I whisper.

Logan's eyes flare and he inches up my body, his thighs now over my chest. He presses the tip of his cock against my lips, and I open. He groans as he presses in, hitting the back of my throat. Leaning over me, he thrusts his hips, filling my mouth over and over, my fingers digging into his ass cheeks. His body is a work of art, every muscle defined and on display. His arms, chest, stomach, legs, back—they are all flexing with each movement. I moan around him, and he halts his movements, pulling out.

His weight disappears, but before I can say anything, Logan's hands wrap around my ankles, flipping me to my stomach and pulling me to the end of the bed. I gasp as a hard, firm slap lands on my ass.

Logan's hand grips the front of my neck as his palm runs down my back between the crack of my ass and a shiver runs over me.

"Maybe another time, baby," Logan whispers into the shell of my ear. His gentle caress is like a whisper against my skin, slowly drifting to the spot I desire most. His fingers enter me without pause, driving in and out. I moan, rocking my hips in time with his fingers. I hear Logan's breath near my ear as his hand tightens around my throat. It sends a delicious tremor coursing through me. In an instant, his fingers are gone, and I am flipped onto my back. Logan's mouth covers my clit and sucks hard, sending a shattering orgasm ripping through me.

I scream into the room, the sound echoing around us as he continues. Before I've recovered, or gotten a breath in, his body is over mine and he is driving into me.

"Fuck, Salena."

Logan's tongue darts out, stroking my aching nipple. I am no longer able to form words or draw in a breath. And when his lips close over my nipple and suck, I feel those pulls echo all over my body.

"Logan," I whimper, feeling my next orgasm building.

"That's right, baby," he grunts, driving in harder, faster.

His lips drop to mine as we both fall apart, his tongue driving into my mouth, swallowing my cries.

"What do you want?" I ask, realizing I have never asked him before.

Logan moves, so he's on top of me and rests on his forearms, but the rest of his deliciously hard body is pressed against me. His head dips, and he whispers against my lips, "You."

Then his mouth takes mine in a slow, torturous kiss. His lips feel like a feather as they trail down my jaw to the hollow of my throat. "This."

His tongue darts out to taste my skin, and I moan, my finger threading into his hair and tugging. I want his mouth back on mine. Logan lifts his head. I gasp at the possessive gleam in his eye. He's telling me without words; I am his. It sends a shiver through me as he recaptures my mouth. I'm breathless when he breaks the kiss.

"I need to shower and get to work."

"Can't you take the day off?" I ask, my fingers tracing the angel wings on his chest.

"Not until we catch this guy."

"We never spoke about Ro."

Logan brushes the hair from my face and pecks my nose. "He was supposed to meet Lola, but she never showed."

"Could he be lying?" I whisper.

"No, baby. I had Sander check the diner, and he was there waiting for two hours.

"Okay."

"We will get the guy." Logan's voice is firm and sure.

God, I hope he's right.

Logan stretches as he rolls out of bed and pads to the shower. As I roll over in bed, I grab his pillow, sinking into its softness as I rest my head. I drift back to sleep because I don't hear Logan again until he wakes me. As I follow him downstairs, I notice the feel of Ghost's fur brushing against my bare legs.

"I'll see you tonight," he whispers just before his lips meet mine. Hot, hard, and unyielding. His hand slides up to cup my jaw and neck, holding me in place as he kisses every thought from my mind, leaving nothing but a riot of sensations.

Logan pulls back, his eyes heated and fierce. He leans in, his lips brushing against my forehead softly, before he steps away and out of the door.

Chapter Forty Seven

Killer

I watch her walk out of the house, a smile stretched across her face as she talks with the tall, dark-haired man. She has my life, the life I was supposed to have. I hate her. The demon will make her suffer for all she's done. At first, I rebelled against the demon's obsession with her, but now I know how she'll suffer. It makes this so much better.

I thought Lola's death would break her more than it did, turn the pack against her. But that's not what happened. They have instead drawn together tighter than before, and she seems to be coping, which only infuriates me more. It's that cop's fault. If he were out of the picture, she'd be running with her tail between her legs. Fucking Jenna didn't do a good enough job at seducing him.

I will let the demon have his fun, and once it is done, I will take my rightful place. I retreat into my mind, giving myself over to the demon inside of me who is begging for fun.

If this meat bag thinks he'll get his body back after this, he can think again. He's having way too much fun.

Salena belongs to him.

That cop may have her in his bed, but she will soon understand the consequences of her decision.

He will teach them all a lesson.

He paces the small house, trying to decide what his next plan is. He is angry and frustrated. Anger fuels him, making his balls throb in need. Someone will pay for her disobedience tonight. He stomps down the stairs into the playroom, the sound reverberating off the walls. He knows it isn't fair to take his anger at her out on them, but fucking and slicing has become his favorite things to do. And when done together? Blissful.

His eyes scan the two girls remaining before him. Poor substitutes, really, but they'll do. One is curled up in the corner, shaking and emitting pitiful cries. The other holds her head high as she glares at him. That one has spirit. He grins and moves over to her; he wants someone with fire in their soul and their eyes. It makes it so much better watching it fade from their eyes.

Grabbing her by the hair, he drags her over to the chair in the center of the room. He straps her to the chair, her eyes glaring up at him. He fucked her last night. Bit every part of her bare flesh, leaving teeth marks and bruises all over her.

Reaching for his favorite knife, he watches as it glimmers in the light.

"Are you ready to play, Salena?"

"It's Davina, you asshole!" she yells, before she spits in his face. He tips his head back, letting out a full-bodied laugh that rings through the air. He wipes the spit from his face, then without a word he presses the knife to her thigh, slowly sinking it in. Her screams are piercing, and he almost comes in his pants just from the sound. Removing the blade, he does the same to the other leg. Blood pooling on the floor only adds to his excitement.

The screams from both women mingle, making him harder. It's going to be a long fucking night of pleasure indeed.

Chapter Forty Eight

Salena

I probably should have called someone—Kai, Felix, shit, even Logan or Sander—but the trail is fresh, and it's the first time I have any type of lead from the killer. The smell is vaguely familiar, but somehow rotten. I can't put my finger on it. I went for a run, taking the track behind the house. But as I was running, I picked up on the scent. I didn't have time to go get anyone. This is what we have been waiting for. It has been two weeks since we said goodbye to Lola, and it was the hardest day I've had since burying my parents five years ago. Lucy's cries still haunt my dreams every night. Her heartache is more than I can bear some days.

I cut through the run-down part of town, sticking in the bushes, my nose following the trail. I stop, ducking under a large bush as a car drives past and disappears around the corner. My paws are silent as I cross the road, heading toward an abandoned house at the end of the street. I circle it twice, noticing it backs onto the small river, and a dingy rests on the shore.

I don't sense anyone is in the house, but I can smell the unmistakable scent of blood. A lot of blood. With one last glance around, I shift into my human form and try the door handle. It's locked, but I crush it in my hand and push inside. I follow the smell of blood to the basement. Shit. Do I really want to go down there?

Taking a deep breath, my heart hammering in my chest, I pull open the door to the basement and make my way down the stairs. I cover my nose and mouth at the smell of blood, vomit, and urine. I feel the tell-tale prickle of magic as I reach the bottom of the step.

Quickly, I pull out my phone and dial the police precinct. I rattle off the address and hang up before making my way further into the room. I gasp as I freeze to the spot. Gathering myself, I step closer. My stomach sinks with dread as I finally realize what I'm seeing.

No . . .

What has he done to her? I stare in horror at the sight in front of me. Blood covers the stone floor, pooling in places where the rock is uneven. The girl in the middle of the floor is so thin and pale, her lips blue. The dress she's wearing is ripped in multiple places, and barely covers her. When I step closer, I realize the rips are cuts. She had been cut, stabbed, and sliced into over and over until she bled out.

My eyes trail down her slim frame, and I swallow roughly, wanting to throw up. Her body is not only covered in deep gashes from a knife. Her, oh my god . . . her thighs are covered in bruises. More precisely, fingerprints. Did he rape her?

I can't even stomach the thought. Who would do this? I spin around, putting my back to the girl on the floor, trying to control my breathing as it saws in and out rapidly. Nausea swirls in my stomach, and I put a hand over my mouth.

A small whimper comes from the dark corner, and I snap my head in the direction of the sound. How did I not hear the heartbeat or breathing before? Oh, I know. My own heartbeat was thumping so loudly in my chest I couldn't hear anything over my own ragged breathing.

"Hello?" I call out, slowly stepping away from the body toward the darkened corner of the basement. I can feel my vision slowly sharpening as my eyes adjust to the darkness.

With a deep breath, I take another step toward where I heard the noise. "I won't hurt you. I'm here to help. The police have been called."

A shuffling noise comes from the dark, and two soft brown eyes stare back at me from a small, frail face. Bruises cover her arms and legs, and her white blonde hair hangs greasy and limp around her face.

"Help," she whispers, her small voice raw, as if she has been screaming for hours.

A quiet sob slips from her lips, and I rush forward, my arm wrapping around her shoulders, pulling her into my side as I slide next to her, my back against the wall.

"Shh . . . it's okay. You're safe now," I murmur into her hair, my body rocking hers back and forth. It's something my mother did when I was young. It didn't matter how old I got, she always rocked me when I was upset. She told me it was a habit, one she got from when we were babies.

I hear sirens in the distance and the girl curls into me, her head resting on my shoulder, crying uncontrollably. My heart breaks for her at what she has been through and witnessed.

Police fill the house with the sound of pounding footsteps in a matter of minutes. I hear them clearing each room and then heading down the stairs into the basement. They shine the torches on us, and the girl huddles closer, burying her head in my chest. I raise my hand, blocking the light from my eyes.

"It's me, Salena. I called it in," I call out.

I sense Logan entering the house a moment later, his fury like a tidal wave of energy. He charges down the stairs, pushing past the officers in front of me.

"Put your fucking guns down," he snarls, stalking toward us.

Stopping a couple of feet away, he slowly squats down, his eyes scanning me and then the young girl, who looks petrified.

His icy blue eyes move back to me, concern shining in the depths. "Are you okay?"

I can see he's restraining himself, he wants to rip me away and shield me from all this. I nod and he turns his attention to the young girl. "You're okay now. Can you tell me your name?"

The girl sits up and looks at me. When I nod, her gaze shifts to Logan.

"Katlin," she whispers, tears escaping her red-rimmed eyes.

I have spent hours in the hospital with Katlin. I'm tired and exhausted, but she asked me to stay, and after everything I've seen I didn't want to leave the poor girl by herself. Katlin is sixteen, and was taken from Colorado Springs three weeks ago while walking to school. Her parents are on the way. They'll be here by morning, and I'll stay til then. Right now, Katlin's going over the description with the sketch artist. I've tuned them out completely, watching Logan's face as he concentrates on what Katlin is saying. He's a good detective. He cares, he listens, he's real.

My heart is overflowing with emotion, and I am filled with a comforting warmth. I love this man.

Katlin's voice breaks and my attention snaps back to hers. I squeeze her hand. "When . . . When I woke up, I was in that basement. He had his hands around my throat. All I remember was trying to scream. His body weight was crushing me into the floor. He– he– he made a movement with his hips pushing against me, and he was hard, he was–

he was getting off on it. I tried to fight him off, but I couldn't. He just laughed at me. I will never forget that sound." Her hands cover her face. "I thought I was going to die," she sobs.

I watch helpless as tears stream down her face. I reach up, rubbing soothing circles on her back until she calms down. My gaze drifts over to Logan.

"Sorry to interrupt, but is this your kidnapper, Miss?" the artist says. I look up at the picture he holds, and my stomach drops out from beneath me.

I draw in a sharp breath. *No. No fucking way.*

My vision pulses around the edges as I stare at what the sketch artist has drawn. This is a dream. A very bad fucking dream. It has to be, right?

Logan straightens from the wall, picking up on my reaction straight away. "You know him?"

My eyes dart up to Katlin's. "Are you sure?" I ask her, my voice wavering.

Her eyes dilate in fear as she nods in my direction.

"It's you he's after," she murmurs. The fear in her eyes makes my blood run cold. I jolt out of my chair and cover my mouth before spinning on my heels and storm out of the room toward the nearest exit. I don't make it very far down the hall when Logan's hand wraps around my wrist and halts my movements.

"Salena, who is it?"

I don't turn to face him. How can I?

I drop my head, squeezing my eyes shut. This can't be happening.

"Salena?"

I turn around to face him, my eyes pleading with him. I open my pack link and feel my brothers in the waiting room.

'Guys.'

Immediately, they pick up on the fact that something is wrong and storm through the doors. A nurse yells at them to come back, but when they spot me and Logan they charge toward us. Logan's face darkens as he slowly sweeps his gaze between us all.

'What's going on?' Kai demands as they draw nearer.

'It's Samuel.'

Both my brothers startle, halting their steps.

Logan's expression is intense, severe, his features sharp, his icy blue eyes hard. "If you guys know something . . . " He lets it hang in the air.

I shift on the spot, and Logan runs his thumb over my knuckles before releasing my hand.

Kai and Felix are both watching me intently, their eyes begging for more information.

"It's Samuel," I croak, my chest tightening.

Kai shakes his head, backing away. "No. No fucking way it's him," he snaps, echoing my first thoughts.

Felix looks torn. "Salena, we would know."

'You banished him. He can't simply return. We would know.'

I turn and walk back to Katlin's room and ask for the sketch. Walking back, I hold up the picture for my brothers. Their eyes widen in shock before they harden like ice chips.

"Motherfucker!" Kai shouts, earning a glare from a passing nurse.

Logan, having had enough, snaps, "You have one minute to tell me what's going on."

I'm the one to speak. "It's our brother."

Logan's eyes widen. "What?"

"Samuel is our brother," Kai says, clearing his throat and running a hand through his hair in agitation.

"Why would he be doing this? Stalking you? Killing girls that look like you?"

"He isn't happy my parents passed on the family business to me after they passed," I say distractedly.

"A bar?!" By the tone of Logan's voice, he doesn't believe me.

Fuck, this is so hard to explain when he doesn't know all the facts. I look at my brothers for help and Felix holds up his hands.

'You're going to have to tell him everything, Salena. I know you wanted to wait until this was all over, but shit's hitting the fan. He needs to know,' Felix says.

'I know.'

Turning to Logan, I gather my thoughts. This is a fucking mess. "Look, I promised Katlin I would stay with her until her parents get here in the morning. After that, I will tell you everything, okay?"

"Salena," he growls. "There's a killer on the loose."

"Tomorrow, my apartment, nine o'clock," I say, my tone firm, though my heart is beating double time as a surge of emotions wash over me, so strong, I think they might bring me to my knees.

Logan narrows his eyes at me, and I feel as if he can see straight through me. He then looks at my brothers. Both hold their hands up and mouth, *sorry*. Logan doesn't realize I'm their alpha. They don't get a say in this.

"I could take you all down to the station. You're withholding information."

"We aren't. I said I'd tell you in the morning," I snap, frustration getting the better of me. I know he's only doing his job, but I need time to process.

"Salena," he sighs, his arms wrapping around me protectively, "I'm trying to protect you."

"I'm fine, Logan," I sigh, and pull from his arms.

I don't wait for his reply as I turn and make my way back to Katlin's room. My heart aches for this girl. She looks so tiny and fragile in the hospital bed, beaten and bruised. The report came back negative to rape, which filled me which such relief I cried silently beside her.

I hear Logan and my brothers in the hall, then the sound of Logan's feet a moment before he enters the room.

"Did you girls want dinner? I can get anything you want," he says, directing the question at Katlin.

Her eyes light up and her lip trembles. "I'd love a cheeseburger and fries from McDonald's," she whispers.

"Done." Logan's gaze finds mine. "And you?"

"Same," I reply.

Logan turns to leave, and I squeeze Katlin's hand. "I'll be right back."

She nods and I jump up and run after Logan. He pauses, sensing me coming, and slowly turns to meet my gaze. His massive frame is strained and worry lines his face. "Is every–"

Before he can finish, I run into his arms, wrapping my own tightly around him. He stiffens for a moment before relaxing into my hold, his arms wrapping around me. His cheek rests on the top of my head, and I feel his body relax as he lets out a long breath.

"Fuck, you feel so good in my arms," he murmurs.

I can hear the thundering of my heart as I squeeze my arms around him. "I'm sorry," I whisper.

"Tomorrow," he whispers back. His chest heaves as he looks directly at me, his gaze charged with an electric current.

I can feel it buzzing around us in the air, and I swallow thickly.

"I care what happens to you. I don't want to see you hurt, or worse," he says.

I flash him a sad watery smile. I am feeling so many things right now.

Disgust at what I saw in that basement. Sympathy for Katlin, for what she's been through, and what she will go through to recover from this. A deep-seated anger at my brother. Trepidation at telling Logan everything. And guilt. So much guilt.

It is all too much.

"I'll be back with some burgers," Logan says, kissing me softly on the lips. I watch him go, feeling a sudden ache in my chest, before I return to the room with Katlin.

The night goes by slowly as I hold Katlin, her small frame twitching in her sleep. Her whimpers break my heart, my own tears tracking down my face. My own flesh and blood is responsible for this girl's misery, and it's all my fault. I stroke her long white, blonde hair, which I washed earlier, after we ate our cheeseburgers. I've tried my best to console her, but it will take a long time for her to be at a place where she feels safe again.

Chapter Forty Nine

Salena

When Katlin's parents arrive, I quietly depart from the hospital. The sound of their sobbing follows me from the room as the three of them cling to each other. I shift when I hit the tree line. I need the run to clear my head, and it will only take me fifteen minutes to get home.

Still, I'm looking forward to a quick shower to wash the hospital smell off me. Walking into the kitchen, I open the fridge as my phone starts ringing. I swipe my thumb over the screen and put it to my ear.

"Hey, Felix. What's going on?"

"Salena, where are you?"

"Home, why?"

"Don't move. We will be there soon." The line goes dead, and I frown at it.

What the hell?

Pulling the milk carton from the fridge, I open it and take a sniff. My face contorts as I gag from the putrid smell.

"Well, I can't use that," I grumble. Looks like it's a black coffee today.

I just finish putting my shoes on when there's a knock at the door. I stroll over, flinging the door open, and steel myself to give Felix a stern talking-to.

I freeze in shock at the sight in front of me. My heart races as I look up at the towering figure with blonde hair and a thick, wild, untamed beard.

"Hey, sis."

I peer down at the gun he has pointed at me, and my stomach plummets to my feet. "What are you doing?"

"You know how hard it's been to get you alone?"

I ball my hand into a tight fist, my teeth gritted in anger. "What the hell, Samuel?"

He chuckles, a low and unpleasant sound. "I want what I've always wanted. What my brothers weren't man enough to take."

"You can't take the pack from me. They won't follow you."

He cocks his head, the corners of his mouth curling into a cruel sneer. "They will if you're a corpse."

Is he serious?

What happened to him? Yes, he was always a little distant from the rest of us, but he was never a bad guy. We all used to be happy until Mom and Dad died, then everything fell apart. A sickening sensation fills me as I see the person my once loving brother has become. Now, as I look back, I realize that we never made any memorable moments together. My memories are of Kai and Felix. I recall how Samuel would always be off to the side, observing. I never thought too much of it growing up, but . . . was he always planning this?

"Kai and Felix won't let that happen."

Samuel shrugs, a wild look entering his eyes. "Then I'll kill them, too. Dad should have left this pack to me. Not you. I didn't go through all the trouble of poisoning them and planning that car accident just to have them hand everything over to you."

I jerk forward, shock and hurt warring in my head and heart.

"What did you do?" I whisper in disbelief, my hands covering my mouth as tears build in my eyes.

I shake my head. I can't believe it.

That my brother could be so cruel.

"Let's go!" Samuel barks, his fingers tightly gripping my arm as he pulls me out the door.

I pull back, ripping from his grasp. "You killed our parents?!" I think I'm in shock, because I can't seem to get a grasp on anything, only his words reverberating over in my head. When he doesn't answer and just shrugs, I ask the next question.

"Lola?"

Fuck . . .

Saying her name out loud is like a dagger in my heart.

Samuel shrugs. "She was in the wrong place at the wrong time. But the power in her blood was much more potent than the human girls, so it worked out better for me. She was a sacrifice worth making."

I blink in disbelief. My body is completely frozen to the spot.

He sacrificed Lola for the power her blood offered. A fresh wave of anger surges through me, and I lunge for him. Samuel lifts the gun and shakes his head. "Trust me, you don't want me to use this."

I stand there, my chest rising and falling with rapid breaths as I try to keep my anger in check.

"Now move!!" Samuel snarls, grabbing my arm painfully and jerking me out the door again.

"Where are we going?" I ask, only to receive a push in the back as an answer.

We walk into the woods in silence, the sunlight filtering through the trees and reflecting off the snow-covered ground. The only thing that breaks the silence is the sound of our feet crunching in the snow.

As we move further into the woods, I take the time to process what he said. Determination wraps around me like a thick cloak. I take a moment to assess Samuel. Even though he's much bigger than I am and has a gun, I didn't earn my position by being weak.

Samuel looks my way, and his lips curl up into a smirk. "After I'm done with you, I think I'll pay that detective of yours a visit."

Something inside of me snaps at those words. "You will not touch my mate," I roar and lunge for him. The gun goes off, but I am already shifting. I collide with him, taking him to the ground. But he doesn't shift, which just confuses me. I bark at him and snap my jaws toward his face. Samuel scrambles back, sweat dripping down his face, as he grabs the gun and points it at me.

"Shift," he orders.

I lower my head and snarl at him. '*Fight!*' I growl back.

Samuel laughs, the sound unhinged. "I can't shift. I made a little deal, you see. You should thank me, you know, for interfering with his plans. At least this way it'll be a quick death."

Confused, I shift back into my human form, needing to speak to him. "What the fuck are you talking about? Who? What did you do, Samuel?"

His eyes seem to burn with madness, and his smirk is unnerving. I blanch as I attempt to control my breathing, my skin tingling with a sense of dread.

"I have the power of an upper-level demon with me." He taps his temple with the gun. "He's in here, and he is *obsessed* with you. But he's taking too long, playing and taunting you. I'm the alpha, and I want my fucking pack!" He screams the last bit, his face turning red in anger.

A shiver of fear trickles down my spine as I stare at my brother in horror. My mouth opens and closes several times. My dickhead brother made a deal with a *demon?*

"Are you mad?" I whisper, knowing full well my eyes are as wide as saucers.

Samuel shrugs and pulls the trigger. Pain blooms in my stomach, making me stumble forward a step. I glance down, my hands automatically going to my stomach. I feel the wetness there as red spreads across my gray sweater, and I look up to meet his gaze.

"Those women . . . he was using them to feed his hunger, playing with them. Testing out the ways he was going to use you. Lola, though . . . She was the perfect sacrifice to boost the demon's power. Shifter and virgin."

"You're going to die," I growl.

Samuel shakes his head. "No, sis. You are."

He fires again, this time hitting me in the shoulder. I stumble back a step as he curses at me. He was obviously aiming for my heart and missed. Samuel thuds his head with the heel of his other hand, growling under his breath. He's acting like a crack addict looking for their next hit. I snarl, my claws extending as I lunge for him. Surprise widens his eyes, and I take us both to the ground. The gun slips from his grip, falling into the snow. I wrestle him for the gun, desperately trying to keep him from getting a hold of it. My claws slash at his face.

"That was for Lola, you piece of shit!" I scream, taking another swipe at his face. Pulling back slightly, I sink my claws into his stomach, leaning down in his face. "That is for Mom and Dad."

Deep-seated hatred burns in his eyes, and I withdraw my claws. With a shout, he reaches up, digging his fingers into my wounded shoulder. I howl in pain. Dizziness swamps me, and I fall backward off him, panting.

Fuck, that hurt.

The bullets must be spelled, because I'm not healing, and I can feel the poison working its way through my body.

I lean to the side and spit out a mouthful of blood before peering up at my brother. He is standing with the gun again, this time pointed at my head. A feral feeling swamps me, and I grin, showing off my bloody teeth.

"You're a dead man," I promise.

I stare my brother in the eyes as he cocks the gun and fires.

Chapter Fifty

Logan

As soon as I pull up to Salena's, I notice her door slightly ajar. With a heavy sense of dread in my chest, I let out a deep sigh and climb out of the car. A prickling sensation washes over me, making the hairs on my arms stand up, and instantly I'm on alert. Something is wrong. I know it. There is an unnatural stillness in the air. I begin to ascend the steps, and hear the loud screeching of brakes as Kai's pickup pulls into the parking lot. Kai and Felix leap from the truck, their feet landing on the snow covered ground.

"Is she here?" Felix says as they approach.

"I just got here," I reply.

I take deep breaths, trying desperately to remain calm as I scan the area. Salena is fine. She knows the dangers. She wouldn't put herself in harm's way. Felix races up the steps and is gone less than ten seconds before he bounds back down.

"She's not here."

Kai opens his mouth and curses, kicking the wheel of his truck. A gunshot rings out from the woods, like a crack of thunder. We all exchange looks before taking off. The snow is fresh and deep, which means we have tracks to follow, but also means we can't get much momentum.

My breath comes out in short, white puffs as we sprint toward the sound of the gunshot. Up ahead, I hear snarling and put on a burst of speed. Kai is in front of me, Felix to my left. We burst into a small clearing, and come to a stop. A tall man who resembles Kai stands a few feet away from Salena, gun aimed at her head.

I unclip my gun without thought and fire, shooting the hand holding the gun. Kai and Felix move faster than humanly possible, tackling the man to the ground. They struggle, and I hear the gun go off again. Felix sags. I sprint over, gun raised.

"Kai, move!" I shout.

He backs up with a feral expression on his face. His eyes dart to Salena who is pushing her way to her feet. Samuel throws back his head and laughs hysterically, his knees still pressed into the cold ground. I keep my gun trained on him as I look at Salena.

"Are you okay?" I ask.

I falter when her eyes meet mine. She's in pain. A lot of pain. Blood covers the front of her body, and a steady stream of it trickles from between her fingers, which are pressed to her stomach.

Salena's eyes widen, and I swing my gaze back to Samuel as he raises his gun. Two shots ring out. One mine, and one Samuel's. Salena is in front of me in a flash, her blue eyes fixed on mine as the bullet strikes her in the back.

"NO!" I grab her as her legs give out and we go to the ground. "Shit!"

For a moment, I glance up and spot a gray and white wolf lunging toward Samuel, its teeth fiercely gripping his neck. I look away, blocking out the noise and focus fully on Salena. Before nausea can take over and send me back into my memories.

Salena slowly blinks those beautiful, sparkling turquoise eyes at me. Blood coats her lips, and she reaches up to touch my face. The world around me blurs at the edges as I concentrate on Salena.

"I'm sorry I didn't tell you."

"It's okay," I reply, stroking her face.

"I love you, detective."

My heart gives a heavy thump at her words, and I drop my forehead to hers. "I love you, too." When I pull back, her eyes are closed. Panic hits me full force.

No. No. Please don't let her be dead. I gently stroke her cheek. "Salena, baby. Wake up."

My heart is racing, and my limbs feel like they're buzzing with energy from the surge of adrenaline. The biting cold of the snow does nothing to numb the anger and fear rising inside me. She has to be okay. I can't lose her. My hand trembles against her cheek, giving away my rising anxiety.

Felix's feet crunch in the snow as he walks up to me, my wild eyes lock on his. I search behind him for Kai, but I can't see him anywhere.

"Where's Kai?" I yell.

"Gone to get help," Felix says, looking pale and in shock.

"What about the wolf?" I ask, looking behind me.

But it's gone.

Only Samuel's body remains.

Chapter Fifty One

Salena

Slowly, I blink my eyes open. Even that slight movement hurts like a bitch. My body feels like one giant bruise. No part of me is spared the ache. I am in a bright white room. A machine next to me is beeping. Without looking, I know Logan isn't here, and my heart and soul ache fiercely for him. I roll my head on my pillow and see my brothers asleep on two chairs that have been pulled next to the bed. I groan as I try to sit up, and Felix's eyes fly open. Within a second, he is up, helping me sit.

"Are you okay?" he blurts out.

"I'm fine. Sore, but fine," I reply, brushing his hands away.

Kai's wide frame towers over the two of us. "You scared the shit out of us."

I press my fingers into my eyes, kneading away the sleepiness. I am bone tired and still sore from dealing with that damn unhinged man.

Giving him a weak smile, I grip Felix's hand, the warmth comforting. "It was only a couple of bullets."

"It was three. And they were laced with poison."

Felix shifts nervously on his feet. He is hovering like a mother hen. "We had to call old Myrtle."

"You were in a coma for three days, Salena," Kai adds gruffly.

The pain in his expression makes my eyes sting with tears.

I clear my throat and scrub my hands over my face. "Where's Samuel?"

Felix looks back at Kai, and they share a look. My heart thumps hard in my chest, and I try to pull myself together. "Just tell me," I croak.

Felix reaches for a glass of water and hands it to me. My fingers shake as I reach out to grab it. The water is cool on my throat, and I sigh as I drain the glass.

"Samuel is dead."

My eyes fly to Kai, and I choke on my water. "What? How?"

Kai's gaze drops as he shuffles uncomfortably. I've never in my life seen him act this way. I push myself to the end of the bed and stand, Felix hovering at my side. I shoot him a glare.

"I'm fine. Stop fussing."

He holds his hands up in surrender and takes a few steps back. I reach out and take Kai's hand. A jolt of anxiety runs through me at the touch.

"What happened after I was shot?" I ask softly.

Kai's sad blue eyes meet mine, and they are red. My heart hammers in my chest and I know what happened. I pull him into my arms and squeeze tight. "I'm so sorry, Kai. I'm sorry you had to be the one to end it."

Kai grips me in his arms and holds me just as tight. "I would do it again. He wasn't of the right mind, and I couldn't let anything happen to you."

"I love you, Kai," I whisper as a few hot tears trace down my cheeks and soak into his shirt.

All of what Samuel said hits me again. I stare up at Kai.

"He killed Mom and Dad," I whisper hoarsely.

Emotions clog my throat, and my fingers dig into Kai's arms as I try my best to stay grounded. I sense Felix approaching, his shock and disbelief flooding our link. I look over at him and he sees the truth in my eyes. Felix crumbles and I reach out, pulling him into a hug, Kai's arms wrapping around both of us. We all bury our heads together, holding each other.

"Are you sure?" Kai murmurs.

I squeeze my eyes shut at the pain in his voice and nod. "He told me."

Felix and Kai jerk back in response to what I said. Samuel killed them to gain control of the pack, and when it didn't go his way, he turned to evil of the darkest kind. In the end, he wasn't our brother. The demon was using Samuel's hatred to get his way. I can't believe my brother would make a bargain with a demon. He hated me that much for taking what he thought was his. But with my brother dead, the demon would have no choice but to return to whatever hell my brother dragged it from.

"There's more," I whisper. I need to tell my brothers about the demon.

"What is it?" Kai asks, taking a step back and leaning against the wall.

Felix stays by me as I look between them.

"Samuel had help."

Kai jolts upright "What?!"

"Who?" Felix snaps.

"They're gone now. But it was a demon, he called an upper-level demon for help."

My brothers stand there, their faces betraying the complex mix of emotions they feel.

Kai's is the first to speak. "Are you fucking kidding me?"

I shake my head, regretting it instantly. I press my fingers to my temples and the world around me spins as I sway on my feet.

"Idiot," Kai spits, starting to pace.

The door opens, and a familiar scent wraps around me. I pull back and take a look at Logan standing in the doorway, his expression a combination of surprise and relief.

"You're awake," he murmurs.

"Yes." I smile hesitantly.

His being here surprises me. I remember telling him I was sorry, and I loved him, and then everything went black. I wanted to ease him into the whole world I lived in, instead he witnessed my brother killing Samuel.

Felix squeezes my arm. *'He didn't see anything. He was so focused on you he missed Kai shifting.'*

With a deep sigh of relief, I feel my shoulders drop, but the dread in my stomach still twists. I still have to tell him. Kai and Felix walk past me, and each gives me a soft kiss on the head before walking out the door. The whole time, Logan doesn't take his eyes from mine.

My emotions begin to spiral out of control the longer he stands there staring at me. Tears escape my eyes, flowing freely down my face, and I swipe at them. In two strides, his arms are around me, and I can feel his warm breath on my neck.

I grip onto him tightly, breathing in his familiar scent like it's the only thing keeping me alive. I wasn't sure if I would see him again. A whole new level of emotions swells when I realize it is over. Samuel is dead. I am finally free to share with Logan the details of my life and our connection.

Logan pulls back, taking my face in both hands, his thumbs gently stroking my cheeks, wiping away the tears.

"Don't cry, baby." His voice is hoarse with his own emotions.

"Sorry," I choke out.

He leans down and his lips brush against my forehead, my cheek, and then my lips in a gentle caress. I cling to his waist, my hands gripping him tightly. Logan rests his forehead against mine and closes his eyes, his breath coming heavily and rapidly against my skin.

"I thought I'd lost you," he whispers.

My eyes falling shut, I can feel the pain in those words. It tears through the silence around us, like lightning splitting the sky on a dark night. It dredges up old memories, reopening old wounds. A dull ache fills my heart, and a lump forms in my throat. Logan has been through so much. So much heartache and loss.

I don't have the heart to tell him now. It can wait a few days. I'll give him time. There's no rush. Though, the longer I wait, the harder it will be. I am basically hiding who I am from him. He has the right to know I'm not human.

Logan pulls away and takes my hand, leading me over to the small sofa near the window. He sits me down and pulls a blanket from the bed to drape it over me, placing another kiss on my forehead.

"Want a coffee?"

I nod, my throat tight with emotion from his tenderness.

Logan exits the room and I sit in silence, waiting, twisting the blanket in my fingers with nerves. Logan enters the room shortly afterward, carrying two steaming coffees. He sits down and passes me my mug. Carefully, I take it and take a deep inhale.

"Your brothers wouldn't tell me anything while you were sleeping." He stumbles over the word *sleeping.* Clearing his throat, he continues, "Can you tell me what happened? About Samuel?"

I look down into my coffee, my chest tightening at my brother's name.

"Samuel . . . he is– *was* my older brother. Growing up, he was always the odd one out. Never quite fit in, keeping himself withdrawn from everyone. He'd just sit aside and observe everyone. He always gave off that impression that he was better than everyone else, that we were simply beneath him. After our parents died . . . " As I trip over those words, I can feel the pain in my heart radiating outward. "He got worse. He thought he would take our parents' place in our family. But it surprised him when he found out that it was me they entrusted everything to.

"The bar?" Logan asks.

I shake my head. "No. The bar was always my dream. I built that from the ground up. It wasn't something that was passed down to me. Samuel was furious, he tried to attack me, so my brothers made him leave town and never come back."

Logan's eyes were like a hawk, studying me closely. I look down at my coffee and run my finger over the rim.

"How did your parents die?" Logan's voice breaks the silence, and my eyes snap up to his. It takes me a few moments to answer.

"The police ruled it an accident."

"But you don't think that?"

I see why he's a detective. I bite my lip and drop my gaze again.

"What do you think happened?" he asks softly.

I raise my shoulders in a half-hearted attempt to answer, unsure of what to say. Samuel confessed to killing them. Despite the state of wreckage, a shifter would have come out of the car accident unharmed, so he had to have taken extra measures to prevent that.

"They died in a car accident, trapped in a burning car," I say.

Logan leans forward and carefully places his mug on the small coffee table, then reaches to grab mine and does the same. Then, wordlessly, he shifts us so we're spooning on the small sofa, the faint smell of leather and fabric surrounding us. His arm was strong and protective as it tucks securely around me, and I can feel his breath in my hair.

"I know I have a lot to explain, and I will, but for now, can you just hold me?" I whisper.

Logan tightens his grip around me. "Of course."

"When we're home, I will tell you everything," I promise.

Logan's lips press to the back of my head, his other arm sliding under my head. The comforting sensation of Logan's arms around me and the rhythmic beat of his heart help me drift off to sleep. Being held by him fills me with a comforting warmth and sense of belonging.

I stir awake as Logan shifts his arms, holding me tightly against his chest, his movements strong and secure as he stands.

"What's going on?" I mumble, too tired and weak to open my eyes.

"Shhh, go back to sleep. I've got you."

I'm placed on the bed, the covers pulled over me. Rolling onto my side, I snuggle down and tuck my hands under the pillow. As Logan's fingers glide through my hair, I feel a sense of calm wash over me, lulling me back to sleep. Logan's lips are soft and tender as they touch my temple.

"Sleep, rest. Kai will take you home when you're awake."

Though I want to protest, I know he has to go back to work.

Chapter Fifty Two

Logan

I can sense Salena is keeping something from me. I want to give her the space, time to herself, but I can't stand the idea that she feels like she can't speak to me. Yesterday I held her close until her breathing had evened out and her eyelids had fluttered shut before I tiptoed out of her hospital room. The need to get to the station and investigate what happened to her parents driving me. To say I'm curious to find out what she's keeping secret would be an understatement. Overwhelmed by the need to create space between us and rebuild my walls of defense. So I'm here hiding, protecting myself from the pain the world can bring. The thought of losing her hits me hard, and I feel a knot form in my stomach. I'm torn between wanting to give her my heart and the fear of losing her. This week has made me realize how easily life can be taken away, and I don't think my heart or soul could take it if she had died.

My eyes move to the mirror behind the bar, and the woman that's still studying me. She's been leaning against the wall near the door for twenty minutes just watching. I hear an internal warning bell as red flags start to appear in my mind. Isn't that she seems dangerous, but just someone who needs to be taken seriously. In the mirror behind the bar, I watch her approach the bar where I'm seated.

She takes a seat next to me, her face set in a stern expression that makes my stomach tighten. She gives a quick nod to the bartender, and almost immediately a glass of amber liquid is placed in front of her. Picking it up, she takes a small sip from it before speaking.

When she speaks, her voice is low and melodic, but with a hint of authority. "Your friends are in need of help."

I pick up my own and grunt as I take a sip. "I don't need help."

"I take a wager you do."

I don't answer her, just take another sip of my drink. I have been sitting here trying to make sense of my feelings, and this ominous feeling twisting at my insides. Seeing Salena almost killed has me flashing back to my brother. Only it is her I'm watching being dragged away. I can't lose her like that. Maybe I should just leave now and save us both. A thick cloud of despair descends over me. I am cursed, I'm sure of it.

I can feel her dark eyes watching me, so I slowly turn to face her. Everything in me freezes. There's something old, almost ancient about her. Wisdom shines in her eyes, contradicting her young appearance.

"Who are you?" I murmur.

One side of her mouth lifts. "Someone who can help."

"Help with what?"

She doesn't answer, and as intrigued as I am, I'm not interested in playing games. Finishing the last of my drink, I stand and throw some notes on the bar. I start to turn away when I hear her voice, my skin tingling with awareness.

"You still have vivid nightmares of that night, don't you?"

I pause without turning back, a chill running down my spine. Her words are like a bucket of cold water.

"You've been marked. It will come for you."

Fear chokes me for a second at the thought of that creature.

"You don't know what you're talking about."

Still not looking at me, she knocks back the rest of her drink. Then she spins on her chair to face me. "Don't I? The creature you faced in the woods as a child, it left you with multiple wounds. Wounds that didn't heal properly. Along with new wounds that appear after the nightmares."

It's a statement, not a question,

"I can smell its taint on you," she adds.

I take a step closer to the darker-skinned woman, her onyx eyes seeing more than I want her to.

"Who are you?" I demand.

She smiles, holding out her hand. "I'm Ash, and I'm going to help you get rid of your demon. The taint on your soul. For a favor, of course."

I look down at her hand and frown, the buzz from the alcohol making my brain fuzzy. Ash drops her hand and stands. "Look, I know Salena. When all this shit started, she called me for help and asked me to keep an eye on Reaper to make sure he wasn't a threat to you. But it's not Reaper we need to worry about, it's you. You have an evil spirit attached to your soul, and if we don't destroy it, it will destroy you. It will come in the night, like a storm, wreaking havoc and destruction on you and those you love."

Disappointment hits me square in the chest. She is either crazy or being paid to make a fool out of me. I turn and make my way out of the small dive bar and onto the street. I round the bend and Ash is leaning against the wall, playing with the feather she has braided into her long black hair. How did she get out here ahead of me?

The moonlight glints off her face as she speaks into the night. "You don't believe me."

"Look, I don't know who you are, but I'm not interested."

"Even if you get Salena killed?"

My stomach drops out and I step into her space. A savage, feral need to protect what is mine fills my veins. "Are you threatening her?" I snarl.

The instant reaction shocks me. I can't believe I ever thought I could walk away from her.

"No, I like Salena. I consider her a friend, and I don't give out that title easily. I'm simply stating that if you ignore this, it will put both her and you in grave danger. It would make a serial killer brother look like a walk in the park. You possess a unique talent, one that few humans can retain beyond their eighth year."

"Humans?"

Ash nods, her long silky black hair glistening in the moonlight as she turns and starts walking toward my car, stopping at the passenger door to wait for me. I curse under my breath as I unlock the car and slide into the driver's seat, the leather creaking beneath me.

"Talk," I demand.

"I have been. Have you been listening?" Ash let out a scoff as she places one of her boots on the dash.

I glare over at her, my jaw clenched as I start the car. I pull out onto the road, having no idea where to go.

"You, Logan Sinclair, are one of those special humans who can see spirits in any shape or form. The veil between the spirit world and the mortal world is transparent to you, and you see things for what they are. You most probably have a great intuition as well, which is why you're a skilled detective and you're hearing me out right now."

"Like I had a choice," I mutter.

"Bullshit. We all have a choice!" she snaps, her eyes whipping to mine, an otherworldly glow emanating from them. "You have a gift. The spirit has marked you as prey and has been feeding off you for years, keeping you a slave to negative emotions and isolation. Salena threatens it. She is bringing happiness to your life, making this spirit angry. It's only a matter of time before it lashes out. Now I can help you, if you'll let me. The last thing I want is for Salena to get hurt."

My fingers tap on the steering wheel, Ash's words mixing with Salena's from a few weeks ago.

"What are you?" I ask.

"I'm many things, but technically I'm a world walker."

"A *what?*"

"In my tribe, I'm classed as a dark witch and shapeshifter. The rest is on a need to know basis."

A chill runs down my spine as disbelief fills me. Am I really listening to this woman? Everything she's saying makes sense, but witch? shapeshifter?

"You need to leave. We must go back to where it happened. Quite literally, face your demons."

My heart thumped wildly. Leave? Go back there…

"I can't just leave," I blurt.

"It's the only way."

I can feel the anxiety rising in my chest, my stomach churning at the thought of facing this demon, this spirit that took my brother. The little boy inside of me is terrified, but the man wants revenge.

"You can't tell Salena where we're going or what we're doing. It needs to be done alone. I cannot help you when your mate is around. She won't let you put yourself in danger." Her voice is firm and unwavering.

I furrow my brows in confusion. Mate?

"What are you talking about?"

Ash's eyes widen, and she raises her eyebrows. "She hasn't told you?"

"Told me what?"

"You really are clueless." She mumbles something else under her breath I don't quite catch.

"Look, we need to leave soon. Say your goodbyes. Salena won't let you go without a fight, so you best make up something good."

"How long will it take?"

Ash shrugs and swings open the car door, causing me to jam on the brakes.

"I will find you," she says, jumping from the car and disappearing.

With a sickening feeling, I know she's right. I have to face this, put it behind me if I want any type of future with Salena.

I hate being this person, fearful and scared of emotions, of loving someone fully. Salena, she stormed into my carefully crafted life and made herself at home. I am losing grip on the carefully constructed walls I built.

With each step we take together, my world tilts even more than before.

Chapter Fifty Three

Salena

I sense Logan the moment he pulls up outside. It's late and I was expecting him hours ago. He has been sitting in his car for fifteen minutes; I don't know what's wrong, but something is bothering him. Ever since he left the hospital yesterday, he has been pulling away. Bit by bit, I can see the distance he is creating between us, and I'm not sure how to fix it.

Kai and Felix are working downstairs at the bar. They are flatout refusing to let me work. Kai was the one to drive me home from the hospital, and I haven't seen Logan since he left the hospital yesterday afternoon. He sent a few vague messages, and called once last night, but his tone was distant and unfamiliar. I had planned to tell him everything when I got out of the hospital, but with how he's acting, I'm worried it'll be the last thing to push him further away. The longer I cling to this secret, the heavier it seems to get, making it more and more difficult to tell him.

It is tearing me up on the inside. I've been pacing all day, checking my phone and the parking lot constantly. Sander dropped by and said he was leaving tomorrow now that the case has been closed.

There's a soft knock on the door, and I frown. Logan never knocks, and I know it's him. My stomach is in knots with apprehension as I approach the door and swing it open.

"Logan?"

"Salena. I . . . " he reaches up, rubbing the back of his neck. He only does that when he's lost and uncomfortable.

"Come in," I say, stepping to the side.

Logan looks at me with a solemn expression before shaking his head.

"Logan, what's going on?" I hate how my voice shakes and my body trembles.

"I'm leaving."

"What? What do you mean?" I grip the door harder to keep myself grounded.

"I'm sorry, Salena, but I can't be what you want. I'm broken and scarred. I have demons." He shakes his head, taking a step back toward the stairs. His clear blue eyes hold a mixture of emotions.

"You don't get to tell me what I want," I whisper harshly. "And who says you're broken, Logan?" I chide, unable to keep the hurt and confusion from my voice.

A myriad of emotions well up inside me, making my throat tighten.

"I'm telling you I can't do this, Salena."

No, no, no.

As I attempt to say the word, I hear a catch in my voice. "Why?"

I wait, but he doesn't answer. I'm not sure he will.

My heart thunders, and I stop breathing. I am stunned silent.

"I'm sorry, Salena."

I watch, frozen as he turns and makes his way down the stairs. A crack of thunder rattles the windows as I stand there staring after him. Life isn't fair. We have finally put my stalker behind us, and he is leaving. Snapping out of it, I race down the stairs in seconds, ignoring the pain flaring in my stomach and shoulder from those damn bullets.

You are strong. Show him you are strong, I chant to myself as I chase after my mate.

The storm bears down, having gotten worse over the last hour. Gusts of wind lash through the trees, sending them whipping back and forth. Lightning lights the sky, showcasing the darkness of the night. The wind howls, and the moon is barely visible through the dark, ominous clouds.

My heart races as I draw to a stop and take in the man who is little more than a shadow beneath the raging sky, his shoulders hitched high as he strides toward his car at a clipped pace.

He is a lost man. He feels out of place everywhere he goes, never able to find that place where he belongs. What he doesn't realize is he belongs with me. I want to carve out a place for him, welcome him, show him what it's like to belong. To be treasured and loved. I thought I had done that, but maybe my secrets have been what was holding us back.

The wind and rain whip my hair across my face as I stand there.

"What if I want you to stay?" I shout over the raging storm. "What if I needed you here with me?"

In the distance, he freezes, as if my words have rooted him to the spot. Slowly, he turns those wintery blue eyes on me. The rain falls heavier as we stare at each other over the distance.

"I told you, I'm damaged. I am not worth loving. You deserve better."

Fire blazes in my chest as I take a step forward. "Don't tell me what I deserve. You're worth more than you know, Logan."

His eyes close, and I watch as he takes in a breath. Hope fills my chest and I'm stupid so fucking stupid. I know it the second he opens his eyes.

"I'm sorry. Goodbye, Salena." With those parting words, he turns and gets in his car.

My heart cracks at the rejection, at the sheer fact my mate doesn't want me. I watch as he pulls out of the parking lot and onto the road. I watch until I can't see his taillights anymore. As soon as they disappear, I break. I struggle to breathe, gasping for air as I double over. Pain lashes me from all sides as I fall to my knees in the snow, rain hammering down on me as I hang my head.

This isn't fair. He belongs with me.

I hear the door to the bar bang open and sense Kai approaching. "Salena?"

I moan, unable to speak through the tears. Kai's strong arms wrap around me, lifting me from the ground.

"What happened?" he asks, his voice low and filled with concern.

"Logan," I hiccup. I can't even finish the sentence. Exhaustion and despair overwhelm me.

Kai curses and carries me around the back and up the stairs to my apartment. He places me on the sofa and grabs me a blanket, wrapping it around my shoulders.

"I'm going to hunt him down," he growls.

My voice is rough and barely above a whisper. "No."

"But he is your mate. You didn't even tell him, did you?"

His words are a knife to my heart. I gasp in anguish as the word *mate* tears through me, leaving behind the tattered remains of my heart and soul.

"I don't want him with me because of the mate bond. I wanted him to choose me!" I cry.

"But it—"

"No!!" I scream.

I stand, throwing the blanket to the floor and shifting. I let my animal take over, snarling at Kai, who holds his hands up, sadness reflecting in his eyes. Before he can say another word, I spin, jumping through the window. Glass shatters around me as I leap to the ground and take off across the parking lot to the woods. The ground is slippery from the rain and snow, and I slide, almost hitting a few cars as ice forms on the road.

I feel a cut along my belly, but I don't care. The pain will give me something else to focus on, and I will heal in a few minutes. I run straight for the trees and along the road, keeping to the darkened woods. Sander is still in town; he's been staying at the motel on the other side of Boulder. I need answers, and I need them now. Something isn't right, and I just can't believe Logan would willingly walk away like that. Something has to have happened. *He said he loved me too. I wasn't imagining that right?*

When I reach the motel twenty minutes later, my breathing is only slightly labored. I skirt the edge of the property, my ears pricked up, and listen. Not hearing anyone about, I quickly move around, smelling each room until I pick up Sander's scent. I look around the empty parking lot and shift before straightening my clothes and smoothing my hair back. Sander swings open the door, and without speaking, grabs my arm and yanks me inside.

"What are you doing here?" he asks, quickly checking out the window. Turning, he takes one look at me and curses. "Are you alright?"

Looking down at myself, I see blood stains from the cuts that have now healed along my stomach. I'm sure my face is red and puffy from crying. I shrug. I'm not hurt, but I'm not alright.

"Where is he?" I ask, my voice wobbling.

Sander shakes his head and paces in front of the door. "He's gone."

My stomach twists, and I feel like I'm going to be sick. "Where?"

"I can't say. I wish I could Salena, I do, but he told me not to say anything. This is something he has to do on his own."

A low growl rumbles from my chest. "Do what on his own?"

Sander's eyes widen. "He didn't tell you?"

Anger replaces my misery. "Tell me what?" I say, taking a menacing step forward. When he doesn't answer, I continue, "If it was your mate?"

Sander huffs out a deep breath and paces the small motel room. "Fine. A woman named Ash told him he needed to face his demons if he wanted to be with you. When he was a boy, he and his brother were walking through the forest at night. His brother was killed by an evil spirit, no trace of his brother was ever found. According to this Ash, the creature marked him and his blood. Attaching itself to him, keeping him isolated and alone, it feeds off his misery. Logan's nightmares have been getting worse since arriving here."

My heart thuds painfully in my chest. "Since he met me?"

"I think that has something to do with it. You make him happy, truly happy for the first time."

"So, he wasn't leaving me?"

Sander's eyes soften. "No, he wasn't. I think he did what he did, so if he didn't return, you wouldn't be waiting."

Anguish squeezes my chest, replaced by resolve.

"Where?"

"Salena."

"He's my fucking mate. He will not face this alone. Where!" I scream, my chest heaving with all the emotions building up inside of me. I will not stand by while he faces this spirit alone. Fuck that, he is mine, and I will stand with him.

Sander sits down heavy on the bed. Leaning forward, he places his elbows on his knees.

"Lake Priest."

"In Idaho?" I ask incredulously.

"Yes." Sander's eyes meet mine. "He left by car with Ash about forty minutes ago."

"Fucking Ash. She disappears for weeks and shows up and takes my mate."

"We can catch up to them if we leave now."

I startle. "You're coming?"

Sander stands, grabbing his jacket and sending me a wink. "He told me to watch you. I can't do that if you leave, and he's my best friend. I hate letting him leave alone."

"Ash is with him, right?"

Sander nods with a slight tilt of his head, his eyes filled with curiosity as he looks at me. "Who is she?"

I turn, opening the door, and Sander walks out to his rental truck. "She's a dark witch, a powerful one. In her tribe she is called a world walker. There's not a lot she doesn't seem to know."

Sander pales. "You're joking?"

"Nope."

Sander's eyes are filled with apprehension as he pulls out onto the road.

"What's wrong?" I ask as I pull out my phone, my fingers flying over the keypad. I send the pack a group message explaining everything and turn off my phone. My brothers will be worried, sure, but I've given them orders to wait for me.

"World walkers are unpredictable. They work in riddles most of the time, and to their own benefit."

I rest my chin in my hand and look out the window. "I know. But Ash can be trusted."

"What makes you say that?"

I see her eyes when she looks at Kai and know Ash won't do anything to mess up a second chance with my brother.

"I just know."

Chapter Fifty Four

Logan

I have managed to evade my reality long enough. I've been pushing what happened deep down into the back recesses of my mind. I could almost pretend that night was just a horrible dream, a nightmare of a young, scared boy. But as I sit here staring out the window of the car, the trees flashing by, all I can see is my brother's terror-stricken face as he's dragged into the darkness. The sound of his screams and the snapping of his bones stabs relentlessly into my head, followed by the deafening silence that tears at my emotional walls.

I haven't faced this in twenty-five fucking years. Which has only added to the pain instead of allowing me to heal. Now knowing that what I saw was real, that it marked me and has been feeding off my misery for all these years, makes anger boil in my veins. I have given too much of my life to this entity. I am taking it back. I have something worth fighting for besides myself now. I have Salena. Or, at least, I did. If I survive the night, then I can work on gaining her forgiveness.

Looking out the front window, eighteen hours into the drive from Boulder, I watch as we wind up the road to the lake. Suddenly the car swerves, just missing a rabbit, then a tree, branches slapping the side of the car.

"Would you watch the road?" I snap, glaring at Ash.

She looks at me, grinning. "Look, no hands."

I look at the road, then my gaze snaps back to Ash. "Are you crazy?"

"Possibly." She laughs, winking at me, her dark eyes holding way too much amusement.

"Do you think this is funny?" I growl.

"Right up until we are dead, it'll be hilarious," Ash says with a grin, then trains her eyes back on the road in front. Thank fuck. I don't want to die when I have finally found something to live for.

But all I can do is sit here simmering in my anger and guilt as she drives us toward the last place I ever wanted to see again. I had to shut my phone off, as Kai and Felix were blowing it up with calls.

I hate how I left things with Salena, but if things go south, I don't want her waiting for me. I want her to be happy. Sander will protect her. I can trust him to watch over the only woman I have ever loved. That realization hits me so hard I can't breathe.

Ash turns her head toward me, perhaps sensing my inner turmoil. "I never asked. What did you tell Salena?" she asks before looking back at the road.

"I broke it off."

Dark eyes swing my way. "You what!?" she screeches, the car swerving.

"You told me to say goodbye."

"I meant as in, *I will see you in a few days.* Tell her you had a sick family member or something."

"I don't have any family," I deadpan.

Ash rubs her temples, muttering something under her breath about the stupidity of males and the human race.

"Hands on the wheel!" I snap.

Ash's eyes flash in warning before she looks back at the road. About five minutes later, she pulls to a stop. The air is thick with tension as she looks over at me with a grim expression. She's already explained to me what needs to be done. I have to draw the creature out and get it to feed on me. It needs to be in its physical form for me to kill it.

When it feeds, the spirit is vulnerable to attack. Once it begins to feed, Ash will contain it with a spell to protect me from the spirit, allowing me to finish the job. Which is to stab it in the heart with a special dagger made of obsidian. Of course, that's easier said than done.

Ash gets out of the car before me and walks to the front, waiting. With a heavy sigh, I open my door. The moment my foot hits the ground, I hear a faint whisper in the wind. With a sense of unease and a great amount of effort, I make my way over to her. She holds out her hand, revealing a glossy, smooth rock in her palm. I frown, picking it up. "What's this?"

"Malachite. It's a protection stone. It absorbs negative energies around you. *And* it will help you stay focused on the task at hand, as opposed to getting caught up in whatever nightmare it shows you."

I pocket the stone, feeling the curves of its surface as I run my thumb over it several times. Ash mutters a few words, and I watch in amazement as shadows swirl and coalesce into an obsidian dagger laying flat in her palm. It shines brightly in the moonlight, its edges looking as if they could cut through anything.

"Where'd that come from?"

"A magician never reveals their secrets," she winks, holding it out to me.

"Use this to stab the spirit in the heart, but only once it has taken solid form. When it feeds, it will be painful, but you will need to push the pain away. Don't let it consume you. This dagger is symbolic. Its sharp edges will pierce darkness to find the light, destroying that thing once and for all."

I swallow roughly and stare into Ash's dark eyes. I hate to admit it, but I am more than a little uneasy. I'm putting my life at risk, and doing so with a complete stranger.

"Let's do this. The quicker we kill this thing, the quicker you can grovel on your knees for Salena's forgiveness for being a shithead."

My shoulders tense, and I let out a menacing growl under my breath.

Ash steps forward, both hands landing on my shoulders. "You got this. Stay focused."

Before I can reply, she spins on her heels, running for the trees, and disappears. I stand here for a few moments, gathering myself. I can do this. Thoughts of my brother and all I've suffered over the years send anger running through my veins. The thought of it coming after Salena makes me vibrate with rage.

I can barely see through the dark as I start down the path toward the lake. I concentrate on putting one foot in front of the other. Everything looks so different now. The moonlight does little to light my way, and I trip several times on exposed tree roots. My hand automatically goes for the stone in my pocket, my thumb running over its smooth surface. I calm somewhat as I stop in a small clearing by the water's edge. Riley and I never made it to the water that night. The water is so still and serene, with a thin layer of fog softly resting on the surface.

I close my eyes and take several deep breaths, my heartbeat slowing down to a somewhat normal pace as an eerie silence settles over the area, lasting several long moments.

That's when I hear it.

The soft sound of a woman singing.

It floats in the air, wrapping around me, but instead of the fear I've been expecting, anger shoots through me like an arrow. I whip around, muscles tensing as I search the woods behind me. All I see is a thick fog rolling over the forest floor toward me.

My muscles tense and my fists clench as I brace myself. The fog reaches me, swirling around my feet, climbing up my legs. My fingers flex, itching to reach for my gun. I know it's of no use, it just makes me feel safer.

The singing started off so soft that at first I thought I was imagining it. But it's growing louder, and now it sounds from all around. I slowly turn in a circle, my growl echoing in the air. The sound of my brother's screams and the cracking of his bones fill my head. Instinctively, I reach up and cover my ears, but it does nothing to stop the sounds from echoing around me.

I sense the spirit drawing closer. The air ripples with its hunger. I can feel its need to consume me. A cool chill covers my entire body, then a soft voice fills my left ear. It's too quiet for anyone to hear, but I understand.

'I knew you'd return one day.'

I spin around, ready to strike out, but there is nothing there. A chuckle fills the air. Burning hot pain slices down my side, and I look down to see red seeping through my shirt.

"Show yourself!" I shout, my fingers flexing on the dagger's handle as I slowly pull it from my pocket.

A shape takes form at the edge of the clearing, the demon coming into focus. It draws nearer, seeming to float just above the ground. Its long claw-like fingernails are dripping with my blood. It looks just like it did all those years ago. I never got a look at it back then. All I saw were fleeting glimpses of shadows.

The demon moves into the moonlight, and I can make out the face of a young woman. Snow white skin reflects the moonlight. Its hair is pure black. But its red-rimmed eyes are what send the tiny hairs on my neck standing on end. The form flickers between woman and shadow. A sick feeling twists my stomach as it smiles at me.

I stand frozen to the spot, unable to move my feet. It's as if they've been frozen solid. Panic rises in my chest, and my eyes close. When I open them again, the demon is a foot away, leaning in closer. I jolt, shocked by its nearness. The demon jerks back and swings its arm, hitting me in the chest with an insane amount of force.

I fly through the air, my body colliding with a tree, before I land hard on the unforgiving ground. Sprawled on my back fighting for my breath, I crane my neck to keep my gaze on the demon. I don't want to take my eyes off it again. If I am to die, I will stare death in the face.

Its crimson gaze burns into me, my vision clouded and unfocused. I can feel a trail of blood dripping down my arm, but I feel no pain. At least not yet. Ash said its claws have a paralyzing effect. That with a few swipes of its claws, I won't be able to do much. It had already sliced my side.

Soft whispers float on the air as I watch the demon stalk closer again. "I've waited so long for your return. You have been my most prized pet over the years," it hisses.

I stumble to my feet and charge forward, intent on taking it to the ground.

"I'm no fucking pet. You are done tormenting me!" I shout.

The demon swirls into a cloud of shadows, her laugh echoing around me. I spin in a circle.

"Come out and fight me," I growl.

I'm breathing heavily, my teeth gritted as I get ready to attack the demon, but then I notice him standing in front of me. He looks exactly as he did the last time I saw him.

"Riley?" I whisper, my voice hoarse.

Riley tilts his head, his dark hair hanging in clumps over his face, partially obscuring his expression.

'You left me.'

Ice fills my veins at his softly spoken words. "No, I didn't."

'That demon took me and you just laid there.'

His words feel like a physical blow to my already wounded heart. His screams still haunt me, bouncing around my head like a never-ending nightmare. I squeeze my eyes close, shaking my head. This isn't Riley. I can't let myself be dragged under by the demon.

As I release a deep breath, I open my eyes to find Riley standing less than a foot away from me. *'Don't you love me?'* he says.

My fists clench as I stare down at the brother I love more than anything. The boy who was taken from me, his memory tormenting me every day since. I could tell that this wasn't my brother as soon as I saw the cruel, calculating look cross his eyes. This is just the demon finding a new way to taunt me, playing with me. My mind clears, and I realize I hadn't let go of the dagger. With surprising speed, I swing my arm in an upward arc, and the demon staggers backward to avoid the blade. Despite knowing it isn't Riley, my hand can't bring itself to harm him. The demon morphs before my eyes, taking on the appearance of the woman from before. The contrast between her striking beauty and her unsettling red eyes creates a sense of eeriness.

A cruel, twisted smile curled her lips. "Your brother was delicious. His screams fed my hunger perfectly. I wonder if you will scream, too."

She disappears, and I feel a sharp, stabbing pain in my back, and can't help but let out a low hiss. Spinning around, I'm met with an empty space. I turn again and my heart thumps hard in my chest as I come face to face with the demon. Before I can react, I'm knocked to the ground. The demon hovers over me. Her long nails sink into my shoulder, keeping me pinned to the ground as her face draws closer to mine. I look to the side and see my dagger lying in the dirt. I reach out my fingertips, just brushing against the hilt. I feel my frustration mounting and a low growl rumbles in my chest.

The demon begins to take shape, a sweet laugh falling from its lips. "You are mine now."

I feel the sweat beading on my forehead as I scrape the dirt with my fingertips, trying to reach the dagger. Where is Ash?

Beads of sweat form on my forehead as I strain against the demon's grasp. I grit my teeth and let out a frustrated yell, the sharp pain in my shoulder making me wince. "You no longer control me," I snarl.

The demon tips its head back. Its laughter is cruel and mocking, and I can feel my heart racing in my chest. But it gives me the chance I need. With a final effort, I stretch my arm those last few centimeters and feel my fingers wrap around the hilt of the dagger. Without a second thought, I thrust the blade into her chest, the force of it taking me by surprise. The demon's red eyes burn with wild intensity. I can feel its anger as it grabs me by the throat, throwing me across the ground. I tumble and roll, feeling the grass and dirt under my hands and body before I come to a stop. Quickly, I roll over to my stomach and snatch up the dagger, pushing to my knees in the dirt. Ash appears out of nowhere, looking me in the eye and giving a slight nod of encouragement. The demon's howl echoes through the trees as it rages against the spell that holds it captive under Ash's control. With a great amount of effort, I push to my feet and stumble over to where the demon is. The demon's eyes bore into me as I approach, each step making me feel bolder.

I stop directly in front of it, my breathing ragged as I fight off the paralyzing effect of its claws. "You no longer command me. You shall never feed from my misery or taint my world with your poison. I am free of you from this day forth. You will leave this world and never hurt another soul."

The obsidian blade glints in the moonlight as I raise it up.

The demon's eyes widen with fear as it jerks and thrashes wildly in a vain attempt to break Ash's spell. Before it can get away, I sink the blade into its heart and mutter the words Ash made me recite the entire drive here. The ancient Latin words spill from my mouth with an ease I wasn't expecting. The demon shrieks as its body turns into black smoke.

Ash's hand gently comes to rest on my shoulder, and I slowly turn my head to look at her. With a soft and confident smile, she nods in approval.

"It is done. You're free now."

I sag in relief, the dagger falling from my fingers. The sharp, throbbing pain from my injuries is becoming more apparent by the second. I lean forward and brace my hands on my knees, taking several deep breaths.

Out of nowhere, a wet nose pushes against my cheek. I tilt my head and my eyes meet the gaze of the white wolf. I let out a rough chuckle and drop my head again, sinking my fingers into its fur for purchase and strength. "How are you here?"

The white wolf whines in front of me, and I tip my head up to stare into its blue eyes, that have flecks of yellow flashing like lightning through them. The sight of them is so comforting, like coming home. It nudges me again and barks angrily at Ash.

I lift my hand and smooth it over the wolf's neck. "Hey, I'm okay. Ash helped me. I'm finally free."

My vision fades in and out, and Ash crouches down next to me. "Are you able to walk?"

"I don't know." I sway on my knees.

Suddenly, a prickling sensation fills the air, and I watch in awe as the white wolf transforms in a swirl of mist. At least . . . that's the best way I can describe it.

Then Salena is kneeling in front of me. I blink several times, confusion making my brain even fuzzier. I must be hallucinating or . . .

"Am I dead?" I turn to Ash.

She laughs, the sound carefree as she shakes her head.

Salena's warm hands cup my cheeks, bringing my gaze back to her. "Are you okay?"

"Did you just. Are you? Was that you? Are you the white wolf?" Damn it. My throat feels tight and my head is foggy, making it impossible for me to express the words I want to say.

Salena's thumbs stroke over my cheeks, and she gives me a weak smile. "Yes . . . I'm sorry I never told you."

"You can shape shift? Are you like Ash?"

"No, I'm not like Ash. But I am a shifter, a wolf shifter."

My head lulls slightly. "So, like werewolves?"

Salena's lips quirk and she tilts her head, silver hair sliding along her delicate shoulders. "No, they are different also."

"I really don't care what you are. I'm just so fucking happy you're here. After everything I said and put you through, you still came for me?"

Tears fill her sparkling blue eyes. "Of course I came for you. You are worth fighting for, Logan."

My hands automatically reach for her face, my fingers sinking into her soft hair. I tip her face up to mine, my lips a breath from hers. "I fucking love you, Salena Cartwright."

I feel her warmth against me as our lips touch, and I swear I can hear my heart pounding in my chest. I deepen the kiss, savoring the sweetness of her lips, and wanting her to know how much I love her.

Salena moves, her sweet scent filling the air as she straddles me.

I groan, leaning forward to nuzzle her neck, breathing her in. My arms wrap around her, pulling her against me. "Say it again," I breathe.

Pulling back, she cups my face, her thumb running over the scars on my cheek. "Logan Sinclair, I fucking love you."

We sit here, arms wrapped tightly around each other for a few minutes until the pain in my shoulder and side become unbearable. I grunt and shift around, trying to ease the discomfort, and Salena springs off my lap with lightning speed, yanking at my shirt as she desperately tries to see my wounds. My hands dart up, grabbing hold of her wrists.

"It's okay."

"No, it's not! You're hurt."

"I'll be fine. Nothing I haven't been through before."

The heat of her anger is evident in her blazing eyes, and my heart warms.

Carefully, I push up from the ground as Salena wraps her arm around my waist, helping me stand. "How did you find me?" I ask.

"Our connection is so strong I could find you in the blackest of nights," she whispers.

A throat clears beside us, and I whip my gaze to the left where Sander stands. "Oh, and Sander told me you'd be here." She chuckles, sending me a wink.

I pull her into my arms and press a kiss to the pulse in Salena's neck, murmuring into her sweet skin, "Let's go home."

My eyes meet Sander's over her shoulder. He has a shit-eating grin on his face. We turn to head back toward the car, and I look around the clearing.

"Hey, where's Ash?"

"Ash disappears all the time. Just slips away without a trace, leaving only a faint echo of her presence and lots of questions behind."

"We can't leave her here."

"Trust me, if she wanted to join us, she'd be here," Salena says, guiding me back toward the cars.

Chapter Fifty Five

Salena

Logan is so exhausted that he sleeps the entire eighteen-hour drive home, his head resting against the car window on a pillow. Every time I glance over at him, and see his bruised and battered body, my anger flares up again.

Sander and I take turns driving again, and we make the drive with only stopping to pee. By the time we pull up to Logan's house, I can barely keep my eyes open from fatigue.

I decide to wait for Logan downstairs while he showers, but I can't relax. Pacing the bottom of the stairs, my hands tremble as I try to think of the perfect thing to say to make everything better. For weeks, I lied to him. The stairs creak and I spin around to see Logan slowly making his way down.

"See, all better," he jokes, holding his arms out.

"I thought I'd never see you again," I confide.

Logan takes the last two steps and enfolds me in his strong, warm embrace. "I will never leave you, Salena," he murmurs into my hair. "I'm so sorry for how I left. I was stupid. Even Ash was pissed when I told her what I'd done."

"She was?" I ask, a small smile pulling at my lips.

"Yeah," he whispers, stroking my hair down my back. "Why didn't you tell me what you are?"

I pull back with a sigh and tug at his hand, making him follow me to the sofa. Taking a seat, we position ourselves to face each other. With a deep breath, I nervously chew my bottom lip.

"None of that. If anyone is biting your lip, it's me," Logan says, reaching over and using his thumb to tug my lip free.

Butterflies dance around in my stomach and I smirk. "Do it, then."

Logan's eyes burn with desire, and he shakes his head. "Stop deflecting."

"Fine. I was afraid that if I said anything, you would take off and never look back. You didn't exactly take the idea of your own gift well."

Ghost jumps onto the sofa and settles between us. She looks between the two of us and meows loudly. I reach out and stroke a hand over her head and she pushes her head into my hand for more.

"Before last night, I don't think I would have believed you." Logan grunts, running his hand over his head, making those arm muscles bulge. "I hate you kept this from me, but I understand why you did it."

"I should have told you sooner, especially with Samuel," I choke out, emotions sitting heavy on my chest. "He killed Ro's dad."

"What?" Logan sits up straight.

"Samuel, he fought me for the pack. He wanted me dead. The thought of living under the rule of a female had him erupting into a fit of rage. Somehow the police were called, and then Samuel . . . he killed Charlie. I wasn't quick enough to stop it." I heave in a breath as tears spill down my cheeks.

Logan scoots forward, Ghost jumping out of the way as Logan pulls me into his chest.

"Hey, it's okay," he soothes, wrapping me up in his arms.

"I'm the reason Ro will grow up without a dad," I cry.

"No. No, you're not. That's on Samuel. Those girls are on Samuel. You did not make him do those things. He did them." Logan pulls back and holds my head in a firm grip, stroking the tears from my cheeks with his thumbs. "You heard me. Don't take this burden on your shoulders. Trust me."

I nod my head and sniffle. "You won't leave me again?"

"Salena, I *need* you. You make me happy, the happiest I've have been in a long fucking time. You chase away the darkness that threatens to pull me under every goddamn day. I knew I was screwed the moment your beautiful eyes locked on mine. I will be whatever you need me to be, because I won't lose you again. I won't walk away again."

Wrapping his hand around my hair, he tugs me forward for another kiss, leaving me breathless. Logan growls and his hands slide down to grip the back of my thighs, lifting me off the sofa as he stands. Wrapping my legs around his waist, he spins, walking us toward the stairs, raining kisses along my jaw and down my neck.

"I need to tell you one more thing?" I groan softly.

"What is it, baby?" he murmurs, kissing along my collarbone.

"You're my mate."

He stops in the bedroom doorway, his eyes snapping to mine and lingering on me before a mischievous smirk graces his lips. My pulse picks up and my stomach clenches in anticipation. What is he thinking?

"Mate?" he replies.

"Yes." I sigh as he gently lowers me to the ground.

Logan shifts, placing his hands around my waist.

"I like the sound of that," he murmurs, leaning down and nipping at my lip.

I gasp in surprise, my hands coming up to land on his chest as I stare into his crystal blue eyes that I've come to love so much. "You do?"

"Fuck, yes."

"You accept me and what I am?" I ask, unsure.

"Baby, I love you. I love you like this, and as that gorgeous wolf."

I can feel the tears beginning to burn my eyes, and I drop my forehead to his chest with a thud. "I'm so sorry I didn't tell you earlier."

"It's okay."

"It's not. You're my mate. I should have told you."

"Is mate like soulmate?" he asks curiously.

"In a way." I shrug and place my palm over his heart. "Our souls match perfectly and recognized each other, causing an imprint to happen. We could feel the connection between us, like two magnets drawn together. But the imprint, or connection, isn't complete until we mate properly." At his confused look, I continue. "Exchange of blood and magic during sex."

"Why me?"

I reach up, wrapping my arms around his neck, my fingers playing with the soft strands of hair as I look up into his gorgeous face. "I saw something in you, something my soul realized it couldn't live without."

I see the doubt and hesitation in his eyes.

"Logan, I love you. I think I loved you the minute you showed up at my door, making sure it wasn't me who had been killed in the woods. I think you know you had chosen me then as well."

Logan's head bends and his lips ghost over mine. "I love you, too. And you're right, it was never one sided."

My fingers sink into his hair, and I pull his mouth to mine. His tongue sweeps inside, and I moan, jumping into his arms, my legs going around his waist.

"Fuck me, Logan," I whisper against his lips.

"Baby, I'm going to fuck you, alright. I'm going to be so fucking deep inside of you, I'll leave a mark," he growls. The fire blazing in his eyes has my core clenching, and I rub against him.

Logan's hands fit perfectly around my waist, giving me a quick squeeze before placing me on my feet. He slowly undresses me, his finger trailing each piece of clothing he removes. Frustrated with the slow pace, I grab his t-shirt and tear it down the middle, running my palms over his abdomen and chest, being careful not to hurt him.

"In a hurry, baby?" he smirks, taking a step back.

My throat vibrates with a low rumble, and I move forward. Logan holds up a hand, stopping me. He slowly pulls down his track pants, standing completely naked in front of me. I reach down, pulling off my underwear and step backward until the back of my legs hit the bed. I beckon him closer and his eyes flare as they watch me lie back on the bed, stretching my body out.

Logan stalks forward, climbing over top of me, and his hand comes up to cup one breast as his mouth descends. My eyes fall shut as his mouth moves from one breast to the other. His hand skims down my body and circles my wetness. A shock wave of pleasure courses through me and my hips lift from the bed.

"Logan."

His fingers move faster against me as his mouth continues to lick, suck, and bite across my chest and neck. I'm panting with need, and a whimper escapes me when he pushes two fingers inside me. His lips move up to my ear.

"So wet for me, baby."

"Logan, please."

"Please what?" he asks, sucking hard on the pulse point in my neck.

"Fuck me."

"Your wish is my command, baby."

His thigh spreads my legs, and he surges forward, burying himself to the hilt. I cry out as an orgasm rips through me instantly, throwing me over the edge. Logan grits his teeth as he moves slowly, milking every moment of it.

"Fuck," he pants, picking up his pace.

I cling to his straining arms as he moves over me, drawing cries from my lips. My heart thrums madly in my chest, this man draws out every emotion and sensation.

"I want you to do it," he pants, his forehead dropping to mine, his nose grazing my cheek.

Confusion rolls through me until I realize what he's saying.

"You want to mate?"

"Fuck, yes. I'm yours."

My canines descend without permission. I groan as I lift my head and sink my teeth into the spot where his neck meets his shoulder, and I claim him. I flip us over so I'm straddling him and reach up, lengthening my nail before dragging it across the same spot on my neck. Then I bend over him, guiding his mouth to the cut. "Claim me," I growl. My magic sings in the air around us, caressing and brushing along our connection.

The moment his lips close over my skin, a sense of harmony and acceptance washes over me and through our bond, our souls entwining and melding together. Logan's fingers dig into my ass as I slowly move up and down over his length, my alpha magic fusing us together. Our orgasm is sudden, and it sends us both spiraling over the edge. I feel his love mingling with mine, a love that runs as deep as the core of the earth.

Once we come down, Logan's bright eyes meet mine.

"*Mine,*" he growls, the sound feral and guttural.

It sends goosebumps coursing over my body. In the next second, I'm being lifted off him and thrown on the bed, my back landing a second before he's on me, filling me again. I cry out and grip his arms as he pounds into me, claiming me his own way.

His lips are soft, his taste addictive. He completely consumes me. His taste, touch, smell. He is everything I have ever wanted.

Chapter Fifty Six

Salena

We spent the next day together as a pack, and I could feel the mate bond, our connection humming in my chest. The feeling of contentment filled me up, like a warm blanket on a cold day. Logan had felt the change too, and he described it as a feeling of finally being in the right place.

When everyone had arrived at Kai's, Logan was shocked, to say the least. He had a lot of questions, so many. Especially for Sander. It still surprises me that he never realized his best friend is a shifter.

Kai and Felix are still mad at me for running off, but they won't stay mad for long. Especially Felix, he's a romantic, and I know he's hooked on our story by the way his eyes light up.

My mind drifts back to my time stuck in the bathroom.

"Help me!" I yell in frustration.

The sound of their hysterical laughter has me fuming. My eyes lock with Logan's, and I scowl at him, which only makes him laugh harder. I love and hate him in that moment, but to hear his deep, full belly laugh does something to my insides.

"Just can someone fucking kill it?!"

Rose laughs. "You sure do swear a lot for a lady, Salena."

"Do I look like a fucking lady to you, Rose?"

A look of sheer amusement crosses her face. "It's just a harmless spider."

Scowling at them all, I bounce on my toes, ready to run through the doorway. The creature of my discomfort is about the size of my palm, and is currently stationary above the door, all eight eyes and legs watching me, ready to pounce the moment I draw near. It has held me hostage in the bathroom for almost an hour, and no one will help a girl out.

Logan steps forward with a chuckle. "Baby, I can't believe you've been in there for an hour."

He has been outside with my brothers having a man on man chat, whatever that is. They all walked in about ten minutes before.

I hold my breath as he walks through the doorway and turns around, looking up at the spider.

"Oh, she is big," he says casually.

Slowly, he reaches up. Fear shoots through me and I can't hold back the shriek as I jump into the shower, closing the glass door, putting a barrier between me and that thing.

Logan's gaze is filled with warmth as he turns to look at me, carefully cradling the spider in his hands.

"I would never let anything happen to you. Trust me?"

I nod, unable to speak while he holds the giant spider. Logan waits until I find my voice, and I cross my arms.

"I'm still not getting out of here until that is outside."

Logan turns the car off and I blink, realizing we're back at his house. We walk in, locking the door behind us and throwing the keys on the hall table. Logan grabs my hand, spinning me around to face him. My stomach flutters at the tenderness in his eyes.

He steps closer, his arm wrapping around me, as he lowers his mouth to mine. I relax into his hold, melting into his kiss. The press of his palm on my lower back, pulling closer, sends a rush of pleasure racing through me. He breaks the kiss, pulling back just far enough to pull my top over my head. His hands are warm and firm on my back, sure and confident in his movements. The kiss is hot, sweet, and consuming all at the same time. I could forget my name when his lips are on mine. Logan somehow manages to guide us to the bedroom without breaking the kiss. His steady hands are always there, like a shield of protection.

I step into the bedroom and Logan breaks the kiss with a smirk. He loosens his tie, and he pulls it off. His chest brushes mine as he steps closer, his hands gripping my wrists and putting them behind my back. He seems to tower over me as his fingers deftly tie my wrists together with his tie. Once he's done, he tests the restraints and smirks. His fingers glide over my ribs, cupping my bare breasts, tugging on my nipples. With a wicked glint in his eye, he lowers his head, covering my breast with his mouth and sucking hard. His touch sends shivers down my spine, and I arch into it, a moan involuntarily escaping my lips as I say his name. Logan moves to the other side, making me squirm, and I tug on my restraints. I want to sink my fingers into his hair.

Dropping to his knees, his fingers undo the zipper of my leather pants, slowly pulling them down my legs. I step out of them with his help and gaze down into his scorching blue eyes as he takes in my naked body.

Lifting one leg, he hooks it over his shoulder, my heart galloping a million miles an hour with anticipation. "Logan," I whisper, my voice shaking with desire.

"Lean against the wall, baby."

He doesn't wait, just hooks my other leg over his shoulder, forcing my upper back to hit the wall. With my hands tied, I can't do much. Sure, I could probably break the tie, but I don't want to. As I surrender to him, my body is filled with an incredible warmth that seems to radiate from within.

Suddenly, his mouth is on me, his wicked tongue gliding over my clit before sucking it into his mouth. I gasp, my legs trembling as he swirls his tongue over and over. I shudder, then rock my hips into his mouth, my hands clenching behind me.

He licks, sucks, and bites, exploring me, then moving lower, he spears me with his tongue. I tremble in his arms, his fingers digging into my ass cheeks, holding me steady, as his tongue works me in circles, drowning me in pleasure. Sparks shoot deep inside me. My orgasm dances around the edges, teasing me. My breath races in and out like I've been running. An electric sensation moves through me, singing along my nerves. I arch into his mouth, chasing it. I scream his name as I shatter into a million pieces floating on a wave of endorphins, my body shaking and quivering.

Logan releases my legs and stands. His powerful arms encircle me, holding me steady. With my arms tied behind my back, my breasts are pushed up, making it easy for him to latch on, biting down on my nipple. I cry out in pleasure, ripping the tie that holds my hands, and gripping his shoulders as I take him to the ground and straddle him. I grind my pussy over his cock as I lean down and return the favor, my teeth clamping down on his nipple. With a deep, menacing growl, Logan flips us with ease. I feel the softness of the carpet against my skin, as well as its slight roughness. Logan's mouth covers mine, his tongue diving into my mouth at the same time as he plunges into me. I gasp at the intrusion. Logan bites my bottom lip and then sucks it hard before releasing it.

"You drive me fucking crazy when you bite that lip of yours," he growls.

"Oh my god, Logan," I cry out as he tilts my hips up, hitting that spot deep inside of me as he fills me over and over.

Chapter Fifty Seven

Logan

The sound of my phone ringing beside the bed pulls me from my sleep, and I feel a deep sense of dread. I stretch out my arm and my fingers wrap around the phone as I answer.

"Logan here."

"Detective, we need you down at the entrance to Mysris trail, ASAP." Milo says. From the underlying tone of his voice I can tell something was wrong.

I throw the covers off and step out of bed, the cold wooden floorboards sending a chill up my spine.

"What's happening?" I demand.

"We found another body."

I pause in the doorway, my body tense as I take a deep breath before replying.

"Be there in fifteen," I snap, unable to keep the hostility from my voice.

I quickly throw on my suit and tuck my phone into my pocket. Salena slowly sits up, the sheet pooling around her waist. I take a moment to appreciate her in her sex-mussed hair and gorgeous body.

Rubbing at her face, she takes me in. "What is it?" she yawns.

"They found a body." I lean down to give her a quick peck on the lips.

Her eyes fly open, the vivid blues and greens swirling with intensity. "What?"

"I have to go, but I'll call you later."

"Okay," she replies, biting her lip.

I reach down and tug it free. "It's okay."

"Yeah . . . " she whispers.

I turn and head downstairs, rushing for my car. I make it to the trail in record time. But I need to make sure. I have this horrible feeling in the pit of my stomach.

Arriving on the scene, I see Milo and Kallie, along with a few other officers, standing around. I make my way over and see a glimpse of Abby's red hair behind them. I stop in front of Milo and Kallie, the icy fresh breeze ruffling their hair. Milo's complexion is almost ghostly, and his eyes are wide with fear. Kallie has an exhausted look, her eyes ringed by dark shadows.

"Who found the body?" I ask, looking at each of them.

"I did," Kallie says, and I take note of her hiking gear under the police jacket she wears.

"What time did you come across the body?"

"About five a.m."

I frown and glance around. "Five a.m, it's still dark. How did you stumble across a body out here?"

Kallie turns and points over to one of the trucks where a large German shepherd sits, quietly watching the commotion.

"Okay, I'm going to talk to Abby, then I'll be back."

They both silently nod without looking back at the crime scene. That isn't a good sign.

I trudge toward Abby, pushing aside a few branches that brush against my coat.

"Hey, Abby," I say, approaching her side. She's staring down at the mutilated body of a young woman. For a moment, all she does is blink. I'm about to ask if she's okay when her eyes snap to mine. Her warm brown eyes brim with emotion, glistening like glass, as she stares at me.

"Who would do this?" she whispers.

For the first time since arriving, I look over at the body placed in a stone circle similar to the one Lola was found in. The body looks to have bled out through multiple wounds at each of her major arteries. There are deep cuts to both her femoral arteries and both her wrists. The girl also has a long, deep cut across her neck. Her lifeless eyes stare at the sky, her naked body still and blue in the snow.

I look at the stone circle and frown. All the rocks are smooth and the same size. Someone went to a lot of effort for this kill site.

"How long do you think she's been here?" I ask.

Abby sniffles and looks up at the sky, the sun peeking over the horizon, casting light across the area.

"I . . . uh. I can't tell with the snow and . . . I think it's best if you wait for the doc to do the autopsy," Abby stutters.

I lightly rest my hand on her shoulder, giving her a reassuring squeeze. Looking around, I search the area. "Where is Doc?"

"On his way," Abby replies, breathing deeply as she brings her camera up.

"Okay, well, take a break if you need to, Abby."

She pulls her face away from the camera and gives me a weak smile. "I'm okay," she whispers before getting back to work.

I turn and make my way to the others.

I look at Kallie first. "Have you given a statement?"

She nods in response, her arms tightly crossed over her chest.

"Alright, then, you should go home," I say, and instantly see the fire ignite in her eyes.

"What? But I found the body. I want to be on the case," Kallie says, stepping forward, her cheeks flushed. Which is much better than the paleness from moments ago.

"Look, we need all hands on deck for this, but you've been here since five a.m. I expect you to be well rested and clear minded. Go home, Kallie."

"But–"

I shake my head. "We have to be smart about this. Go home, unwind, relax and sleep. You're no good to anyone tired. That's when mistakes are made."

Kallie opens her mouth to argue when the captain speaks up from behind her. "He's right. Go home, Kallie. I don't want to see you for at least six hours."

She gives a solemn nod before heading back toward the cars. I slowly twist my body to face Milo, seeing determination in his eyes. "I need you to stay and help Doc and Abby with anything they may need."

Milo gives a curt nod before springing into action and walking toward the crime scene. I turn to the two other officers whose names I can't recall.

"You two, I want you to sweep the area, see if you can't find any sign of a struggle. Just anything. I'm going to call the dogs in."

I turn to the captain, who looks as if he's aged twenty years overnight. "Logan, I thought we had the guy?" he mumbles.

"Me, too. Samuel admitted to killing those girls."

"You think he had an accomplice?"

"Fucking hope not," I growl, frustration making my stomach tighten with dread.

"Do what you have to to find this piece of shit. You hear me?"

"Yes, captain."

I hear the crunch of the snow under his boots as he turns and walks away. Then I pull out my phone, making two calls, one to the canine squad, and one to Sander.

Chapter Fifty Eight

Salena

A dozen questions are perched on my tongue, anxiously waiting for my mouth to open so they can fly out. I hold on to them tightly, desperately settling for silence. I closed the bar tonight, so only pack are here, all of us waiting on Logan's return.

Logan looks defeated as he takes a seat. His blue eyes haven't left mine since he walked through the door a couple of minutes ago. He came straight for me, wrapping me in his arms. He closes his eyes and leans his forehead against mine, taking in my scent.

'I missed you,' I whisper down the mate bond. We haven't tested whether we can communicate telepathically yet. I'm not sure if it will work with Logan being a human.

Logan's eyes, bright and blue like a glacial lake, suddenly open, and I see shock ripple across his face.

'I missed you more,' he replies in my mind.

Happiness explodes inside me, and I rise up to my toes, giving him a slow, sweet kiss.

"Go sit down. I'll get you a beer. It looks like you need it," I say, pushing him toward the bar where the others are waiting.

Now sitting at the bar, everyone is waiting. Lucy and Grady are seated to his left, Rose standing next to them. Since Lola's death, Rose has lost her spark. She has barely left the house, something I know I need to fix. Mercy bursts through the doors, a gust of cold, snowy wind pushing against her, making her long blonde hair whip around her face as she turns and slams the doors shut.

"Shit, the weather's turned to crap out there," she grumbles, stamping her boots at the entrance.

"Storm's rolling in tonight. Looks like it's come early," Felix says, walking over and helping her with her jacket.

I survey the room, taking in the sound of my family. My pack isn't large, but we are family. Declan, Mercy, and Felix sit at the table in front of the bar where Logan, Lucy, Grady, and Rose are. Tyler, Kai, and I stand, the anticipation setting our hearts racing.

"As you've all heard, we found another female body early this morning. On Friday night, she left a party, and was reported missing later the next day. She was only nineteen."

Butterflies dance around my stomach, and not the good kind.

Logan continues, "The crime scene was a perfect match to the one where Lola was found."

Lucy gasps, covering her mouth, and Rose's eyes instantly well with tears. I take a step forward, looking at Logan, a question burning on the tip of my tongue.

Logan meets my gaze. "Whoever it was bleached her hair to make her look like you."

My breathing picks up and I shake my hands out. "How? Samuel is dead," I say, shock rippling through me.

Logan shakes his head. "I don't know. We are working on the assumption that he had an accomplice. The crime scene was too perfect to be a copycat, and those details were never leaked."

I shake my head. "Samuel mentioned no one else."

"The only other people who we know of are the PI and Jenna. Maybe she was his accomplice?" Kai says.

My blood runs cold at the mention of her name. A deep-seated anger swells to life in my chest, and I hear a low rumble in my throat as the beer bottle I'm gripping breaks apart in my hands.

"Don't say her name," I snarl, unable to contain the anger boiling in my blood.

Kai freezes, speaking through gritted teeth. "I'm just saying she could know something."

I attempt to think rationally, but my mind is filled with images of the two of them. Closing my eyes, I take a deep breath. With my emotions this high, I am a danger. I sense Logan get up and approach me. When I open my eyes, he is standing directly in front of me, barely a foot away. Guilt fills his eyes, and he reaches up, pushing the hair from my face and tucking it behind my ear.

"Salena, you don't need to worry about her."

I still, heart pumping with rage. "Where is she?"

Logan hesitates, and I narrow my eyes.

"Salena, let me do my job," he says carefully, his eyes searching mine.

I storm around the bar and grab a cloth, muttering under my breath. I don't want Logan anywhere near that woman. When I glance up, I hear the sound of Rose and Declan's voices as they work together to pick up the broken glass.

Every bone in my body is screaming at me to go hunt whoever this is down. I need revenge. I need to stop the killings. Katlin flashes through my mind and my heart lurches. Logan's arm wraps around my waist, and he turns me to face him.

"Baby, we will get whoever this is. I won't stop until they are fucking gone."

"I just can't believe it's happening again."

"You were right. It was two people all along," Felix says.

"What should we do?"

"I want to head out and see if I can pick up a scent, or a track, anything," I say.

Logan shakes his head. "Please don't."

"Logan, I need to. I will take Felix and Kai with me."

"And me," Mercy pipes up.

Before anyone says another word, there is a loud bang on the front door.

We all exchange looks, and Logan lets go of my waist, approaching the door with Kai. Unlocking the door, they open it, and Ash is standing there with Sander and . . .

"Ro?" Logan says, confusion swirling in his voice.

My body locks up, tension bleeding out of me. Rose's eyes dart to mine, panic filling her features. I watch as Declan grabs her hand and pulls her over to a table.

Sander walks in first, followed by Ash, her dark eyes immediately landing on Kai. My brother swallows roughly and looks away. Ash smirks and heads my way.

"I leave for a few days and shit hits the fan again," she jokes.

"A girl is dead, Ash," I snap.

A ghost of a shadow passes over her eyes. "I know."

Logan's voice pulls my gaze, as he speaks to Ro.

"Ro, what are you doing here?" Logan asks.

Sander takes off his jacket and speaks first. "Found him banging on your door about ten minutes ago."

"You were looking for me?"

Ro looks uneasy as he scans the room. "My mum's gone."

Logan ushers him in and shuts the door, keeping out the snow. "What do you mean gone?"

Ro shakes his head. "I don't know. I haven't seen her since yesterday. She never leaves the house."

"Shit." Logan turns and looks at me.

I can feel his rising anxiety. I don't need to read his thoughts to know he's worried she might have been taken.

I turn to Kai, but his attention is solely on Ash. With a long, deep breath, I try to steady my heart before I make my way over to Logan and Ro.

"Where was your mom the last time you saw her?" Logan asks.

Ro shuffles on his feet, shoving his hands in his jacket pockets. Poor kid looks freezing, his face pale and lips almost blue from the cold.

"Home. She only leaves the house on Tuesdays to shop. Other than that, she doesn't leave."

I feel a deep pang in my heart hearing that.

"I need to go over and check your place out and I will call it in," Logan says, squeezing Ro's shoulder.

I give him a weak smile. "Want to stay here where it's warm? You're more than welcome."

Ro looks around at the mismatch group I call family. His eyes lock on Rose's and widen. I feel a sense of unease and distrust there. Why?

Felix walks over, pecking me on the head. "I will go with Logan to check out the house. You stay here."

"Who's in charge here?" I snap, turning on him. Felix puts his hands up and smirks at me, then points at Logan. I give a low growl and Logan clears his throat, reminding me of present company.

"Ash, will you go with them?" I ask.

Logan and Felix both go to interrupt. But I raise my hand, my gaze firmly fixed on both of them.

"No. It's all I ask."

Ash strolls forward, tipping back a bottle of whiskey she has nabbed from the bar, saluting me. "It would be my pleasure," she says.

"Thanks."

I peek over at Logan and the set of his mouth and the hardness in his eyes tells me he's barely keeping his anger in check, so I decide it's best not to say a word.

Logan steps forward and pulls me into his embrace. His touch feels protective and strong, and I just want to sink into him.

I watch as he, Ash and Felix walk out into the storm. Then I turn to Ro and offer him a smile. "Come on, sit down and I'll get you a drink."

Chapter Fifty Nine

Logan

It seems like this day will never end. It has been cursed from the start, with one disaster following another. I am so tired; I miss Salena, and I just want to go home. Ash's smartass comments only serve to exacerbate my mounting frustration. Still, I understand why Salena asked her to come along. I noticed Kai's body stiffen and felt the air become heavy with tension when she walked in. You don't need to be trained in body language to see that.

I slowly come to a stop outside the front of Hayley's house, parking at the curb. Felix leans forward from the backseat, resting his elbows on each of the front seats. "I'll take a look around the area, see if I can pick anything up."

I give a slight nod of my head in agreement. "Okay, Ash and I will check out the house."

We all pile out of the car, and Felix disappears in seconds. I just catch a flash from the corner of my eye. "Shit, he's fast," I murmur.

Ash smirks. "You're not freaking out, are you?"

I scowl in her direction. "No."

We do a lap of the house, looking for any signs of forced entry or a struggle. Hayley's car remains parked in the garage. So, wherever she went, she did so on foot, or someone picked her up.

With a deep sigh, I call it in. Officers arrive on the scene a little later, Mack and another I'm not familiar with. Both have given Ash a wide berth, and I don't blame them. Her presence is intimidating, and her sharp gaze misses nothing.

"All we can do is file a missing person's report and hope she turns up."

"I know."

"Where is Ro?"

"Right now, he's at Salena's."

Mack arches an eyebrow. "The bar?"

I narrow my eyes in challenge. "Problem?"

Mack holds his hands up and shakes his head. "Nope. No problem."

"Good."

With that, they get in the patrol car and drive off. The minute the red from their tail lights disappears around the bend, Felix appears next to me.

"Nothing," he says before I can ask.

I let out a low growl and run a hand through my hair in frustration. "Fuck," I snap.

"Alright, sunshine, I'm sure she's fine," Ash says, crossing her arms, looking completely bored by the whole thing.

I take a step toward her, my anger flaring. "Do you always have to be–"

"Adorable?" Ash cuts in, her eyes sparking with what I assume is magic.

"I was going to say *smartass*," I grumble.

Felix shifts on his feet. "Look, let's go. Things will hopefully look better in the morning."

Ash and I stare at each other for another beat before she breaks out in a grin. Stepping forward, she lightly punches my arm. "I like you, Logan Sinclair. You are a fine mate for the alpha."

With that, she turns to Felix. "Tell Salena I will be in touch."

Then she turns, and I watch in amazement as she seems to be swept up in a cloud of shimmering white snow, and then I'm staring into the eyes of a beautiful timber wolf. Before I can process it, she turns, running faster than a normal wolf down the street and out of view within seconds.

Felix lets out a deep breath. "That woman is intense."

The sight of Salena riding me, her head flung back, firm round breasts on display, has my fingers digging into her hips. I can't help but grind her down on my lap while thrusting up, going as deep as I can. Fuck, she feels good. She always does. It has been different with Salena from the start. She burns as hot for me as I do for her. Everywhere we touch leaves a scorching path of heat and desire.

Leaning forward, I swirl my tongue around her dusky nipple, drawing it into my mouth. A loud moan slips from her lips as she rocks against me, and I can feel she is close, her muscles tightening around me in the most delicious way.

My fingers flex and squeeze the soft skin of her ass. I dip them lower, curving around until I feel the wetness from where we are joined. My fingers gather it up, and I circle her tight ass. Her breathing hitches and she pushes into my hand.

My eyes find hers. "You want that baby?"

I feel her pussy clench around me, and I grit my teeth.

"Yes. Yes, Logan," she groans, moving over me, not slowing her pace one bit. I see the need in her eyes. A need I have no problem fulfilling.

I reach my other hand up and fist the hair at the back of her head, slamming her mouth to mine as I slowly push my finger into her ass. Salena bucks in my arms, a loud, sexy moan ripping from her throat. I swallow it, working her ass as she fucks me. Her body trembles and shakes, making my balls draw up tight. With a loud cry, she clenches tightly around my cock, sending me over the edge. I grunt, flexing my hips, and break the kiss as I bite down hard on her shoulder where our mate marks are. She cries out, her words unintelligible, and I wrap my arms around her waist as we ride out the orgasm together.

Once we both have our breathing back to normal, Salena slides off my lap, collapsing on the bed next to me. She throws her arm over her face, and the corners of her lips curve up in a contented smile. I slide down next to her, laying on my side. I tug her arm down and she rolls her head to the side to meet my gaze.

"Salena, you're my heart, my life, my entire existence. I want to spend my whole damn life with you. And damn it, if I don't know this is a really shitty time, but will you marry me?"

Her smile is blinding. "Yes, of course."

I reach over and open the drawer beside the bed, feeling around until my fingers close around a velvet box. Pulling it out of the drawer, I roll to face her fully.

"I got this the day after we mated," I murmur.

Her turquoise eyes widen in surprise and then drop to the box in my hands. I flip open the lid and she gasps, her hand gingerly reaching for it and pausing. When our eyes meet, I feel a tug in my heart as I see tears lining her eyes.

"Logan, it's gorgeous."

"Not as gorgeous as you, baby," I say, leaning forward and kissing her softly.

I discovered the ring in a vintage store in Denver. The beautiful pear-shaped cornflower sapphire is nestled with three diamonds on each side that catch the light. I draw back and take the ring from the box then grasp her left hand. The gold band feels cold and smooth to the touch, glittering in the light. Sliding the ring on, I look into her eyes. "Will you, Salena Cartwright, marry my brooding ass this weekend?"

A wave of shock washes over her face, before her joy lights up her features, shining brighter than the sun. I can sense her happiness and excitement in my very core.

"Yes!" she exclaims, ripping her hand from mine and launching herself into my arms.

As she rains kisses all over my face, her giggle fills me with contentment that radiates through my heart and soul. I never imagined I would experience these emotions.

Chapter Sixty

Salena

I'm in the process of securing my earring when I hear a knock at the door. I'm at home alone, getting ready for the wedding. Logan is at Kai's house with the pack setting up in a large tent we've rented. Lucy and Rose are on their way to get me, so they can take me there. I take one final glance in the mirror before I answer the door. I've chosen to keep my long silver hair down, and I've done my makeup with a smoky look and a statement red lipstick. It matches my outfit perfectly.

The red sweetheart strapless dress has a beautiful shimmer that sparkles in the light. The top of the dress is a dreamy satin, and as it falls from my waist, it's adorned with shimmering sequins in a mermaid style skirt. I feel a rush of excitement when I find the matching jacket. Every inch of me is adorned with glimmering red sequins that glitter and shimmer in the light.

My heart races with elation as a huge smile takes over my face. I slide my hands over my waist and hips, and turn, heading to the door. A wave of emotion crashes over me as I swing open the door, expecting to find Lucy and Rose. My heart stalls in my chest and before I can react, Hayley lunges forward, plunging a needle into my neck, the world around me instantly fading to black. I vaguely hear her whimper, "I'm sorry."

I wake slowly, my limbs heavy. I crack my eyes open and lick my lips. They are so dry. My head is throbbing, and I squint to avoid the bright light above me. I tip my head to the side, seeing the shape of a man standing over a workbench. Panic surges. My fingers curl, scratching the wooden table beneath me. I lift my body bit by bit, swinging my legs over the side of what I think was a hospital bed. Looking down, I realize I'm only in my underwear. I suppress the growl that climbs up my throat, and stare at the figure across the room. I tilt my head as I narrow my eyes. That is no man. The humanoid creature has fucking horns and coal black skin. He doesn't look to have any hair, and is only wearing a pair of tattered shorts.

As I move, something in the corner catches my attention, and I see my wedding dress ripped to shreds. My vision blurs with rage as I feel the anger surge through my veins.

Screw modesty.

I am about to kill this fucking demon.

I land on weak, shaky legs, the noise drawing the attention of the figure across the room. He spins, dropping what he held in his hands, an evil smile creeping over his face.

My eyes dart around the room. It has the workbench, table, leather chair, and two doors. One exit, the other must be a bathroom.

"Ahhh, you're awake. About time, now we can have some fun."

"Who are you?" I scowl, my senses barely functioning as I try to reach out to my pack.

The demon's eyes are devoid of color, just a lifeless gray pit of despair that sends a shiver racing down my spine.

"Your brother made a deal with me. Get him the pack back, and I could have my own fun here in this world."

"My brother is dead, so the deal's off."

"Yes, I'm fully aware. He was my vessel, and when he died, I was able to take on my true form. Through some sacrifice, that is. Blood of a virgin is quite powerful." He smirks, licking his lips.

"Your brother let me have my fun with those girls, not that he could stop me. Samuel spent a lot of time watching you. So much so that I became obsessed. You can blame him for this. His seething contempt for you stoked my burning appetite to consume you. I plan on making our time together very . . . " he pauses, as if trying to think of the right word " . . . memorable."

I recoil in revulsion, my fingers digging into the mattress behind me.

He continues as he starts toward me. "I have been practicing with the others on how to make the body last longer. But with you being a shifter, you will heal over and over after I inflict my torture. Watching you bleed will be so fucking sweet."

His soulless gray eyes seem to gleam with delight. The smile that stretches across his face makes my body tremble in fear. I feel an icy chill run down my spine, and I know I have to leave. My legs feel like jelly, but I have to try to get out of here. I would rather die trying to escape than stay in hope of rescue.

I make for the exit, but he is fast and on me in a second. His hand wraps around my throat, the claws puncturing my skin. I feel the blood trickling down my neck.

"Trying to leave, my pet?" he growls excitedly.

My toes are barely touching the ground as I thrash around in his grip, trying to kick him with my legs. He draws me in close to his body, so close I feel his erection.

Whispering in my ear, his rotten breath skates across my neck. "Keep fighting. It only makes me enjoy it more."

I feel his tongue slide up my neck, licking up the blood. My body revolts in disgust, and his head tips back on a laugh as he throws me across the room. My back hits the wall hard, and I hear more than I feel my back break. Dizziness swamps me as I crumple to the ground, dark spots dancing in front of me. I blink as I watch the creature's dark figure approach me.

"I'm so glad you're not as easy to kill as those weak, pathetic humans," it hisses.

Grabbing me by the hair, it drags me over to the corner of the room. I feel a searing pain and let out an involuntary scream, unable to move. I try to shift, but something is blocking it. The world slowly fades out of focus and darkness carries me away.

Chapter Sixty One

Salena

I am so fucking hungry, and my body aches something terrible. Yes, I have healed, but it has been a slow process. I was able to shift once a couple of days ago, and took a chunk out of the demon's leg. Since then, he has been injecting me more often with something to keep me from shifting again. Without being able to shift, I don't heal as quickly and I'm vulnerable. My body quivers uncontrollably, no matter how hard I try to steady it. It has been three days since Hayley showed up at my door, and I know my brothers and Logan must be frantically searching for me.

I hear the pounding of feet on the stairs, and my body locks up. The smell of the demon overwhelms me, and I fight to control my nausea. I sit up slowly, my senses on alert as he draws closer. Pulling a key from his pocket, he silently reaches for the chain that is wrapped around my neck, undoing the lock. The moment it falls to the ground, I surge forward, my forehead connecting with his nose. The demon is momentarily stunned. I don't give him time to recover. I launch to my feet, running for the stairs. Taking them two at a time, I push through the door into the kitchen. Turning, I slam it shut like my life depends on it. I flip the lock, hands shaking madly, and drop my forehead to the wooden door and take a breath. A simple door and lock isn't going to stop the demon, though. I feel a heavy exhaustion settling in my bones, and I know I have to keep going.

I turn, pushing from the door and my heart sinks when I see the door leading outside has been boarded up.

Fuck.

I dart through the house, my heart pounding in my chest as I move toward the front. I pause, sensing something move in the house. I am only a few feet from the front door. I turn, walking backwards to the door, keeping my senses on high alert. Whatever it is, it is dark and wicked, saturating the air with its stench. The air rushes around me, tossing my hair about. I slowly turn, feeling the wood of the door against my back. My heart is pounding in my chest, my lungs heaving with each quick breath.

Suddenly, I'm lifted into the air and thrown across the room, a loud yelp escaping me. My body smashes into the coffee table, sending it crashing over. Before I can get my bearings, I'm lifted again by an invisible force and thrown into the nearest wall. I groan on impact, my body landing in a heap on the floor. I slowly open my eyes and take a sharp intake of breath at the sight before me. Hayley stares me down, her lip curled in a menacing sneer. Her face is contorted in a cruel expression, but the lack of emotion in her eyes reveals she isn't really there.

The demon saunters into the room behind Hayley, his hand landing on her shoulder. She doesn't so much as flinch, just stands there. I sit up, leaning my back against the wall as I stare between them.

"She was so easy to manipulate. So full of grief and self-loathing. I told her all about you and your pack and how you killed her husband. It was so easy. Too easy, really. Then I simply brought my friend in to take over her body. By the time she realized I had lied, it was too late. Any fight she had left faded when I threatened her son."

My heart races and my stomach drops as a wave of horror washes over me. Hayley and Ro have been through enough. They don't deserve this.

Squatting in front of me, the demon snaps his hand out, and grips my jaw painfully in his hands. When his lips curl up into a wicked grin, I know he's savoring the thought of my punishment. He'll have something extra in mind tonight. My eyes drift shut as his clawed hand wraps around my throat and he lifts me to my feet. My hands fly up to grip his wrists, my nails biting into his flesh. From the corner of my eye, I see Hayley's body twitch; her gaze snapping to mine. Brown eyes flicker with the void of the demon. She's fighting it; she's still in there.

The demon tightens his grip around my neck and walks back through the house. I see the door to the basement swing open. Dread settles in my stomach, and before I can react, he throws me straight through the door. The world tilts and spins, my body rolling down the stairs. My back takes the brunt of it, the stairs pounding into my back as I flip over. My head smashes against the wall before I come to a stop at the bottom, my eyes looking at the ceiling. I gasp for breath, trying my best to breathe through the pain racking my body.

I roll my head to the side, looking up the staircase I've just been thrown down, and see the demon's shadow moving about. I close my eyes, struggling to draw in enough air. I don't want to die here. I just don't see a way out.

I drift off to that special place in my mind, a place that takes me away from all this, from the nightmare that awaits me.

"Oh, no you don't," snarls an ugly voice.

My face is gripped painfully in his hand, his long fingernails digging into my cheeks. I can feel the blood trickling from where they are puncturing my skin. I force my eyes open and shoot a menacing glare at the demon. But his eyes are following the path of my blood, mesmerized. Leaning forward, his long tongue darts out, licking the trail of blood. I quiver in repulsion, too weak to fight back.

"You are not drifting off tonight. No, I have special plans for you."

I can't help the small whimper that escapes me, and the demon grins in satisfaction.

Chapter Sixty Two

Logan

Startled, I jerk back a step, my hands raising. I recognize her immediately. It's Davina Jacobs, one of Samuel's murder victims. The young woman stares at me, her eyes furious, as her blood pools at her feet, turning the carpet in my room red.

"You need to hurry," she speaks urgently.

A tear slides down her face and blood begins trickling from the corner of her mouth as her eyes take on a far-off look. "I just landed an internship at my dream job."

She blinks, a determined expression hardening her features.

"He took that from me."

"And he paid with his life. Samuel is dead," I reply gently.

Davina has fire in her eyes even as blood flows from wounds across her stomach, breasts, arms, and legs. The smell of it permeates the air in my bedroom, and I swallow over the rising nausea.

"But he's not," she adds, looking me straight in the eye, unblinking. "I can take you to them, but we must hurry."

My heart is thumping so loudly in my ears I swear I misheard her. "You know where Salena is?"

Davina nods, her body fading in and out of view like a mirage. Her gaze goes over my shoulder, and I sense someone stepping into the room. I turn and see Sander standing there, his worried expression etched on his face.

"Davina will take us to Salena," I tell him.

Sander glances around the room, his eyes sweeping the space. I know he won't see her.

"The dead girl?" he asks uneasily.

"Yes," I snap, growing irritated.

"We must hurry," Davina says, appearing in the doorway next to Sander. I feel my eyes widen in surprise as I watch Sander's face pale.

A shiver runs over him as he speaks in a raw, hoarse whisper. "She is right behind me, isn't she?"

I glance at the ground and my fingers instinctively move to the back of my neck, kneading the tight muscles. "Uh . . . kinda."

"Great. Well, I came to tell you I called my alpha and luna to help. They will be here any minute."

"Really? How? Aren't they in Portland?"

"Yes. Nesrin, my luna, has a sister who can portal them here."

"Portal . . . " My voice hangs on the word.

Davina flickers out of sight, and I panic, pushing past Sander and out of the room. My feet pound the stairs of my house into the open living area. I sigh in relief when I see her standing near the front door.

I hear Sander follow me down just as Kai shouts from the kitchen. We race in, and I'm startled by the sight of three unfamiliar people standing there.

There's a man who matches my size with black hair and green eyes that glow yellow behind the iris. In front of him with a sweet, gentle smile stands a tiny woman with long wavy auburn hair and amber eyes. The woman next to her is taller and has brighter red hair, but you can tell they're sisters. These must be Sander's people. Sander confirms it by going up, wrapping his arms around each person in a tight embrace.

The small woman steps forward, her hand landing on my scarred cheek. I don't flinch or snap, which I think is more of a shock than a stranger touching me. Her palm feels warm and soft, and her eyes seem to see more than I want them too.

"You, Logan, are a good man. Now let's go and get your woman back," she says with a look of pure determination on her delicate face.

I blink as if coming out of a trance and give her a firm nod.

"And later, if you want me to, I can heal those scars. But if you ask me, they suit you, sexy and rough, right? I bet you're a big teddy bear." A soft chuckle escapes her lips.

I can hear a deep, menacing growl come from the large man's throat and Sander's snicker in response.

"That is Nesrin, and this is her mate and my Alpha, Lukas. And this here is Leila," Sander announces, pointing out everyone around the room.

"Guys, this is Logan, Kai, Felix, and Mercy."

Leila steps forward, her eyes narrowing in concentration as she focuses on something behind me.

"Davina is growing impatient. You must leave now," she says.

I stare at her, shocked. "You can see her?"

Leila's intense eyes lock with mine, and I can almost feel the emotion radiating from her as she nods.

"Right, then. Let's go," Kai says, moving for the front door.

As we all move outside and head for the car, I notice someone leaning against the driver's side door of my car. The moonlight bounces off a dagger as it flips gracefully in the air. Ash is standing there, her dark hair gleaming in the light.

Kai storms forward. "What are you doing here?" he snaps.

Straightening, she dismisses him and looks directly at Lukas and Nesrin, bowing to them before turning to me. "I'm here to help."

I nod, not wasting time fighting, and move past her to get into the car. We take three cars and Davina sits in the front with me, while Kai and Felix in the back.

Chapter Sixty Three

Salena

My vision is hazy at best, blackness dancing around the edges. I wish my sight would just go, so then I wouldn't have to look at him, his evil, sadistic grin hovering over me. Observing and analyzing each one of my reactions to determine which one produces the loudest scream.

I want to tear him to shreds, ripping each limb from his body. It's these thoughts which kept me going. That and seeing Logan's face again.

This demon belongs in hell, and I'm glad my brother is dead, because I would kill him myself for bringing this creature here. The demon's strength grows, and its features become increasingly grotesque and terrifying. Its skin—if you'd even call it that—has turned ashen in blotches, fingers have stretched into almost talons, the cheeks have hollowed out, and his vacant gray eyes have scarlet veins pulsating in their depths. It looks creepy as fuck as it stares back at me.

Hayley stands in the corner, her eyes vacant and her face expressionless. I think she's given up fighting the demon who has taken her body hostage.

One of the demon's nails drags down my stomach, and I suck in a deep breath. I feel the warmth of my blood spill over my stomach and pool under my back. I kick out with my legs, feeling the force of the impact as I connect with his face. Rearing back, he hisses at me before grabbing my leg and twisting it violently, breaking it. I let out a loud, anguished cry, my breath coming in short, shallow gasps. His laugh is pure evil as he relishes in the sound of my screams. Tears stream down my face, and for the millionth time I wish I could shift and tear him to pieces. Whatever he's injecting me with won't allow it.

Suddenly, the air in the room shifts, and the demon is flung off me. Unable to do much else, I roll my head to the side to see a woman standing across the room. Her auburn hair is in a wild disarray around her head, but it's her glowing white eyes that make my breath catch. Her hands are extended in front of her toward a white ring of magic surrounding the demon on the floor. He lunges for the woman, and I cry out only to see the demon hit an invisible barrier. The white ring on the floor vibrates and splits into another ring, then another. These rings spin around the demon as magic saturates the air. From behind the woman step two figures. One is Ash, the other a formidable black wolf. He stands tall, an intimidating figure with eyes the color of liquid gold that glints in the light. The wolf turns his head, his eyes locked on mine, and I immediately know who is here to rescue me.

'You are safe now,' the black wolf speaks to me.

I look up at the ceiling, feeling the warmth of my tears as they slide down my face. The feeling of being found is so overwhelming that it's beyond words.

Ash's voice rings out around us, and I roll my head back toward the group. Ash is speaking in her native tongue, her voice growing louder and louder. She approaches the demon trapped in Luna Nesrin's magic and raises her hands to the ceiling. Before she can finish the banishing spell, a figure darts across the space, slamming into her. They roll across the dirty floor, and I catch a glimpse of Ash's dagger. A chill runs down my spine.

"Don't hurt her!" I scream.

Ash freezes, and Hayley snarls harshly, the sound barely human.

"She is possessed!" I shout, my voice breaking, my throat raw.

I feel a flutter in my chest and along my mental shields, and whimper. Logan is here. I hear him shout at someone, then he's pounding down the stairs. Tears threaten to spill from my eyes again, and my throat tightens painfully as I watch him come into my line of sight.

I lie motionless on the ground, unable to move. My leg and back are broken. My body is unsure what to heal first. Logan's gaze is fixed on the demon in the circle. Then his gaze frantically searches the dimly lit room before his eyes find me.

Before he can make a move, Ash calls his name. He hesitates and then looks at her.

"You need to hold Hayley. She is possessed, and I can only work one spell at a time." She grunts from the effort of holding the demon at bay.

Nesrin has the other trapped, and Lukas is watching her back. He won't leave his mate exposed.

Logan glances back at me. I can see he wants to tell her to get fucked, but I nod.

Help her, I mouth.

That's all it takes. He runs over and pins a thrashing Hayley to the ground, his knee on her back and her arms wrenched behind her.

Ash stands, looking ruffled for the first time ever. She moves back to the edge of the circle, the demon inside pacing angrily, its eyes fuming with hatred. Ash's voice echoes around the room, her hands rising before she throws them down, her final words ringing in my ears. The demon screeches and thrashes about. I watch as parts of its body begin disintegrating, disappearing piece by piece. When he's gone, the white ring disappears, and Ash turns back to where Logan has Hayley pinned.

The woman with the wild hair runs over to me, her hands hovering over my body. Her beautiful, kind eyes lock on mine, warmth radiating from every pore as she smiles. "I'm Nesrin. Let's get you out of here."

"Thank you," I weep.

The second our hands clasp, a warmth flows through my hands and works its way up my arm, spreading through my entire body. I gasp as my injuries begin healing, and I can feel my body become whole again. A sense of peace washes over me, and I can breathe easily for the first time in days. Tears move down my face, soaking into my hair as my eyes fall shut.

There is commotion behind Nesrin, and I see the black wolf shift into his human form. His back is to me as he speaks to someone. "She is fine. Calm down."

As I whisper Logan's name, a warmth spreads through me, and I feel a flutter in my chest.

"Salena," he answers.

Lukas steps aside for him, and my gaze lands on him standing behind Nesrin. She smiles, stroking my face, and stands, giving Logan room. He drops to his knees, his arms wrapping around me tightly. The chain is still tight around my wrist, and I can feel the rough links pressing into my skin.

Nesrin quickly steps forward, waving a hand over the lock, and it clicks open, falling uselessly to the ground.

Logan gathers me in his arms and stands. "I'm getting you out of here," he states, storming through the room and up the stairs. I catch a glimpse of Ash helping a sobbing Hayley to her feet. Ash appears completely drained, her eyes glazed over from fatigue. Which isn't surprising. I can't imagine a vanquishing spell would be easy.

We emerge into the cold night air, our breaths visible in the crisp chill, snow falling thickly all around. I see Sander jog over with a thick blanket in his hands.

Logan helps tuck it around me without letting me go. I can see the shadows caused by concern, and protectiveness, and a sliver of vulnerability on his face. Logan moves toward the car and gets in the backseat with me on his lap. He stares at me long and hard for a beat before dropping his forehead to mine. We take a moment to breathe in. Then, taking my face in his large palm, his lips crash down on mine, stealing the breath from my lungs. My hands cover his and I melt into his touch. God, I missed this. *I was so afraid I'd never see him again.*

"Don't say that," Logan murmurs, breaking the kiss.

I focus on him, stroking his scarred cheek. *'I love you, Logan.'*

"I love you, too, baby."

"Are you alright?" I ask, smoothing my fingers over his forehead.

Logan's eyes widen, and he seems speechless. "Me? Are *you* okay?

I snuggle into his warm arms, his heartbeat steady under my cheek, and sigh in contentment. "I'm in the only place I want to be. Your arms. How did you find me?"

Logan stiffens, and I pull back, peering up at him.

"Davina."

I frown. "The dead girl?"

Logan nods. "She came to me, said she knew where to find you. I wish she told me what I'd be walking into, though. A fucking demon?" he blows out a ragged breath.

I peer out the car window and see Ash standing there, looking vulnerable for the first time ever. She stands off to the side, her arms tightly wrapped around her middle, as she watches Felix and Nesrin guiding Hayley to the other car. I watch as Kai stalks toward her, and I'm silently praying that he'll remember his manners, considering she just saved my life. I'm shocked speechless, though, when Kai steps up to her and takes her face in his hands, dropping his mouth to hers.

"Oh, shit," I blurt, covering my mouth.

Logan follows my gaze and smirks. "They are perfect for each other."

I laugh, because he isn't wrong. The front door of the car opens, and Sander jumps in. "Let's get you two home."

Chapter Sixty Four

Salena

The next morning, I watch as the sun rays slowly paint Logan's face with a gentle, golden light. I can't help but reach up and gently trail my fingers over his features, feeling the warmth of his skin. His beautiful blue eyes blink open and his gaze moves over every inch of my face as if committing it to memory. He moves closer, our bodies facing each other, and our legs tangled together, his strong arm gently wrapped around my middle, providing a comforting sense of security.

"I'm never letting you out of my sight again," he murmurs against my lips.

My eyes don't leave his when I whisper, "I can get on board with that, but I prefer to go to the toilet alone. Gotta keep the mystery alive."

Logan squeezes my waist. "Baby, I was so fucking scared I'd lost you."

My heart speeds up and my soul cries out at the pain in his voice. I don't have the courage to tell him I was afraid of that very same thing. I wasn't so sure they would find me before my body gave out, succumbing to the multiple injuries. Thanks to Nesrin, my body has been fully healed, but the phantom pain still lingers.

"Did he?" Logan asks softly, looking lost for words. A frown appears on my face as my mind tries to make sense of what he's asking. Then it hits me. What the other girls suffered. I reach up, cupping his cheek.

"No, honey, he didn't get that far. He did other things, but never that."

Logan's breath whooshes out of him, his whole body sagging in relief. Gripping my head in both hands, he smashes his mouth over mine, his fingers tangling in my mess of hair. The kiss is consuming, lighting that fire in my chest that burns just for him.

Logan rolls on top of me, bracing himself on his arms. His blue eyes swirl with more emotions than I can count as he stares down at me. His love and adoration for me flow through our mate bond, warming my heart and caressing my soul. I also feel all the pain of almost losing me again. "I don't know what I'd do without you in my life, Salena," he says, rubbing his nose along mine.

"Good thing you will never have to find out, detective."

A small grin tugs at his lips as he dips down for another kiss, his warm, soft lips moving gently over mine. When he pulls away, a wave of sadness washes over me.

"He tore up my wedding dress. You never got to see it," I grumble, disheartened.

"Baby, I will pay any amount of money to get it remade. You deserve the best, and I will give it to you."

"I really want to marry you," I whisper, my hands tracing the muscles of his back.

"Fuck," he curses.

Logan drops his mouth to mine in the most delicious kiss. The moan that escapes me sounds desperate. I can sense the tension radiating off his body and feel the solidness of his muscles against me. He's restraining himself. I don't want him to hold back; I want him to love me the way he does best. So I bite down on the lip, and a deep rumble comes from deep in his chest as he grinds his cock against me.

"Logan," I breathe, my voice sounding needy even to my own ears.

His eyes hold mine as he searches them, like he's trying to uncover a secret. I know what he's looking for, but I am ready. More than ready.

Logan must sense that, because he pulls down the neck of my tank top, sucking a nipple into his warm mouth. My fingers dive into his thick hair as I arch my back, pushing my breast into him.

"Yes," I moan.

He moves to the other breast before sliding the top over my head. His warm hands move down my sides as he takes my underwear off, the feeling of his touch coating me in goosebumps. His fingertips softly glide over my center, his eyes sparkling with raw intensity.

"Fuck, baby, you're wet already?"

"I want you, Logan," I say, moaning as his fingers enter me, sliding in and out at a slow pace. My eyes fall shut, the bed moving under his weight, suddenly his mouth is covering me, sucking and licking on that sensitive bundle while his fingers plunge inside of me. Bright sparks of pleasure roll through me as I lift my hips, needing more. I cry out in pleasure as he bites down on my inner thigh before running a slow, torturous lick over my clit. I look down into his wickedly sexy eyes as his mouth covers me again and sucks hard, his fingers curling and hitting the spot deep inside of me. The tips of my fingers and toes tingle as ecstasy rises inside me, lighting my body up like electric currents running under my skin. Pleasure tears through me so hard and fast white spots dance in front of my eyes as I scream his name.

I feel Logan move away, and I whine, instinctively reaching for him. Then his body is covering mine, his knees pushing my legs apart, and then he is slowly pushing inside of me. My muscles clench and contract around him as another orgasm comes from nowhere, taking my breath.

"Fuck, Salena," he groans, his forehead dropping to mine as he plunges in over and over, sending me higher and higher. I feel my senses slipping away as his body moves over me.

A sense of frenzy hits me, my fingers digging into his back, clawing, as if I need him even closer. I lean up and bite my mate mark on his neck, and Logan groans low and deep, moving even faster than before. His fingers tangle in my hair, tipping my head back as he lavishes my throat. Pulling back, he speaks roughly.

"Open your eyes, baby."

When I open my eyes, his blue eyes are filled with such emotion that I can feel his love and adoration washing over me.

"Come with me," he growls, sweat beading his forehead.

He grips my hair tighter, the sting sending a pleasant shiver over my scalp. This time he bites down on my mate mark.

"Logan!" I scream as pleasure bursts from every cell in my body like a tidal wave. I hear his groan in my ear as his movements become jerky. He takes his time, allowing us to savor and enjoy the pleasure. Without pulling out, he rolls over to his back, pulling me with him so I'm laying on his chest. Our breathing is heavy and erratic as we try to catch our breath.

I don't know how long we lay there in silence, our breathing in perfect harmony. It is so good to be home. So good to be back with my mate. I feel a warmth in my chest, as if my heart is glowing with contentment.

I am anxious about one thing, though.

"What will happen to Hayley?" I whisper into the silence.

Logan lets out a sigh, his palms gliding over my back. "Felix and Kai sat Ro down and told him everything. It wouldn't be fair if he thought his mom was crazy and tried to kill you. He and Hayley are going to be fine. It will take time, but with our help, everything will work out."

"Is she okay?"

"Nesrin healed Hayley's physical wounds, her mental ones will take a while longer."

My heart breaks for her. She doesn't deserve that, no one does.

"Lukas, Nesrin, and Leila left last night after everything was settled. I'm so grateful Sander called them."

I am, too. I should have taken Sander up on the offer sooner. Maybe none of this would have happened.

"Don't think like that. You didn't know," Logan whispers, reading my emotions correctly.

I snuggle into his arms, my head nestled in his chest, as I lightly trace the wings tattooed over his chest.

"Thank you for loving me." I whisper, softly into the dark.

Logan's fingers grip my chin, tilting my head back so he can read my expression. "Thank you for loving me. You fought for me when no one else ever did."

I lean up and gently kiss him, my heart fluttering wildly in my chest. When I pull back, I rest my ear against his chest. I can feel the strong, steady thump of his heartbeat as I snuggle back into him, his arms tightening around me as I drift off to sleep.

Acknowledgements

Without my support team, completing these books would have been impossible. Whenever I feel like giving up, they are there to give me the boost of confidence I need to keep pushing forward. You know who you are and how much you've helped keep me on track for my goals. I appreciate it all.

Marica, my editor, deserves my deepest thanks for her patience and understanding, despite my scatter brain approach to writing. You're a gem!!

I want to give a special shout out to my amazing husband for always having my back. Without you, none of this would be possible. You have been my rock, always there to encourage me in my pursuits.

I want to express my gratitude to my beautiful readers for the encouragement and support you've given me. I'm loving this journey. xxxx